I0612742

HEART OF HYTHEA

Suzanne Francis is a captivating author. Her writing
pulls you from the realm of reality and places you
into the world of imagination so smoothly that
you may not know you have arrived there.
Dianna Doles Petry, Sage Fire Reviews

Ms. Francis paints her setting with specific, colorful
details that completely drew me into the land of Yrth
and its ongoing civil war. I recommend it highly.
Dandelion, Long and Short Romance Reviews

Suzanne Francis, author of the "Song of the Arkafina"
Series, is one of the best small press authors. In a group
that is sometimes tarnished with low-quality offerings,
Suzanne delivers an exceptional, unforgettable story
every time. Her worlds are filled with colorful details and
captivating characters that kept me turning the pages.
Pat Bertram, author of *A Spark of Heavenly Fire* and
More Deaths Than One, from Second Wind Publishing

Also by Suzanne Francis

Ketha's Daughter
Dawnmaid
Beyond the Gyre

HEART OF HYTHEA

Suzanne Francis

Published by
Bladud Books

For my husband Michael,
And my children
John, Heather, Fiona and Joel,
With love

First published in 2008 by Mushroom eBooks

This Edition published in 2008 by Bladud Books,
an imprint of Mushroom Publishing, Bath, BA1 4EB
United Kingdom
www.bladudbooks.com

ISBN 978-1-84319-641-9

Printed and bound by Lightning Source

Contents

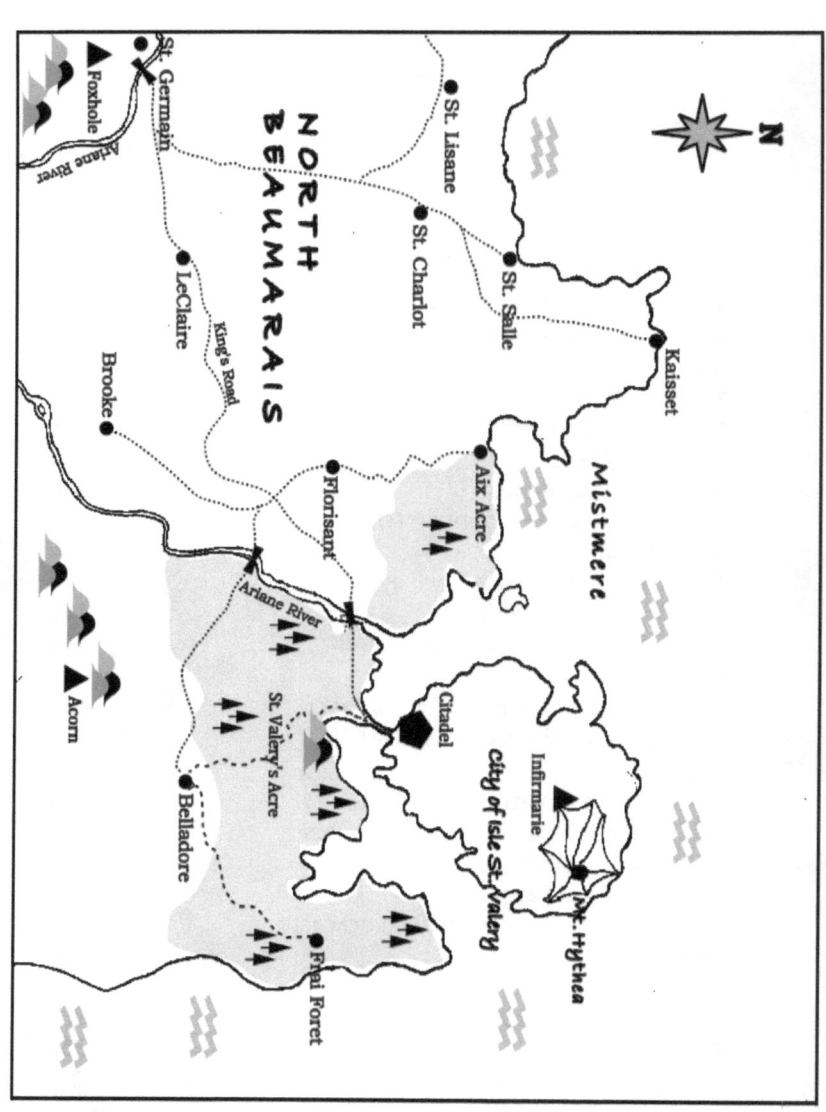

1

The Innocent, Citchet

(The Arkirish Dynasty, Eight)

Geya sits before her silver mirror, outside of time and space. Carefully, she removes a worn sheaf of circular tokens from a silk wrapping and fans them out on the table in front of her, then selects three at random. After placing the tokens face up, she studies them for a moment.

This is what she reveals...

The first token, a blue one, is the tenth from the estate of Naer, Beginning/End, in a standing position. The second, with a green back, is from the Tollyn. Geya sighs. It is Varing—the trackless marsh. The third card has a red back. It is The Innocent, Citchet, from the Arkirish Dynasty.

~~~~~~~~~~~~~~~~

The girl was crying and muttering to herself as she walked across the field, lugging a valise much too large for her small frame. The sun beat down on her chestnut curls, and she stopped for a moment to mop her face with a carefully embroidered handkerchief. Then she shaded her eyes with her hand, and looked this way and that, searching for some familiar landmark. She saw none, and the realization that she was well and truly lost brought a fresh welling of tears to her eyes. After setting the valise down on the ground, between two furrows, she sat down forlornly, and began to sob in earnest, her face buried in her chubby hands.

"Well now, little Miss. And what seems to be the trouble?" The voice seemed to come from nowhere and the girl's head snapped up in alarm. She had dropped her handkerchief, so she hastily dried her eyes on her pinafore before looking up at the boy who had spoken to her. He seemed very tall, but then she was only six, and small for her age.

Her lip trembled, but she answered bravely enough. "No trouble at all, kind Sir. I am merely a stranger in this land, pausing for a moment's respite before continuing on my way again."

The boy regarded her gravely, and did not laugh, as she had feared he might. His gray eyes were thoughtful. "And where are you bound, Traveling Lady?" he asked her. "If you do not mind my asking," he added politely. The girl studied him for a moment before answering. He had long, very dark brown hair, cut haphazardly, so that it grew in a shaggy mass of curls down his back. His patched clothing and bare feet were worlds removed from the fine frock and sturdy leather boots she wore. She had half-decided to run from him—after all her mother had warned her many times not to talk to strangers—but then he smiled, and the gap between his front teeth utterly charmed her.

"I am on my way to the country of Ruboralis." She paused for a moment, uncertainly. Until just now, the girl hadn't given her destination much thought. "To visit... the King!" she declared, triumphantly. "He has invited me to live in his palace and eat cake all day long." She glared at the boy, daring him to challenge her, but he just grinned again, good-naturedly going along with her tall tale.

"Well then, you'll be knowing that the path you are on now leads directly to the worst den of robbers this side of the Bresla River, eh? Did you mean to come this way? You aren't lost by any chance?" He squatted down beside her and removed an apple from his pocket. Digging his thumbs into the flesh, he tore it in half. The girl looked at him wide-eyed, much impressed by this casual display of strength. He handed her a piece of the apple and she accepted it graciously, trying not to show her hunger. It was well past dinner time and she had been walking for what felt like many hours.

"I am certainly not lost," she insisted, when she had devoured her share of the apple. "I mean to fight the robbers before supper and take their booty as a tribute to the King. My weapons are hidden in this valise I am carrying with me," she added, in case he should think to question her story.

But the boy only nodded sagely. "Indeed. The King will be most impressed with you, Lady Traveler, I can see that. I think I should warn you though—the robbers are all out at the moment and won't be back until well after dark. In the meantime, perhaps you would like to come home with me for awhile? I know it isn't the sort of fancy place a rich lady like you would usually stay, but I happen to know Ma made a fresh seedcake this afternoon and I am sure she would give us some, and a drink of cold water from the well." He stood and offered her his hand. "What do you say?"

The little girl smiled and nodded. "Well, I am just the tiniest bit hungry. Perhaps I could stop, for a while. But then I must get back to my travels," she firmly insisted. Then, remembering her manners, she said, "My name is Katkin. Thank you for your kind invitation, good Sir. Will you tell me your name?"

The boy grinned again. "I am Jacq," he said, pointing to his chest, "and Jacq is me. Will you allow your humble servant to carry this bag for you, my Lady? I am ten years old and very strong for my age, so it would be no trouble at all." Katkin nodded, her eyes shining with admiration. As they walked across the bare, brown field, until recently planted in fodder for the cattle-beasts, Jacq asked her, "Have you traveled far today?"

She nodded tiredly. "I left my home at Tintaren a long time ago. My journey has taken me many miles since then. I expect I have passed through Mardonne and Secuny already. Soon I will reach the ocean, and there I must find a ship to carry me across the Gulf, to Ruboralis." Then she looked up at him, her green eyes wide and serious. "Can you keep a secret, Jacq?"

He nodded gravely, and she continued, "I am running away from home. I hate my mother and father!"

Jacq did not have the heart to tell the girl that she hadn't even left the wide fields of Tintaren yet, so he asked her gently, "Why, Katkin? What have they done?"

"I want a pony, and they say I am not old enough to have one. I am almost seven years old! That is plenty old enough." To his dismay, her lip began to tremble again, and he quickly took her hand.

"Don't cry. After we have some cake, I will take you to the barn and show you Nestor. He used to be my father's horse, but now he is mine. Would you like to ride him? He is very big and can easily bear both of us on his back." When she smiled, it felt to Jacq as though the sun had come out from behind the clouds again. He put down the valise and did a handstand. After she clapped and cheered delightedly, he impressed her further by taking several wobbly steps forward on his hands.

"Can you show me how to do that?" she wanted to know.

"Well... I could, but it takes a lot of practice. You would have to stop your travels for a good long while, and maybe even go back home. Then we could visit each other and I could teach you all sorts of tricks."

She shook her head decisively. "Oh, no. I couldn't do that. It is such a long way. And I don't..." Katkin did not want to admit she was lost. "Still," she sighed, "it might be nice to go home again. Willow will miss me when she comes home from school. And Nurse might get in trouble if I am gone too long."

Jacq had a sudden inspiration. "After we go to my house, I will show you a magic shortcut back to Tintaren. Even though it took you many days of travel to reach this place, it will carry you home in just a few minutes. But Tintaren is a very big place, so you will have to show me which house you live in."

"The biggest one of all, up on the hill above the little cottar houses," Katkin answered, with naive disdain.

Jacq gave her a sharp look. "The Lord's house? You live in Tintaren Manor?"

She nodded in agreement. "The Lord of Belladore is my father." Then, because Jacq had dropped her hand abruptly, she asked, "What is wrong? Don't you want to take me to your house any more?" Her lower lip began to quiver.

He gave her the gap-toothed smile again. "Course I do. You just surprised me, that is all." He grasped her hand once more, and they set off across the fields towards Jacq's home. "Did I ever tell you the tale of the pirate named Scallywag Pete, and how I fought him to the death on the shores of Ghiria?"

She laughed. "Of course you haven't, silly. We just met. But will you tell me now?"

"Indeed I will. It was like this, see..." By the time they reached his cottage, Katkin and Jacq were laughing and talking like old friends, the brief moment of awkwardness between them forgotten. His mother made the lonely little girl very welcome, as he had known she would.

Now as they sat together, happily munching seed cake on the sagging front porch of the house that he shared with his mother and three brothers, Katkin asked, "Where is your father, Jacq? Does he labor in the fields like mine does every day?"

Jacq's gray eyes flashed at this and he said resentfully, "Your father does no work, except to tell the foremen what to do. And my father is dead. He died in an accident two years ago."

Katkin defended her father loyally. "He does too! Every night he comes home muddy and tired. But he still plays his vielle for me, and sings songs. My father is the best daddy in the world. But I am sorry about your father," she added.

But Jacq would not let it go. "Do his hands look like this?" The boy had huge hands, and they were rough and calloused from field work. "I labor in the fields and so do Ma and Barlow and Nathan. Thad is still too young, but when he is older he will too. We all have to work, Katkin. That is what cottars do. But you don't work, do you?"

She seemed to accept this disparity without question. "No, I have lessons with Nurse in the mornings. In the afternoon I play by myself. I get very lonely sometimes, because Willow has gone away to school in the City. I don't have any friends now. She sighed deeply and took another bite of cake, then carefully brushed the crumbs off her pinafore. After a moment she said thoughtfully, "Let me see your hands again." Jacq held out his hands. She stared at them for a few seconds, and then frowned at the open blister weeping on the left palm. "How did you do that?"

He shrugged. "Digging holes for the new vine stock. I don't have any work gloves." She looked so distressed at this that he spoke quickly to reassure her. "It is all right. It doesn't hurt very much." To his immense surprise she grasped his hand and kissed the palm softly, on the blister, then looked at him, her vivid green eyes luminous with unshed tears.

"There," she whispered. "Now I have made it all better."

Later, Jacq Benet would always say it was at this exact moment he fell everlastingly in love with Katrione du Chesne.

After a moment he said quietly, "I will be your friend. If you want me to, that is." She had smiled at that, through her tears, and said she would be very pleased to have him as her friend.

Later, Jacq walked her home again, carefully avoiding the route that she had used, so she might not feel ashamed of her childish notion that she had passed beyond the borders of Beaumarais.

Katkin said goodbye to him by the kitchen gate. "I will see you again tomorrow, Jacq. Don't forget, you promised to show me where you saw the robin's eggs!" She gave him her brightest smile, and then ran through the gardens, her braids flying.

Jacq watched her go, and then walked back through the fields, whistling thoughtfully. He was going to find his mother and tell her he had just met the girl he was going to marry someday.

Later that evening at dinner, her quarrel with them forgotten, Katkin was telling her parents of her adventures that day. Her mother looked horrified when told she had been to one of the cottar houses.

She spoke sharply. "Katrione, such low persons are only our laborers. We do not associate with them as friends. I forbid you..."

Katkin's father Gaspard interrupted her. "Let the girl be, Anwen. I know that family. Jacq is Francois Benet's oldest boy. He is a good lad and a hard worker. Katkin needs someone to look out for her now that Willow is gone." He dropped his voice and the girl had to strain to catch his next words. "Gilles Savoyard told me some of the cottars down south have been raiding storehouses, stealing and looting. The Guard have put down the uprising for now, but who knows when it might start up again? We can't keep an eye on the girl all the time."

His wife replied, not bothering to lower her voice at all. "Then we should send her to the City to school with Willow. She would be safer there *and* less trouble to me." Katkin's eyes went wide with horror.

But Gaspard wouldn't hear of it. "Not a chance, Anwen. She is much too young for that. This place would be a mausoleum without her, anyway. Wouldn't it, little Kitty Kat?" Her father turned to her, laughing, and ruffled her hair. "But you have to remember, Jacq has a job to do here, and you must not interfere with him when he is working, all right?" Katkin nodded happily. "Now, let's get my vielle. I know a new song."

Father and daughter left the table together arm in arm, leaving Anwen behind, muttering angrily.

* * * *

As he had promised, Jacq showed Katkin the robin's nest, and where the squirrels kept their nuts and the badger's den, and a thousand other hidden places. Tintaren was a huge maze of vineyards and cellars, for the wealthy Lord of Belladore owned the only expanse of land suitable for viticulture in Beaumarais. Katkin and Jacq explored every inch of it together, and never grew tired of each other's company.

Nevertheless, there did exist one secret place that Jacq was very reluctant to reveal to her. Katkin found out about it quite by chance. One winter's day, after finishing her lessons, she went looking for Jacq out in the wide daisy-studded meadow behind Tintaren Manor. She caught sight of him some distance away, hurrying down a path between two recently ploughed fields. Katkin was about to call out but fell silent as she realized someone else was looking for him too. She saw Jacq's head lift sharply as the foreman shouted his name. Katkin watched in surprise as Jacq stopped abruptly, stepped sideways, and then completely disappeared from sight. She looked around wildly, refusing to believe the evidence of her own eyes, but it was as if he had ceased to exist.

Katkin jumped when the foreman came up beside her. "Hello, Little Shadow." He had given her this nickname some time ago, after he noticed that everywhere Jacq went she seemed to follow right behind. "Have you seen Jacq?" he asked. "I need him to help me shift some barrels."

Katkin looked up at him and answered uncertainly, "No, Rene. I haven't... seen him, not lately."

"Well if you find him, tell him I am looking for him, will you?" He stalked off and Katkin walked over to the place she had seen Jacq vanish. After a few moments she heard a strange sound, like the puff of displaced air, and Jacq once more stood beside her. He looked surprised and slightly annoyed to see her.

"What are you doing here, Kat?"

"Where did you go just now, when you disappeared?" Katkin asked excitedly.

Jacq tried to pretend ignorance but she would not allow it. Finally, exasperated by her questions, he snapped, "There is a very secret place I can go to. Don't ask me how I do it, because I don't know myself. The first time I went it was an accident, see? I was running from some boys, when I was much smaller than I am now. I tripped and fell sort of sideways, and then I found myself somewhere else, and they weren't behind me any more."

"Take me there, now," Katkin insisted. "I want to go with you. Jacq, please..."

"No. I won't take you," he said flatly. "I don't even know if I can."

But she had badgered him and sulked for days until finally he gave in.

Katkin skipped along beside Jacq as they crossed the brown fields to a place out of sight of the Manor House and the barn. After checking to make sure they were unobserved, he took her hand firmly in his, closed his eyes for a moment, then stepped forward and a little to the left. Katkin felt such a sickening moment of vertigo, she closed her eyes against it. After she opened them again and looked around, she said with disappointment, "Oh well, you said it might not work."

Jacq said quietly, "Oh, it worked all right. Look, Katkin."

He pointed upwards and she saw the dull whiteness of the sky above their heads. It had been a bright, sunny day a moment before. Now there were no clouds, just this uniform lack of color and form, as though the firmament just stopped. Her heart began to pound in fear.

She asked shakily, "Where are we? What is this place?"

He shrugged. "I already told you, I don't know. Are you ready to go back?"

Katkin did not want Jacq to know she was afraid, so she said carelessly, "No, let's walk around for a bit. Have you seen any other people?"

Jacq scratched his head. "There are white things here, but I wouldn't call them people. I don't think we should explore any further. I tried that a few times when I first came here, but I always felt as though I didn't belong. Like I was trespassing somewhere very sacred. We should go back."

"Show me one of the things, and then we can go back, I mean it."

He looked at her doubtfully.

"Please, Jacq. You never have to bring me here again."

He sighed. "All right. But you have to promise you won't tell anyone else about it. Swear on the Goddess Lalluna." She crossed her hands over her chest, as she had seen the Daminem[*] of the Unity do once on a visit to the Infirmarie in the City, and solemnly swore an oath. Then he took her hand and led her across the brown field to a ramshackle house.

"I know this place," said Katkin. "It is the old Bell cottage. No one lives here now. The old man died last year."

"Yes," said Jacq. "He did. Come inside, Katkin."

The tiny house was neat as a pin within, as though nothing had been touched since the owner passed away. Katkin stood still, nervously waiting for Jacq to show her the thing that wasn't exactly a person. The silence was so oppressive she thought she could hear her own heart beating. "Back here," he whispered, seemingly as afraid of the stillness as she. He pointed to a curtained alcove that hid the old man's bed. They walked forward together, and Jacq parted the curtains slightly so Katkin could peer within.

As Jacq had promised, something white lay on the bed, on top of the faded blue counterpane. Katkin suddenly understood what Jacq meant about trespassing.

"Jacq," she whispered urgently. "Let's go."

The creature heard her, and lifted its head. Katkin gave a moan of fear, for it had no face, just a flat whiteness, as blank as the sky outside. She turned and fled, and Jacq followed behind her, shutting the door firmly, in case the terrifying being inside should decide to pursue them.

Once they were well away from old man Bell's cottage, she begged, "Take me home, right now. Please..."

Jacq took her hand, and stepped sideways again. After the same horrible feeling of dizziness, they stood once more in the living world.

"I told you," he said simply, "but you wouldn't listen to me, would you?" But then he had to comfort her frightened tears, and he forgot to be angry with her.

Time passed, and still they remained the best of friends. Jacq was fourteen, and towered over eleven-year-old Katkin. They

---

[*] The Elder Sisters of the Unity, who have made Abiding Vows. (pl.)

spent what time they could together, rambling through the fields of Tintaren, with Jacq on Nestor and Katkin on her new pony, Brinna.

But Jacq seldom had time for such adventures. As he grew larger and stronger his work at the vineyard had grown much more demanding, and the foreman less tolerant of interruptions. He often sent Katkin away with a curt admonition, and her busy father just ignored her pleas to lighten Jacq's workload. Sometimes Jacq seemed angry, and would go for hours without talking, especially if he saw Katkin reading or writing in one of her schoolbooks. Katkin worried endlessly about his moods and would try hard to coax a smile from him when she thought he was unhappy.

Her mother and father seemed troubled too, and there were whispered conversations about a man named Nicholas Reynard, and something called the Rising. Katkin paid much less attention to this. Her world revolved firmly around Jacq and the endless fields of Tintaren. With a faith borne of childhood innocence, she believed both would be with her forever. She could not have been more wrong.

One late summer day, Katkin waited impatiently behind the barn for Jacq to finish his afternoon work in the fields. They had been planning this ride to the lakeshore for weeks, and now Jacq was very late. As the sun slowly dipped lower in the sky, Katkin felt her own spirits sinking. The grape harvest would begin in just a few days and she knew Jacq would be far too busy then to spend any time with her. As she was about to give up and return to the Manor house she saw him hurrying around the corner of the barn, and she hailed him with a cry of delight.

"At last! I was beginning to think you had forgotten all about me, Jacq Benet!"

He looked tired and a little dispirited as he rinsed his hands and head under the water pump by the horse trough. "Rene was watching me like a hawk. I couldn't sneak away early. Come on, we'll have to move if we are going to make it down to the Mere and cook supper before dark. Did you manage to find us something to eat?"

Katkin grinned and held up a box containing half a dozen eggs and some potatoes, stolen earlier in the day from the kitchen gardens.

"Did you tell your father anything of our plans?"

She shook her head. "I didn't want to chance it. He might have said I couldn't go."

Jacq shrugged and accepted this. "You will catch it if we are late back then. Come on, let's get the horses."

Katkin led Brinna from the barn while Jacq saddled Nestor. They set off together down a well worn path that led to the shores of the Mistmere. Autumn was in full flight and the hills were awash in the yellow leaves of the oaks, with occasional bursts of flame red from maple and sycamore. There was a nip in the air that presaged the coming of winter, but the sun was warm in the brilliantly blue sky. Katkin thought it a perfect afternoon, despite a bank of heavy-looking clouds that were massing to the east.

Once they reached the shores of the lake, where a stony tributary rushed down to meet it from the hills, she lit a small fire with her tinder and flint while Jacq dug a deep hole in the side of the bank. Katkin scrambled down into the river to retrieve some rounded stones, and then tossed them into the fire. Once they were hot enough, Jacq carefully piled them in the makeshift oven along with the food. In the meantime, Katkin poked about the hillside and discovered some ripened fruit in an abandoned apple orchard. She carried back an apron-full of bright red apples which she and Jacq munched in companionable silence as they waited for their late lunch to roast.

After a time she said, "I heard my parents arguing last night. My mother wants to send me away to school in the City, but my father will not let her."

Jacq lay on his back, chewing on a piece of grass, and stared up at the sky. He turned his head to smile at her, and he seemed untroubled. "Don't they have that argument every year about this time? He always wins, does he not?"

She shrugged. "I am not so sure he will this year. It was quite serious. They have been acting very strangely ever since that man Nicholas Reynard started attacking the Lord's houses. But he will never defeat my father," she continued confidently. "And someday, when I am Queen..."

Jacq hooted with laughter at this. "You? The Queen of Beaumarais?"

She responded with dignity. "Of course I shall be Queen

someday, and you will be the King and rule by my side, Jacq. Then I will put Nicholas Reynard in prison for a thousand years, and decree that no children have to go away to school if they do not wish it."

Jacq suddenly stopped laughing and sat up. He looked over at her and said seriously, "If I am to be king then we would have to be married."

Katkin nodded serenely. "Whom else would I marry, Jacq? I love you. I always have. You are the bravest and strongest boy I know and my best friend in the whole world."

He seemed at a loss for words for a moment, and then he took her hand, holding it gently in his. "It won't be that easy, Kat. Life isn't always fair. When you are older, maybe you will understand."

Her head flew up in alarm. "What are you saying? You don't want to marry me?" Katkin's eyes quickly filled with tears.

Jacq shook his head violently. "No! I am not saying that, not at all." Then he continued, more softly, "Listen to me, Katkin. What I want and what you want—it might not matter—that is what I am saying. Your father is a powerful man. I don't think he will want you to marry the son of a cottar. He will do everything he can to prevent it."

She looked genuinely shocked at this. "My father wouldn't do that. He wants me to be happy!"

But Jacq just shook his head once more. "I hope, one day, that things will be different. Some of us are working to make it that way. In the meantime, I can only make you a promise."

She stared up at him, suddenly aware of how much he had grown in the last year. There was the suggestion of facial hair on his upper lip and jaw now, and a breadth to his shoulders that spoke of manhood. Though she was still only eleven, Katkin intuitively understood that this promise, whatever it was, was no childhood game between them. She took a deep breath and said slowly, "What do you promise, Jacq?"

He met her green eyes with his own steady gray ones. "I promise I won't marry anyone else, Katkin. I will wait for you as long as I have to. Do you understand?"

She nodded and said softly, "I hope you don't have to wait *too* long." Then, for the first time since they met, four years ago, she felt suddenly shy in his presence. She turned away to see to the lunch and he grinned, shaking his head wryly.

"We had better head back now." Jacq pointed up to the sky. "See those clouds up there? It looks like a storm is brewing." They had finished lunch some time ago, and now were unsuccessfully trying to lure a large water rat from her nest in the bank with various scraps of food. A fine drizzle began to fall as he spoke, and Katkin hurried to collect her things. Soon it began to rain in earnest, and they rode back up the valley with their heads down, each lost in private contemplation, as thunder rumbled away in the distance.

A bolt of lightning split the sky with a deafening boom. A tree beside the path exploded into sheets of flame and Brinna reared in terror, throwing Katkin off her back. Jacq jumped down from Nestor and ran to where she lay on the ground, limp and unresponsive. He shook her gently, crying, "Katkin! Katkin, wake up. We have to get back to your house." As Jacq brushed the hair away from her face, his hand felt something warm and sticky. Blood poured from a gash on her forehead, and he knew he would have to move her despite the fact she was still unconscious. After binding the wound as well as he could with his handkerchief, Jacq carefully picked Katkin up and draped her across the broad back of Nestor. Though he rode as quickly as he could for Tintaren, it still took him over an hour to get there.

By that time her family was in a panic, and Katkin's mother and father both met Jacq at the gates of the main house. Anwen took one look at her daughter and shrieked, "You see, Gaspard! I told you this would happen. What has that lout done to her? Look at her! Look at your daughter..."

Jacq opened his mouth, and tried to explain, but Gaspard du Chesne had already instructed two of his men to get the boy off his horse and into the barn. The last thing he heard, before they dragged him away, was Katkin's voice, crying hysterically, "Jacq! No, I want to stay here with Jacq!" The sound of her screaming his name stayed with him for a long time afterwards.

2

Hithluel, the rocky shore

(The Tollyn, Six)

They have entered this turn of the Gyre. We must stop them, once and for all. Do you agree, my sisters? *The beautiful, dark-haired woman in the mirror nods. Then she becomes three.*

You are the Moon.

One face in the mirror changes, becomes even more striking; white wings gleam from behind her shoulders. Moonlight smiles. I am the pretty one—this time.

And you... Raven. *Raven looks distastefully in the mirror—sees her black, matted hair and sharp rat's teeth.*

Now we must search for the Innocent. She is the key to this turn of the Gyre. Find her, Moonlight.

Moonlight touches the tokens, still scattered on the table before them, and shakes her head. You can see the future without these old luckcast* tokens, Geya. Why do you bother?

Geya smiles. *I know it. But such things remind me of what we once were. Now I would draw one more, so I may see what this turn of the Gyre holds for us, my sisters.*

---

* The luckcast is an ancient divination system of unknown origin. It could not have come to Yr with the traveling peoples for it has a different structure than both the water runes of the Dalvolk and the Triske stones of the Firaithi. It consists of forty-five round tokens, traditionally made from thin pieces of wood, or bone. The tokens are notched on each side and bound by a thong of leather. Each sheaf of tokens is divided into three domains. Traditionally, the seer draws three or nine tokens, an equal number from each domain, and interprets the tokens based on their orientation. The first domain, the Estate of Naer, is comprised of fifteen pairs of opposites: love/hate, courage/fear etc. The second domain, the Tollyn, is a mythical terrain. The third domain is the Arkirish Dynasty—the King, Queen and the court add still more depth to the readings. For a complete listing of the luckcast tokens and their meanings, see Appendix I at the end of this volume.

She draws another token from the luckcast. It is the fifteenth card of the estate of Naer, in the Reversed position—*Death*.

So, it begins...

~~~~~~~~~~

Frost still rimed the grass in the late afternoon as Katkin made her way through the forest called St. Valery's Acre. She rode with care, alert to every sound from the undergrowth on each side of the path following the riverbank. Her pony, Brinna, snorted anxiously. Katkin firmly held the reins, afraid the pony would shy at a birdcall or some other small noise. Patting her mane, she said, "Come on, Brin. Settle down now. There is nothing here to be frightened of. I hope..."

The catch in Katkin's voice gave her own fears away. Since the War between the Soldiers of the Rising and the King's Guard began, the forest surrounding the huge inland sea known as the Mistmere had become a haven for brigands and deserters from both sides. She knew the dangers well, yet traveling the forest path remained the quickest way back to the City of Isle St. Valery from the village of Belladore, after spending the day with her sister Willow.

Her sister's husband, Yannick Abelard, had sent a message to the Infirmarie last night, begging for help with the delivery of their first child. Katkin was not a proper healer, not yet, but she was all the poor family could afford. Fortunately, the birth went well, except for a long labor. Her sister had borne a beautiful baby girl, and named her Roseberry after Yannick's mother.

But now Katkin might be late back to the Infirmarie. There would be the devil to pay if the Maitress found out she left the City without an escort.

Katkin stopped before she reached the steepest part of the path, leading up to a bluff by the side of the river. There, the forest fell away to reveal a grassy meadow, studded with daisies and buttercups. The track here was narrow and stony, with high banks on either side. It would be the perfect place for an ambush. "We will take it slow, Brinna. There will be no surprises ahead for us, girl, I can promise you that." Katkin spoke aloud and then smiled, wondering if she was reassuring the pony or herself. She urged Brinna forward and climbed the rocky rise with care. Katkin held herself in readiness, one hand on the reins and one on her bow, an arrow in her bowstring, but nothing disturbed their passage.

When she had reached the meadow safely, she breathed a sigh of relief and stopped to admire the view. From this vantage point, she could see the entire City on its peninsula and the walls and battlements gleamed in the low winter sun. She remembered the first time she had passed this way, as an unhappy eleven-year-old, traveling to boarding school in the City. That had been before the beginning of the War. Before Nicholas Reynard murdered her parents and utterly destroyed her home.

Katkin looked further down the path and saw a man gazing out over the cliff edge. Immediately, she jumped down from Brinna, bow at the ready. The stranger's back was towards her and she did not think he was aware of her presence. He wore the elaborate uniform of a cuirassier, a horseman, with red epaulets on a jacket of midnight blue. The crested dragoon's helmet on his head bore a long plume of black horsehair that mingled with his own long, straw-colored queue. He carried a broadsword and a flintlock pistol stuck into his belt. Despite these weapons, Katkin found nothing particularly threatening about him, perhaps because she could see he stood with the aid of crutches. It appeared he had no companions, other than a black horse standing nearby, patiently waiting for its master. Perhaps he was merely a traveler, like herself, pausing to admire the view of the City from the top of the sandstone bluff. She decided to approach him, after convincing herself she faced no real danger.

Grasping Brinna's bridle, she walked boldly forward, intending to greet the stranger and continue on her way down to the shores of the Mistmere and into the City. Suddenly she stopped again, and watched in agitation as the soldier removed his crutches and threw them angrily over the edge of the bluff. They clattered down the rocks before finally coming to rest somewhere out of sight.

Katkin began to think she should get back up on Brinna and ride quickly past the distraught soldier. She hoped he would not try to follow her, though it did not seem likely now his crutches lay at the bottom of the cliff. But might this man need her help? After all, as a Juvenie* at the Infirmarie she ought to be ready to

---

* Younger apprentice of the Unity of Lalluna. One who has made Prime Vows, but is not yet old enough to make the Abiding Vows at age twenty-one. Pl. Juvenet.

use her training at any time. She had to approach him cautiously, that much was certain. Frantically she tried to remember what she had learned. Something about remaining calm, and not making any sudden movements, or was that the treatment for shock? Perhaps, if she didn't do something soon, it wasn't going to matter at all.

As she took a few tentative steps towards him, his horse caught wind of her and whinnied. The blond man turned sharply and almost fell. Katkin forgot to be cautious. With a cry of alarm, she broke into a run, with arms outstretched, determined to save him from joining his crutches at the bottom of the cliff. But after a few seconds he regained his balance and regarded her silently as she drew up with him, out of breath and red-cheeked.

His look was dismissive.

She was nothing like the sort of women he usually associated with—neither the spoiled and wealthy daughters of the fellow gentry he called his friends nor the languid courtesans who now and again received his business. On the street he wouldn't have given her a second glance, even though her dark-lashed green eyes were large and luminous, and her chestnut hair curled fetchingly round her face. Her mouth was far too generous, for one thing, and that ridiculous sprinkle of freckles across the bridge of her unremarkable nose made her look like a farmer's daughter. He wondered what on Yrth she was doing in the Acre alone, especially since she was wearing the simple vesture of a cloistered Unity Juvenie—a white long-sleeved shift, ending just below the knee, covered by a blue-striped apron, embroidered with the winged symbol of Lalluna on the bib. A worn fichu, meant to be tucked round the neck and shoulders, had come loose in her hurried advance across the meadow, giving her a disheveled look the stranger found both strangely appealing and somehow oddly familiar.

She blushed and re-tucked it quickly as soon as she saw his appraising glance.

Katkin, normally irrepressible and confident, could think of nothing at all to say. She drew herself up to her full height, but she still felt miserably childlike next to this tall soldier. He seemed to possess the battle-weary air she often saw in the injured Guardsmen at the Infirmarie. She took in his ice-blue eyes, and fine, straight nose. His elaborate uniform marked him as a wealthy and probably high-ranking officer of the King's Guard. The man appeared to find her confusion amusing, for his eyes held a spark of merriment and his lips twitched slightly. He did not speak either, but seemed to be waiting to see what mad thing she might do next.

Katkin cleared her throat and said nervously, "Good day, Sir. As I was making my way through the Acre just now, I noticed you..." a pause here while she struggled to find the least threatening phrase, "accidentally dropped your crutches over the edge of the cliff back there. I can fetch them for you, if it would please you."

"Do not trouble yourself, Miss." He had a deep voice, obviously accustomed to giving orders. "Miss?"

As she scrambled down the steep path to the river's edge, Katkin called back up to him, "It is no trouble, I know a way down." She made her way to the bottom and retrieved the crutches from the bank. Fortunately they looked to be undamaged by their fall. The same could not be said for Katkin's composure by the time she fought her way back up the cliff face, through many clumps of gorse and blackberry. Once back at the top, she handed over the crutches, and smiled awkwardly at him.

"Thank you for your help," the man said softly. "You must think it very careless of me to let them... fall like that." Again, his lips twitched and she knew he mocked her obvious discomfort. Then he removed his helmet, cradling it under his arm as he bowed stiffly.

"Captain Tomas Jean de Vigny at your service, Miss."

Katkin smoothed down her apron as best she could and wished her knees had not gotten quite so muddy. She finally found her voice. "Katrione du Chesne at yours." A disturbing sensation of *déjà vu* made her ask, "Have we met somewhere before, Captain?"

He ignored this question and posed one of his own. "May I ask what brings you into the St. Valery Acre's in the evening? You should return to the City. There are many dangers here, Miss."

Despite her now bedraggled appearance, she tried to answer him with adult dignity. "I am on my way to St. Valery now, Captain de Vigny. I have been in Belladore attending a birth, and I must return to the Infirmarie immediately."

"You are a healer?" he asked her, looking skeptically at her torn frock and ripped stockings.

"I am a Juvenie, of the Unity of Lalluna."

"Then you *are* cloistered. Are you not meant to have a chaperone? Why are you out alone?" he asked, raising his eyebrow at her.

Katkin swallowed uncomfortably, surprised at his knowledge of her order's precepts. "A pressing emergency called me away. I had no choice but to go alone." She glared at him defiantly. "Anyway, I can take care of myself. I am armed." She pointed to her bow and quiver lying on the ground next to Brinna.

The Captain shook his head. "So, you stayed longer than you should and had to take this risky path to get back to the city before curfew and the closing of the gates? I think you made a mistake. Your pathetic little bow would be no help against a man such as me. It is fortunate for you I am a gentleman."

Katkin spoke calmly, though his conceit annoyed her. "I will be punished severely for this mistake, as you call it." Despite her efforts to sound untroubled, her voice faltered as she looked worriedly about her, the stranger's plight almost forgotten. With nightfall imminent, she had little chance of getting back to the Infirmarie undetected. The Maitress would be furious with her. "I will never make it back in time now. I could lose my place with the Unity."

Tomas looked at her sympathetically. "You shall not be punished for stopping to help an injured man in distress. I will accompany you and speak to the Maitress myself."

"You would do that? Why? You don't even know me," she said, a bit surprised by his generosity.

"It is nothing. As a matter of fact, I was on my way to the Infirmarie for treatment when I paused here and, as you observed, dropped my blasted crutches. It is the least I could do after you have put yourself out for me. Now, if you will fetch your faithful steed, we can be on our way." He stood quite still, waiting for her to turn away.

Instinctively, she knew the proud Captain felt shame at his disability and did not want her to see his awkward movements. Dutifully, she turned her back on him and retraced her steps toward Brinna. She heard his deep voice from behind her, saying,

"Hold, Pollux. Stand ready." Katkin stole a glance back and saw his agonized expression as he scrambled ungracefully onto the animal. He righted himself on the saddle and carefully composed his appearance before leaning down to collect the crutches on the horse's flank. Katkin, shivering now in the early evening chill, paused to cover herself with her woolen cloak, and throw the hood over her head. Climbing on to Brinna, she urged the pony forward until she stood close to Tomas' horse. The Captain looked down upon her and said, "Shall we ride together?"

Katkin did not bother to hurry now she had the wounded man in her charge. Reasoning he could very well be her patient once they arrived, she decided to try and find out more about him. She wondered how to bring up the subject of his injured leg and strange behavior on the cliff edge. Not wanting him to feel ill at ease, she decided to take an indirect route.

"You said you were on your way to visit the Infirmarie? Do you intend to take the healing waters there?"

"Unfortunately that is so. I do not wish it, but my superiors have ordered me to. I would rather stay at the front than be fussed over by a coterie of goddess-worshiping harpies." His bitterness surprised and offended Katkin. She stared up at him with burning cheeks.

"So am I a 'goddess worshiping harpy' as well? After all, I am a Juvenie, and I have made my Prime Vows. You speak of something of which you obviously know nothing, Captain. We have a fine history of cures among those who believe in the healing powers of Lalluna."

He replied arrogantly, "Take no offence. I know more than you think. You are naïve and I would hardly expect you to understand. When you are older, as I am, you will have no time for such fairy tales."

Katkin snorted in derision—she felt sure he could not be more than a few years older than she. She felt her temper rising so she decided to change the subject. "Captain, will you tell me of the wound that has caused you to be in such a distressing situation? If it is not too private a matter, I mean?" She knew, as a Juvenie, she should not be asking such questions of a patient.

"It is, as you say, a private matter, yet I feel I owe you some explanation for my strange behavior back there on the bluff.

What did you think when you saw me throw these damned crutches over the cliff? Did you think I intended to follow them myself?" He looked at her questioningly, and Katkin nodded her head, realizing to her chagrin he had seen through her act from the very beginning.

"How do you know what I saw? You had your back turned."

He looked at her with a raised eyebrow and answered wryly, "I am a professional soldier, Miss. I would not have been promoted to the rank of Captain without some rudimentary ability to know when I am being crept up on. Also, your quite priceless expression gave you away." At this he smiled mockingly, but his face did lose its pained expression for a brief moment.

"You are making fun of me." Katkin said sullenly. "I truly thought you meant to throw yourself off the cliff after the crutches. I only wanted to help you." She looked up at him, sitting so far above her, resplendent on his steed. "Did you think of jumping, Captain?"

His smile disappeared. "No, I did not. I have seen too much death in my time to wish to add my own life to its number. But I am angry and frustrated and I let my feelings get the better of me on the cliff top. My utter failure to overcome my injury makes me behave so. I am no good to my country like this. Though I have suffered through the ministrations of many physicians, none has been able to cure me. When my commander ordered me to find the Daminem of Lalluna and endure more treatment, it did not please me—to put it mildly. I have no faith in any healing, and wish to find nothing but an honorable death on the battlefield." His cold blue eyes, so filled with pain and sadness, pierced her to the core.

She said softly, "I am sorry. There are many who have suffered in this war and the Daminem do what they can to help. Please tell me, if you will, how your leg came to be injured."

The Captain rode silently for a moment, and then said condescendingly, "If it troubles you to hear of warfare, you will not find this story a pleasant one. Such things are not proper subjects of conversation for young girls."

Katkin sharply declared, "I am not a child! Have I not told you I am one of the Juvenet of the Unity? Continue, Captain, I have heard many tales from the soldiers in my care. Yours can be

21

no worse." Katkin sat back on Brinna, hoping she had at last convinced him to treat her with some respect.

"As you wish. About six months ago, my men and I found ourselves trapped in a narrow gully on the west side of the Ariane, held down by musket fire from some of Reynard's cursed peasant rabble. We were taking heavy losses and I decided to make a break for the head of the gully and see if I could draw their fire, allowing my men to escape downwards."

Katkin looked up at him, amazed. Riding out alone against a host of enemies and he made it sound all so mundane. She remarked admiringly, "That was a very heroic thing to do."

He smiled ruefully. "Heroic, you say? Of course it was. That is a part of my duty, as a Captain in the King's Guard. But perhaps damned foolish would be a better choice of words. I took a pistol ball directly in the knee and it shattered the joint. I felt such agony, I cannot describe it, and I have not been free of it since that day. The battlefield surgeon wanted to amputate my leg from the knee down but my father prevented him from doing so. He insisted it would have ruined my chances for promotion. But my leg has not healed properly and now I am a cripple. Completely lame! I cannot walk without the aid of crutches, nor can I ride far. I am useless. Truly useless to the war effort or for anything else."

"Even if you can no longer fight, there are other ways you can help with the conflict, are there not?" Katkin suggested softly. "I cannot wage war either and I have lost much, yet I do what I can. Do you understand? Nicholas Reynard has hurt many people." Katkin thought she might shake him out of his self-pity with her words, but that was not the case.

Instead, he rounded on her, furiously shouting. "You are just a child. What could you have lost? Some pretty doll house or play toys? How could you understand what it is like to be an officer of the Guard? Do you know what expectations are placed on my shoulders, and what the price of failure is?"

Katkin drew a shaky breath, and stared at him, surprised at his vehement reaction. She might have told him more of her own catastrophic loss, but she had no intention of provoking him further, given his questionable mental state. Instead, she replied quietly, "I beg pardon, Captain. I have obviously spoken out of turn. Can you forgive me?"

He nodded curtly. "Of course, Miss du Chesne, but I should be apologizing to you instead. I have been a heel. I have only my injury to blame, and therefore myself."

She smiled up at him reassuringly. "It is nothing, really. I think we are both a little tired, that is all."

They traversed the last steeply winding section of path and reined their horses at the entrance to the Yoke. Katkin eyed the gate, which was shut and barred. She said, "Oh no! The curfew has already begun. They won't let us in now. What are we going to do?"

Tomas did not answer her. He rode close to the closed gate on Pollux and pounded loudly on the boards with the hilt of his sword to rouse the keeper within.

A small window opened. Beyond it, a head appeared, clad in the shining steel helmet of a Guardsman. The gatekeeper said, "The gate is closed until morning. You must show a pass."

Tomas drew himself up straight and barked, "I am Captain Tomas de Vigny of the Fourth Company, King's Guard. Open the gate and I will show my pass when we are safely inside. I have urgent business within the City." He glared at the gatekeeper, who blinked in surprise. Katkin looked at Tomas in dismay. She thought the Captain had spoken very rudely to the Guardsman, who only wanted to carry out his duty to keep the City safe. She wondered if he would refuse, but a moment later she heard the heavy bar drop to the ground and the gate opened wide to admit them.

A cobbled courtyard and a small hut filled the space between the inner and outer gates. A low fire burned in a brazier. Katkin noticed a tin bowl of beans and a chunk of brown bread lying next to a three-legged stool by the fire. Apparently, they disturbed the gatekeeper's evening meal, such as it was. Looking toward the other side of the courtyard, she could see the inner gate, as well reinforced as the outer one, leading to the Yoke.

Without dismounting, Tomas reached into his saddlebag, pulled out a small rolled parchment, beribboned, and sealed with red wax. He dropped it into the gatekeeper's outstretched hand, saying, "Here is my pass, boy. Now let us proceed immediately."

The young Guardsman unrolled the document and read it laboriously, his lips shaping each word. Tomas looked on with mounting impatience. Finally, the Guardsman said, "I am sorry

23

for the delay, Captain. Your papers are in order and you may cross into the City. But the young lady? Does she have a pass? Otherwise, I must ask her to return tomorrow morning."

Tomas swore explosively at the young Guardsman. "This young woman is my companion and is a resident of the City, who could not return by curfew time through no fault of her own. She is coming with me now. Do not argue with me further, Private."

"Sir, I am under strict orders from the Sergeant not to admit anyone who does not have the proper papers. As much as I would like to, I cannot let her pass the Yoke with you." The young Guardsman looked up at the Captain and swallowed nervously.

Katkin felt very sorry for the lad, who was probably a farm boy from the sunny fields beyond the City, not yet fifteen summers old. He had been called up to fight in an incomprehensible war, taken far from home and left to carry out his duties as gatekeeper on this dark and cold night as best he could. How could the Captain be so unfair? She tried to defuse the tension. "Captain, please, let it rest. I can easily find lodging in one of the houses near the mouth of the Yoke."

Tomas ignored her plea and jumped down from his horse to confront the Guardsman face to face. Only Katkin knew how much the effort would have cost him. He said angrily, "Call your Sergeant. I would speak with him." The Private backed away, and walked quickly into the hut.

In a moment, the boy returned with an older man, whose sour expression indicated he did not appreciate the interruption of his evening meal. After wiping his mouth on his uniform sleeve, he said, "Well? What can I do for you, Captain?"

"I wish to travel the Yoke in the company of this young lady, who does not have a pass. She represents no threat to the City. Will you allow her to cross, or must I call for *your* superior officer?"

The Sergeant scratched his head. "Well now, Captain. Rightly speaking I ought not to."

Tomas swore impatiently and said, "Did you serve with Major General Charles de Vigny in the campaign against the Mardonne?" The Sergeant nodded warily. The Captain continued, "He is now the Lord of Havenwood. A very powerful man. He is also my father. Surely you can trust my judgment in the matter of one small girl?" Katkin colored at this dismissive description, but said nothing.

The Sergeant considered this for a moment then said gruffly, "Very well, I will allow her to proceed in your company. But go carefully—the stones on the Yoke are slick with frost. You should lead your mounts across."

The young gatekeeper produced a ring of large brass keys from his pocket. He opened the inner gates and waved them through. Katkin turned back as they continued on to the Yoke, to see the Guardsman staring after them, shaking his head and muttering before he slammed the inner gate shut.

Katkin paused while Tomas retrieved his crutches from their strap on the saddle. Brinna stamped restively on the narrow Yoke, obviously eager to get back to her stable. Katkin felt the same way, despite the trouble she knew waited for her at the Infirmarie. Though the Captain had promised to plead her case with the Maitress, she decided to leave him and travel the rest of the way alone. Grasping Brinna's bridle, she urged her pony forward into the darkness and listened for the ringing sound of his horse's iron-shod hooves on the stones to show he followed.

After a moment, Tomas called out tiredly, "Katrione, please. Do not proceed so quickly. I am unable to keep up with you."

Perhaps the sound of Brinna's feet on the cobbles drowned out his voice, for Katkin did not slow her pace, nor did she look back.

Tomas forlornly watched her disappear into the darkness, as he struggled along with a single crutch, gripping the bridle of his horse with his free hand. Despair at the hopelessness of his injury overwhelmed him. His glorious career had effectively ended the moment he took a musket ball in the kneecap, plunging him into a daily grinding battle with pain that he could never win. Alcohol deadened the worst of it, but only for a little while. He began thinking how easy it would be to slip over the edge of the Yoke into the sanctuary of the Mere, away from the agony of his shattered knee and the pity of his comrades. If he could not die in battle, would that not be an honorable end? As Katkin made her way across the Yoke without him, he left the side of his horse and staggered to the edge. He clung to the railing as a wave of nausea left him chilled and sweating.

"*Come to me...*" The water called to him now, in a cold and terrifying voice that froze him to the marrow. "*I will take away the pain for you in no time at all...*"

As he stared down into the blackness of the Mere, Tomas unaccountably began to think about his childhood—winters in the City and golden summers at the country estate, with servants to wait on his every whim. His parents seldom saw him, of course, being always busy with the social whirl of the privileged. Tomas' father, a highly decorated General, took a young, foreign-born bride after his retirement from the King's Guard. His mother, although kind enough, did not seem to want to have much of anything to do with her son and he grew up with a succession of nannies and governesses. The General had a stormy relationship with his beautiful, blond wife, and when a jealous rage overtook him, he would often strike her. When she died suddenly, giving birth to a stillborn son, he had almost gone mad. He drank to excess and lashed out at everyone around him. Tomas grieved deeply, but unobtrusively, and avoided the old man as much as he could. He matured quickly after that, fiercely independent, spoiled by his wealth and neglected by his father. A stint in military school hammered much of the independence out of him, but he gained something much more valuable—a fanatical devotion to the King's Guard that pleased his father immensely. He still spoke proudly of Tomas' field promotion to Captain, after a particularly long and bloody campaign against Reynard's soldiers.

Now, as he felt tears well up and spill over onto his cheeks, Tomas knew just what his old man would say. "Tears are for the women, boy; we men have to show discipline, keep up the side. Stop this damned self-pity." But his father didn't understand him—no one did, really. Tomas could see the hazy form of his father on the bridge now, striding towards him, shouting something. Suddenly he realized that all he had to do was fall forward over the railing and the water would do the rest. His father would no longer be able to see him, would not be able to mock his despondency and pain. Slowly, he removed the dragoon's helmet from his head and placed it on the railing. As the black horsehair plume stirred in the wind, he let himself pitch head first into the water.

* * * *

Katkin hurried along the Yoke until she reached the stone-walled bay in the middle. She paused there and listened again for the sound of Pollux's hooves, but heard only the slapping of the waves on the breakwater. Katkin left Brinna and walked back to look for the Captain, guiltily regretting her angry impulse to leave him behind. She spied the larger, dark form of his horse first, and then, more vaguely, Tomas leaning dangerously far over the railing. Katkin broke into a run, heedless of the icy stones, anxiously calling his name. While she was still some distance away, he fell forward and hit the rocks of the breakwater, then sank, silently, into the inky blackness.

Once she reached the place where his helmet lay, she anxiously scanned the water, praying he would surface, but he did not. Katkin threw off her cloak and climbed over the railing. She jumped wide to clear the rocks, praying none lurked beneath the surface. The freezing water hit her like a physical blow and drove the breath from her lungs, temporarily disorienting her. She surfaced and began to tread water, trying to decide where to dive down, knowing she had little time to spare. Already her extremities felt almost numb. Doggedly she dived, using her hands to grope blindly in the water for any trace of him. She found nothing.

Katkin went under again and again, without success, until her strength was almost gone. It felt as though the water became thicker with each dive—until it was like syrup she could barely push her way through. As she kicked furiously to try and bring some feeling back into her frozen legs, her foot struck something in the water. Steeling herself, she plunged down and cast about for the thing she had touched. She found the Captain! Wrapping her arms around his middle, she tried to raise him to the surface, but his boot seemed to be caught in something close to the bottom of the lake. Her lungs and heart exploded with pain and she began to see stars swimming in the blackness around her. Katkin realized dizzily she would likely perish if she stayed under much longer. Just as she felt she must to let go and surface again, he floated free. With a reserve she did not know she possessed, Katkin forced her way to the surface with Tomas in tow, exploding from the water and gulping great breaths of air. Her head cleared immediately.

In the almost pitch darkness, Katkin could just make out the vague line of the Yoke in the distance, lit at intervals by dim lanterns. She felt her strength fading rapidly and called out for help, though she did not believe the gatekeeper would be able to hear her. Tomas felt like a thousand pound weight in her arms. She decided she had better swim for the breakwater, but each time she tried to close the distance it seemed to move further away. The water was growing warmer and now felt so comforting she felt as though she could sleep in its embrace forever.

Katkin called out again, although this time it sounded like a whisper. She sent a desperate prayer to the Goddess Lalluna, and to Ancamma, Goddess of the Mere, and then closed her eyes for a few seconds to rest. She woke with a start when her head slipped under the water. Coughing and choking, she struggled to the surface, but could no longer keep moving her legs. Katkin knew she must be close to death as an unearthly, glowing mist began to dance in front of her eyes. Her conscious thoughts began to glide away from her, like beads from a broken necklace. As her face sank once more below the surface of the Mere, the last thing she saw was the insubstantial figure of a winged woman emerging from the formless mist.

3

The Priest, Taleyear

(Estate of Naer, Standing Seven*)

Death will not appreciate your meddling, Geya.

Then Death can take the soul. I have another to give.

Moonlight looks stricken. But what will happen to him when he dies again? He will be lost forever.

Geya is unmoved. We need him this turn of the Gyre. The survival of the Autochthones depends on it, and our survival depends on *them*, my sisters.

~~~~~~~~~~

"Will she live, Maitress? I heard that when the patrol found her on the Yoke, she was very nearly drowned."

"Katrione is young and strong, and I think she will survive, Goddess willing."

"What about the man with her? Do you have any idea how they ended up in the water?"

"No, I do not. Nor do I know why Katrione would be out of the Infirmarie at such a late hour. Do you have any information you would like to share about that, Becka?"

Rebecca Kent was Katkin's best friend and roommate at the Infirmarie. She was a short, slightly plump girl from the countryside west of the City. With her mass of stringy yellow curls and slight overbite, she reminded the Maitress of a recalcitrant pony.

Becka fiddled with the mobcap covering her blond curls. "Kat told me she needed to go to the village of Belladore to attend to her sister's pregnancy, and she promised to be back before nightfall. She asked me to cover for her and I didn't think it would do

---

* The fifteen Estate cards are twinned. Depending which way they are drawn, they may describe a thing or its opposite.

any harm. Willow is the only family Katkin has left, and she and her husband Yannick are very poor."

The Maitress frowned. "Too poor for the sister to make her own way here to the Infirmarie? Katrione knows we make no one pay if they have a hardship."

"Quite possibly, Maitress. She went into labor suddenly. Her husband sent word to Katkin last night, and she left very early in the morning on Brinna, before rounds or even Lauds."

The Maitress looked grave. "Until Katrione awakes, the situation will remain a mystery. In the meantime, all we know for sure is that the young man's name is Tomas de Vigny."

"How do you know that? I thought he had not regained consciousness yet." Becka's unquenchable curiosity always exasperated the Maitress after a few minutes.

"Do not be impertinent, Becka. Too many questions are very unseemly," she snapped. "He carried identifying papers with him, though I needed them not. I knew the son of Charles de Vigny on sight."

"Charles de Vigny?"

"Yes, girl, of the Havenwood de Vignys. What do they teach you in history these days? General de Vigny led the campaign against the Mardonne, when the City herself almost fell to their forces during the long siege. After the war, the king rewarded him with a Lordship. Much later, his wife Lara stayed here for a few days and the boy came to see her once." The Maitress appeared to find the memory of this upsetting and Becka saw her sigh heavily. She fell silent, but Becka, ever inquisitive, wanted more information.

"Was he the old man outside the gate yesterday morning demanding to see you?"

The Maitress looked up, unhappy at this interruption of her reverie. "Eh? Must you know every detail? Yes, indeed, I received him and his retinue after breakfast. The de Vignys are very wealthy and it brings great honor to our Infirmarie that the boy is recuperating here. Though the old man is a terror still and demanded his own doctor be allowed to treat his son. I told him Captain de Vigny carried orders from his commanding officer placing him in our care and he would be given the best possible treatment during his stay with us. He looked moderately satisfied and went back to Havenwood to wait for him to awaken."

"How long will he have to wait?" Becka asked.

"Goddess only knows, my child. They must have spent a long time in the icy water and it could have meant the grave for both of them."

"Did you speak with the gatekeeper, ma'am? Perhaps he knows something about why they came into the City at such a late hour," Becka said, hoping she might somehow vindicate her friend.

"No, the gatekeeper could add very little to the story. He mentioned they passed through on his watch on their way to the City, and the Captain rudely insisted Katrione be allowed to accompany him."

Katkin wandered once more through the silent and forbidding land that Jacq had taken her to, long ago.

She found herself this time on the Yoke, and as she looked out over the Mistmere she saw many more of the faceless white creatures floating on its surface. They looked almost like mermaids, for they had no legs, only worm-like bodies covered in translucent scales. Katkin felt drawn to one in particular, and though she felt very afraid, nevertheless she approached the edge of the breakwater so she might get a closer look at the thing it held in its arms. A body lay there, wearing the blue uniform of a cuirassier. Katkin knelt so she could see the dead man's face and then gave a surprised cry. It was Tomas de Vigny. She reached out a trembling hand, but the creature before her said softly, "You must not touch the astrelet*. His anafireon resides there and I must keep it safe, until we may leave this place. But why do you wander the Vastness? You are not among the dead yet. Go back to the mortal world, *Fenacrist*. Go back, Living One." The other creatures took up the cry and Katkin backed away from them in terror. As she turned to run, her foot caught on the uneven stones of the Yoke and she plunged headfirst into the icy Mere. With a scream of panic, she woke. The Maitress and Becka stood over her, their faces grave and attentive.

"Maitress! I am sorry I overslept. Please don't punish me. I will start work right now," she said anxiously. Katkin looked about her with confusion. The room, though very familiar, did

---

* Spirit body

not belong to her. It contained only a bed, a bedside table and a padded bench for visitors. She struggled to rise, feeling curiously lethargic after what was surely a long sleep. The Maitress pushed her gently back down on the bed as Becka spoke eagerly.

"You don't remember anything, Kat?"

The Maitress spoke sharply. "Hush, child. There will be time for remembering later. Now she needs rest. How do you feel, Katrione?"

Katkin looked around wildly, asking, "What has happened? Why am I in the wards? I dreamed I heard someone talking about death. I am not dead, am I?"

Becka smiled, relieved to see her friend animated and talking after so long in a deathlike sleep. "Nay, you are not dead. It would take more than a dip in the Mere to kill you, I guess, though you had us worried for a little while."

Suddenly, the whole horrible experience came flooding back to Katkin—Tomas falling, and the icy water, and her desperate struggle to get to the breakwater. Beyond that everything was a blur. "How did I get back to the Yoke? I could not have swum another inch."

The Maitress answered her question. "The young man managed to swim to the breakwater with you and called for help. The patrol heard him and brought you both into the Citadel. We..."

Katkin, unable to contain herself, interrupted the Maitress, something she would normally never dare do. "Is the Captain all right now? What happened to Brinna and his horse, Pollux? Did someone fetch them?"

"Do not trouble yourself, my dear. The animals are here in the stables, and are being well cared for. Captain de Vigny is here also." The Maitress spoke briskly. "I should go and check on him. I will leave you here with Becka for company. Who, I should add, is not to tire you by asking questions about your experience." She delivered these instructions with a black look to Becka, who quailed visibly.

"Yes, Maitress, of course. I will be as quiet as a mouse."

"I want to talk," said Katkin irrepressibly. "Also, I have to make a confession. I must tell you why I left the Infirmarie without your permission."

"Now is not the time, Katrione. Instead, you must take a little food and then rest. You have been through a difficult experience, young woman, and we must allow the body to heal itself. I will excuse you from duties until further notice. We can discuss the fact you were out of bounds when the accident happened after you are stronger." The Maitress left, shaking her head.

Abruptly, Katkin felt very tired once more, and said, "Just let me rest for a little while, Becka, and I will have some broth..." She drifted off to sleep, feeling warm and protected in the comfortable confines of her room. Becka smiled softly at her friend and settled down on the bench to wait for her to awaken.

The Maitress walked down the long hallway deep in thought.

One of the senior healers, Damenie[*] Beneficence, met her and said, "Maitress, I was just coming to find you. The Captain that came in with Katrione, Tomas de Vigny, has regained consciousness. He insists you come at once and answer his inquiries. Should I send for his father?"

The Maitress shook her head, saying, "Not yet, Damenie. Come, take me to him. There are things I wish to ask of him as well. As soon as I have seen him you may send word to Havenwood."

Tomas had awoken in a similar room to Katkin, but did not make himself comfortable. In fact, he loudly and angrily demanded immediate discharge. Upon entering, the Maitress spoke forcefully to him, saying, "Captain de Vigny, be quiet this instant! This is a house of healing and I will not have my other patients disturbed by this childish display of petulance. Now if you will please lie back in your bed, I will endeavor to answer your questions and ascertain when you may leave."

"You have no hold on me, Madam. I shall leave when I see fit. Now bring me my uniform. The sooner I get it, the fewer disturbances the other patients will have." Tomas sat up straighter, impatiently waiting for the harpies to obey his command.

"I am afraid I must disagree with you, Captain," the Maitress said firmly. "We found in your possession a set of sodden but perfectly readable orders, which said in no uncertain terms that you must report to the Infirmarie and place yourself in the care of the healers. No doubt you find this inconvenient, but the matter is closed as far as I am concerned."

---

[*] A healer of the Unity of Lalluna who has taken Abiding Vows.

Tomas had the grace to look abashed and lay back on the pillows with a heavy sigh.

"Captain de Vigny, I understand you wish to have news of the Juvenie, Katrione du Chesne. I can report she is recovering well, and should suffer no ill effects from her midnight swimming expedition with you." She spoke dryly with an even gaze towards the Captain. "Can you provide me with any further details about that?"

Tomas shifted uncomfortably in his bed, trying to avoid the old woman's stare. "As I told the patrol, ma'am, my recollection is unclear. I remember passing through the gate and proceeding on to the bridge. The girl's pony slipped on the frosty cobbles and bumped her. She fell into the water and I jumped in to rescue her. After I found her unconscious in the Mere, I swam with her to the breakwater and shouted for help, attracting the attention of the causeway patrol. By the time they carried us back to the Citadel, I must have passed out from shock."

The Maitress' gaze did not waver. Tomas could not tell if she accepted his fabrication or not. Perhaps it was stupid to lie about what really happened, but he did not want anyone, least of all that snot-nosed gatekeeper, to know he needed rescuing by some chit of a girl after trying to take his own life. Tomas cleared his throat guiltily, aware the Maitress still waited for him to continue his story.

"That is all I remember. The girl and I met in the Acre. I knew she should not be there alone so I escorted her back to the Yoke. I would like very much to speak with her and see her condition for myself." He looked hopefully up at the Maitress, who shook her head quite firmly.

"I am sorry, it will be impossible for you to visit the Juvenie. I must confine you to this area until you complete your treatment. Katrione has been relieved of her duties until she has made a full recovery and can explain why she left the compound in direct contravention of her primary vows. Please be assured I will personally see to her treatment and she will receive the best of care until she can answer this serious charge against her. Now, Captain de Vigny, with your cooperation, we will begin the examination."

"Maitress, will you be doing the assessment yourself?" Damenie Beneficence asked.

The Maitress looked away from her. "No, Damenie, I feel a little under the weather. Please begin when you are ready."

Tomas watched as the younger healer moved to stand by his bedside. Closing her eyes, she placed her hands on either side of his forehead. He immediately felt great warmth flowing from his fingers. Passing her hands downwards, she moved them to his chest and paused there.

At that moment, the door flew open to reveal three flustered-looking Juvenet and a tall, white-haired man in full military regalia. The lead Juvenie, Trechelle Peletier, fairly fell into the room in her haste to stop the old man from entering.

She blushed deeply. "I am sorry, Maitress, we couldn't prevent General de Vigny from coming to see if the Captain was awake yet."

The Damenie opened her eyes as she took her hands away from Tomas' chest. She said, "The patient's lungs are clear, Maitress. There is no aspirated water or other damage I could perceive."

The Maitress said, "Very well, that will be all for now. Trechelle, please allow the General to enter." She turned serenely to the old man, who opened his mouth to speak and at first merely spluttered in his haste to make himself heard.

"I should have been told the minute my son awoke. You have delayed me unnecessarily. I am due to meet with the Mayor in a few minutes. What kind of an operation are you running here? No order! No discipline!"

He drew a breath to continue his tirade and the Maitress cut him off, noting with some amazement he had not seen fit to greet his son or ask of his condition. "Welcome, General de Vigny. I was going to send for you directly, after we finished your son's examination. You may stay with him now, but please limit your visit to a few minutes, as he still requires a great deal of rest." Watching Tomas out of the corner of her eye, she saw him pale visibly and begin to sweat as the old man approached his bed. The Maitress said firmly, "Escort the General back to the waiting area in five minutes, Trechelle, not a minute more. In the meantime, wait outside so they may have some privacy." Trechelle arranged the pillows so Tomas could sit up comfortably and left with the Maitress.

Charles de Vigny made his way towards the bed, his cane tapping out a tattoo on the scrubbed floorboards. Tomas looked like death, but the old man appeared not to notice. "Well, boy, how do you feel? I hope the harpies are keeping you comfortable here," the General said, giving Tomas a rare smile.

"Fine, Sir." Tomas knew better than to complain about the pain from his injured knee.

"Good lad. I am proud of you, boy, very proud. Did you know your story was in the Gazette this morning? The headline says 'Injured Hero Saves Girl From Icy Death.' The fellows at the club talked of nothing else." His father patted his arm. "I will get you out of this misbegotten hole as soon as I can. Why would you want to stay here when you could be recuperating at Havenwood, instead? Is there anything you need in the meantime?"

Actually, Tomas did not want to go back to his father's mansion at all. There he would be alone with the old man, with no well-meaning harpies to protect him. From long experience, Tomas knew his father would force him to recount his heroic deed over and over again while he relentlessly questioned every detail. He feared that eventually, after some slip up, the old man would discover what actually happened the night Tomas went into Mistmere. Now he considered the alternative it was a much better idea to stay here, in these peaceful surroundings, and see the General for five or ten minutes a day. He could pretend to be tired when he did not want to answer questions. Anyway, he must figure out a way to see Katrione again, to make her change her story to match his. Maybe the old man could help after all, especially given his good mood. Tomas suddenly possessed the beginnings of a plan. He said, beseechingly, "Father, perhaps there is *something* you could do for me..."

Later the same evening, the Maitress sat at her desk figuring the budget for the coming year. One of the younger Juvenet appeared at the doorway and tapped softly. "Come," she said, looking up from the mound of unattended paperwork in front of her. "Please be brief, Amber. I am very busy, as you can see," she said wearily.

The young girl curtsied respectfully. "I am sorry, ma'am. There is a General Charles de Vigny here to see you. He is waiting in the blue sitting room and says he will not leave until you have spoken with him, as he has an urgent matter to discuss. He was not very polite, ma'am."

The Maitress sighed and put down her pen. "Yes, I dare say he was not. I am sorry the old dragon spoke rudely to you. I will go to him now. Please bring up some tea and perhaps a bun or two. It seems I will not have the opportunity for dinner any time soon." She struggled up from her chair, her old bones stiff from sitting still. Reaching for her cane, she began the slow trek down the hall to the receiving rooms.

General de Vigny rose stiffly and greeted her with a curt nod as the Maitress entered the small sitting room, warmed by a cheery fire in the hearth. Comfortable, though threadbare, couches and chairs furnished the room. Before either could speak further, Amber arrived with the tea and a few currant buns arranged on a wooden tray with a posy of wildflowers in a vase. She placed the tray on a low table between two armchairs.

"Will there be anything else, Ma'am?" she said, eying the General distrustfully, as if she truly expected him to belch fire like a dragon.

"No thank you, Amber, you may go for the evening. I might be working *very* late and there is no need for both of us to be tired in the morning." With another, stiffer, curtsy, Amber took her leave.

The General seemed oblivious to the Maitress' hint and sat silently as she busied herself with the tea. Finally, as the stillness grew uncomfortable, she said, "General, I hope you are keeping well? To what do I owe the pleasure of this visit?"

The elder de Vigny looked at her levelly, his blue eyes still clear and piercing, even at his advanced age. Although he officially retired some twenty-five years ago, he still wore full military regalia, including a chest full of gold and silver medals. His thinning white hair was neatly brushed back from the temples. His skin color tended rather alarmingly to blotchy redness, especially when he was angry. Charles de Vigny spent a lot of his time being angry.

He spoke abruptly. "You have a Juvenie here, named Katrione du Chesne, correct?"

The Maitress nodded patiently, now aware that she could not distract the General by pleasantries from whatever he wished to discuss with her. She told herself firmly he would not goad her into losing her temper, no matter what he might say next.

"And my son saved this girl from the Mere, correct?"

Again she nodded, wondering at the reason for this examination, but unwilling to interrupt his questioning. The General's legendary temperament had not softened with age and she did not wish to run foul of it.

"My son tells me she has been suspended from her duties as a Juvenie, pending the outcome of an investigation. I wish to know..."

This was too much. The Maitress interrupted brusquely, forgetting her earlier resolution to try and humor him. "General, I must ask you not to interfere with a purely internal matter here at the Infirmarie. I can provide you with no further details about the girl, Katrione, or her status. It has nothing to do with your son's care, which should be your only interest at this point."

She sat back in her chair, hoping this would satisfy the old man, but she was disappointed.

"Madam, I beg to differ with you. As you say, my interest is with my son's welfare. Tomas has spoken to me at length about this girl and her abilities as a healer. He wishes his care be given over to her and I am here to make sure that happens, as much as it pains me." The General's disdain for the healing arts of the Unity was also legendary.

The Maitress choked on a mouthful of hot tea, not believing what she heard. "That is impossible. She is not even qualified and will not be for another three years, assuming she will be allowed to complete her training, which is by no means certain at this time."

"Be that as it may, my son wants to make use of her talents, limited though they are," the General said, intractably.

"Are you aware of the Unity's history and training programs at all, General de Vigny?" The Maitress spoke in even tones, trying with some difficultly to keep her rising temper in check.

"I don't see what that has to do..."

The Maitress spoke softly, but determinedly. "Allow me to continue. You may be aware some girls born in Beaumarais are given a special Gift of healing from the Goddess Lalluna?"

Here Charles snorted derisively. Of course, he heard rumors

of such gifts, but no rational man believed in them. "Bunch of fairy stories, if you ask me. Still, if it keeps the ladies happy at home, I suppose it is harmless enough."

"I do not recall asking you, so please attend to me as I try to explain. Girls who possess this Gift are tested and then may join the Unity, usually at the age of twelve."

The General frowned as the Maitress paused to sip her tea. "I don't understand what all this rot about gifts has to do with my simple request."

"Patience, please. All may become clear with time." The Maitress decided, though it pained her, that she must try to talk some sense into the old reprobate. Perhaps if he knew something of the history of the Unity he would understand why she could not possibly grant his request. "The Unity goes back to the origin of the City itself. Just after the trader, Antoine St. Valery, discovered the calefactive springs in the heart of the mountain, Hythea, and founded the City, we Daminem began to create this facility, using our Gifts for the good of all who need healing. Over the years, our numbers have grown, through an unwavering dedication to the Goddess and to the care of the sick and injured. Our training program for Juvenet must be followed religiously, as it is necessary for a healer to have a most thorough education. She learns every system of the body and its care. Patients stay here many weeks as a rule and we provide traditional medical remedies as well as the healing water. But our treatments go far beyond the conventional. A Juvenie learns the method of stilling her mind to enter a trance-like state. By placing her hands on the patient she is able to see inside the body and visualize the area of injury or disease."

The General gave her a skeptical frown but she plunged on regardless. "Katrione, at nineteen years of age, is in her seventh year of training here. Although she does undoubtedly have strong skills in Sight, she does not have the complete medical training necessary to treat your son's injury. I hope you understand now my refusal of your request."

She stopped talking for a moment, and ate one of the buns which had lain undisturbed on the plate as she made her argument. The General said nothing. After another bun had disappeared, he spoke quietly. "Tell me something, Maitress. Do the people who come here and avail themselves of your services always recover?"

The Maitress paused in her pursuit of a third bun. Such a question from Tomas' father might be perilous indeed, given his wife had died at the Infirmarie of a hemorrhage. "General, why do you ask such a question, when you already know the answer? Most people who come here for treatment experience a little improvement over a long period of time. Others show a significant improvement. In rare cases, there would be a complete remission of symptoms. Tragically, there are always those whose conditions deteriorate and they die, as did Lara, your wife." She stared at him, the food forgotten, unsure where he might be heading with this new line of questioning.

He looked back at her, his eyes narrowed shrewdly. "And to what do you attribute your success or failure? Is the Goddess so capricious that she only heals those who please her in some way, or punishes those who displease her?"

In her deep dismay, the Maitress involuntarily made the sign of the Goddess by crossing her arms over her chest. She spoke sharply in reply to his blasphemy. "Of course not! Though we give everyone the same careful treatment, some patients are too ill or too horrifically injured by the time they come to our care. Invariably some will die. In those cases, the Damenie in charge of treatment feels a great deal of remorse, but we are trained to deal with this and not allow it to interfere with our duties."

"So how *does* the Damenie represent the Goddess? Or does she make herself known to the infirm directly?"

More blasphemy. The Maitress felt she was losing control, so she must act decisively to bring the conversation to a halt. She spoke with finality, "General de Vigny... Charles, I appreciate your sudden interest in our theology, but I don't have the time at the moment to discuss the finer points of our healing procedures. Perhaps you could come back at some later date, and I will be more than happy..."

He rose to his feet, medals jangling, and telltale signs of blotchy redness showing around his stiff white collar. "Answer my question immediately," he thundered. "How does the Damenie represent the Goddess?"

His stick thumped the floor repeatedly and the Maitress

feared his tantrum would disturb the sleeping patients below.

She spoke quietly, trying to calm him. "Please, sit down and I will answer your question as best I can. Of course, very occasionally, the Goddess appears directly to a patient. However, in most cases she relies on us to serve as an image of her." The Maitress paused and struggled to find the right words. Never before had a layman asked her to explain something so fundamental to the faith of the Unity. "In effect, the Damenie becomes a vessel of the Goddess in the eyes of the one being healed."

"So it is vitally important for the patient to have faith in the Damenie, because she represents the Goddess, is that correct?" The General leaned forward and stabbed his finger in the air, emphasizing his words. "Although, like any rational man, my son has no truck with this so-called Goddess of yours, he does seem to believe the girl, Katrione, can help him. Your job as the Mother Superior of this Infirmarie is to provide him with whatever he needs to make a full recovery. Having failed me once, Maitress, it would not be wise to let it happen again." Here Tomas' father spoke more softly, as he produced the carrot to go with the stick. "If my boy recovers and can lead his troops to another glorious victory, you will not find me or the City ungrateful, Maitress. I don't need to mention, I am sure, that I have great influence with the Mayor. We could make sure the Infirmarie is well looked after when the next budget is discussed. But if this simple request of mine is not granted..." His voice trailed off, the threat unspoken between them.

The Maitress paused before answering him, remembering the scene in Tomas' room. She realized Charles de Vigny's main interest in life, now he had retired, must be basking in the reflected glory of his son's prowess on the battlefield. The General, thinking her still ambivalent, spoke again. "You know, my friend Gaspard du Chesne died at the hands of the Rising. What happened to that family is a terrible stain on our history. I don't think we should even be considering any sort of sanction against the daughter of so prominent and hapless a family, do you, Maitress? The Council would not take kindly to that at all." He played this trump card decisively. The Maitress was not discomfited. She had been quite sure Charles would bring up the tragic du Chesne story eventually.

Allowing herself a moment to gather her thoughts, she sat back tranquilly and poured herself another cup of tea. She recalled what she knew of Katrione's history. The girl had been born into wealth and privilege at Tintaren, the du Chesnes' vast vineyard to the south of the City. Her father, Gaspard du Chesne, the Lord of Belladore, had many families in his employ, but paid poor wages for long hours. Nicholas Reynard, seeing the opportunity to exploit the unrest of the cottars, had chosen the lands of the du Chesnes as one of the first strikes of the present War. The ensuing battle left many casualties, including Lord and Lady du Chesne, who died defending their home from the Rising. When Reynard claimed Tintaren for the Rising, Katrione and her sister Willow had been attending school in the City. The exclusive academy summarily expelled them once word arrived that their fortunes were reversed. They moved to the village of Belladore to live in a one-roomed cottage. Willow, a talented seamstress, made just enough money to keep them.

But the girl's Gift had first made itself known in that country village. After her cat was found drowned in a well, onlookers from the village reported Katrione went into a trance and laid her hands on the unmoving animal. Shortly afterwards, it sat up and washed itself—as alive as any other cat. The astounded Willow had brought her sister to the Unity for testing, and she had been admitted as a Juvenie. Of course, the Maitress did not believe, then or now, that Katrione had completely and instantaneously healed the animal, for no healer in the long history of the Unity had ever possessed such power. The cat, made deeply unconscious by the near drowning, simply revived at her touch. Nevertheless, until the last few days, the Maitress had thought Katrione an exemplary student, for she had finished top in her class for the last three years.

The Maitress looked over to the General, now sitting back in his chair smugly, as though he had already won the argument. Knowing he could be very helpful to the Infirmarie if he chose to be, she decided to give it one last effort. She laid a hand on his sleeve and spoke softly. "Do you know what the Rule of Lalluna is, Charles?"

"No, and I don't think I need to know." The neck around the collar reddened again.

She spoke hastily, hoping to forestall another tantrum. "If you will be so kind as to allow me to explain, my dear General." The Maitress had thought of a possible compromise and wanted to keep the old man occupied while she straightened the details in her mind. Having the patronage of de Vigny could mean much more money and influence with the Council for the Infirmarie. She wanted to please him. But the precepts of the Unity required the Maitress to remove Katrione from the ranks of the Juvenet. How could she do both? "The Rule of Lalluna is the vow we make when we are accepted into this Unity." She dropped her voice low. "You know, Charles, having the Gift can be a terrible burden."

The General looked confused. "I would have thought it a great boon, if it were real. Not that it is, of course."

"So do many who have not the experience of it. That is why Lalluna created the Unity; to guide those endowed with the Gift in the healing arts. Otherwise, they have the desire to practice, but no control over the outcome. Madness and death lie at the end of that path. That is why we allow no one to practice the Gift outside the auspices of the Unity. All must adhere strictly to the Rule, and keep themselves upon the straight and narrow way. When a maiden comes to us in her twelfth year, it is before menarche and before she has known any man."

The General looked distinctly uncomfortable at this. The Maitress rose and moved towards the fireplace. She spoke thoughtfully. "The Gift of Healing is precious, and must not be squandered. We who have the Gift bow to the Rule of Lalluna— to remain childless and give our bodies only to the Goddess for her use as a Vessel of healing. Obedience and chastity must become our watchwords—otherwise we become unfit to serve as her representatives and the Gift leaves us. Do you not see how difficult this situation is? The girl, Katrione, left the compound without permission and traveled through the Acre with a young man, unchaperoned."

The General growled, "Surely you don't suspect my son of contributing to her delinquency?"

"Of course not. I make no accusations. But the Rule on this matter is clear." During this last exchange, the Maitress had determined she could indeed curry favor with the General and also follow the Rule. She spoke decisively. "I believe I may be able to grant your request after all. The Goddess herself will decide. I will allow Katrione to attend to you son's care here at the Infirmarie, assuming she is well enough to undertake it. If she is able to help him, through the use of Lalluna's healing waters, I will allow her to finish her Juvenead* and continue his treatment. If she has lost her Gift, she must depart and Tomas will be given a more experienced healer for the remainder of his stay."

The Maitress wondered privately how fair this test would be for Katrione, who, unless one believed the crazy talk about the cat, had no actual experience with using her Gift for treatment. Still, as the head of the Unity, she had faith in the discernment of the Goddess. Lalluna would tell her if the girl still had her Gift.

General De Vigny smiled thinly, pleased he had made the old woman capitulate to his demand. "Very well, Maitress, I accept your conditions. I have no doubt my boy will recover, if he sets his mind to it; he is a de Vigny, after all. He doesn't need you or any of your harpies to make that happen. Now he will have the girl as his nurse, he will use his own strength to be victorious."

The General rose and bowed once more. He left the room without a backwards glance. The Maitress remained long afterwards, staring into the dying fire. She thought about the vanity of old men, who desired nothing except total victory, no matter what the cost, and how it fed the beasts of war and kept them satiated.

---

* Apprenticeship

4

Arrereons, the verdant plain

(The Tollyn, Eight)

Geya turns over more colored tokens and sighs.
Dai, where have you got to, traitor?

~~~~~~~~~~~~

Katkin shook her head, trying to rouse herself. Diffuse light seeped under the curtains until Becka opened them, filling the space with brightness. She bustled about the room, placing the tray containing breakfast on the table beside the bed. Katkin yawned, and stretched. After lying sleepless most of the night, trying to reconcile the recent events in her mind, the picture still felt maddeningly incomplete. She remembered jumping into the water to save Tomas, and finding him there. But beyond striking out tiredly for the breakwater, she could remember little else. Tomas had been cold and unresponsive in her arms and she thought him almost certainly drowned. How could he have woken and saved them both, especially with his injured leg? It did not seem possible, yet the gatekeeper's story was incontrovertible.

Now, a strange request from the Maitress had added to her already considerable confusion. She went back over the conversation in her mind. It had been late—very late—when the Maitress had come to her room. Katkin thought how old she looked. Old and mortally weary. She had entered the darkened room alone and did not bother to light the gas lamp mounted on the wall near the door. Instead, she carried with her the stub of a candle in a small, brass holder, which she placed on the bedside table.

"Katrione, do you sleep? I must talk with you," she said, her voice hardly above a whisper. Katkin already had her eyes wide open, but the Maitress' sight was failing, especially in the dimly lit room.

"I am awake, Maitress. I could not sleep, after all that has happened. I keep going over it in my mind."

"It is of the Captain and his plight I wish to speak, if it will not distress you unduly."

"No, I would like to talk about it. Maybe it will help me clear things up." Katkin thought she knew the reason for this late visit. "I feel terrible about breaking the Rule. You have to come to tell me I have been dismissed from the ranks of the Juvenet, I expect."

The Maitress had other ideas. She said quietly, "Suppose I told you there is a way you could avoid dismissal, and help the Infirmarie as well."

Katkin leaned forward in bed, asking eagerly, "What must I do? I will undertake anything, if it means I may stay and complete my training."

"I have been speaking this evening with Charles de Vigny, the father of the soldier you met in the Acre." Briefly, she told Katkin of the conversation that had transpired between them. "I have agreed to allow you to try and help the boy, Tomas. I did this, not because the General insisted, but because I thought you deserved a second chance."

Katkin looked at her in amazement. She had expected the Maitress to enforce the Rule without recourse but now she had been given another chance in the form of this odd test. "I would be happy to treat the Captain, but I have never tried to heal anyone, before now. Do you think the Goddess will look kindly upon my efforts?"

The Maitress smiled encouragingly. "That is up to her. If she does, you deserve to stay here."

"When will I be allowed to see him? The Captain, I mean." She broke off, aware that too much eagerness would look unseemly given the circumstances involved.

"General de Vigny indicated his son wished to start as soon as possible. Would tomorrow be too soon, do you think?" Privately, the Maitress wondered if Katkin would still be too weak.

But Katkin answered her immediately, saying resolutely, "I will be ready and I will do my best to help the Captain."

"Very well. Get some sleep, my dear. I will send Becka for you in the morning with some breakfast." The Maitress rose and turned to go, then paused to ask a question that still weighed heavily on her mind. "Who went into the water first, you or the Captain?"

"Why do you ask? I thought I told you that already. He fell or perhaps jumped over the side and I went in to save him. You do believe me, do you not?" Katkin looked at her imploringly.

The Maitress replied, "There has been a certain amount of confusion—the Captain has told another version of events. Tomorrow perhaps, we will be able to find out what happened, when you have a chance to speak with him. Don't let it trouble you tonight."

She turned to leave once more. Katkin stopped her by asking, "What did Tomas say? There is so much I cannot remember. I need to know the truth."

"So do we all, my dear. Now sleep, for you will need all your strength for tomorrow."

Of course, she thought she hadn't slept a wink, worrying about what the next day would bring. Nevertheless, later, when Becka bade a cheery good morning to her, the sunlight streaming in through the open curtains surprised Katkin. She must have managed a couple of hours of sleep after all. The breakfast on the tray made her stomach lurch, and her nerves jangled at the thought of seeing the Captain and the trial the Maitress had set for her. She picked listlessly at the food as Becka looked on impatiently

"You must hurry, Kat. The Captain has been asking for you since just after sunrise. The Maitress insisted we allow you to sleep. He sounded quite annoyed when I passed his room on my way here with your breakfast. They say he is bad-tempered, just like his father." Here Becka's voice dropped conspiratorially, her curiosity getting the better of her. "He *is* very good looking though, don't you think? And also very interested in you. What were you two up to in the Acre, anyway? You can tell me, I swear I will not breathe a word to anyone."

Katkin blushed bright red, shocked at the implication of this question. "Nothing happened in the Acre, I can assure you. He merely escorted me back to the City. I cannot say I even noticed his looks, his wound occupied my full attention." This sounded prim and wasn't strictly true, but she had been trying to be more concerned with his injury. Katkin quailed inwardly, wondering if she would be the victim of vicious gossip on top of everything else. She had heard stories of other Juvenet who left the compound for assignations with the young men of the City. Even though they could sometimes hide their indiscretions for weeks, the Gift would invariably leave them and that could not be disguised for long. Katkin prayed silently she would not find the same had happened to her—the prospect was terrifying, nonetheless.

"Did the Maitress say anything to you about why I am to see the Captain this morning?" she asked Becka.

"No, she just told me to bring you breakfast and then see you to his door."

Katkin gave a sigh of relief. It seemed the whole Juvenie hostel would not be discussing her upcoming test then. That was a blessing. If she failed, she prayed the Maitress would allow her to leave quietly.

After dressing, Katkin followed Becka down the hall to the Captain's room. It surprised her to find that despite her near-drowning she felt strong and perfectly well this morning. Becka stopped before the door to Tomas' room. From inside, they could clearly hear a heated exchange going on between Tomas and an unknown Damenie. Evidently, the Captain had grown even more tired of waiting. Becka knocked on the door and after giving her arm a reassuring pat, left her on the threshold, though not without a curious backward glance.

The door flew open and Damenie Beneficence, looking uncharacteristically flustered, peered out at her. "Katrione, thank goodness. I was beginning to think we would have to restrain the Captain, such is his eagerness to see you. The Maitress said you are to be allowed to remain in this room unsupervised, although I will be outside if you have need of me."

The Captain spoke hurriedly. "That won't be necessary, Damenie. I am sure the thought of you skulking around outside the door would be a distraction for Miss du Chesne. Isn't that correct, Katrione?" He looked at her, and silently implored her to concur.

"Um, I..."

He did not allow Katkin to finish her reply. "Well, that is

settled then. Run along, like a good harpy. Katrione will send for you when she has finished."

Tomas lay back on his bed, looking smug, as Katkin entered the room and closed the door behind her. She studied him without speaking for a moment and his blue eyes held hers in defiance. Finally, she tore her glance away and moved over to fuss with the curtains at the window, to hide her embarrassment and confusion.

Katkin cleared her throat and sat down on the chair by the bed. She looked at her hands, willing them to stop trembling. The silence remained unbroken, until finally she said, "Tomas, I don't understand why I am here. I thought you did not believe in the healing waters."

He spoke sharply in return. "You are here because I desire your presence. I asked my father to bring pressure to bear on your Maitress and he did so. I told him I needed healing and I thought you could help me. I made him believe, I almost begged!"

His fervor surprised her and she wondered when he had acquired this sudden faith in the works of the Goddess.

"Do you truly believe I can help you?" Katkin asked, watching his face for some sign he mocked her again.

Tomas reddened slightly, and looked out the window instead of making eye contact with her. "No, I do not. Not at all. I am sorry. I suppose that disappoints you, Katrione."

She looked at him in surprise. "Please explain yourself, Captain. You begged for my presence here and now you tell me you don't think I can do anything for you?" Katkin shook her head in confusion. What kind of game did he think he was playing?

"I had to make up something, so they would let you come to me. The old woman, the Maitress, she did not want to allow it, and I needed to talk to you urgently."

"What about?"

He still wouldn't look at her, and instead transferred his gaze to the fireplace, where a small fire blazed in the hearth. "I... I wanted to find out what you remembered. My own memories of our rescue are hazy. Will you tell me?" He lay still, hoping against hope she would not recall what had happened. He was disappointed. Katkin proceeded to recount his fall from the Yoke in exacting detail.

"But I don't remember how we made it to the bank or the patrol coming to our aid. Do you?"

Tomas cleared his throat and his hands played fretfully with the bedclothes. He said firmly, "That isn't what happened! I seem to remember your pony bolting and knocking you into the water. I jumped in to save *you,* then swam to the breakwater and raised the alarm." He stared at her belligerently, daring her to disagree with his account.

Katkin shook her head, wondering if the shock of his near drowning had further unhinged him. She said gently, "That is not possible. My memory of your fall is very clear. I saw you quite deliberately take off your helmet and place it on the railing. Then you fell. Or jumped. Anyway, I left Brinna far up the Yoke, by the resting bay. She was nowhere near us."

Tomas, realizing his ploy had failed miserably, abruptly changed tack. He reached for her hand and grasped it feverishly. "When the patrol rescued us from the breakwater I told them a different story. I said I went into the Mistmere after Brinna bumped you into the water. Do you understand why? I had no choice. If anyone found out I had broken down like that my career would be over and the old man would never forgive me. You have to back me up. Please, I will do anything." Her stunned silence seemed to disturb him even more. "What do you want from me? Gold? I have plenty..."

Katkin stared at him, shocked he would do such a thing. The Maitress had been confused about the events of that night because he had lied. Now, he wanted her to do the same thing—to change her story to match his. That would be just as bad, wouldn't it? Yet, Tomas' distress felt so real and heartrending she hardly thought she could refuse. And what of her test? If he did not want her to heal him she would be required to leave the Unity. Suddenly, she knew what she must do. Turning to face Tomas, she forced him to look directly at her. "I have a proposal to make to you, Captain. I think it will benefit us both. At least I hope so."

He looked at her with interest. "Name it, Katrione."

"Because I broke the Rule, I have to undergo a trial. If I am successful, I may stay. If I fail, I must leave the Unity forever." In a few words, she told him of the Maitress' visit of the night before and the conditions of the trial.

He said scathingly, "But this is ludicrous! I have a shattered kneecap. You cannot possibly think your 'mystical powers' can help me. I will not be a party to this."

Katkin began to get angry. Her whole future hung in the balance and he seemed not to care at all. "You said you would do anything! You are asking me to lie for you. This is what I ask in return. Why won't you let me try? Are you afraid?"

Tomas looked at her mildly, plainly surprised by the outburst. "My dear Katrione, indeed I am not afraid. Why would I be? You are just a girl, after all. I merely think you are wasting your time."

His willful ignorance was galling. "Don't patronize me. You asked for my help, and that is my condition. I have no use for your gold or any other reward. This Infirmarie is my life and I will do whatever I have to in order to remain here. Do we have an agreement?" She glared at him fiercely and he seemed taken aback.

"Yes, of course. I suppose I can understand how important this is to you. What do you wish to do?" Tomas stirred restlessly under his covers, thinking whatever she proposed would probably be painful. The knee flared into agonizing life again, just through this simple movement. Katkin watched him try to master his pain and her conviction grew she had to do something to help him.

"We will begin with a simple examination. I want you to remain still, and try to place your trust in me. Do not be alarmed if you see my expression change as I search your wound. Sometimes we feel the patient's pain as we use our deep empathetic skills." Tomas snickered at this, and Katkin pointedly ignored him. "The left leg is the injured one, correct?" He nodded his assent, wearily.

She rose and pulled the curtains firmly shut. Katkin knew she must will herself into calmness by finding her center and calling upon the Goddess. A sudden feeling of confident assurance washed over her, and her hands, as they moved aside the covers to expose the bandaged and splinted left leg, felt steady.

Tomas closed his eyes and lay back on the pillows. Examinations, however painful, had to be endured stoically. He flinched when she touched the knee, though he did not make a sound in protest.

51

Katkin went deep inside herself and saw through her fingers as she searched the wound. She inched her way forward, examining the area on either side of the patella. Katkin had been steeling herself against the burning shock of the badly injured knee she was sure she would find. Now she redoubled her concentration, unwilling to believe what her vision revealed. A few seconds later, she pulled her hands away with a cry.

"What is it? What do you see?" Tomas asked her, a little frightened by her agitation.

Katkin shook her head violently, trying to clear away the image. "I saw... nothing."

"Nothing? Explain yourself. Or have you already given up on this hopeless folly?" he asked angrily.

That stung, and pushed Katkin back into action. "I am sorry. I must have been distracted momentarily. I will try again. This time I am sure I will be successful."

Again, she searched the knee with her fingertips and this time Tomas watched her intently. Her expression, so calm and peaceful, gave him momentary hope. Almost... almost, he felt himself believing in her, trusting in her to do something. But again her eyes snapped open and she quickly withdrew her hands. Once more, the wound failed to show itself and she came to the unhappy realization that her Gift from Lalluna must indeed be lost.

In a choked voice she said, "Excuse me, I have to... to... step outside for a moment," and turning away, fled the room.

Katkin wandered aimlessly until she found herself in the small chapel room reserved for patients. A beautifully carved wooden statue of Lalluna stood in one corner, and smiled serenely down upon her. Katkin sank down on a rough wooden bench, and placed her head on one of the embroidered pillows scattered around for the comfort of those sitting. She felt tears pricking at the back of her eyelids and sent a prayer of thanks to the Goddess that the chapel had no other visitors at this early hour.

The morning sunlight streamed through the leaded windows, and the colored glass made lovely abstract patterns on the floor. The chapel, silent and warm, possessed a sense of quiet possibility that pervaded everything. Katkin felt comforted. Suddenly, she rubbed her burning eyes and found herself fatigued beyond measure. The colors on the floor appeared to rise around her, until they formed a rainbow of whirling motes. It seemed she slept, for she heard a voice speaking to her. A woman's voice echoed in her mind, unknown to her, and yet at the same time as familiar as if it were her own.

"*My vessel*," the Voice said softly. "*Do not fear. There is meaning in what you see. Search your heart and you will find it.*"

The voice faded away and she woke with a start. The sun had passed behind a cloud and the Chapel looked almost monochromatic in the relative darkness. As Katkin pondered the words from her dream she knew she must return to Tomas at once and find out their significance. Nevertheless, one thing was certain—she no longer feared she had lost her Gift.

"I was beginning to think you would never come back," Tomas said impatiently as Katkin re-entered the room. "I am sorry this whole charade has been upsetting, but you cannot say I did not warn you."

His self-satisfied tone had no effect on Katkin, who still felt calmed by the reassurance of her dream in the Chapel. "I am sorry I had to leave you, Captain. What I saw caused me great confusion, yet I think now I understand and I will try again in a minute. First tell me this—did any of the other Daminem examine you when you were brought here?"

"Not as far as I know. My father interrupted one of the Daminem before she had a chance to begin. What difference does that make anyway? Now you have failed, I assume you are still willing to keep your end of our bargain?"

Katkin shrugged. "Naturally, I intend to keep my word. But are you so sure I have failed? I am not. I wish to make another attempt, by your leave."

"Very well, but I don't see..."

"Please be quiet and, just perhaps, we will both see what we have been missing."

This time when Katkin went in to her trance, she searched without fear. The Goddess must have sharpened her inner senses somehow, because she saw at once the faint red lines of scar tissue in the wound and the vibrant blue of freshly mended tissue. The answer came to her abruptly. *Someone has healed this man already.* But how? It seemed an incomprehensible puzzle—until she remembered the presence of the mist on the water just before she lost consciousness. Katkin recalled her childhood experience with the drowned cat in Belladore. When in her trance, she had seen the same mist then, and a vague outline of the Goddess, though no one else had. Was it possible Lalluna had come to them in the water and healed Tomas' leg?

Almost not daring to believe, she asked him, "Captain, is your knee very painful now? Could you move it if I asked you to?"

"Of course it is, you stupid girl. You don't think you have actually accomplished anything useful this morning, do you?" he snapped, frustrated by her failed attempts to help him.

"No, I do not, yet I do think some miracle has occurred, by the grace of the Goddess. Please be patient while I remove the splint." She did so as carefully as she could. By his sharp intake of breath and compressed lips she could tell he manfully struggled with what she hoped must be imaginary pain. "Now try to bend your leg," she requested.

"No, I will not. I am tired of your stupid games. Put the splint back on and leave me in peace." Although he had little faith in her, there had been a tiny spark of hope in his heart. All at once it died and his sense of disappointment infuriated him still further.

Katkin begged him. "Captain, please. I truly believe the Goddess has made your leg whole again. Will you not try to move it a little?"

He shook his head firmly. "Go away, little girl. Why do you pretend you have cured me, when all the time my knee hurts like blazes? Can you just not admit the truth? You have failed."

Katkin faced this new quandary. If the Captain had been healed in the Mere by Lalluna, but could not release the fear of his injury from his mind, he might still feel pain because he expected to, after six long months of nothing else. How could she make him see the truth? Katkin knew trying to reason with him would be useless. He obviously still thought of her as a child, and in his arrogance felt himself to be vastly superior.

At once Katkin conceived a bold and risky plan.

She said acidly, "I don't believe your knee hurts so badly. I think you are a coward. You don't want to fight any more. You are just craven. Do you hear me, craven!"

The ire that overtook Tomas with these words made his earlier bad temper seem like a sunny day. At once he sat up in bed and threw aside the covers, his face a twisted mask of rage.

"You little bitch!" he spat at her. "How dare you say I am a coward? I saved your life by swimming with you to the breakwater. I am not to blame for your pathetic failures. Get out and don't come back here again."

Although his anger frightened her, Katkin could not stop now. She continued to taunt him, praying she was right about his knee.

"I am not the pathetic one. At least I don't hide behind my injury like some child."

"Be gone, girl or I will not be responsible for my actions. You have tried me beyond my patience, you impudent stripling." He looked almost incandescent with wrath, but to her disappointment, he did not get out of bed.

Katkin knew she must press him still further.

"You don't scare me with your threats. I am not afraid of you! Come and make me be quiet, you big baby!" With this last stinging insult, Katkin grabbed the jug of water on the bedside table and threw the contents directly in Tomas' face. "Here is your healing water!"

As she turned to flee, Katkin reflected she might have gotten a little carried away, especially after she heard his bellow of pure rage. A second later, she ran out the door and down the corridor as if her very life depended on it. More quickly than she would have thought possible, he came up behind her. Grabbing her shoulder, he spun her around so hard she lost her footing and fell backwards. She looked up breathlessly as he loomed above her, his hands clenched in fury. Katkin scrambled ungracefully to her feet and backed away from him slowly, and he kept advancing until her back pressed up against the wall. The empty hall gave her no protection.

She said, nervously, "Tomas, I..."

She did not finish her sentence. The blow came out of nowhere, striking the side of her face and sending her right back down to the floor again. Katkin shook her head to clear away the stars, but the ringing in her ears continued. No one, in all her life, had ever, ever struck her like that. She sat back on her heels, gasping for breath, trying not to cry.

"That will teach you to call me a coward! Now I would hear you beg for my forgiveness, wench. Or will you have another taste of this?" Tomas straightened himself fully and strode forward to where she cowered next to the wall—his fist raised threateningly.

Stiffly, Katkin rose to her feet and stared up at the Captain, thinking ruefully that she should now be very happy because Tomas de Vigny had just proved to her, beyond a shadow of a doubt, that he was no longer a cripple. But she seriously wondered if she would be alive long enough to even tell him about it.

"Captain! Look at yourself," she shouted at him. "How did you get here? You ran, do you see? Your knee is whole again." Then, because her words did not seem to penetrate his rage, she cried in despair, "Why do you not understand me?"

Finally, he dropped his fists, shaking his head and staring at her in confusion. "By the Gods, girl, what have you done to me?" Tomas reached a trembling hand to the wall to support himself. At first, he looked as though he might fall, but after a few seconds he removed his hand and stood unaided. Carefully and slowly, he bent his knee and straightened it again.

"Does it hurt you, Captain?" Katkin whispered to him, her green eyes still full of fear.

"I feel nothing. No pain..."

Abruptly, Tomas understood why she had insulted him and thrown the water in his face. It had all been to get him on his feet. Suddenly, he felt physically ill. Turning away from her, he stumbled back down the hall to his room and emptied his stomach into the china washbowl inside the door. He sank down on the bed, and carefully removed the last of the bandages. Gingerly, he touched the joint, feeling the smoothness of the unbroken skin, and the solidly reassuring bone underneath.

Tomas understood that he should be filled with joy, but instead he felt only dismay – and shame. The girl had healed his knee, to be sure, but now he suffered from a new and much more intractable pain—something broken so irretrievably that no touch from her or anyone else would ever be able to mend it. Like a twisting blade lodged deep in his belly—the knowledge that he had struck Katrione after she risked everything to help him walk again. Entwined with this lay the memory of his mother's desperate cries for help, and his father's fist raised above her as she cowered before him. *Now I have become my father, who I utterly despise.*

His eyes filled with tears. Letting them fall unheeded down his cheeks, Tomas looked up and saw Katkin standing in the doorway. It horrified him to see the beginnings of a fresh blu-ish swelling where his closed fist had connected with her cheek. She did not speak, just stared at him with those deep green eyes, her expression unreadable. He found himself captivated by her disheveled chestnut curls and slender body. Somehow he had been blind to her loveliness before this moment. Had he ruined everything with his rage? Perhaps it might not be too late...

Wiping away his tears, Tomas stood up slowly and approached her, his hands raised in peaceful submission. The knife in his guts twisted a little more when he saw her expression change to one of fear, and she tensed to flee from him once again.

"Katrione, please don't run away. I will not hurt you, I swear it." Carefully, because he did not yet fully trust it, he bent the healed knee and knelt before her. He took her trembling hand and placed it to his lips. "Can you ever forgive me? I must have been mad to go after you like that."

To his vast relief and amazement, she rewarded him with a little tremulous smile. "I wanted to make you angry enough to chase me, Tomas. I just did not expect to succeed quite so well. You shouldn't have knocked me down. Still, I forgive you. I did say some pretty awful things to you, but you must know I did not mean any of them. Now for heaven's sake let go of my hand and get up from that ridiculous position before someone comes along and finds us. I would never live it down..."

Katkin and Tomas looked up at exactly the same moment after hearing an abbreviated cough. It appalled them both to see the Maitress standing in the open doorway, regarding them with rapt interest.

5

Pencathe, a natural harbor

(The Tollyn, Thirteen)

Moonlight watches intently. What do the cards say now?
Geya turns over another colored disk from the luckcast sheaf she holds. She reveals a token from the Arkirish Dynasty.
He comes, do you see? The Hero, Aages—to strive with the Knave, Dindal. Only Moera knows who she will choose.
Moonlight mutters and turns away. At least she has a choice. I never do.

~~~~~~~~~~

"Goddess! What did the Maitress say? Was he actually kissing your hand when she walked in?" Becka's eyes shone in romantic bliss as she huddled close to Katkin in the tiny room they shared in the Juvenet hostel. The simply and sparsely furnished attic room, like all those surrounding them, housed the two girls in austere style. It held only two narrow beds, a small set of drawers and a washstand with a white porcelain bowl and pitcher. But Becka's flair for decoration insured the room would never be dull. Bunches of dried flowers in discarded medicine bottles decorated every empty surface. Tiny embroideries and a picture torn from a book hung on the white plaster walls. The room had little space for anything else, except Katkin's most prized possession—the battered vielle that had once belonged to her father. It lived in a dusty leather bag under her bed. The alcove window gave a view of the City and even beyond, to the wooded shores of the Mistmere. Katkin looked now to St. Valery's Acre, as she and Becka sat on the window seat enjoying the weak winter sun.

"Yes, he was, and she saw everything. I thought she would be angry, and make the Captain leave at once. Instead she merely asked about his health and when he said he was able to walk again without pain she looked very pleased and said he could go home whenever he was ready."

"And she said you could stay, of course? How clever of you to pass the test like that," Becka declared.

Katkin shook her head. "I did nothing, Becka. The Goddess healed him."

"How modest you are, my dear. What you did was amazing. I have never heard of anyone being completely healed—just like that! It usually takes ages and lots of trips to the Springs." Becka sighed. "I wish I had been there."

"What!?" said Katkin. "Why?"

"To see the handsome Captain kneeling in his nightshirt, of course! It must have been priceless!" Becka turned to her friend, eyes narrowed suspiciously. "Why did he kneel like that? Is there something between you two? The Maitress can't be very pleased about that."

Katkin studied the bluish smudge of trees across the Mistmere while she considered her answer. Could there be something between the two of them? Although it might be said the Captain was very handsome, she did not find his arrogance particularly appealing. Anyway, she would probably never have the opportunity to see him again.

"The longer you wait to answer me the more suspicious I shall be, Katrione du Chesne!" Becka's words broke through her reverie and Katkin gave a guilty start.

"Oh, Becka, really... you are being so foolish. There can be nothing between us. I have completed my test and now life can go on as usual. If you will stop pestering me with endless questions, that is..."

Becka laughed irrepressibly. "I shall—but I have just one more for you. What have you done to your face?"

It pleased Katkin that the Maitress had chosen not to question her about the bruise, though she had undoubtedly noticed it. But if Becka knew the truth it would be no time at all before everyone else in the hostel did too.

She transferred her gaze back towards the Acre again. "I slipped and banged it on the door frame. It looks worse than it feels."

Katkin stole a glance at Becka to see if her roommate accepted her story. Becka's eyes looked wide and trusting and Katkin felt iniquitous for lying once more to protect the Captain. She had already changed her story about who went into the water first, in accordance with her agreement with him, and though the Maitress had given her a piercing glance, she had not challenged Katkin's revised version of events.

A knock interrupted their conversation. Trechelle stuck her head in the door and said impatiently, "Katkin, you have a visitor in the receiving room. The Maitress sent me to fetch you."

Becka's eyes lit up. "I bet it is the Captain, come to pay his respects. Do you think so?"

Trechelle snapped at her. "It is none of your business who it is, you little gossip-monger. The Maitress gave me a message for you, too. She said for you to get to work right now or you would have night soil duty for the next month!"

With a squeal of dismay, Becka ran from the room. Trechelle sighed and asked, "Why do you put up with that gossiping little snip?"

Katkin spoke up loyally for her roommate. "She just wanted to know because she cares about me. She is a good friend, and I won't hear you say anything against her." She paused, and after a moment spent smoothing down her frock carefully as she rose from the window seat, willed her voice to normality. "Is it Captain de Vigny?"

Trechelle shook her head. "Nay, Katkin. The visitor is not in uniform and I have never seen him here before. Now we must hurry, as he has been waiting for some time, while I searched for you."

After Trechelle left her at the door of the downstairs receiving room, Katkin knocked softly, wondering who her unknown visitor could be. Stepping through the doorway, she saw the Maitress occupying one of the armchairs. A tall man wearing black knee breeches and a patched but tidy linen shirt stood next to her. He had high cheekbones, wide set gray eyes, and a prominent nose that looked as if it might have been broken more than once. Katkin stared at him for a moment, nonplussed. Why did she think she knew him from somewhere?

"Come in child, and close the door. You are letting in the draft. And don't stand there gawking like some moonstruck cow. I thought you had been taught better manners than that," the Maitress snapped pettishly.

Katkin came into the room and, stepping forward, gave a stiff curtsy to the young man.

"That is better, girl. Now we will continue with the introductions, if you please."

The young man spoke, his voice deep and slightly gruff. "There is no need, Ma'am, for Miss du Chesne and I once knew each other well, though it was long ago." He thrust his hands deeply into his coat pockets and grinned shyly at her.

The gap-toothed smile gave him away. Her eyes widened with sudden recognition. "Jacq? Jacques Benet, is it really you? This is incredible—I haven't seen you for ages and ages." Katkin beamed at him and hurried forward to offer her hand, which he took gravely. His huge rough hands still dwarfed hers, just as they had all those years ago. Looking into those steady gray eyes that regarded her so seriously, she did not know what to say.

The Maitress cleared her throat in annoyance, obviously feeling excluded from this reunion of old friends. "So, how is this possible? You two must have met some time ago, or is this some *other* man you rescued in the Acre?"

Surprised by the Maitress' petulant remark, Katkin waited for Jacq to speak. When he did not, she had to take up the explanation herself. "Jacq and I were friends long ago, Maitress. We grew up together at Tintaren. His family..." She paused, unsure how to express the connection between them properly.

Jacq unselfconsciously supplied the necessary relationship. "... slaved for the du Chesne family in the fields. We were cottars." His awkward smile smoothed over the sting in his words.

Smiling back at him, Katkin continued the story. "Once I decided to run away from home. Jacq found me, lost and crying in the fields, and we walked back to his house. His mother gave me a piece of seed cake and made me feel very welcome. So after that, every time I found myself unhappy or lonely, I went to find Jacq. We became best friends even though he was four years older than me."

"But we lost track of each other quite some time ago," Jacq said simply, and did not elaborate further. Katkin thought back unhappily to the dark day they rode down the valley to the lakeshore together. After her accident on Brinna, her mother had won the argument about boarding school once and for all. She had packed Katkin off as soon as she was well enough to travel, and had not let her see Jacq again, even to say good-bye.

Katkin forcibly brought her mind back to the present. She did not want to linger on what had been the saddest episode in her life, other than the loss of her own home. It seemed incredible Jacq stood before her now—grown into a tall, broad shouldered man.

The Maitress broke the silence. "Aren't you going to ask Mr. Benet why he is here, Katrione? Honestly, I never met anyone as scatterbrained as you are today, child."

Jacq answered her before Katkin could frame the appropriate question. "I bear a message from Captain Tomas de Vigny." The Maitress' eyebrows shot up, but she said nothing.

Katkin stared at him in wonderment, and asked, "How on Yrth do you know the Captain?"

"Captain de Vigny is in command of the Fourth Company of the King's Guard. I serve as their blacksmith and farrier. When the gallant Captain walked into the garrison yesterday, free of his crutches, his men rejoiced. I asked him about his miraculous cure and he told me of his stay here. It pleased me to discover that my childhood friend has become so adept in the healing arts." Here Katkin blushed hotly and looked at the floor. Jacq continued, unaware of the effect his words had on her. "When the Captain found I knew you, he chose me to bear this message to the Infirmarie, for he wanted it delivered to Miss du Chesne and no other."

"And what is the message, young man?" the Maitress asked, with sudden interest.

Jacq recited mechanically, "Tomas de Vigny wishes she would do him the honor of dining with him tomorrow evening at seven o'clock at the Boar's Head Inn. He apologizes for not coming himself but he finds he is busy with many pressing matters since his recovery."

Katkin shook her head firmly. "You must convey my regrets. It is not possible for me to dine with Captain de Vigny. He knows I cannot leave here again, for any reason."

The Maitress waved her hand in Katkin's direction. "Do not

be so hasty child." Then she spoke softly to Jacq. "Please tell the Captain Miss du Chesne accepts his invitation with pleasure. If he would be so good as to send a carriage for her, she will be ready at seven o'clock. Now, if there is nothing else, I will ring for a Juvenie to escort you to the kitchen where you may sup, if you wish, before returning to the garrison."

To Katkin's disappointment, he nodded his head.

Picking up a small bell, the Maitress sounded it once and Amber appeared in the doorway.

"Thank you for delivering the message, Mr. Benet. Go with the Goddess."

Katkin shook hands with Jacq once more. She blushed and stammered, "Good-bye, Jacq, it was so nice to see you again after all these years."

He smiled back at her and his eyes were very kind. "Good-bye, Miss du Chesne. It was nice to see you too."

Jacq bowed to Katkin and the Maitress and followed Amber out of the room. Katkin desperately wished the Maitress had given her more time to talk to him. But now the Maitress had sent him down to the kitchen like some tinker's helper, for a glass of ale and one of cook's pies, she had lost her chance.

She turned to her Mother Superior, full of confusion. "I don't understand, Maitress. Why do you wish me to see the Captain again? Am I not still cloistered?"

The Maitress smiled at her, her old eyes glittering shrewdly. "There are many things you do not understand, my dear. Perhaps when you are older the ways of power and influence will mean more to you. For now, let us leave it that the Captain desires to show his gratitude by escorting you to dinner and we would not wish to offend him by refusing, would we?"

Katkin thought she knew rather more about the ways of power and influence than the old woman gave her credit for, given her unfortunate experience with Jacq. A sharply spoken rebuke punctured her reminiscences. "You haven't been listening to a word I have been saying! Where has your mind wandered off to now?" The Maitress peered at her questioningly.

"I am sorry, I was thinking about Jacq. We used to be very close, and it has been so long since I last saw him. Almost eight years, in fact. I have had no news of him since I went away to boarding school. After Tintaren Manor burned down I tried to find him again, but his old house was empty. I wonder..."

The Maitress interrupted her. "You should not be wasting your thoughts on a lowly blacksmith. Not when the Captain has asked you to dine with him. This could mean very good things for us here at the Infirmarie, girl. Lord Charles de Vigny has great power and influence in the City."

Katkin began to feel uncomfortably like a pawn in a chess game the Maitress wished to play with Tomas' father. She could not help thinking the old woman had ceased to care about what was best for her. Her only interest appeared to be exploiting Captain de Vigny's gratitude for the benefit of the Infirmarie.

"Now you must return to your duties. Remember what I have said—it will be to our advantage if you befriend the Captain."

With a distracted wave of her hand, the Maitress dismissed her.

Katkin made her way along the hallway and outside into the cold afternoon sunshine. She crossed the greensward on a brick-lined path that led to the baths. The Springhouse was one of the oldest buildings in the Infirmarie complex, built just after the founding of the Unity. It was shaped roughly like an upturned boat, with broad roof beams exposed on the inside of the high ceiling. The thermal springs came directly from the heart of the mountain, Hythea, channeled by a series of pipes and cisterns. A beautiful verdigrised copper statue of the Goddess Lalluna, with wings outstretched, overlooked the bathing pool and formed part of a complicated fountain with sprays and waterfalls that served to cool the water to blood heat.

Katkin spent the next few hours contentedly helping the sick and injured to bathe in the healing waters. She loved the pungency of the aromatic steam in the cavernous bathing room, and the plangent sound of the running water. The vague worries about her rendezvous with the Captain and the Maitress' unspoken expectations slipped away unnoticed.

Much later, as she lay in her garret bed in the winter darkness, those concerns began to gnaw at her again. She turned over and sighed as Becka lit the candle on the little table between their beds.

"What's eating you, Kat? You are as restless as a windmill

tonight. Did your meeting with the Maitress go poorly this afternoon?"

Katkin answered thoughtfully. "The meeting went all right, I guess. At least a part of it, anyway. The visitor turned out to be a childhood friend of mine, Jacques Benet. I have often wondered what happened to him after we last saw each other. Now he is all grown up. Somehow, I still pictured him in my mind as a fourteen year old boy."

Becka, anxious to get to sleep, tried to encourage her friend to speak of her difficulty, whatever it was. "So you saw Jacq. What happened next?"

Katkin did not answer her directly. Instead, she asked thoughtfully, "Becka, if the Maitress asked you to perform some task—something you did not feel comfortable doing—would you do it anyway?"

Becka, with her head propped up on one hand, looked over at Katkin in surprise. "Of course I would. The Maitress is the wisest woman I have ever known. Anything she asked me to do would be the right thing, I am sure. How could it not be?"

Katkin wished she shared Becka's child-like trust in the Maitress. "I don't know. I suppose you must be right..."

"Tell me what she wanted. Maybe then I can help you decide."

Knowing full well what the hopelessly romantic Becka would think of the Maitress' request, Katkin decided to keep it a secret for now. Instead, she turned over and feigned a yawn. "It is nothing. Just forget I ever mentioned it. Good night, Becka."

Becka blew out the candle and soon was snoring gently.

Katkin lay in the darkness, waiting and hoping for the forgetfulness of sleep. She eventually passed into a fretful slumber, tossing restlessly. During the night she woke many times, sure she could hear someone calling her name. Then, just before dawn, she found herself dreaming of Jacq.

Katkin stood on a barren heath and the Goddess Lalluna stood by her side. The sky above them was low and white—no clouds— just the seeming absence of anything else. In the distance, on a naked hillside, she could see a great spiraling tempest that tore the whiteness above it into streaming shreds. Such a cataclysm should have produced a violent rushing of wind, but instead there was deathly stillness, and this stillness made her very afraid. From the bottom of the vortex a steady stream of black figures issued, and rapidly moved downhill towards them. She looked to Lalluna for help, but the Goddess only cringed and stepped behind Katkin. A shining figure dropped from the sky in front of them and the black things scattered and flew away, shrieking curses. Though he had somehow grown dove-gray wings and carried a mighty sword, Katkin did not question Jacq's appearance. In the dream, it felt perfectly right that he should look so. As Katkin walked forward with her hand outstretched, Lalluna cried out, "Dai! I forbid you to enter this place. Leave here at once." Katkin stared at her in confusion. Why had she called him Dai?

He spoke, and it was definitely Jacq's voice she heard. "I come for her, Moonlight. The girl and I are destined this turn of the Gyre. Do not interfere."

Lalluna said sharply. "It is you who interferes, Dai Irrakai. Go back to your chaos, traitor."

He shook his head. "I cannot. The battle continues."

Katkin stood quietly to one side, listening to this exchange, wondering who they were talking about. Suddenly, Jacq stepped towards her and folded his wings about her protectively. She felt a moment of incredible peace. Then she heard Lalluna's voice quite clearly, "My vessel is a part of me. She can never truly be yours, Dai."

She looked up at his face and saw the tears as Jacq sighed and let her go. Katkin fell to the ground. As she stared up at him, he produced a glowing green orb from between his fingers. The light from it increased until it almost blinded her, and as it increased, she could see Jacq's form dissolving into nothingness. She cried out, "Jacq, come back. I love you. Don't leave me..."

Lalluna coldly repeated, again and again, "You cannot love the traitor," as Katkin woke, crying..."

"No!" She sat up in bed, her heart pounding.

"No, what, Katkin? Are you all right? You are as white as a sheet." Becka's voice brought her fully awake. The morning sun filtered through the alcove curtain. Seeing her roommate standing with one foot suspended awkwardly in the air, a stocking dangling from her hand, gave her a reassuring feeling of normality.

Becka said impatiently, "Are you getting up or what? You are going to be late for Lauds if you don't stir yourself."

She rose hastily and began to dress herself in her blue shift and white mobcap. Already her dream had begun to fragment, like the shards of a broken mirror, but Katkin would have been only too glad to forget the feeling of peace she felt in Jacq's embrace.

6

Passion

(Estate of Naer, Standing Four)

Did you send her a dream, Moonlight?
Moonlight shakes her beautiful head. No, Geya. I do not know where
that dream came from. But I wonder..."
What, my sister?
I wonder if Dai speaks to us, through her.

~~~~~~~~~~~~~~~

The Maitress gave Becka the afternoon off to help her roommate
get ready for her dinner engagement with Captain de Vigny. She
used her considerable talents to tame Katkin's unruly chestnut
tresses into a becoming style. Then from somewhere deep in her
bottom drawer she produced a little pot of rouge, an item that
was, of course, strictly contraband for future Daminem. "We will
just use a little to make your cheeks sparkle and to shine those
lovely lips of yours. No one will ever know, and you will look all
the more divine."

Katkin snorted at this. "Becka, I hardly think the Captain will
even notice."

"Oh, hush Kat. Of course he will notice. Honestly, I am wasting all my efforts on you. I don't think you want to go to dinner
with the Captain at all!"

"That is not true. He wishes to show his appreciation to me
and of course I must be gracious and accept. The Maitress made
herself most clear on that point."

Becka said, a little enviously, "I still think he is in love with
you."

Katkin laughed merrily at this. "Honestly, the rot you talk
sometimes!"

She sighed happily as she hovered over Katkin, artfully

arranging little tendrils of hair to frame her face. "You look so beautiful, and so grown up. I think the Captain will simply melt into his boots when he sees you. What a pity we don't have anything else for you to wear..." The Maitress had given Katkin a tattered, cast-off gown from out of the Infirmarie's wardrobe of donated clothing.

The Maitress called Katkin down to the office half an hour before her departure, both for an inspection and an interrogation. Katkin stood in front of her, and could not help feeling like a different person, not a plain Juvenie of the Infirmarie but rather some exotically coiffed and made up creature. Katkin wondered what the old woman thought of her appearance, and dared not ask.

For a moment, she sat behind the overflowing desk, staring at Katkin, silently. Finally, she spoke. "Well, my dear, you do look lovely. Any man would be proud to step out with you on his arm. I am sure I don't have to tell you how important this evening could be for you."

Katkin could not help thinking the Maitress really meant to say, "For the Infirmarie."

She seemed to sense Katkin's thoughts, because she asked sharply, "Do you know what it costs to run this place every day, Juvenie? How much to feed, shelter, and treat all those who come to us in need? And we never turn a single soul away, even if they cannot pay. I would like to think we would be able to continue that tradition, but with the war dragging on, I do not know where we will find the resources. Old De Vigny has money, and influence with the Council. We can use that influence, Katrione. All you have to do is be kind to the Captain. Make him think you care for him, just a little..."

"Maitress, I do not wish to lead him on. How can friendship between us even be possible when I am cloistered here within the Unity?"

"If I, as the head of the Unity, am prepared to countenance such a friendship, you should have no objection," she snapped back. "Has the Captain not always treated you with the utmost respect?"

Katkin grimly appreciated the irony of this. She had twice deceived the Maitress to cover up the Captain's misdeeds and she could not take back those lies now. The Maitress honestly believed Tomas was a gentleman of irreproachable honor. But now he no longer suffered the pain and distress of his crippling injury, perhaps he would become such a gentleman. For her own sake and his, she fervently hoped this to be true.

Katkin tried to look attentive as the Maitress continued to instruct her. "Remember, a young lady always lets the gentleman take the lead in conversational matters. A demure spirit is the hallmark of quality behavior. Now go, the carriage will be outside soon. Do not disappoint me..."

She dropped her eyes and curtsied obediently. "Yes, Maitress. I will try."

Now, as she stood outside on the busy thoroughfare, Katkin scanned the passing coaches, looking for the de Vigny crest—a white stallion racing over a field of green. The number of both carriages and riders hurrying back and forth in the early evening surprised her. It seemed life went on much as usual while the City fought her War with the Rising. Vendors filled the streets, hawking papers and little parcels of food to the passers-by scurrying home in the winter cold.

Katkin took all this activity in with interest. Only rarely, in her seven years of residence, had she been given permission to leave the Infirmarie. Occasionally, one of the Daminem had entrusted her with a prescription for the compounding apothecary. Feeling both important and a bit scared, she would clutch the little purse containing a few francs to her chest, convinced every one who passed her on the sidewalk might be a ruffian trying to steal it. Even as a young girl, she had found the City both fascinating and dangerous.

As she scanned the row of rather run down houses on the opposite side of the road, she remembered forbidden visits to a little sweet shop there, run by kindly old Mrs. Apple. Though she rarely had any money, occasionally when she tidied a recently vacated room she might find a centime or two left behind by a patient. Then she and Becka would sneak out and buy a piece of Mrs. Apple's heavenly caramel, sharing the sticky treat in hiding behind some tree in the grounds of the Infirmarie. Once a Damenie caught them and the Maitress had thrashed them both. She smiled ruefully, remembering how difficult it had been to sit down for several days afterwards.

A carriage pulled by four white horses stopped in front of her, driven by a coachman in handsome black and red livery. A footman jumped down from his seat next to the driver and opened the door of the carriage before bending down to unfold the steps. Katkin stood on the sidewalk, uncertain as to what she should do. It had been a very long time since she had traveled anywhere in such style. At that moment, she sincerely wished Becka, who would have loved every minute of this pomp, could have taken her place.

Tomas de Vigny hurriedly made his way on to the pavement. His face had lost many careworn lines, and he greeted her with a dazzling smile as he bowed low, his feathered tricorn cap sweeping the ground. He looked resplendent in his formal uniform, fairly dripping with gold braid and silver buttons. Katkin clutched her black woolen cloak closer, suddenly realizing that her threadbare clothing might look very out of place in his splendid company.

"Miss du Chesne, I am deeply honored you have chosen to accept my humble invitation to dine with me this night. May I assist you in the ascent of the carriage steps?"

Proudly, he offered her his arm, and she felt obliged to take it, remembering the Maitress' warning about demureness.

"Thank you, Captain, I appreciate your help."

After settling down in the plush green velvet-lined interior of the de Vigny carriage, she stole a glance at Tomas. He looked as handsome as ever, yet she could not help thinking Jacq's strong, homespun looks were more to her own taste. Katkin shrugged this thought off as hardly useful and tried to focus on her companion. Mindful of her instructions, she attempted to engage the Captain in friendly small talk as they made their way down Lampwright's Street, crossing the western part of the City towards the Citadel.

"How have you been keeping, Captain? Jacq... That is, Mr. Benet, said you had been very busy catching up with your work at the Citadel?"

"Indeed, I have, Katrione. Now I am well again, I have much to occupy my time. However, I am not too busy to pay attention to the person who made this recovery possible." He turned to her and leaned closer as the carriage swayed on the cobbled street. "I owe you much, and I shall so enjoy discharging my debt. You and I will be seeing a great deal of each other in the coming weeks, my dear."

He sat back smugly, completely secure in the belief she would find the idea of such contact pleasing.

"Are you so sure the Maitress will allow it, Captain?" Katkin could not resist trying to discomfit him a little.

"Hah! My father has that old woman wrapped around his little finger," Tomas said confidently. "She will do as she is told to do." Katkin rather sadly feared he spoke the truth, and she kept this thought strictly to herself.

As the carriage passed in front of the Citadel, Tomas proudly described its features to Katkin, who listened without much enthusiasm. The designers had chosen a pentagonal shape, for its strategic value, with thirty-foot high masonry revetments. Punctuating the length of the curtain walls were five bastions, which projected from the pentagon like the points of a star. These allowed the defenders to fire upon any enemy attempting to scale the walls with siege ladders. A parapet providing protection for the musketeers ran along the top of the revetment. Two of the five sides faced the Mere, and indeed the revetments plunged smoothly down into the water, with no banks, making attack by boat very hazardous for the enemy. A wide grassy ditch that could be flooded in times of attack protected the two sides of the Citadel that faced the City itself. Several bridges spanned the ditch—the widest one led to the main gate with its huge portcullis and tunnel leading into the interior of the fortress. All could be cut, if necessary, to protect the Citadel from invaders. The main gate faced the Citadel Commons. The final face of the revetment contained the well-reinforced and guarded gate to the Yoke.

Tomas spoke lovingly of the magnificent engineering achievements of the Citadel, saying no invader would ever be able to take the City of Isle St. Valery because of its strength. Katkin, who had little interest in military matters at the best of times, tried unsuccessfully to smother a yawn as the carriage pulled up to their intended destination.

The Boar's Head Inn had become a popular establishment with the officers of the King's Guard. Inside the low-roofed structure, Katkin thought it both dark and smoky, though many candles burned in sconces scattered about the walls. On the chimney piece hung a magnificent stuffed boar's head, bearing an impressive set of tusks and bristles. Tables and benches filled the dining room, all set with snow-white tablecloths and napkins. Silver napery glinted mutely in the firelight. Dashing uniformed officers gathered at the bar, chatting with elegantly dressed ladies who stood decorously beside them.

Katkin looked around her in wonder. She had never imagined she would be allowed to frequent such an establishment, especially as a Juvenie of an order sworn to poverty.

Tomas exchanged loud and cheery greetings with the other officers of his battalion as he removed his greatcoat and plumed tricorn to give to the waiting servant. The servant turned to her expectantly and Katkin realized she would have to remove her own cloak. She lowered the hood to her shoulders and undid the clasp at the front. The Captain paid no attention to her, being busy still with his compatriots. Slowly she let the cloak fall from her shoulders, praying perhaps he would not notice her lowly frock until she had a chance to sit down and cover up most of it behind the table. Katkin had never felt the pain of her humble state quite as keenly as now in the company of the proud Captain.

Tomas turned to her, smiling, intending perhaps to introduce her to one of his fellow officers. His smile died when he surveyed her clothing and his expression grew stormy.

He dropped his voice to a furious whisper. Leaning close to her so they could not be overheard he said, "What in the god's names were you thinking, coming here dressed like that? I brought you here to show you off and you look like a... ragamuffin!"

If the floor had opened and swallowed Katkin up, she would have been only too pleased. Flushing scarlet with dismay and humiliation, she hissed back, "This is the only dress I have, Captain!"

Ignoring her explanation, Tomas impatiently snapped his fingers, recalling the servant carrying their coats. "The young lady and I would prefer a private dining room. Please ready one, immediately."

"Of course, Captain. If you and the lady..." he paused here fractionally "...would care to accompany me, I will be more than happy to seat you in a more secluded location." The servant turned smartly and led the way across the crowded inn, and at each table their procession passed Katkin could feel every pair of eyes boring into her back like so many sharp little knives.

He led them to a cozy parlor, with a single table set for dinner in the centre. A much smaller fireplace took up one wall. The servant deposited their coats on a hook just inside the door as Tomas gave the order for dinner.

Katkin wandered over to the fire, staring into the flames and wondering what else could possibly go wrong with the evening. She felt tears stinging her eyes and angrily rubbed them away, determined not to humiliate herself further by giving way to her emotions.

The servant departed, closing the door with a soft click. In the uncomfortable silence that followed she turned back to look at Tomas from across the room. Finally she spoke, determined to try and salvage something of their time together. "Captain, I am sorry if I embarrassed you. Honestly, this is the only dress I had to wear. I lost everything else in the fire that destroyed my home."

He looked at her skeptically, seemingly unable to believe she told the truth. Suddenly, he laughed uproariously, shaking his head in wonder. "Oh Katrione, being with you is so good for me, I swear by the gods. Every man should have such a woman to prick his inflated pride now and again. Come sit by me at table, and talk, and I will forget the rest of the sorry world even exists."

Pulling out a chair beside him, he motioned for her to sit. She did so, privately still seething at his boorish behavior out in the main part of the inn.

Katkin did not really feel like talking, and as it turned out, that did not bother the Captain at all. He monopolized the conversation with tales of his heroic exploits on the battlefield. She had merely to nod her head admiringly from time to time and he was content.

Uniformed waiters brought the food, served in silver chafing dishes, and the sheer size and richness of the repast staggered Katkin. The meal began with foie gras, followed by roasted pheasant with a creamy sauce with wild chanterelles. More dishes followed in dizzying succession, and Katkin, unused to such fare after years of eating the simple, nutritious diet provided by the

Unity, soon felt more than a little ill. Tomas had also given her a glass of wine, insisting she try a little, although she had asked the waiter to serve her water. The wine made her head spin, and the room felt as though it was getting warmer and warmer. He contentedly finished the rest of the jug and called for another. With the disappearance of the wine be became even more voluble, until Katkin felt she might scream. Only the stern warnings of the Maitress kept her from making some excuse to leave the table and run all the way back to the Infirmarie.

Just when she felt sure she could neither eat another bite nor sanely listen to another tale of heroism, rescue arrived in the most unlikely form. A tap at the door interrupted another interminable story. Tomas paused mid-sentence to bark drunkenly, "Come in, if you must disturb us."

Jacq strode into the room, and stood at attention, watching the Captain gravely. He did not greet or even look at Katkin, but kept his eyes straight ahead. Tomas seemed most annoyed and asked curtly, "What is the meaning of this intrusion? Stand at ease, man and deliver your message, whatever it may be."

Jacq relaxed slightly and crossed his hands behind his back. "Begging your pardon, Captain. A runner has returned from the front with news of Reynard's movements and Colonel Deschamps requires your presence at a council of war. The Colonel asked me to fetch you because he could find no one free at the Garrison to carry the message. He sends his apologies, but requests you return there immediately."

Tomas reddened and swore softly. He rose from his seat and turned to Katkin. "I am sorry, my dear, I must leave you. Duty intervenes and we will have to end this pleasant interlude for now." He paused and gave her a sly smile. "Be assured I shall soon be calling for you again, and next time, perhaps you *will* have some other little frock to wear. Yes, I am sure of it."

Katkin rose as he bowed. After clicking his heels together smartly, and taking her hand, he pressed it firmly to his lips. Jacq colored and quickly looked away.

Turning, he addressed Jacq in supercilious tones. "Your name escapes me, boy."

Jacq said evenly, "Benet, Sir," but Katkin saw the flash of anger in his eyes.

"Very well, Benet. I charge you with the escort of this young woman back to her home at the Infirmarie, as to my great misfortune I am unable to do so myself. Make sure she arrives safely and then report back to me at the garrison. I will have the carriage sent round to the back so you may leave in private." Obviously, despite his now excellent humor, he had no desire to repeat the scene which transpired when they arrived.

"Good night, Miss du Chesne, until we meet again."

Katkin smiled at him, quite unable to believe her luck—now she would be able to leave with Jacq and talk with him privately. She felt positively giddy with relief at the Captain's premature departure. Once back at the Infirmarie, she intended to write a letter telling him unequivocally she never wanted to see him again. But she would not embarrass Jacq by making a scene with the Captain now, so she merely said, "Good night, Captain, and thank you for this evening. It has been truly... enlightening."

Tomas turned with a flourish and left the room. Katkin still felt dizzy, and as soon as he had departed, she sank back down into her chair. Jacq was at her side in a second, his face a picture of concern.

"What troubles you, my lady? Are you unwell?"

She looked up in surprise, not expecting him to address her so formally. "I will be all right in a moment, Jacq. It is the wine, I guess."

He nodded and said stiffly, "I will see if the carriage has arrived."

"Jacq?"

"Yes, my lady?"

"Do you think it is possible we could walk back to the Infirmarie? I suddenly feel the need for some fresh air. And Jacq?"

"Yes, my lady?"

Perhaps the wine made her more forthright than necessary. "Could you please stop calling me by that ridiculous title? You used to call me Katkin. I wish you would again."

He smiled at her, shaking his head. "You haven't changed a bit."

The bitingly cold night air felt heavenly after the closeness of the smoky inn. Jacq waited for her on the empty sidewalk and as she slipped her arm through his she felt entirely content, the memory of her unpleasant evening with the Captain slipping away completely. They strolled through the Citadel Commons, heading back towards the corner of Lampwright's Street. A million tiny white jewels spangled the clear night sky. Her breath made a frosty cloud in the air around her.

She still could not quite believe the tall, grave man striding beside her had once been her childhood friend. They talked of inconsequential things at first, still a little shy with each other after such a long separation.

Finally, Katkin asked him a question for which she had been longing to know the answer. "How is your mother? I have had no news of her since I left Tintaren to go to school in the City."

"Her life was pretty difficult for a while. The autumn after you left to go to school the potato crop failed and a lot of us had nothing to eat. My mother had a new baby then, named Jessie, but she died of starvation." He delivered this devastating news in a matter of fact way, trying hard not to upset Katkin, who walked silently by his side.

"I am so sorry. I never even knew you had a baby sister. When did your mother get remarried?"

"She didn't," was all Jacq had to say to that.

Katkin sighed. "Things must have just gotten worse when Reynard came and burned Tintaren down."

She looked up at him with her green eyes full of sorrow.

"With your parents gone, mother had no income, and we all suffered during the first winter. I knew I had to do something to earn some money, otherwise my brothers were going starve as well." Jacq, as the eldest child of Elisabeth Benet, had always taken his responsibilities towards his family very seriously, especially after his father died. "Though I was only fifteen, I was... well, big for my age." Katkin smiled, remembering well how he had towered over her as a child. "I lied about my age and signed on at the Citadel as a blacksmith's apprentice. My family could eat on the pay I received and I lived at the garrison rent-free. Now, though, things are much improved. My mother has a better house and a few acres of land, and she is able to grow what she needs to feed herself, Thad, and Kadya. The older ones are grown up and gone now. She even owns a cow!"

Katkin's head snapped up and she stopped walking. She asked

sharply, "Where did those few acres of land come from? Who gave them to her?"

Jacq turned and looked at her steadily, his gray eyes clear. "Old Tintaren land, given to her by Reynard."

She felt rage boiling up inside her and after taking a deep breath, fought it back down again. "My lands? He gave her my land, the land he stole from my father?"

"If you want to look at it that way, yes, I suppose so."

"How else should I look at it? I have no home because of that murderer. I hate him."

Jacq began to walk again and she fell in step beside him. He spoke quietly. "Do you know much about the history of this war? How it started, I mean?"

"Not really, I was just a little girl back then. My mother and father talked about it but I didn't pay much attention." But she did remember the haunted fear in her mother's eyes when she talked of the Commander of the Rising. Katkin looked up at Jack and asked, "Do you know anything about Reynard? I thought he was supposed to be this mysterious figure that appeared out of nowhere to lead the cottars to victory."

Jacq shrugged. "Just what I have heard the men saying in the garrison. Rumor has it he used to be an officer in the Guard, and he quit to fight for the cottars instead, because he believed strongly in the cause they had taken up."

"Yes, no doubt you are right," agreed Katkin. "A murderer such as he would be a traitorous cur."

"Cur or not, since he took command they have become much better organized. They win many battles against the Guard now, though they are frequently outnumbered. The cottars have legitimate grievances, Katkin. Children were starving—my own sister among them, because of the inequality of the arrangements between cottar and Lord. Why should they not try to change things?"

"Because the cottars have been in the employ of the Lords for hundreds of years. It always worked well in the past. The Lords took good care of all the people who tended the land for them. Everyone benefited."

"Did they? Just because people have always done something a certain way does not make it right or fair. I never attended a school. While you were in your classroom learning to read and write, I was in the fields—day in and day out. Does that seem fair to you?"

She sighed. "I lost my chance to go to school because of Reynard's attack on Tintaren. That wasn't fair either. So I suppose we are even now. But there is something I do not understand— if that monster Reynard has been so good to your mother, Jacq, why are you working against him? Even if you do not serve in the King's Guard, you still assist them in their efforts, as a blacksmith. Reynard is their sworn enemy. Does your family not feel anger at this?"

He answered thoughtfully. "My family understands why I do what I do. They are not angry with me." He would say no more and they walked on in silence, the earlier carefree mood between them lost.

Finally, they drew up to the gates of the Infirmarie. Katkin looked up at Jacq, sad she had allowed her anger to make things uncomfortable between them. Impulsively, she reached high, threw her arms about his neck, and hugged him, burying her face on his capable shoulder. At first, he stiffened uncomfortably, but then he returned the embrace, giving her a sudden, hard clasp that almost took her breath. He released her abruptly and quickly turned away so she could not see his face.

"Jacq, I am sorry I lost my temper. What happened with Reynard is in the past and I cannot change it. I am glad your mother is well and happy." She touched his broad back and he turned to face her again, his expression carefully controlled.

"You don't have to apologize. I understand what the loss of your home meant to you. I am sorry it happened. Sorry for everything. We never had a chance to..." He stopped and shook his head sadly.

"Never had a chance to what?"

"Nothing. It is over now, anyway. I should be going, or the Captain will be wondering where his report is." His voice sounded bleak as he turned away from her.

Katkin laid her hand on his arm. "Thank you for walking back with me. It has been by far the best part of the whole evening for me. I shall forever think of you as my hero."

She meant it teasingly, but Jacq did not smile in return.

His gray eyes looked down at her seriously and he said softly, "I would always be that for you, if only I could." She looked up at him in surprise and then, at last, she understood.

She asked, with sudden urgency, "Jacq, when can we see each other again?"

His voice sounded troubled in the darkness. "I don't know, Kat. You have your vows to think about."

She took his hand and said quietly, "I have only made the prime vows, not the abiding ones. They don't happen until I am twenty-one. I still have time to change my mind."

Still he did not allow himself any hope. "But Captain de Vigny is…"

Katkin laughed. "…awful. And no competition at all."

This time his embrace was unrestrained and joyful, and almost swept her off her feet. She grasped his calloused hand and brought it to her cheek and then her lips, kissing the palm softly.

Jacq suddenly had to take a very deep breath to steady himself. "Kat," he whispered. "Oh, my beautiful girl, do you understand what your caresses mean to me now? This is no childhood game between us."

She nodded silently, eyes wide, and stood on her toes, to bring her face close, so she might receive his mouth on hers.

7

The Princess Arellen

(Arkirish Dynasty, Standing Four)

Look now, she has chosen. Are you happy, Raven?
Raven's eyes are sad. Better for him if she hadn't, maybe.
Moonlight sighs. It would be better for Fyn. He always loses, and so do I.
Geya speaks sharply. Hold your tongue, Sister. We do not have the right to judge. Moera deals the tokens we all must play.

~~~~~~~~~~~

Katkin, true to her resolve, duly wrote a polite missive to Captain de Vigny telling him in no uncertain terms that while she valued his friendship highly, she did not wish any further contact with him outside the walls of the Infirmarie. Though she wanted to send it right away, she had no money for a messenger and the letter languished under her pillow. It seemed it might not be necessary after all. As the weeks passed with no news or communication, she began to wonder if the Captain intended to spare her any further attention, despite his words to the contrary the night they had dined together.

Jacq did not call on her either, or send any message, and Katkin found this lack of attention far more distressing. Becka, aware of this secret unhappiness, despite her roommate's concerted efforts to hide it, pried relentlessly. The Maitress had given her a private order to keep her ears and eyes open for news of Katkin's relationship with the Captain.

After news arrived that the King had ordered the Fourth Company to the west of the City to engage Reynard as he attempted to consolidate his hold on the area, Becka offered the following report to her Mother Superior. "Katkin is checking the incoming patient manifest every day, Maitress. I think she is worried for

Captain de Vigny's safety." The Maitress sent Becka on her way with a pleased smile and a pat on the shoulder. But it was not for Tomas' name that Katkin scanned the list so anxiously, but rather Jacques Benet.

One night in the refectory, during the evening meal, Becka tried fruitlessly to get her friend to confide in her. They sat together at a long table with benches on either side. Around them, other low conversations buzzed in the background.

She lowered her head, whispering conspiratorially. "I heard the Maitress had a visitor today from the Citadel. He brought a big, fancy box and left it in her office. Amber told me it had the de Vigny crest on it. Do you know anything about it? It might be a gift for you."

Katkin looked up from her plate of boiled potatoes and cabbage, her mouth full. Sometimes Becka's curiosity annoyed her, and she felt in no mood to talk, least of all about the Captain. She swallowed her food and replied angrily. "I have no idea who or what that box is for, and I don't give a damn about it. Now stop asking me questions!"

Becka quailed in her seat, shocked at Katkin's sudden outburst. Her eyes watered emotionally and Katkin immediately felt guilty for snapping at her friend. "I am sorry, Becka. I shouldn't have spoken to you like that. I am just tired, I suppose. I spent all day in the Springhouse, hefting fat ladies in and out of the water." She smiled at Becka, who could not help noticing the smile did not quite reach her eyes.

Katkin's heart sank when, just a few minutes later, Trechelle stood before them, bearing a message she should come to the Maitress' office immediately. Becka's knowing smirk was infuriating, and Katkin left without speaking further to her. Becka watched her go, nodding her head in silent satisfaction.

Once inside the office, Katkin stared moodily at the fancily wrapped package that took the central place on the Maitress' desk. It was addressed to "Miss Katrione du Chesne" in a bold and flowing script that undoubtedly belonged to the Captain.

"Aren't you going to open it, girl?" the Maitress snapped at her, obviously impatient to know the contents of the box.

"If you wish, Maitress," Katkin replied dully, not the least bit interested in any gift from Tomas. Taking the letter opener, she cut the string. After removing the wrappings, she revealed a box made of thick, golden paperboard. Katkin hesitated briefly.

"Go on, child! Such a fine box must contain a fine gift."

She removed the cover of the box and examined the contents. On the top lay a folded note card, addressed to her in the same flowing hand and bearing the de Vigny crest. A mysterious bulky object enveloped in scarlet silk filled the rest of the box. Putting the note aside for a moment, Katkin lifted the silk shrouded object and unfolded it carefully. The contents made her gasp out loud. The silk protected a stunning gown of emerald green taffeta, with a narrowly fitted bodice, and a sumptuous gold-trimmed stomacher. The puffed sleeves, edged in turquoise satin, fastened with pearl buttons, and had cunning designs embroidered with gold thread. Another long row of pearl buttons fastened in the back. A hooped petticoat filled the bottom of the box, along with a pair of turquoise silk shoes with high slender heels. Katkin had never seen a lovelier or more costly outfit. Putting the dress down slowly, her trembling hands reached for the missive from Captain de Vigny. Opening the note, she scanned it silently and then passed it to the Maitress, who was making impatient clicking sounds with her tongue. The Maitress read it out loud:

"General Charles de Vigny requests the presence of Miss Katrione du Chesne at a ball to be held in her honor on the 15th of December at Havenwood." The invitation had been printed in a fancy script on the card, but a handwritten note was scrawled on the bottom:

I told you I would arrange something becoming for you to wear on our next engagement. The dressmaker will come to the Infirmarie tomorrow for a final fitting. Until we meet again, I am your most humble and ardent servant, Captain Tomas Jean de Vigny.

The Maitress looked absurdly pleased, her old face wrinkling into a smile. "This is marvelous. They are holding a ball in your honor. Did you hear me? In your honor! Katrione, you have performed even better than I imagined possible."

Katkin sighed deeply. "I don't want to go."

"What? What do you mean you don't want to go? The ball is for you. Look at this beautiful gown the Captain sent. What girl wouldn't want to wear a dress like this?" The old woman looked at her in angry confusion.

Katkin shook her head violently. "I don't care about the dress, nor do I particularly like Tomas de Vigny. He humiliated me at the Boar's Head in front of a roomful of people, drinks far too much and brags about himself constantly. I don't want to go with him, to this ball or anywhere else. I made up my mind on that point after our dinner together. Anyway, Jacq Benet and I..."

The Maitress drew herself up, her mouth working, furious with Katkin's refusal. "Impudent girl! Stop this at once. What does it matter what you want? I am the Mother Superior of the Unity and you have vowed obedience to me. You shall go to this ball and there will be no more argument."

For a moment, it looked as though Katkin might protest further. She locked eyes with the Maitress and the two women stood across the desk from one another, the dress between them, forgotten in the heat of the moment.

"Need I remind you, little fool, you have nowhere else to live? We took you in when you had nothing." A real and present threat echoed in her words.

Katkin did not cry, although she felt like it. Never had she felt so alone, and so utterly friendless. She had no one to help her—no one to make the Maitress understand why she did not want to see Tomas again. Even Becka had taken the Maitress' side. Blinking back the tears that threatened to spill over at any second, Katkin took a deep breath and decided she had no choice. "I will go to the ball, if you wish it," she said listlessly.

The Maitress smiled, her victory over the hardheaded, imprudent girl assured. "I am pleased you have chosen to see reason. Come, child, let us not quarrel or exchange any more harsh words. The Captain may have his faults, but surely you can see how his favor is to your advantage. Can you not be happy?"

Katkin said stubbornly, "I don't wish to have his favor even if it conferred every advantage to me in the world. If you order me to see him, then I have to comply, but it will not bring me happiness. You will not make me change my mind."

"As you wish, Juvenie. I would be as a mother to you, and guide you in the ways of the world, if I could. So if you persist in this willful disobedience, then I must discipline you accordingly. I am confining you to your room until the evening of the ball. Now go there at once. I will have your meals sent up to you."

Katkin turned and walked out, leaving the hated dress behind her without a backward glance.

The five days until the Ball passed very slowly, and she felt bored and lonely in her tiny room. She spent the time reading and occasionally playing her vielle. Becka came and went as her duties allowed. Katkin spoke little to her, after deciding her roommate had become just another pawn in the Maitress' chess game with Charles de Vigny.

Her journal became her only friend and companion, and she poured her heart out to it. She toyed with the idea of going to the ball and behaving so awfully the Captain would never want to see her again. But having had first hand experience of his violent temper, it seemed a risky undertaking. Finally, she decided she must tell him something close to the truth, but in such a way that he could salvage his honor and pride. She would lead him to some quiet corner and somehow convince him that though she had the utmost regard for him, she could not see him again because her work at the Infirmarie must come first.

The day of the ball dawned clear and cold. Ice formed on the inside of the tiny attic window and Katkin scraped it away with her hand before looking out, thinking of her five-day imprisonment. She had missed her work, very much, and she wondered if the Maitress would ever allow her to resume her training. Perhaps she would not give up until Katkin was married to Tomas de Vigny. Privately, she swore to herself she would run away before she let that happen. She sighed deeply, thinking of the trials that lay before her.

Sometime soon, Amber would climb the stairs to the Juvenet hostel, bringing up the gold box. Then Katkin would have to step into the elegant green and gold gown, which had been made just for her, feeling all the while as if it was truly meant for someone else—the worldly aristocrat Tomas must think she was, but that she could never be. Becka would do her hair and once again she would find herself trapped in the green velvet interior of the De Vigny carriage. The thought brought her nothing but unhappiness.

Later, coiffed and beribboned, she waited outside the gate with the Maitress standing by her side, obviously on guard to make sure she did not run away. When the carriage pulled up and the footman stepped down and opened the door, Katkin saw, to her surprise, the interior was vacant.

She turned to the driver. "Where is the Captain?"

He touched his cap respectfully. "Detained at the Citadel, Lady. He begs your indulgence and says he will join you at Havenwood."

As she boarded, she listened to the Maitress' last words of advice, spoken as the old woman hobbled back through the gates to the Infirmarie. "Katrione, I know you think I am being too hard on you. But sometimes one cannot listen to one's head—one must instead follow the heart. If you listen to your heart I am sure you will find the right answers to the questions we face together."

Later, riding alone in the darkened carriage, Katkin reflected sadly that her heart held only the words of a common blacksmith of the King's Guard, who had told her not long ago he would always be her hero if he could.

She found the carriage ride unexpectedly relaxing, for she hadn't been forced to make polite conversation with her absent suitor. Katkin took the opportunity to gaze out the windows as they passed street after street, climbing steadily to the heights above the City, to the shoulders of Mount Hythea herself. The finest houses in St. Valery perched here on the steeply sloping mountainside, above the smoke and dirt of the City, like so many fancy eyries. She would have enjoyed this unaccustomed view of the City, spread out before her like a fairy world of twinkling lights, if she wasn't dreading the ball quite so much.

Presently, they turned on to a long winding drive, after passing through a set of magnificent gates emblazoned with the white horse crest and bearing the name "Havenwood." Katkin leaned forward, straining to catch a glimpse of her intended destination. Even given her memories of her own earlier life of privilege, it was a truly magnificent edifice. The main house rose three stories high with lower wings stretching out on either side. Katkin could not begin to count the number of windows. Her carriage slowed to a stop in a line of others, as they discharged their passengers in front of the commanding set of entrance doors, manned with servants in the red and black livery of the de Vignys. She felt her heart begin to pound as the carriage moved slowly forward until it had drawn up to the doors.

Tomas waited for her on the steps, his eyes lit expectantly with the thought of seeing her in the dress he had sent. He was not disappointed. A breathtaking vision of beauty stepped slowly and nervously from his father's carriage, the gown a perfect fit for her slender figure. Hurrying forward, he bowed low before her, pressing his lips to her hand. "Welcome to Havenwood, my dear. You are beyond magnificent. Such a beautiful woman as yourself should always be dressed as you are tonight. Come, my father desires to meet you at once. All this..." Here he spread his hands, encompassing the brightly lit house, the still-arriving carriages filled with richly dressed people, and the scurrying servants. "All this is for you, Katrione. And you deserve every bit of it."

Katkin did not think Tomas would be so happy with her after he heard the message she meant to deliver to him sometime during the evening. But she knew the talk she dreaded would have to wait until they had a quiet moment alone. So she turned to him and smiled, saying politely, "It is a fine house, Captain, and I look forward to thanking your father for this occasion he has so thoughtfully planned for me."

Taking his arm, she ascended the steps to the door, flanked on either side by tall footmen. Inside the hall, where the ornately painted and plastered ceiling towered high above their heads, the butler announced them in dulcet tones as, "Captain Tomas Jean de Vigny, recently returned from a successful campaign in the West, and his lady, Katrione Estelle du Chesne, in whose honor this occasion is celebrated." Hundreds of heads turned and stared at the two of them and a wave of polite applause drifted across the floor. Katkin, taken aback by both this introduction and the attention from the crowd, had to be almost dragged along by Tomas, who eagerly made his way through the mass of people in the salon to where his father sat at the far end of the room, in an elaborately carved chair that looked almost like a throne.

The old man rose as they approached him, and Katkin immediately saw his similarity to Tomas. They shared the same aristocratic nose, firm jaw and icy blue eyes. Those eyes took in every inch of her now, making her feel distinctly uncomfortable. Finally, he nodded and spoke approvingly, though not to her.

"Glorious. Son, your description did not do this fair lady justice. But I think, perhaps, there are no words that would." Then he, too, bowed and kissed her hand. "Welcome, my dear, to Havenwood. It has been many years since such a picture of loveliness has graced this floor." Remembering her manners at last, she curtsied deeply in return, and thanked him for his welcome.

The chamber orchestra began a minuet and Katkin worried she might be pressed into dancing one of the complicated steps that were all the rage among the elite ranks of the City. Of course, she had taken dancing lessons as a child, long ago, but she remembered nothing of them now. It seemed she would be spared this trial for the moment, however, for Tomas wanted to show her off by introducing her to as many people as possible. Katkin looked around her in wonder. The conspicuous wealth she saw everywhere around them staggered her. She thought of little Jessie, Jacq's sister, who had starved to death in the countryside not twenty miles from where she stood right now in this ostentatious mansion. Suddenly she felt ashamed, knowing she had once been a part of this lavish lifestyle, and had never given a thought to those around her who were not as fortunate.

"And this is the Marquis Ameloy and his wife Beatrice. I say, Katrione, are you listening?"

Katkin started, guiltily aware her attention had wandered once more from the endless introductions Tomas seemed willing to inflict on her. She apologized and tried to keep smiling and make polite chatter. Finally, unwilling to continue with this tedious round of meeting people who all appeared to blend together in a blur of titles, rotund bellies and garish dresses, she asked, "I wonder if we might have some punch, Captain? My throat is exceedingly dry."

"I am sorry, my love. Where are my manners? You shall have some at once and then very soon the servants will call us in for dinner. It will be a magnificent feast and you and I will sit at the head of the table. Do you not find all this thrilling, Katrione?" Katkin rather thought she did not, but the question might have been rhetorical, so sure was Tomas of her answer.

"Of course you do. And who wouldn't, after all?" As they made their way to the table where a highly polished silver punch bowl gleamed in the light of the twin candelabra flanking it, a young woman suddenly blocked their way. She wore a bright blue silk dress even more revealing than the one the Captain had chosen for Katkin. Her heavily made up eyes hardened unkindly after giving Katkin a frankly appraising look.

"So this is your new little pet, Tomas? Why do you not introduce me?" The girl's voice dripped sarcasm and Katkin wondered what the relationship between them could be. But her presence seemed to throw Tomas off his stride a bit and Katkin became aware of a somewhat guilty pleasure at the thought. He colored slightly and his voice lost its bright tone.

"May I present my... friend, Lady Simone Beauchamps. This is Katrione du Chesne, Simone. Now if you will excuse me for a moment, Katrione, I will fetch us some refreshments." He bowed and left the two of them alone.

Simone stared at her brazenly as Tomas hurried away, and the look reminded Katkin uncomfortably of a cat eying a dish of cream. She affected a little girl's articulation. "Yes, Tomas and Simone used to be ever such good friends but now the gallant Captain doesn't have time for his little Simone, does he? Not since he met you." Her voice grew hard. "But I must congratulate you on your new dress, Katrione, it is lovely. You must be so pleased to have changed tailors. That little number you wore at the Boar's Head didn't do you justice at all. I can certainly understand why Tomas was ashamed to be seen with you in the dining room." Her knowing smirk gave no doubt the words were intended to sting, and they found their mark. Katkin blushed hotly at the mention of the horrible scene at the inn and felt glad Tomas no longer stood by her side.

Presently he returned with a silver cup of punch for her and a large goblet of red wine for himself. Simone, perhaps intent on creating an impression of friendliness now that Tomas had rejoined them, said sweetly, "Now you are one of us, Katrione, you must come and call on me sometime. I live at Beauchamps House, on Melliton Way. I am sure we could find lots to talk about." Katkin could not think of a single polite thing to say to this, but fortunately she was spared the need for a reply by the announcement for dinner.

Tomas, taking her arm, steered her towards the dining room. As he had promised, the servants seated them at the head of a long table, covered with an unbelievable array of fine porcelain dishes bearing the de Vigny crest, cut crystal wine goblets, and solid silver and gold plated cutlery.

After they had been seated a few moments, a footman approached Tomas and stood respectfully to one side. "Begging your pardon, Sir," he murmured.

Tomas drank another large swallow of red wine before answering. "What is it, man?"

"Cresson just sent word from the stable. Electra is about to foal. He's real worried. It is early, and he thinks it may be turned. He wants to send for Benet, over at the Citadel."

Katkin, who had been ignoring the conversation until now, suddenly pricked up her ears.

"Benet?" asked Tomas, obviously confused. "Who's that?"

"The blacksmith, Sir. You know—very tall, strong as an ox..."

Tomas helped himself to a generous forkful of sliced pork, and spoke with his mouth full. "That hulking dim-wit? What on Yrth for?" He continued eating, oblivious to the angry glance the woman at his side suddenly gave him.

The footman said, "He isn't dim. A lot of people think that about him, because he never talks. But there is no one better in Beaumarais for horses. It is uncanny how well he knows them."

Tomas shrugged. "Very well, you can take my carriage. But mind he rides on top with the driver, not inside. I just had the bench re-upholstered and I don't want stable muck all over it." He returned his attention to his food, and drained his glass of wine.

Katkin sat at his side, fuming at his haughty attitude. The meal that followed seemed endless. The Captain drank wine like water and several times his hand strayed under the tablecloth to explore her thigh. Each time, she seized it firmly and pushed it away.

Now Katkin knew Jacq was at Havenwood, she found she could bear Tomas' company no longer. She wondered if she might slip away to the stable and ask him why he had not called on her as he promised he would. When the General announced that the ladies could retire to the powder room, while the gentlemen went to the smoking lounge for cigars and port, Katkin found her chance. She quickly slipped away from the others, and headed towards the back of the house. A young lad passed her and she stopped him. "Where are the stables, if you please? I left my... powder in the carriage and I must fetch it."

He gave her a curious look, but accepted her story readily enough and directed her to the left wing of the house. Katkin crept through the darkened hallways and out a set of double doors to an untidy cobbled courtyard full of crates and barrels. A low stone building stood across the way.

She crossed the yard quickly and paused just outside the arched entrance, for she could hear Jacq's voice from inside, murmuring instructions to another man. Peering anxiously through the door she saw the two men, with their backs to her, standing before a mare, who had obviously just been delivered of a foal. Jacq was stroking her flank gently. A lantern, hung from the exposed beam, lit the scene from above. Carefully, Katkin eased her way into the stable, hoping her ungainly hooped skirt would not brush into anything and give her away. She slipped into the stall nearest the door, which thankfully was unoccupied.

Jacq had obviously just completed some complicated piece of work, for the other man said admiringly, "You are a marvel, Jacq." As Katkin watched from her hiding place, Jacq stood, picking up the newborn foal that lay on the ground in front of him with the utmost gentleness, cradling it to his chest. The foal rested perfectly quietly there. Jacq turned, obviously searching for something, and caught sight of Katkin before she could duck behind the dividing wall. His eyes went wide, but he said nothing to her.

Turning quickly back to the other man, he said, "Can you find me a few old rags or something, Henri? I need to get this little fellow cleaned up. See if you can get us some ale from inside while you are at it. Looks like there is a big party going on in the main house."

"Sure thing. I might be gone a few minutes."

"No hurry. Take your time." The man disappeared out the door, and Jacq carefully laid the foal down again on a pile of hay. He whispered, "Come out, Kat. He is gone." She stepped carefully out and stood before him. He stared at her, and shook his head in disbelief. "My Gods, Kat. Where did you get those clothes? I hardly recognized you."

Katkin answered carelessly, "Tomas gave them to me to wear

to the ball tonight. I didn't want to come, but the Maitress made me, because General de Vigny was giving it in my honor. Now I am glad I did."

Jacq raised his hand to touch her face. "You look so beautiful. Like a queen. But you shouldn't be in here, your dress will get filthy."

She shrugged. "I couldn't care less. I heard Tomas say you were in the stable and I wanted to see you. Why haven't you been to the Infirmarie? You promised me you would come and visit."

Jacq looked down at the ground and did not answer her. He appeared to be thinking about something else. After a moment he said, "You had better get back now. The Captain will be wondering where you are."

She didn't move right away, not until she heard the sounds of footsteps crossing the cobbles, and Henri's voice calling out, "I've got the rags, and the scullery maid is bringing the ale in a minute." Then she gave Jacq a stricken look, lifted her skirts high, and fled out into the night.

Jacq watched her run and then crouched back down over the foal, so that Henri would not see the tears on his face.

Back in the main house, Katkin wandered the halls aimlessly, wondering unhappily why Jacq had not answered her question. She was absently studying a particularly hideous portrait of one of the de Vigny ancestors mounted on a rearing stallion, which hung between two tall windows, when she heard the Captain's voice, deep in conversation with his father, drifting down the gallery towards her. Not wishing to meet him again just yet, she slipped into an alcove behind the heavily brocaded velvet curtain and waited for him to pass by. The old man spoke as he limped along next to the Captain, the sound of his cane muted by the rich Aubusson rug at their feet. Katkin reddened, glad of her hiding place, when she heard the topic they discussed.

"I am very proud of you, my son. The girl is indeed everything you described and much more. She will be the shining jewel in the de Vigny crown. You must marry her at once, and you have my full blessing."

Tomas said earnestly, "Thank you, father, I am so pleased you approve. Katrione will make a fine wife, as you say."

Charles de Vigny dropped his voice and Katkin had to strain

to hear his next words. "And once you defeat Reynard, well... the bargain gets all the sweeter, eh boy? Her holdings will be returned to her, and you will become the Lord of all Tintaren. The de Vigny's will hold the title to the best wine-producing lands in all of Beaumarais. Who will stand in our way then, eh? I will see you crowned King before I die." Katkin, her eyes wide with horror, gave such an audible gasp at this she almost gave her secret position away.

She heard Tomas protest. "But, Father..." and then they passed beyond her hearing. Katkin stepped out from behind the curtain, thoroughly shaken.

When Tomas found her a few minutes later, after she had returned to the Salon, she looked so pale and ill he found a chair and forced her to sit down at once. He said, with concern, "You must recover your strength, my love. Soon the orchestra will strike up again. My arms ache to hold you on the dance floor." Indeed, she could hear the orchestra tuning up above the din of conversation.

Katkin, now panicked by the elder de Vigny's plan to usurp her lands, said urgently, "Tomas, I must talk to you privately. Can we go somewhere quiet for a few moments?"

He looked at her with such fervid interest she realized her request had been totally misconstrued as a desire on her part to be alone with him. Regretfully, he shook his head, saying, "As much as I would like to, my dear, we are expected to lead the gavotte. We must not disappoint my father."

Once the music started, Katkin had to allow him to escort her to the dance floor. She acquitted herself much better than she thought she might, with Tomas merely hissing to her at one point that he would appreciate it if she might not tread on his feet quite so hard. His own dancing, though he had consumed at least two bottles of wine with dinner, was graceful perfection. After an interminable hour, spent twirling in the arms of what seemed like every man in the Salon, she felt she could endure no more.

"Tomas, I am tired and I wish to go home now." Katkin's look was imploring and he swallowed his disappointment manfully.

"As you wish, my love. I will call for the carriage and we will ride together."

"There is no need for you to escort me. I can go alone," she said, hopefully. Even though she knew she desperately needed to talk to him, she could not face the thought of another minute in his company.

"I wouldn't hear of it. I would spend every minute I can with you, my lady."

After stepping into the waiting carriage, Katkin sank into the velvet seat as the footman slammed the door. They set out at a good clip. Tomas sat down heavily next to her and immediately put his arm around her waist, pulling her close. His eyes lingered on her face hungrily, and he lowered his mouth to hers, kissing her wetly. She struggled violently away and threw herself to the other side of the carriage, not daring to look at him. He merely laughed drunkenly and joined her on the opposite side, his hands searching in the darkness and finding her breasts, which he mashed unmercifully as his mouth sought hers once again.

Revulsion gave her the strength to break his hold on her. Backing away, she delivered a stinging slap across his cheek, causing him to sit back abruptly. He regarded her with amusement.

"What a fiery little vixen you are, my Katrione. So you would refuse my attentions? No woman who wears a dress such as yours should be surprised when a man cannot keep his hands away from her body."

She snarled in return, "You bought me this dress and I loathe it. I wish you would take it back."

He leered at her. "By all means, my dear, remove it right now if you wish."

This remark infuriated her even more than his drunken kisses. She snapped, "Go to hell, Tomas."

"Ah, my little Katrione, but your anger excites me all the more. I would ravish you right now if you would allow me. If you will not, it is of no consequence." Here, he gave her a self-satisfied little smile. "I will have you soon enough."

She realized if she was ever going to tell him the truth, it had to be now, in that darkened carriage. After taking a deep breath, she said, "I would speak with you on a topic concerning us both. Will you not honor my request and listen to me?"

He regarded her with surprise. "Of course I will, my dear. I always want to know what you are thinking. Please enlighten me."

"Tomas, there is something I must say. As much as I would like to continue this relationship, I..." At that moment, the carriage halted outside the gates of the Infirmarie and Katkin realized with a sinking heart she had lost her chance. Tomas had already risen to escort her outside.

"I fear I must leave you now, my love. We will have to postpone our talk for another time, and I shall look forward to it very much. Right now, I must hurry, for the Colonel expects me back at the garrison. We prepare for another major offensive against Reynard and I may be away for a few days. When I return, we will meet again—nothing is more certain—and I will also have something important to talk to you about. Until then..." Tomas bowed again and bid her adieu.

She alighted, and her eyes filled with tears as the carriage pulled away. General de Vigny wanted her lands and Tomas selfishly thought only of his own need for her. The Maitress seemed determined that they should both get what they desired.

Katkin honestly did not see how she could stop them.

8

Gessach Mebd, the meandering river

(The Tollyn, Three)

Raven sighs. Do we guide the girl wrongly in this, Geya? She does not know what terror lies in store for her this turn of the Gyre. Dai says...

Geya's reply is sharp. Speak not the name of him who betrays us all. The Amaranthine use her kind for the benefit of all living things, throughout the worlds between worlds. What does it matter if it is beyond their understanding? We give them protection and counsel in return. Without the thaumaturgical, their world would be a place of lesser wonders. Do you believe they would be the happier for it?

Raven shakes her head doubtfully.

~~~~~~~~~~

Katkin presented herself in the Maitress' office first thing in the morning, after passing a sleepless night. The old woman looked up as she knocked.

"Well, Katrione. I hope you enjoyed yourself last evening in the company of Captain de Vigny?" She smiled briefly as she shuffled through a pile of papers on her desk.

Katkin did not smile in return. "I did not, Maitress. My opinion of the Captain has not changed in the least."

The Maitress' expression darkened. "That is a great pity, because I intend for you to continue seeing him, as long as he wishes. He has invited you to a luncheon at Havenwood in one week's time, with his father, Lord de Vigny, and the deputy Mayor, Robert Grassle."

Katkin groaned aloud at this. The Maitress slammed her hand down on her desk. "No more impertinence, young lady! Go back to your room."

But Katkin had had enough. She said forcefully. "You leave

me no choice, Maitress. I am leaving the Unity. If I cannot practice healing, as I vowed to, then why should I stay here any longer?"

The Maitress sat quietly for a moment, surprised at this open rebellion from her former star pupil. She decided to try and reason with the stubborn girl once more, using the argument she had saved if all else failed her. "My dear Katrione, did you know I have selected you to succeed me as Maitress one day? I still think you are the best Juvenie we have ever had at the Infirmarie. No other healer in the history of the Unity has your power."

Katkin, baffled by this unexpected compliment, felt immediately wary. "Why do you tell me this now? I have told you I am leaving."

"Because, child, I think you should consider the advantages of such a prestigious position. You want to help people; I feel it in you strongly. Is that not so?"

"Of course. I just don't see how..."

"Perhaps you also want to marry and have children. I do understand those are powerful urges. Did you know such desires are not incompatible with being Maitress?"

By now, she felt thoroughly confused. "What are you saying? How is that possible, when once I bear a child I will lose my Gift? How could I be a healer then?"

The Maitress asked her softly, "When is the last time you saw me use my Gift, Katrione?"

"I... I do not know, Maitress. I am not sure I ever have."

"That is because I lost it—long ago. After the first summer solstice, it left me, as it has all the other Maitresses. This is not something told to everyone, Katrione, but you must know it so you may make up your mind to stay and marry the Captain."

Katkin, shocked by this admission, asked, "You mean, you are the head of the Unity of Lalluna, yet you have no Gift?"

The Maitress looked at her calmly. "That is correct, child. My job, like that of the Maitresses before me, is purely an administrative one, with the exception of the observance at the solstice time."

"Why do Maitresses lose their Gift then? What do they do at the observance?"

The Maitress shook her head. "That I cannot tell you, unless you decide to stay. It is a secret passed down from the Maitress to her successor and vital to the continuation of the Unity."

Katkin tried to make sense of what she heard. "Are you saying I could be Maitress and be married, and it wouldn't make any difference?"

"That is correct, my dear. There have been isolated examples in the history of our Unity of just such an occurrence. Just think of the good things you could accomplish with your Gift and the de Vigny fortune. When you marry Tomas, as he so ardently desires you should, you may stay here and continue in the great tradition of the Unity to help the infirm, and with such resources at your disposal! How could you possibly refuse such an offer?" The Maitress looked at her expectantly.

Katkin sat down abruptly, stunned by this new choice placed before her by the head of the Unity. "I... I will need some time to think about this. May I return to my room?"

The Maitress gave her a benevolent smile. "Of course. Take as long as you like. But there is no need for you to be confined to your room any longer. Why not return to your duties now? I am sure you are eager to get back to work after your suspension. Amber will walk back to the wards with you, to keep you company."

Katkin nodded gratefully, and turned away, then looked back over her shoulder, saying, "Maitress, my friend Jacques Benet, the blacksmith, hasn't been here to see me, or sent a message, has he?" She tried hard to make her voice sound disinterested.

The Maitress shook her head. "No, Katrione. You have had no visitors or messages, other than those from Captain de Vigny. Now run along and consider carefully what I have told you. Remember, you should not be wasting your thoughts on a common blacksmith."

After Katkin left the office, the Maitress whispered to Amber, "See that she goes straight to the wards, and keep an eye on her. If there are any soldiers from the Fourth Company there, don't let her talk to them. I don't want her asking questions about that man, Benet. Do you understand?"

"Yes, Maitress." Amber curtseyed and followed her charge out into the corridor.

Katkin moved through her responsibilities as if in a dream. Damenie Beneficence reprimanded her, "I said drain the left vesicle, Katrione! Where has your mind wandered to? If you cannot assist me properly, then at least go to the supply room and bring back some more bandages. And tell Amber to come in here and help me while you are away." Katkin apologized and backed out of the room.

She reached the supply room and gathered up an armful of rolled gauze bandages. On her way back down the corridor, she passed an open doorway. A cheerful voice called out, "Excuse me, Miss..."

Katkin peered through the door in surprise and asked, "May I help you with something?" She beheld a young man, in his early twenties, with long brown hair, parted neatly in the middle. He sat up in bed, with his right leg bandaged and splinted. His green eyes had a merry twinkle as he grinned back at her.

"I hope so. I would dearly love a drink of water, but my leg is out of commission at the moment. A pistol ball caught me when I wasn't looking, see? There is a jug over there. I wonder if you wouldn't mind?"

Katkin smiled, pleased to be able to help. "Of course. What is your name, soldier?" She put down the bandages and poured a mug of water from the jug. He drank thirstily before answering her question.

"Jamie Trudeau. Do you have a name, or shall I just call you my angel of mercy?"

She shook her head and laughed at this. "My name is Katkin. Can I get you anything else before I go? I need to take these bandages—"

"Did you say Katkin? As in Katkin du Chesne?"

"How did you know my name?" Katkin asked in amazement. "Have we met somewhere before?"

Jamie stared at her and whistled in appreciation. "So you are the one that Benet's been swanning around over. Well, I can see why, now."

Katkin felt the blood rushing to her cheeks. "You know Jacq? Has he spoken of me?"

"Well, yes and no, if you get my drift. Benet keeps very much to himself, see, and none of the lads knows him very well. Hardly talks at all usually. But a few weeks ago, he comes in late, looking like he'd just ate a steak dinner. He wouldn't say anything much though." Katkin guessed this must have been the night he walked her home from the Boar's Head Inn. "Then a few nights later he got out the old polish kit and got himself very tidy, and me and the lads figured he was going out to see a young lady. So we asked him about it, and he finally admitted he was. He told us your name and that you was at the Infirmarie. Later on he came back, looking very doleful-like, and said you was too busy to see him." Katkin inhaled sharply at this but said nothing. She sat down on the edge of the bed, and tucked her hands underneath her so that Jamie would not see their trembling. "He went again a few more times and each time it was the same old story. Now I happen to be one of the few people Benet actually talks to sometimes, so he says to me one day, 'Trudeau, what can I do? I want to see her again, more than anything, but how can I, when they say she is always so busy?' So I says to him, 'Why not write her a letter?' He didn't think much of that, because Benet can't spell too good, see? Neither can I. But I knew that Corporal Jonas could write real well, so we went to him, and he wrote the letter."

Katkin asked, in a choked voice, "What did it say?"

He looked at her in surprise. "You ought to know! Benet told Jonas what to write, and when the letter was done he carried it over here and gave it to some girl to give to you. Becky, I think he said her name was." Katkin looked so distressed at this he said, "Do you mean to say you never got it?"

Katkin shook her head in despair and burst into tears. Jamie patted her back sympathetically. After a moment she demanded, "How long ago did he bring the letter?"

He said, "I dunno exactly. Maybe two or three weeks ago. We got called away to some fighting after that." Just then, Damenie Beneficence strode into the room and spoke sharply to Katkin.

"There you are, Juvenie! I need those bandages. What have you been doing?" Katkin jumped up and hastily wiped her eyes on her apron.

Jamie gave her a winning smile. "I'm right sorry about that, Damenie. I stopped her for a drink of water, that's all. Please don't make a fuss." Damenie Beneficence nodded vaguely in his direction and turned to go. Then he winked slyly and said to Katkin, "The next time I see your friend, shall I say hello for you?"

Katkin turned back to him, and her eyes filled once more with tears. She whispered, "Yes, please, Jamie. Tell him I... care for him, very much." She hurried from the room as a forceful rebuke from the Damenie drifted back down the corridor.

Jamie watched her go. He answered softly, "That I will, Miss. That I will."

Amber stood outside the Maitress' door and blocked it as Katkin tried to push past her. "She has a visitor. You will have to wait."

"No, Amber, I will not. I want to speak with her right now." Katkin's anger boiled over and she grabbed the younger Juvenie by the shoulders and threw her out of the way. As she burst in through the door, Tomas de Vigny had just risen, and was in the middle of a bow.

The Maitress said in a shocked voice, "Katrione! What is the meaning of this intrusion?"

She stared at them both wide-eyed. "You lied to me! You said he hadn't been here or sent a message, but he has. How could you do such a thing, Maitress?"

Tomas said crisply, "Calm yourself, my dear. I am sure whatever your Mother Superior did she had a very good reason for it."

The Maitress said serenely, "You may as well come in, child, and close the door behind you. I will endeavor to explain."

"Do not bother." Katkin said bitterly. "You wish to say I should not be wasting my thoughts on a common blacksmith. So you sent him away when he came to see me, and you told me he had not come to call."

"Yes, my dear. I did only what I felt was necessary for your well-being and ultimate happiness. Of course one always regrets when one must shade the truth somewhat, but..."

"You lied to me. He came to see me and he sent a letter," Katkin interjected vehemently.

"But..." the Maitress continued, giving her a look of exasperation. "I did what I did with the very best of intentions. I sent the young man away several times, but I swear I know nothing of any letter."

As Katkin began an angry retort, Tomas stood abruptly and said, "Come, Katrione. You look as though you could use some fresh air. Let us go for a walk." Then, to the Maitress, "We will not leave the grounds, I give you my word."

The Maitress nodded. "Of course, Captain. But Katrione will need a cloak. I will send Amber to her room for one."

He shrugged. "No need. She can wear mine."

"I don't want to go for a walk with you," Katkin retorted angrily, and then stopped, realizing how childish this sounded, even to her own ears. So she allowed him to take her arm and guide her out the door and into the anteroom. The Captain paused and carefully placed his heavy greatcoat over her shoulders before opening the door and ushering her outside into the chilly afternoon sunshine.

He led her across the green sward and up the back of the Springhouse, on a winding path that led to the cemetery. As they walked, Tomas asked her questions about her work at the Infirmarie, and Katkin found, to her surprise, that he had learned a great deal about Lalluna and the Unity since the first time they met in the Acre and seemed eager to know more. She wondered at this and asked what had happened to change his mind.

They stopped before a level area of the grounds, just below the stone wall that surrounded the cemetery. It was once a memorial garden, with raised beds of shrubs and flowers, but the overworked gardeners had neglected it. Now, thorny, dry rose canes poked mournfully out from the unkempt yellow grass. In response to her question, Tomas said quietly, "I thought I should know a little something about the Infirmarie, since I am going to be living here."

Katkin's eyebrows shot up. "Living here? Why would you do that? Are you ill again?"

He smiled and touched her face, very gently. "When my wife is made the Maitress, then she must be able to carry out the duties of her office at any time of the day or night. That means we must live here, on the grounds." Katkin blushed hotly, but could think of nothing at all to say. He continued. "The present Maitress has offered us this piece of land to build a house on, Katrione. That is what we were discussing when you came in, just now."

Katkin could not believe what she was hearing. "But... But what about Havenwood?"

"Havenwood belongs to the old man. I can't stand him. That is the last place I would want to live. It is too big, anyway." He took her hand and led her to the site. When they turned around, they could see the whole Infirmarie laid out below them, and the white stone buildings looked very beautiful in the late afternoon sunlight. He said softly, "I want to build a house here. For you. That we can share with our children. Nothing would give me more happiness."

Katkin looked up at him in confusion. When had this soft-spoken man replaced the drunken boor who accosted her in the carriage last night? Which one was the real Tomas de Vigny? There was but one way to find out.

She took a deep breath and said, "Tomas, I am much honored you wish to marry me, but I must tell you that while I hold you in high regard, I do not love you."

He blinked at this, and looked away over the rows and rows of plain white gravestones before answering. His voice remained gentle. "I know you do not, Katrione. And I thank you for your honesty. But I believe you will... grow to love me, given the opportunity. I want to take that chance, my dear. All I ask is that you try."

His answer to this was so unexpected that Katkin gave the only reply she could. "I don't know what to say, Tomas." They stood for a moment in silence, facing each other in the long grass. Katkin accidentally grasped at a rose stem in her distress and confusion and a thorn embedded itself deeply in her flesh. She gave a cry of pain, and Tomas took her hand in his, saying, "Here, let me." A drop of blood lay on her palm like a ruby, surrounding the thorn. He carefully removed it and wiped the blood away with his handkerchief, then softly kissed her hand.

The longing in his eyes was plain. "Will you try?"

Katkin thought once more of Jacq's gentleness, cradling the newborn foal to his chest, and the feeling of his mouth on hers. How could she possibly make up her mind? She begged him, "Give me a little time to think on it. Until tomorrow."

He sighed. "Very well, love. Until tomorrow."

They turned away from the garden and began to walk back down the hill. When they reached the door to the Juvenet hostel, Tomas said, "Katrione, last night you said you had something you needed to discuss with me. Will you tell me now?"

She looked at him for a moment and then she said slowly, "It wasn't important. In fact, I can't even remember what it was I wanted to say."

As she turned to go, Tomas announced suddenly, "Your friend—the blacksmith, Benet—he quit this morning. Just packed up his tools and went."

Katkin tried hard not to cry, though she felt like it. "Did he say why? Or where he was going?"

The Captain shook his head. "He might have been annoyed about something, but he never talks to anyone, so I doubt I could even find out for you. I am sorry."

She shook her head numbly and turned away with a heavy heart. She walked slowly up the winding staircase to her room on the third floor, dragging her fingers along the spindles of the banister, considering Tomas' unexpected news about Jacq's departure. Katkin did not know whether to believe the Captain or not, given what she knew of his character.

When she arrived back to the room she shared with Becka, it was empty. She immediately began rifling through her roommate's possessions, looking for Jacq's letter, hoping it might give her some clue to his whereabouts. After a time, she found a square of parchment, deep beneath a pile of clothing in the back of a drawer. It was addressed to Katrione du Chesne in a neatly printed script. Katkin hurriedly unfolded it, noticing to her dismay that the seal had already been broken. As soon as she began to read, she placed a hand over her mouth to stifle a cry of despair.

My dearest Katkin,

> *I have been to see you four times since the night we walked together from the Boar's Head, but the Maitress always tells me you are busy. I do not believe her and I wonder now if she has even told you of my visits. There is so much more I would tell if I could, my beautiful girl. But for now, I can say only that you are in my thoughts every minute and I am anxiously awaiting your reply. Please send a message back to me somehow.*

Yours faithfully,
Jacq

PS. I paid Corporal Jonas to write this for me. JFB

The message was dated three weeks ago. Jacq had obviously grown tired of waiting for her answer and had left the Citadel, perhaps forever. She found herself slightly piqued that he had not chosen to wait a *little* longer, especially since he had seen her just last night at the ball. Why did he not say something in the stables, when she asked him why he hadn't called on her? Perhaps he had changed his mind, or even regretted sending the letter? Katkin considered this for a moment and then thoughtfully left the Juvenet hostel again, heading for the wards.

She went back to Jamie Trudeau's room, intending to ask him about Jacq. He lay facing the wall, and appeared to be sleeping. She shook his shoulder gently, saying, "Jamie? I am sorry to wake you, but I must ask you something. It is very important." The man in the bed rolled over and looked confusedly up at her. She had never seen him before.

"Did you call me Jamie? You've got the wrong gentleman, Miss. My name is Arthur." Katkin apologized for her mistake and left the room. After making inquiries, she found the ward Damenie did not know where they had sent Jamie Trudeau, only that he had gone that afternoon and would not be back. She walked back to her room dejectedly, wondering if Jamie's transfer had been deliberate. Becka, now off-duty, greeted her at the door, and Katkin pushed past her without a word.

She sat down on her bed and Becka immediately joined her, saying, "What is bothering you, Kat? Tell me about it. You know you can trust me."

Katkin stood up immediately, enraged at this transparent lie from her roommate. She quickly slapped Becka's face, before drawing Jacq's letter from the pocket of her shift and waving it in front of her.

"*Can* I trust you, Becka? Why did you not give me this?"

Tears sprang to Becka's eyes and she looked too stunned to speak for a moment. Then she said petulantly, "Because it wasn't fair. You already had Captain de Vigny, and then this other man came to see you as well. I didn't have anyone, so I pretended he sent me the letter instead!" Her lower lip began to tremble. "What difference does it make anyway? The Maitress says you are to marry Tomas and it will be very good for the rest of us when you do. Don't you see how lucky you are? The Captain is so rich and handsome, and he has chosen you to be his wife." The look she gave Katkin was frankly envious.

Katkin turned away from her, saying, "Get your things and get out. You are no longer my roommate."

"But Katkin... I am sorry about the letter."

"I don't give a damn. Just go." Becka put her hand over her mouth and ran from the room. She did not return. Katkin felt sure one of the senior Daminem in charge of the Juvenet would come up and chastise her for her actions, but she was left alone. When the dinner bell rang, she made her own way down to the refectory. The other Juvenet avoided her, and Katkin found herself eating alone at the end of a long table. She had little appetite and only picked at the plate of barley and swiss chard in front of her. When she returned to her room, after the compline service in the main chapel, Becka's things were gone.

When Captain de Vigny came to see her in the morning Katkin could only beg him for a little more time in which to make up her mind. Two more days passed with the same result. She knew both he and the Maitress were growing ever more impatient with her indecisiveness. That night, as she lay in bed, sleepless, wondering once again what she should do, a quiet tap on the door got her out of bed. It was the Maitress.

"I must speak with you, Katrione. May I come in?"

"Of course, Maitress." Katkin got back into bed, and the Maitress settled heavily on the edge, and placed the candle she carried on the table.

She spoke crisply. "I will get right to the point, Juvenie. I see my seventieth winter this year. I don't expect to have many more. Some day very soon, I will have to leave my position. As you probably know, the new Maitress is always chosen from among the Juvenet, so she may have as long a tenure as possible. You are the one I want." The Maitress' voice grew hard. "So, you must stop this foolish irresolution and accept Captain de Vigny's proposal, tomorrow."

"But, Maitress..."

"No more buts. You have had ample time to make up your mind." She stood and walked back to the door. "The Captain will be in my office at noon. You will tell him then."

Katkin said nothing in response to this, and the Maitress left without wishing her a good night. She shut the door very firmly and Katkin could hear the tapping of her walking stick gradually fading away as she made her way back down the hallway towards the stairwell. It sounded just like the ticking of a clock.

Katkin jumped up from her bed, crying, "Lalluna, my Goddess, please help me! Tell me what I should do."

She walked over to the ewer by the washstand, and poured some water into the basin. Katkin splashed her face, hoping it would help her think more clearly.

After pulling the eiderdown off her bed, she wrapped herself up, and sat down on the window seat. Katkin peered out the glass, across the darkened rooftops of the City she had called home for the last eight years. Her thoughts were a desperate jumble. She seemed to be caught in the balance—between her calling at the Infirmarie and her love for her childhood friend Jacq.

At that moment, she heard someone whisper her name, and she looked up. The water in the basin had begun to glow, and its light cast flickering shadows across the walls of the room. Katkin approached the washstand, unafraid—sure this was some sign from Lalluna. As she stood over it, the water clouded and became dark, then cleared abruptly. A faint image flickered across the surface— of a single rider on a white horse, galloping across a field thick with smoke. Then the smoke cleared abruptly and Katkin could see the Infirmarie. It looked to be overflowing with casualties. Daminem scurried to and fro, bearing wounded men on pallets and stretchers. She could see the handsome house that Tomas had promised to build for her up on the shoulder of Mount Hythea, overlooking the main buildings. The water gave her a bird's eye view, and now carried her up the hill and close to a window looking into a lavishly appointed sitting room. She saw two blond-haired children tussling in a corner. A group of women, Simone Beauchamps and Becka Kent among them, lounged around a table, playing cards and drinking tea, oblivious to both the screams of the children and the frantic activity going on below them at the Infirmarie proper. In the center sat a short, dumpy middle-aged woman in a fancy, low-cut gown. Jeweled rings adorned each of her puffy fingers. Katkin stepped back in revulsion as the water brought her closer to the fat woman's face. There could be no doubt—it was her own.

107

With a cry of horror, Katkin tipped over the washstand and spilled the water onto the floor. The light and the image vanished abruptly. She threw herself back down onto her bed, sobbing. Katkin knew the Maitress would never give her permission to forsake her vows, not with the de Vigny fortune at stake, so she made up her mind to run away, as soon as it was light.

She lay on her back, staring up at the ceiling, wondering where she would go now that Jacq had left the City. In the end, she decided, it did not matter. She could stay at the Infirmarie no longer, now she knew what the future held for her. After a few minutes, she rose again, lit a candle, and began to move purposefully about the room, gathering up her few possessions. She dug underneath the bed for her ancient leather satchel and placed her clothes inside. Then she packed her father's vielle on top. The dress Tomas had given her, now packed away again in its golden box, she left lying forlornly under the bed. Wrapping herself up once more in the eiderdown, she sat on the bed to wait for the dawn. Exhaustion and unhappiness overtook her and finally, she slept...

Katkin wandered through the halls of the Infirmarie, frantically looking for something, though she knew not what it could be. She felt a sense of anxious foreboding spurring her forward. Gliding along the unlit passages, her unshod feet seemed to only skim the smooth surface of the flagged stone floors. The moon shone full through the curtained windows, sharply outlining the shadows and forming liquid white pools of light. She moved to the French doors off the refectory leading outside to the sloping green lawn. Moonlight bathed the lush grass and a warm wind stirred the dry flower heads, causing them to click and nod quietly. Katkin stepped onto the path that led to the Temple of Lalluna, the holy cavern forbidden to all except the Maitress. In her dream, the way looked quite familiar, as if she had trod it many times. White pebbles lined the path and shone palely in the moonlight. Passing through a rusted iron gate, she found herself in the old cemetery. The Daminem and Maitresses from ages past found their final resting place here. Their unadorned graves, marked only with roughly shaped, square marble stones of purest white, also reflected the moonlight. Holly trees grew in wild profusion everywhere and their thorny leaves snagged and caught at Katkin's unbraided hair and her bare arms and legs. The path wound on and on, going steeply uphill, switch-backing up the side of Mt. Hythea.

In a dense grove of cedar trees, she wandered into a tiny enclosure surrounded by a low stone wall. Flowers grew in abundance here, and their perfume gave a heady scent to the night air. Snowdrops, lilies, roses and jonquils competed for space on the floor of the grassy dell, high on the mountainside. In her dream, she knelt to pick the flowers and found they had somehow been changed into bunches of tiny arm and leg bones, with fleshless hands and feet instead of flower heads. With a cry of horror, she dropped the grisly bouquet and ran from the dell up the path to where it passed through an arched rocky face high on the mountainside.

Inside the tunnel entrance, the white stone path continued to shine, providing an eerie phosphorescent light to the rough walls. She hurried downwards as the tunnel opened out into a cathedral-like cavern, festooned with stalactites and stalagmites, glistening like so many pastel colored layer cakes. The place felt familiar to her and yet somehow strange—both hauntingly beautiful and a little frightening.

In the center of this huge space, a statue of the Winged Goddess Lalluna stood high on a plinth. The same unearthly glow lit the figure from above. Her normally serene expression had become one of raw anguish and Katkin felt very afraid. Blood red tears coursed down the stone cheeks and dripped onto her breast. The statue sang or perhaps chanted some unknown song. Her softly keening voice sounded as though it held the sorrows of all the ages of mankind. Katkin could not make the words out at first. She moved closer to the plinth, straining to catch their meaning.

"My children cry out to me. Who will stop the slaughter of my innocents?" The voice died away after a heart-wrenching cry. Katkin looked down abruptly as she felt something moving in her arms. It was a baby girl. The child clutched at the heavy gold moonstone pendant Katkin wore, as the symbol of her office as the Maitress of the Infirmarie. It was the day of the Solstice, the time of the Observance. She dropped the baby and fled from the Temple, weeping. When she woke, she was still crying.

If Katkin had harbored any doubts about her decision to leave the Infirmarie, this dream destroyed them utterly. Drying her eyes, she rose and dressed in her uniform, then checked her bag one last time. Outside her door, she heard the sleepy murmurs of the other Juvenet as they made their way downstairs for Lauds and breakfast. Very soon, she knew, the upper floor would be empty, and she planned to leave quietly down the back stairs. The stable man knew her well, and Katkin felt sure she could convince him she was going to take Brinna out for an early morning ride.

She planned to head first for the Citadel. Although she dreaded the encounter, Katkin felt she had no choice other than to tell Tomas her decision personally. Sighing at the thought of his reaction, she crossed the floor and retrieved the gold box from under the bed. Perhaps if she returned the dress to him he would not be quite so angry with her.

Katkin stood quietly in the center of the room, and thoughtfully looked about her, one last time. Then following some compulsion she did not understand, she took one of the medicine bottles Becka had filled with fresh flowers and water. Smiling grimly, she dumped out the contents into the middle of her ex-roommate's bed and put the phial and the stopper in the pocket of her shift.

Shouldering her bag, she turned and grabbed the door handle. She rattled it uselessly several times before discovering the Maitress had locked her in after her late night visit. Cursing roundly, Katkin backed away from the door and crossed the room. She examined the attic window and tried to remember what she knew of the roof above her head. The tiny aperture opened inwards. It seemed the Maitress did not consider it a possible escape route and so had not bothered to lock it.

She stuck out her head and looked down. A sheer drop of three stories stretched below her onto the grassy quadrangle. Looking upwards proved more helpful. There was a sturdy looking gutter running along the roof edge. She only had to hang on to that for a few feet until she could kick in the window of the room adjoining hers and escape. Taking a deep breath, she scanned the empty lawn below. By now, Cook would be serving breakfast in the refectory. She should be able to pass across undetected. After making sure she had tied the box securely, she pushed it out the window and watched it fall down to the grass below. It landed with a soft thud and attracted no attention. So far, so good.

Katkin shifted the satchel so that it rested on her back and took a deep breath to steady her nerves. Then she climbed from the window onto the sill and grasped the guttering with both hands. It was slimy with algae, and, on closer examination, looked somewhat rusty. But Katkin had no intention of going back, not now she knew the truth. She lowered herself down, and her feet scrabbled for purchase on the smooth stone wall. Just as she was sure she could hold on no longer, she found a ledge, and rested for a moment, taking deep breaths of the bitter winter air. Already the icy iron of the guttering was numbing her fingers and she knew she did not have much time before her hands would be useless. She began to inch her way along, praying all the while that the room next to hers would be unoccupied. The cold metal painfully stuck to the skin on her hands. The passage felt as though it took forever, but at last she saw the window before her. She pushed at it with her knee, but the previous occupant of the room must have latched it shut.

Katkin said, despairingly, "Come on, let me in, you stupid thing. I can't hold on much longer." She could see the open door of the room lying just on the other side of the glass. Her freedom was so close, yet seemingly impossible to reach. Raising her foot, she brought it forward, intending to kick in the pane. Just then, the guttering shuddered and pulled away from the roof. With a scream of sheer terror, Katkin lost her grip and fell backwards, hurtling down towards the green sward thirty feet below.

Caesura

Though she did not feel the impact with the ground, Katkin was sure she must be dead, for the Infirmarie shimmered and then disappeared from her vision. A rush of dove gray wings surrounded her and then he was there, bearing her up. She forgot her fear in an instant of joyous recognition. Here was the God from her dream, who bore Jacq's face. She stirred in his arms and asked, "Do you carry me to death's kingdom, Jacq? Are you now an angel?"

Through the uniformly gray mist surrounding them, Katkin could see huge trunks faintly on either side, like the columns of some enormous building. In a moment, they reached the ground, carpeted in soft evergreen needles. Though she stretched her head well back, she could not see the tops of the trees encircling them. He put her down before answering her question. "I am not he who is called Jacq. Nor am I an angel."

Katkin said reverently, "I had a dream about you once. You were with Lalluna, and she called you Dai. Is that your name, God?" She studied his face for a moment. He had Jacq's strong features, and high cheekbones, but his eyes were the color of moonlight—if the moon were ever to ride high in a sky of deep lavender.

He replied, "I am not a God, Katkin. Never call me that. I am only Amaranthine."

She stared at him in confusion. "But you must be a God. Look at you. You are immortal. You have wings. You have the power to cross the heavenly plane."

"I know how it must seem to you, in your time, but you must believe me." He turned from her, paced in the mist, and muttered, almost to himself, "Geya and the others, they would keep the truth from you. Sometimes I think they have forgotten that we were once as you are now. They revel in the worship of the people of your age, and ages past. They would have you believe in magic. Here is the truth—in the future we Amaranthine learned ways to change ourselves, and cross between the continua, but it is not magic, only science."

She looked at him wide-eyed. "And my Gift from Lalluna? Is that... science, too?"

He looked at her for a moment without speaking. Then he shrugged his shoulders with a rustle of feathers, and Katkin was struck by the humanness of the gesture. "I do not know. You see—it is as I said, we are not Gods. We do not know everything. In many ways, we are still very much the same as you. We make mistakes. We dream. We feel... love."

Katkin whispered, "Why? Why did you rescue me then, if you are not a God?"

"I had a need to speak with you, so I brought you here. Geya does not know of this place."

Katkin looked around her. The mist lay thick amongst the tree boles, and prevented her from seeing more than a few feet in any direction. But the balminess of the air made her sure—wherever they were—it was no longer winter. "Where did you bring me?" she asked him curiously.

He smiled at her, and for a moment he looked so like Jacq she felt her heart wrench miserably. "So many questions! Would it make a difference if I told you the answer? You would not understand."

She said stubbornly, "I would have you tell me anyway. Did you not say I should stop believing in magic?"

"Very well, then. We are in the third azimuth of the eighteenth pellicle. A place called Rythis."

Katkin looked askance at him. "And what is that, pray tell?"

"Another continuum. I said you wouldn't..."

She continued doggedly, "Are there many of these... continuums?"

"Continua," he corrected gently. "Maybe an infinite number. They are all around you, and you part them like a sea of long grass as you move about in your world. Do you see?"

She nodded. "Yes, I understand. And you... Amaranthine can travel between them, so it looks as though you appear in my world where ever and whenever you want to. Is that right?"

He looked at her with dawning respect. "Truly you are the bearer of many gifts, not just the one of healing."

She sighed and said sadly, "I liked it better when I believed in magic. It makes things much simpler. Are there no Gods at all? The world seems a much duller place."

He smiled. "Only Death might be called a God, in your language, although that is a small word for so great and mysterious a thing. No one among us, Amaranthine or human, understands what Death is. Many have asked, but he does not speak, and the answer will never be known."

Katkin looked very surprised at this. "But you have conquered Death! Are you not immortal, all you Amaranthine?"

He shook his head and said quietly, "No, we can die, believe me."

"Even Lalluna?" Katkin asked forlornly.

He nodded. "Yes, even Lalluna, though she would not want you to know that."

"Is that why she called you a traitor in my dream, because she knew you would tell me the truth about her?"

He shook his head. "No. That tale is much longer and I cannot tell you all of it now. Once, in the future, we fought a battle against a terrible enemy."

"The black creatures from my dream?"

He shook his head. "Nay, the Angellus are not the true enemy, despite what Geya and the others believe now. This enemy was far worse, and the battle raged for many turns of the gyre. They used up countless lives of your people, without remorse, in the conflict. Because I would not help them, they thought I took the enemy's side. That is why they think I am a traitor."

"Why would you not help them?" Katkin wanted to know.

Dai Ben'aryn sighed. "There are many Amaranthine, Katkin. Some want nothing to do with the physical continua, and spend their time in perfect, eternal dreams amongst the outermost pellicula. Others, like Geya and Lalluna have become very intimately involved with the continuum of your home, Yrth. They have gained great power from the worship of your people. Belief gives them strength and the more they have, the more they desire. I do not agree with their subjugation of another race, even in the name of giving aid."

Katkin gave him a look of utter confusion.

He smiled gently. "But perhaps I have said too much already. I am sorry if I have distressed you, but I will do what I can to make it right again."

She said softly, "Thank you for saving my life. I do not understand what you are, but if you are ever in need, you must call on me, and I will help you if I can."

He looked at her with a peculiar intensity. "I will not forget," he said. "Now come, we must return to your world. I will bear you back to the grounds of the Infirmarie." He stepped forward, intending to catch her up in his arms again. She stopped him with a question.

"Why do you look like Jacq?"

"Because he and I are related, in a way," he said.

"Like brothers?"

Dai Ben'aryn sighed and touched her forehead. Katkin immediately fell into a deep sleep and he caught her as she slumped forward. He paused and looked down upon her face for a few moments, and spoke gently, though she could no longer hear him. "I am sorry, my love. I should not have told you all the things I did. My loneliness clouds my good judgment sometimes. But how could I explain about Jacq, anyway?"

He looked up sharply, as though he could hear someone approaching. Working quickly, he removed a curette from a glass phial and gently scraped the flesh on the inside of her cheek. Then he carefully placed the curette back in the phial and sealed it. With a shimmer of dove gray wings, he reappeared in the living world, and hovered just over a sturdy privet bush, a few feet from the place Katkin would have fallen to her death. With careful aim, he dropped the sleeping girl so she landed squarely in the hedge.

9

Happiness

(Estate of Naer, Standing Five)

Did you search her mind, Moonlight? Does she have no memory of her fall?

No, Geya. I can find no trace. But I still believe someone must have helped her.

Who?

I do not know. If Dai were here...

~~~~~~~~~~

Katkin's eyes flew open as the impact with the privet sent her bouncing down to the ground. She crawled into the space behind the hedge, and took a quick survey to see if she had suffered any injury in her terrifying fall from the third floor. Her tongue found a place on her cheek where she must have bitten down when she landed. It was rough and sore. Miraculously, it seemed she had escaped with that minor wound and just a few other scratches, though she could not quite figure out how she had managed to fall in the hedge, which grew a good six feet from where she should have landed. Shaking her head in amazement, she scrambled to her feet and searched the ground to make sure she had not dropped anything. A single dove-gray feather caught her eye, and as she picked it up, she felt a disturbing sensation, as though she had just dreamed something that still resided on the edge of her memory. She studied the feather for a moment, and then brushed it against her cheek. Its softness felt like a caress. Sighing, she tucked it down the front of her shift between her breasts and then surveyed the empty quadrangle. The box containing the dress still lay where it had fallen, close to the wall, and Katkin picked it up.

After crossing the lawn hurriedly, she peered into the

Springhouse through the side entrance. The Juvenet and Daminem must still be busy with the morning meal, for the building was empty. Katkin went to the largest copper bathing pool, and ran her still-frozen fingers through the steaming water. They warmed immediately, and the pain from her broken skin left her. After taking the phial from her pocket, she filled it with the sacred water, stoppered it firmly and added it to the contents of her satchel. Katkin paused for a moment and regarded the verdigrised statue of the winged Lalluna, perched in the middle of the fountains. The Goddess' face looked back at her serenely.

She said softly, "Forgive me, my Lady. Though I do not know why, I believe I may have need of your water someday and I will care for it well. I wish I did not have to leave you, my Lady, but I do. I know you understand my reasons."

The statue's expression did not change, nor did she expect it to. She gave the sign of the Goddess and left quietly, heading towards the stables. The bells chimed again, and Katkin knew she had little time now to make her escape. She followed a brick-lined path that wound through the kitchen garden beds and entered the stable yard through the rear gate. It seemed deserted. She found Brinna inside and rubbed the pony's head briefly before turning for the tack room. Katkin swore softly as she almost ran head first into the stable man, returning with a bale of hay.

He gave her a curious glance as he threw the bale down in the corner for Brinna to breakfast on. "Well, Miss Katkin. Where might you be going so early in the morning?"

She blushed and stammered. "Just for a ride, Pierre. I won't be out long."

He gave her an appraising glance before replying, taking in the box she carried, and the bag slung across her back. "A ride, eh? With all your bits and pieces in tow? I don't think so." Pierre frowned and stepped between Katkin and Brinna, blocking her way. "Don't lie to me. You are running away, aren't you?"

Katkin's eyes filled with tears. "Please don't tell anyone. Please... Just let me take Brinna and go. I will never trouble you again, I swear it." She took a step towards Brinna, but Pierre did not move.

He shook his head. "I need this job, Miss Katkin. The Maitress told me just the other day. 'Pierre,' she says, 'that Juvenie du Chesne—keep an eye out for her. You must not allow her to leave the Infirmarie on her pony. It means your position here if she does.' So you see, Miss, I can't let you go. Unless..." His eyes narrowed.

Katkin swallowed. "Unless what? What do you want from me?"

He shrugged. "A couple of gold pieces would tide me over until I could get another job."

She stared at him, dumbfounded. A couple of gold pieces? He might as well ask her for the moon. "I don't have any money. You know that." A sudden inspiration struck her and she tore open the gold box. "You can have this dress. It is worth much more than two gold pieces. All you have to do is sell it." Katkin held the box out to Pierre, and silently prayed he would take it.

He shook his head, and spit copiously into the hay. "Garn! I don't want no fancy dress. Sell it yourself, and bring me the gold. I won't raise the alarm if you leave now. I warn you though. The Maitress ain't going to be happy. You had better bring me the money by tomorrow. Otherwise, I will sell your pony to the mines, understand me?"

Katkin put a hand over her mouth, horrified at the thought.

"You had better get moving. A work detail will be here in a few minutes to start mucking out the stables. Remember, bring me the gold by tomorrow morning. I will wait for you by the side gate at sunrise."

With a cry of despair, Katkin turned and ran back the way she came in, across the stable yard and away to the high fence that surrounded the Infirmarie grounds. After climbing a tree that grew close by the wall, she shimmied out onto an overhanging branch and dropped down to the other side. She stayed on her hands and knees for a moment, her thoughts a desperate jumble. She needed to find someone to give her money for the dress in time to save poor Brinna. But where? She did not know anyone in town with that kind of wealth, except for Tomas. He would hardly be interested in buying the dress back from her. Then she thought of Simone Beauchamps. She had admired the dress, after all, even though she had been awfully catty about it. Though her heart quailed at the idea of seeing the supercilious girl again, Katkin decided that she must take up Miss Beauchamps' invitation to visit her, right now. After a moment of grim reflection, Katkin decided she did not care what Simone thought of her as a result, as long as she could save Brinna from the pit.

Katkin knew it would take her quite a long while to walk to Melliton Way, but she could not afford to hire transport. As she trudged wearily along the streets of the City, she passed vendors hawking papers to the people hurrying to work in the business district. Carefree children sang and chattered as they made their way to school. Katkin envied them. She could not remember the last time she felt happy enough to whistle a tune as she went about her day. Cutting through the park, she paused for a moment by the duck pond. The ducks crowded hopefully around her feet, but she had nothing to give them. The thought of food made her stomach rumble but there was no money to buy a sweet roll or coffee from the bakery next to the park.

Katkin had to stop and ask directions of several passersby before she found the way to Simone's neighborhood. After a steep climb that took her back up the slopes of Hythea, close to Havenwood, she turned on to Melliton Way. Luxurious town houses lined the street, set well back behind high railings. She found Simone's house, an imposing pillared structure, with a discreet brass placard on the gate announcing it as the residence of the Beauchamps family. Taking a deep breath to calm her unsteady nerves, she walked through the manicured garden to the ornate black lacquered door and knocked firmly. A butler opened it and stared down at her superciliously. His very fine clothes spoke eloquently of the wealth of his employers, the Beauchamps family. After looking disdainfully for a moment at her threadbare Juvenet's uniform, the butler obviously thought she had made some terrible error in judgment by coming to the front door.

"May I help you, Miss? The trade's entrance is around the back, through the kitchen courtyard, if you are looking for work. Although I doubt very seriously you will find a welcome there, either."

Katkin looked up at him in confusion. "I am not looking for work. I have come to see Lady Simone Beauchamps."

This earned her a raised eyebrow. "Indeed, Miss, and why would Lady Simone wish to make the acquaintance of a person such as yourself, if I may be so bold?"

"I have already met her. She invited me to visit her any time I liked. If you would be so good as to fetch her, I am sure she will see me. Tell her Katrione du Chesne is calling."

"This is impossible, for Lady Simone has not yet risen from her bed. Perhaps you could return after luncheon, although I am not sure she will see you even then."

She could not wait until after lunch. Katkin said, rather sharply, "Look, I just need to talk to her for a minute. Please go and get her now."

The butler gave her a withering glance. "I am afraid I cannot do that, Miss du Chesne, if indeed that is your real name. Now please remove yourself from this doorstep or I will be forced to send for the police."

Katkin pleaded with him. "You don't understand. It is very important. I have to see her."

At that moment, a sleepy voice drifted past the butler, and looking past him into the house Katkin could see a woman in a richly embroidered silk robe making her way down the stairs. "Who is it, Gerard?" A second later Lady Simone herself stood at the door, looking surprised and a bit annoyed.

"Well, Katrione, this is a bit of a shock. We civilized people normally don't go calling on one another until a little later in the day. I suppose you wouldn't know that though. You had better come in before the neighbors see you hanging about on the doorstep. Gerard, bring us some coffee in the breakfast room."

Passing the butler, who despite his professionally blank expression managed to convey his utter disdain of her, she followed Simone through the lounge into a sunny glassed-in breakfast room furnished with a small table and some bentwood chairs. Huge, potted palms filled the room. Gerard brought a tray with a silver coffee service and a plate of rolls, bowed, and left them alone.

"So, what brings you here so ridiculously early in the morning? I must say I am disappointed to see you have gone back to your old dressmaker again. I thought you looked rather stunning in that dress of yours the other night. Tomas did too—he never took his eyes off you all night. What a disgusting spectacle he was."

Ignoring the implied insult, Katkin answered her politely. "It is the dress that I have come to see you about. Since you admired it, I thought you might like to buy it from me. I have it in this box."

Simone laughed cruelly. "What on Yrth? Buy some cheap rag that Tomas de Vigny gave you! You must be mad. Is that the only reason you came here this morning?"

Katkin tried hard to answer her with dignity. "I really need some money. You would be doing me a great favor, if you could—"

Simone interrupted her, saying rudely, "Why would I want to do you a favor, you little brat? That you stole Tomas from me is bad enough, and now you come here begging for money? I cannot believe you would be so brazen."

Katkin replied hotly, "I didn't steal the Captain from you! I don't even want him—so why don't you take him back?"

"Don't you think I would if I could, you fool? Now he only has eyes for his pretty little nursemaid Katkin. If you need money so badly, why don't you go and ask him for it? I have no doubt he'll be more than happy to give you some, providing you open your legs wide enough for him, my dear."

Simone's vulgar remark shocked Katkin and she blushed hotly. Gathering up her shredded dignity, she stood without speaking and picked up the unopened box that lay on the table between them. She walked away from Simone, who called after her merrily, "We must get together again some time soon, Katrione. It has been so delightful to see you again. Give my regards to Tomas when you go begging to him." Mocking laughter followed her out the door and down the steps.

Simone, spying from behind a sheer curtain that hung in the front window, saw her walk back down the road, head down, looking miserable. She looked on in surprise as Katkin suddenly tossed the gold box out into the busy street, in front of a delivery cart. The box burst, disgorging its contents out on to the cobblestones. She and Katkin both watched as the gold and green dress entangled itself in the wheel of a passing carriage. Eventually, torn and muddy, it passed from sight. The piece of red silk remained in the road, looking like a puddle of fresh blood. Simone, thoroughly pleased with herself, went back to bed.

Her impulsive destruction of the dress Tomas had given her did not lift Katkin's spirits at all, and she had yet to deliver her unhappy news to him. Once she reached the Citadel Commons, it took all her courage to walk underneath the big iron portcullis and approach the gatehouse, inquiring where she might find Captain de Vigny. The gatekeeper gave her a curious glance, but directed her politely enough. She passed through the tunnel into the interior courtyard and immediately began searching for the Fourth Company barracks.

She found Tomas in his office. He lounged lazily at his desk as a young soldier knelt on the floor shining his boots. An open decanter of brandy stood front of him, next to a half empty glass. He looked up sharply as Katkin knocked, and his annoyed expression quickly turned to one of surprised delight at the sight of her standing in the portal. He barked an order to the Private to leave at once, and immediately crossed the room to meet her.

"My dearest Katrione, I had no idea when the Maitress said you had an important message for me that you meant to come here today. I thought I was to see you at noon in her office. But this is a most welcome surprise. I must warn you, though, I am busy and can spare only a few minutes for you."

Katkin thought to herself that he had not looked busy at all, and the smell on his breath confirmed her fear that he had once again been drinking heavily, though it was still only mid-morning. She sighed and said, "I did not want to meet you in the Maitress's office. What I have to say, I wish to say privately."

His eyes lit at once with prurient interest. "Oh? What have you to say then? No, wait—let me close the door first, so that we may be assured of seclusion." He got up and walked past her unsteadily, then shut the door to his office. She could hear hoots of laughter on the other side, and could well imagine what the men must be thinking. Katkin licked her lips nervously. She had no desire to be shut in a room with Tomas de Vigny, given the news she was about to deliver. Her courage failed her.

"Look, Tomas. You said you were busy. Perhaps we should meet later at the Infirmarie after all. I should be getting back there now." She turned to go, and he took her by the arm, firmly, and dragged her over to the leather sofa that lay against one wall.

"Don't be silly, Katrione. I told you, I am always interested in your thoughts." He slumped down and patted the seat beside him. She sat as far away from him as practical, and he immediately slid over to narrow the distance between them. "Now," he said, eyeing her hungrily. "What is it you wish to tell me, so very privately?"

Katkin took a deep breath. "I came to tell you I do not love you and I cannot marry you. Nor am I going to become the Maitress of the Infirmarie. I left there this morning and I am never going back."

He stared at her, and she could almost see his anger gather and rise until it filled him to the brim. "What!? After everything the Maitress and I have done for you? You ungrateful little bitch." He stood and paced the floor, his fists clenched. But after taking a deep breath, he said, "No, by the Gods. I will stay calm. I forget sometimes how young you are. I understand."

She looked at him uncomprehendingly. "You... You do? You are not angry with me?" Katkin had been so sure the Captain would be unreasonable, her relief brought tears to her eyes.

He shook his head. "Of course not. You are still little more than a child. We should not expect you to make such an important decision. It is too much for you—you are frightened, uncertain of yourself. Why don't you just leave everything to me?" He sat down beside her again, smiling drunkenly, and took her hand. "Now we have that straightened out, I think we could spend the rest of your time before I take you back to the Infirmarie very agreeably, don't you, my dear?"

"Take me back? Were you not listening? I just told you I am not going back." Katkin stared at him, and the comfort she felt a minute ago evaporated abruptly. She hastily snatched her hand away and started to rise.

He made a grab for her, and pinned her down on the couch, then said forcefully, "No, *you* were not listening. I said I would take care of everything and I will. Right now, I am going to prove to you, once and for all, that you will find love with me pleasurable, and then we are going back to the Infirmarie in time for our meeting with the Maitress. She and I have already decided what will happen after that. You have no cause to worry, my dear. Everything is settled."

Katkin tried to scream, and Tomas put his hand securely over her mouth. Though she struggled violently, she could not escape, for even in his drunken state he was far stronger than she. He ripped the fichu away from her shoulders and kissed her throat and neck, all the while begging her to stop fighting him, saying she would enjoy what he had to give her. Katkin, more angry than frightened, bit the hand he held over her mouth and he cuffed her, saying firmly, "If you will act like a child, I must discipline you."

As Tomas' free hand groped downwards, trying to remove her underclothes, someone rapped sharply on his office door. He looked up in alarm, and let her go, immediately. Katkin backed away from him, with her clothes in wild disarray. Tomas seemed to see her for the first time. He cried, "Gods, what have I done? Katrione..." As soon as the door opened, and his aide entered, muttering apologetically about an important message from the Colonel, she darted through and into the corridor.

Tomas ran after her, calling her name. As she fled down the corridor he ordered his men to prevent her from escaping at all costs. One private managed to lay a hand on her, and she felled him with a savage kick to the groin. Then Katkin, with a tomboyish agility that astonished both her and Tomas, made her way down the endless hallways and out the portcullis to freedom.

Once outside, she lost herself amongst the busy market stalls on the Citadel Commons. Many of Tomas' men followed and began to search the crowd. Katkin tried to stay hidden among knots of people as she worked her way towards the edge of the Commons, away from the Citadel. After half an hour of this exhausting cat and mouse pursuit, Katkin had hoped they would give up the hunt. But as she passed between two narrow stalls, a Guardsman caught sight of her and raised the alarm. She looked around wildly, but the open booths offered no concealment. Katkin broke into a run, and dove behind a row of ragged wagons belonging to the market gardeners who had come into St. Valery from the countryside.

"Quickly, Katkin! In here!" The voice came from behind her and Katkin whirled to see an old woman holding open a door cloth. She could hear the shouts of the pursuing Guardsmen and did not stop to question her unlikely savior. A single leap took her up onto the backboard of the wagon and into the safety of the cover. She lay on the wooden-slatted floor, panting wildly. Seconds later, she heard heavy boots pass by on the pavement, but they did not pause.

Slowly, Katkin stood, her legs trembling, and looked about

her. The tiny room was obviously home to the old woman, for it held an improbable collection of objects and furniture, including an oil-burning stove and a rumpled bed. An ornate mirror hung precariously on one wall. The old woman seemed to be untroubled by her unexpected company. After making a pot of tea, the woman patted the bed beside her and Katkin sank down again and accepted a cup with thanks.

"Why did you help me?" Katkin asked her curiously, after she had taken a few sips and found the taste sharp but agreeable. "And how do you know my name?"

"They told me," she answered matter-of-factly, and pointed to a folding table that Katkin had not noticed before in the jumble of bits and pieces. It held a sheaf of luckcast tokens, fanned out, as if she had been in the middle of a telling. She reached over and picked up two of the tokens, which lay face up on the table. "You see, here is Naer Two, Dread. It means there is trouble approaching. I had only to look out my door and see you running to know that was true. And here is Queen Elleranne of the Arkirish Dynasty. She is the healer." The crone's blue eyes were very bright and she stared at Katkin, as if to challenge her to disagree.

Katkin looked back at her, and the wrinkled face seemed somehow familiar. "What is your name? Have we met before?"

The old woman cackled. "Perhaps in a dream, pretty Katkin. Yes, I think that must be it. As for my name? You may call me... Madame Eidolon."

She proffered the tokens to Katkin, who studied them with interest. Such oracular devices were frowned upon at the Infirmarie, of course—the Maitress thought them backward, mere superstition. But this sheaf was unlike any other she had seen before. The tokens were made of some very thin, flexible substance with a burnished, silver sheen. She ran her fingers along the unusually stylized design thoughtfully. "Madame... Eidolon? Could I stay here with you? Just for a few days? I need somewhere to hide until I can leave the City."

The old woman shook her head. "I am leaving here today on a long journey, for I have other tasks to complete." Katkin sighed disappointedly, and Madame Eidolon patted her hand. "Why don't we see what the third token says? Perhaps it will give you some assistance."

She reached across and flipped over the remaining luckcast token. It was Thanis, the wide ocean.* "You see? You must stay. Your love is searching for you."

Katkin grimaced. "Ugh. I don't wish to be found by *him*."

But Madame Eidolon laughed and said there was more than one fish in the sea. Then she reached over to the fruit bowl to offer Katkin an apple. As she did, Katkin saw her reflection in the mirror. The mirror showed a beautiful dark-haired woman, with flawless skin. Katkin blinked in surprise and looked again, but Madame Eidolon had moved away to lift the door curtain and was motioning for her to leave. Tomas' men seemed to have abandoned the chase, so Katkin slipped through unseen and headed for the docks.

She spent the rest of the day a few blocks from the Citadel, staying hidden in the district of wharves and warehouses next to the shore, where the many independent ferries docked. After asking each of the ferrymen in turn, she found none willing to pole her across the Mere on the promise of future payment, no matter what sad tale she concocted. That meant until she could raise the money for the fare, she could not escape Isle St. Valery, for she knew Tomas would have the Yoke watched during the daytime. She had planned to head for Belladore, to her sister Willow's house. Though she knew Willow's circumstances were hardly better than her own, she had hoped she and Yannick might be able to keep her for a few days until she could find Jacq again.

Clutching her leather bag close to her chest, she wandered aimlessly, passing weaving men, laughing and shouting in the moonlit night. Wharf Lane had a sinister reputation—a place where tough sailors and soldiers mixed in the taverns lining the street. Stopping for a moment, she looked out at the Mere, past the forest of masts and riggings belonging to the boats occupying the wharves. Somewhere across the water lay the Acre, and past that, her former home, Tintaren—now just a burned out shell of a building. Jacq's home lay there too, and she hoped against hope he might still be there when she managed to make her way across Mistmere.

She felt bone tired and a little dizzy, and the pain from her empty stomach would not leave her alone. Somehow, she must

---

* The vast ocean. Thanis presages all aspects of romantic love.

find some money for Pierre and a way out of the City. But how? Katkin felt her fingers growing numb in the freezing wind, so that she could hardly hold on to the satchel. After another savage gust of wind mixed with rain whipped at her cloak, she decided she had a more pressing problem—food and shelter for the night.

Looking to a rustic building across the way, she saw a wide door thrown open, spilling light out on to the pavement. Inside, she could see a fireplace and rough wooden tables. Uniformed soldiers passed in and out, singing and talking together. She crossed the street to examine the sign hanging over the door. It said "The Compass Rose" in fancy script. Katkin remembered Jacq telling her about this tavern, as they walked back to the Infirmarie together on the happy night the Captain had left her to return to the Citadel. The men of the Fourth Company often went there, to flirt and talk with the kindhearted female barkeep. The sight of the fire roaring away inside drew her in like a moth. Gathering her courage, she stepped through the door and found a vacant seat on a bench next to the wall, trying to make herself as small as possible in the hopes no one would notice her. She sat in a large and low-ceilinged room, nothing like the refined luxury of the Boar's Head. Here common soldiers and sailors mixed it up with brawls and drinking contests and the battered wooden furniture looked much repaired as a result. A long bar with a polished brass foot rail stretched across the room. Heavily used spittoons were scattered about the floor. Men stood at the bar, their flagons of ale in hand, drinking, smoking, talking and guffawing loudly. No one appeared to take her order for a few minutes and she began to relax into the warmth of the fire.

Katkin sighed, desperately wishing she could buy something to eat. Trenchers containing home cooked food lay on almost every table except her own. The smells tortured her with their promise of a full belly. Suddenly a tough looking youth wearing an apron appeared before her, a pad of paper and the stub of a crayon gripped in his hand.

He spoke brusquely, "What'll it be, Miss, and don't be all night about it. I've other people to serve, you know?"

Katkin tried a smile on him. He pointedly ignored it and remained staring at her with a stony expression, pencil poised over the pad. "Well?"

"I don't want anything. That is, I don't have any money. I would just like to sit here for a few minutes and get warm. Please?" She gave him a look of pure supplication.

The boy scowled at her. "Look, we need this table for paying customers. So clear off."

"Please, I won't take up much room. It is so cold outside..."

His look was hardly sympathetic. "We have a rule here. If you don't pay, you don't stay. So do I need to send for the police or are you leaving quiet like?"

Sighing, Katkin stood up and collected her satchel. She could not imagine how things could possibly get any worse. Putting on her cloak slowly, she delayed her departure into the bitter night as much as she could. The boy stood beside her, telling her to get a move on with loud impatience.

Presently, a rough looking older woman joined him. She wore a faded red dress, the neckline cut low to reveal her ample décolletage. With her frizzy red hair tied back in a kerchief, Katkin thought she looked something like a tough, female pirate. But her strangely accented voice, when she spoke, sounded kind enough. "Now, Jimmy, what's the trouble here?"

"Madame has no money, and thinks she ought to be allowed to stay anyway. I told her to get out, that's all." He stared at her defiantly. "We're running a business here, ain't we? Not a charity hall."

The barkeep stared at Katkin, taking in her threadbare appearance and pinched look of hunger. "You're from the Infirmarie, aren't you? I saw you there, when I visited my ill mum a couple of years back. A Juvenie, are you?"

Katkin decided not to put too fine a point on her status at the Infirmarie at the moment. She made up a story quickly, one she thought would generate the maximum amount of sympathy for her plight. "Yes, ma'am. I am a Juvenie there. I sneaked out tonight to be with my young man, you know how it is..." She paused and the barkeep nodded understandingly. "He left me here on the docks, just like that, with no money and no way to get home. I cannot walk back all the way alone in the dark and even if I did, they lock the gate at midnight and there is no one to let me in. I just need somewhere to stay tonight, and tomorrow I will be on my way." Here Katkin burst easily into very real tears, hoping against hope the woman would not question her story too closely. She might not know the Infirmarie gates were open all night...

The woman clucked sympathetically, "You poor dear. Of course, I would love to help you, but as Jimmy said, we are very busy in here. I do have a spare room upstairs, nothing fancy mind you, and I let it out now and again for the soldiers and their ladies who want some privacy of a night." Katkin could well imagine the sort of privacy she meant. She continued, "As much as I would like to, I can't just give it to you for nothing. I am running a tight ship here and everyone has to pay their way." Seeing Katkin's disappointed look, she said, "Now I know you don't have any money. But is there something else you could do in exchange for the room? Can you sing, girl? Or dance, perhaps? A new face to entertain the patrons is always a welcome sight around here and the men toss coins up onto the stage after a good show. You give me some money for the room and if there is any left over, it is yours to keep."

Katkin's face brightened at this. She might be able to leave St. Valery tomorrow after all, with Brinna! She smiled at the barkeep and nodded. "I can sing a little and I know how to play the vielle I have with me."

The barkeep patted her maternally. "That's the spirit, dearie. Now you just follow me and I will show you the room." Katkin stood once more and swayed alarmingly, her face pale.

"Goodness, you look famished. Jimmy, bring up a bowl of soup and some bread for the poor girl." Turning to Katkin, she said, "Don't worry, dearie, dinner will be on the house, but I will need a good performance from you to cover the room for the night. The soldiers usually only rent by the hour."

Katkin, bemused by the woman's shrewd but generous nature, followed her up the narrow wooden staircase to the top floor of the building.

The room contained a deep armchair and table, as well as a double bed in the corner. The barkeep, who had finally introduced herself as Maggie Fenty, chatted amiably about her business as she lighted the sticks piled high in the little fireplace. Presently Jimmy arrived with the loaf and a bowl of stew, thick with chunks of gristly meat and turnip. Sullenly, he dropped the tray on the table and stalked out again. After a day without food, the meal looked heavenly to Katkin. Maggie looked on at her, obviously pleased by her appetite.

"You just sit right there and eat every bite of that soup and I will pop downstairs to my wardrobe and dig out something else for you to wear."

The spoon paused on its hurried way to Katkin's mouth as she asked, "Something else to wear? Why can I not just wear this dress?"

Maggie laughed heartily. "No offense, dearie, but the men we get in here, they expect something a bit more... well, entertaining than that little frock, nice as it is, I am sure. Don't you worry, pet. I have loads of stuff, and some of it is too small for me. I am sure I can find something that will fit you a treat."

Katkin had just mopped up the last of the stew with the remaining bread crust when Maggie returned, a dress folded over one ample arm. Holding it up she said, "Try this one on, dearie. I am sure it is going to be just right."

Katkin eyed the dress distastefully. It featured a garish combination of pink and blue satin fabric, with a tightly fitted bodice and obviously plunging neckline. The skirt, slashed at intervals, revealed a black lace slip underneath. A feathered headdress completed the outfit. Katkin's heart sank to her toes at the thought of making such a spectacle of herself, though she realized she had little choice. If it meant a bed for the night and money for Brinna and the ferryman, she had to wear the horrible thing and entertain the men downstairs as best she could.

Undressing self-consciously, she took the gown from Maggie, slipped it over her head, and fastened up the hooks in the front. Maggie smiled encouragingly. "That is more like it! You look fine. Now just a little powder and paint and you will be ready to go..." She led Katkin over to the chair and proceeded to make up her face with rouge, eye shadow, lipstick and a generous dusting of white powder. She produced a hand mirror so the girl could see the finished product. Katkin's dismay was complete when she saw the Jezebel's face staring back at her.

"Now are you ready to start? The boys will be getting restless. I have promised them a new treat and they do hate for anyone to keep them waiting. Makes them start breaking heads and we don't want that, now do we?" Katkin agreed they did not, but said she must tune the vielle before she came down. "I'll leave you to it then. Just come downstairs when you are ready and go straight up onto the stage. Don't be too long about it."

With trembling hands, Katkin removed the vielle from her leather bag and tried to tune it up as best she could. The strings needed cottoning, but she did not have time for that delicate job at the moment. Turning the crank, the wheel spun underneath the strings and she played a quick scale, pressing the keys firmly to get her fingers warmed up. She tried to think of songs she could play to entertain the unruly crowd below well enough to earn her the use of the room for the night, and some extra coins for Pierre. The children's folk tunes she knew, taught to her by Jacq or her father, might not be terribly appropriate, but they would just have to do. Taking her courage in both hands, she went out the door and down the stairs. The soldiers and sailors in the audience greeted her with howls and catcalls as she nervously took the stage.

Jacq, sitting close to the back of the Compass Rose, did not even bother to look up as the cheers filled the tavern. He rested his head in his hands, behind a veritable forest of ale bottles. Judging by the noises coming from the area around the stage, some tart had just come on to entertain the crowd. Wearily, he stood, preparing to leave, in no mood to listen to music this night. He had a long ride ahead of him, back to LeClaire, in the cold and dark. Then abruptly his head snapped up and he listened intently to the song the girl had just started singing.

"My love has gone for a soldier,
My soldier has gone for a love,
She is a beauty in satin..."

Though it seemed unbelievable Katkin should be in the Compass Rose, he recognized her voice right away. He remembered teaching that song to her and he wondered angrily why she sang it now in front of a bunch of drunken men.

The music stopped abruptly as a soldier lurched drunkenly on to the stage. He shouted, "That's her... That's the whore who pegged me! You're coming with me, girlie, the Captain wants you back."

Katkin backed away as the man who had tried to prevent her

flight from Tomas' office appeared and began to threaten her, his fists raised menacingly. Suddenly a tall figure strode between her and the Private and landed a blow that sent him crashing back off the stage and into a table, which broke under his weight. The fallen man scrambled to his feet, and his friends wisely restrained him from going after Jacq, who stood above him, breathing hard, his fists clenched in a murderous rage. Maggie Fenty shouted over the din for calm.

Turning away, Jacq grabbed Katkin by the arm and furiously dragged her off stage and back towards the stairs. "What in the god's names are you doing here dressed like that? You look like a harlot," he hissed at her.

He made to push her up the stairs but stopped as Maggie's strident voice rang out across the bar. "Young man, the room upstairs is not yet paid for. If you want the use of it, the girl will have to sing some more or I will need to see some money up front." Giving Katkin a very black look, he stalked back across the room and threw some coins down on the bar. Maggie counted them and asked sweetly, "Will that be for the night or just an hour?"

"All night," he snarled at her.

She nodded her head, smiling and saying, "Enjoy yourselves, you two."

Katkin watched him walk back across the room, the other men giving him a wide berth, given his size and thunderous expression. Grabbing her elbow again, he steered her up the stairs and into the room without uttering a word. Jacq pushed her roughly away from him, and she careened down onto the bed and sat there, her breasts heaving in the low cut dress.

Immediately, he turned his back to her and said harshly, "Take off that whore's costume and put on something decent. And wash that muck off you face!" Katkin did as he ordered, too afraid to argue or utter a word in her own defense. Not until she wore her own Juvenet's vesture once more and had scrubbed her face raw in the cold water of the basin did he speak to her again. His voice was icy.

"What in the hell are you doing here, Katrione? You are supposed to be at the Infirmarie."

She found her voice at last. "I ran away this morning."

Jacq still would not look at her. "Get your things together. I am taking you back. The Maitress was worried sick, wondering where you are."

Katkin shook her head violently. "I am not going back there. Ever."

He grabbed her arm roughly and shook her. "Yes you are! That is where you belong. With your fiancé, Captain de Vigny."

She looked at him in shock. "Jacq! What are you saying? I thought... after the night you walked me home, that you truly cared for me." Her eyes filled with tears.

He stared back at her and shook his head. "I do care for you, more than anything. That is why I am making you do what is best for you. When I saw you in the stable at Havenwood..." He paused and clenched his fists in frustration. "Gods, Kat. You looked so beautiful in that gown. I can never buy you anything like that." He faced her and said despondently, "I am an illiterate blacksmith. You deserve a far better life than the one I can give you. Now get your things."

Katkin drew herself up as tall as she could and shouted at him. "You listen to me, Jacq Benet. Everyone in the whole world seems to think I ought to marry Tomas de Vigny. Becka, the Maitress, even you! No one has bothered to ask me what I want to do. Well, I do not want to marry him. Why won't anyone listen to what I have to say?" She slowed and said each of her next words with emphasis. "He is a drunkard and he tried to ravish me. I think he is detestable. And I hated that dress!"

She paused to catch her breath and Jacq's expression changed quite suddenly. He repeated angrily, "He tried to ravish you? By the gods, he won't get away with that."

"It doesn't matter anymore. I am never going to see him again, anyway," she said, wearily, and walked to stand by the fireplace, watching as the logs collapsed in a shower of red sparks.

He came to stand beside her, and after a moment, gently took her hand in his.

She looked up at him and asked softly, "Why did you leave the Citadel without saying goodbye?"

He sighed. "I guess I let my pride get the better of me. When you didn't answer my letter, I thought maybe you had decided you preferred de Vigny after all. How could I blame you? Then when he offered me that job..."

133

Katkin looked baffled. "What job?"

Jacq scratched his head. "The day after the ball, he came to me in the smithy. He told me he was going to build a house at the Infirmarie, for the two of you to live after the wedding. It was to have a big stable with a lot of horses, and he wanted me to take care of them. I turned him down flat, and left that day. I thought it would be better for both of us if you and I never saw each other again. I am sorry, Kat."

She moved sideways so that she stood closer to him, and rested her head on his shoulder. "Then why did you come back? How did you find me?"

"I ran into Trudeau four days ago, in LeClaire. He told me you had not seen the letter I gave to Becka. So I came back to St. Valery, as soon as I could. I wanted to make sure... that you really were happy with de Vigny. I went to the Infirmarie first thing this morning and they said you had gone. Since then I have been all over the City looking for you." He grinned sheepishly. "I only stopped at the Compass for a bite to eat and some ale before I rode back to the country. Too much ale." He shook his head, ruefully. "I certainly didn't expect to find you here. When I saw you up on the stage, in that costume, I just lost my temper completely. Anyway, I should never have pushed you like that. By now you have probably decided I am no better a man than the Captain." He sighed deeply and stepped away from her again, then thrust his hands into his pockets.

Katkin shook her head. "I don't think that, Jacq." She turned to face him, wondering why he seemed so unsure of himself. "Did Jamie not give you the rest of my message?"

Jacq stared over her head at the fire for a few seconds before answering her. "No. I guess not. Only the part about the letter. He was... in a hurry."

"I told him to tell you that I cared for you very much. My feelings have not changed."

Though he put his arms around her and drew her into an embrace, still he asked, "Are you sure about this? We have not seen each other for a very long time. You hardly know me anymore. I won't hold you to the promise you made as a little girl."

She laughed softly. "I know everything I need to know. When *are* you going to kiss me, Jacq Benet?"

* * * *

"Kat, I have to leave now." He had been kissing her, for the better part of an hour, in the armchair they pulled up next to the fire.

She looked at him in surprise. "You don't have to go. We have the room all night, do we not?"

He shook his head regretfully. "If I stayed I would make love to you. I wouldn't be able to stop myself."

Her gaze was unwavering. "I am not afraid. Stay with me. Share my bed."

"It wouldn't be right. Not until I make you my wife. That, I hope I can do very soon, but there are some things I must take care of first." He stroked her cheek softly. "Do you understand why I have to go?"

She nodded, but not without a disappointed sigh.

He continued, "I hate to leave you in this place alone, but I think you will be safe enough as long as you lock the door behind me when I leave and do not open it until I return for you in the morning. I dare not stay with you, Kat, even to sleep in the chair. For all my fine words, I would not be able to keep my hands away if I stay in your company a moment longer." Jacq smiled gently. "I fear there will be no sleep tonight for me anyway. Yet tomorrow will come, and we will be together, and I will never leave you again, until death comes for me on his black horse."

Suddenly Katkin's eyes went wide. "Horse?! Oh no, poor Brinna! I was so happy about finding you again, I completely forgot about her. Pierre is going to sell her to the mines. I have to go back to the Infirmarie right now and get her." Katkin struggled to rise from the chair, and Jacq spoke quickly to reassure her.

"Don't worry about Brinna. I will take care of everything. Gently, he brushed a tear from her cheek and she smiled up at him.

"Promise?"

He nodded gravely. "Yes, I promise. Now try to get some sleep."

With a final kiss, he left her and she dutifully locked the door. Leaning back against it, she said, "Good bye, my love, until tomorrow."

Though she, too, thought she might not sleep a wink, the events of the day had left her bone weary and she slept peacefully and dreamlessly.

135

10

The Hero, Aages

(Arkirish Dynasty, Standing Five)

I wish...
What?
I wish we could stop now.
Will they stop?
No, I suppose not.
Then neither may we. The hands of Moera are busy at the loom, Raven.

~~~~~~~~~~~~~~~~~

The banging on the door woke Katkin, and she sat up blearily in the double bed. She could hear cockerels crowing outside in the yard of the Compass Rose and knew by the low light it must be just after dawn. Remembering she had begged Jacq to come as early as he could in the morning, she threw on her robe and rushed over to the door. She turned the heavy brass key in the lock, smiling expectantly at the thought of seeing him again. But her joyous greeting died on her lips when she saw the identity of her early morning visitor.

Tomas de Vigny stood before her in the open doorway, unshaven, unwashed, and looking very, very angry. He carried his pistol in his right hand and a mostly empty bottle of whiskey under his arm. She stared at him, in a paralysis of fear, clutching her thin, flannel nightdress protectively. Overcoming her shock at last, she grabbed the door and made to slam it in his face. He stepped forward smartly, easily stopping the door with his fore-arm, and then roughly shoved her across the room. She fell to the floor by the fireplace. He closed the door himself with a decisive click, locked it and pocketed the key.

Katkin had never been more afraid in her life. Tomas stood

above her, and snarled menacingly, "Where is he, you bitch? Where's Benet?"

"He is... He is gone, Captain. He left last night." She saw the hand holding the pistol relax, and he put the weapon back in its holster on his belt. Suddenly the meaning of his question hit home. He had arrived with pistol in hand to kill Jacq, should he have found them together. Katkin sent a prayer of thanks to the Goddess that Jacq would not stay with her last night, even though she had asked him to. But she knew it might be hours before he returned for her again. How long would Tomas de Vigny keep her trapped in this locked room before he would decide to kill her and then lie in wait for Jacq?

She tried to distract him with conversation, hoping somehow to defuse his rage. "How did you find me? I told no one where I was going, because when I ran away from you yesterday at the Citadel, I did not know myself."

His lip curled in disgust. "Did you think you could arrange a meeting with your lover, Benet, and I would not know of it? My aide came to me early this morning to tell me of your behavior here last night. He told me Benet paid to take you upstairs to this room. My Gods, Katrione, have you no decency? Are you such a whore that you would lie with a common blacksmith on that filthy bed?"

He aimed a savage kick in her direction and she scuttled away on the floor until she backed up against the chair. She raised herself up slowly into a sitting position, hoping he wouldn't go after her again. Katkin swiftly decided this was not the time to argue with Captain de Vigny. His insane possessiveness could be the death of her and Jacq as well. Calculatingly, she assumed a contrite expression, and held out her hand in supplication.

"Don't be angry with me. I made a mistake, I know, and I am very sorry. If you will just leave for a moment and let me get dressed, I will go with you right now, wherever you wish."

He laughed mockingly at this suggestion. "What makes you think I would want to go anywhere with you, now you are damaged goods? Do you know how many people saw you leave last night with Benet? My men would never respect me if I married such a whore. I am sorry, Katrione, but now you are only good for one thing, and I intend to have my fill of it before I leave this room."

After putting the whiskey bottle down on the table, he advanced towards her, his hands already drunkenly fumbling for his belt buckle. Katkin sprang up and sprinted past him, trying to get the table between them. He caught the top of her nightdress as she went past, and ripped it violently. The thin material came away in his hands.

Smiling at her crudely, as she gathered up the torn garment, he said, "Well, that is a good start, anyway. Why fight me? I will have you now, just as Benet did last night. You shouldn't be so fastidious, my dear. One man is much like any other, I am told."

Standing on the other side of the table, she stared across at him with loathing, her earlier resolve to placate him forgotten. She screamed, "I will fight you as long as I have to, you bastard. I hate you, and your conniving father. I will die before I let you take me!"

He recoiled at this and repeated, uncomprehendingly, "Conniving? What in the devil are you talking about?"

Katkin kept talking, aware that the longer she could distract him, the closer Jacq might be. "I overheard the old man's treacherous plan the night of the ball. You did not see me but I was hiding behind the curtains when the two of you walked past the gallery. Your father said you should marry me so you could take over my lands when the Guard defeated Reynard. He said he would see you crowned King! It is obvious you don't care about me, Tomas. Why don't you just admit it?"

He seemed genuinely perplexed at this. "Of course I loved you, Katrione. I told him so that night. I said I did not care about the land at all. Did you not hear me say so?"

"You are lying."

"I am not, I swear it. Is that what this is all about? Did you think to revenge yourself on me, for some fool plot my father imagined? He is power hungry, and has always been so. Ever since I was a child, he has had grandiose dreams for my success. I could never please him enough. That is why I wanted to build us a house at the Infirmarie, so that you and I could be happy somewhere away from him."

Katkin, though still horribly afraid, began to think he might be telling the truth. Perhaps now he would be more reasonable. She willed her voice to calmness, and clutched her torn nightdress tightly around her breasts. "I am not here just because of that. I have tried to tell you on several occasions I do not love you. You wouldn't listen to me because you always wanted to believe I returned your feelings. I am sorry, but it is Jacq Benet I love and he loves me. He is the one I want to be with. Do you understand?"

Tomas, who had been lost in thought during her speech, sprang to life again. "Yes, Benet," he growled, "I shall be calling him out, as soon as I have finished with you. He will be dead before the morrow, do not doubt it. And who knows? Perhaps... yes, when things have quietened down a little, and I make a few judicious transfers, I shall marry you anyway. Why not? You will have no one to save you once Benet is gone, my dear, and I can get the old woman at the Infirmarie to lock you up until all the talk has died down."

On hearing this new plan on the part of the Captain, Katkin decided she could reason with him no longer. Snatching the heavy glass whiskey bottle off the table, she smashed it over Tomas' head before he could fumble for his pistol. The chair broke under him as he slumped to the floor. He did not struggle when she reached into his pocket and pulled out the key, but the blow did not incapacitate him for long. He lunged at her as she tried to reach the door, key in hand. Katkin screamed and threw a vase of flowers at him. It missed his head by inches. He punched her hard, in the face, and she crashed painfully to the floor, her head spinning.

Suddenly, the door handle rattled violently as Jacq tried to force it open. He called her name, pounding on the door, frightened by the noises he could hear coming from inside the room. Tomas reached for his pistol, a knowing smile on his face.

"Jacq, don't come in, he has a gun," she screamed, praying he could hear her through the heavy panels. But outside in the hall, Jacq had already begun his charge towards the locked door.

He smashed into it with his shoulder down, running flat out. Pieces of wood showered the room as the panels gave way. Jacq let out a furious roar as his momentum carried him straight towards Tomas, who quickly raised his pistol. He never managed to fire a shot. Katkin rolled out of the way as Jacq sent the Captain to the floor with a ferocious blow to the head, then picked him up bodily and threw him against the wall. He landed with a sickening thud and his pistol fell from his limp fingers. Jacq kicked it under the bed and then hurried back over to Katkin. He gathered her up gently and held her as she apologized again and again for opening the door to the wrong person.

"None of this is your fault. It is all de Vigny's, and now he must answer for it."

Turning from her, he walked slowly and deliberately to where Tomas lay against the wall, still only semiconscious. Seizing him by the throat, Jacq lifted him up with one powerful hand, and held him against the wall, with his feet dangling six inches off the floor. The Captain's face quickly turned red and then an alarming shade of blue as he struggled weakly to free himself.

Katkin, very much afraid that Jacq, in his rage, would do something he later regretted, said quietly, "You must stop... Please, Jacq. You are going to kill him. He hasn't hurt me. Let him go."

He relaxed his grip a fraction and Tomas took a gasping breath. His eyes bulged with fear, but he could not speak. Jacq, his voice an angry whisper, said, "Nay, do not worry, I will not kill this... worm, even though he deserves it. For it used to be a man I admired." Addressing the Captain, whose terrified face was only inches from his own, he continued, "Do you remember the day you rode out alone against the Rising when the soldiers of the Fourth Company lay trapped below in the gully? Because of that deed, I once thought you the bravest man I had ever met. You saved the lives of many of your men that day." Lowering his arm slowly, he allowed Tomas' feet to touch the ground, though he did not release his grasp on the Captain's throat. He said, "Now I let you walk away, in payment for that debt." His voice grew lower, an intense menacing growl Katkin found truly frightening. "But if you ever touch her again, I will hunt you down and tear you to pieces with my bare hands. Nothing is more certain. Do we understand each other?"

Tomas nodded painfully and Jacq released him, saying finally, "Now get out, before I change my mind." Jacq turned away, and walked back over to Katkin.

The Captain stood still, blinking hard, and looked as though he might fall. Then, with slow, precise movements, he began to smooth down his disheveled uniform. After a moment he spoke, and his voice was loaded with menace. "You won't get away with this, you know. Attempted murder of an officer of the Guard is punishable by hanging. You are the one who will be hunted down, you whoring son of a mongrel bitch." Jacq whirled and raised his fists, then took a step back towards de Vigny. The Captain threw off his jacket unsteadily, and growled, "Come on, do your worst. I am not afraid of you, scumbag."

Katkin hurriedly stepped between them. "So is treason," she said quietly.

Captain de Vigny dropped his hands and stared at her. "What did you say?"

She cleared her throat and spoke a little louder. "I said, so is treason, punishable by hanging, I mean." Katkin drew a shaky breath and continued. "I am sure King Benedict would be very interested to hear of your father's plans for your succession to the throne, Tomas."

He laughed nervously. "You little bitch! You couldn't... Anyway, the King would sneer at the suggestion."

"Are you so sure? I seem to remember only last year two officers in the King's Guard were executed for plotting against the king." She stared into his eyes and she could see the doubt there, so she pressed on, trying to give her voice a surety she did not feel. "Give me your word you will not file charges against Jacq, and I will keep his filthy plot to myself."

He said nothing for a moment, and his eyes darted back and forth between Katkin and Jacq, who still stood by with his fists clenched, obviously ready to continue their fight. Katkin urged him, "Do it, Tomas, or I will tell the King everything. I mean it."

Finally, he gave her a curt nod. "As you wish, my dear. But don't think for a moment you have won, Katrione. That drooling behemoth you claim to love is a poor prize. And don't come running back to me when you find out your error, you lying little trull." As he flung this final insult at Katkin he marched across the room with his head held high, stepped over the fragments of the door, and was gone.

Jacq would have followed, but Katkin caught his arm. "Let him go, Jacq. He *has* lost, and he knows it."

Jacq took several deep breaths, trying to conquer his anger. After a moment he produced a handkerchief from his pocket, and dabbed at the dried blood on Katkin's nose.

141

A smothered cough interrupted him. Looking up, they saw Maggie Fenty standing in the doorway, scratching her head. "Who's going to pay for all this, I'd like to know? And what have you been doing to my good door, Mr. Benet?"

"My apologies, Ma'am. Unfortunately, I needed to enter quickly and it was locked. I will pay for the damage."

She smiled at him and shrugged. "It is always the same around here, I can't keep the place from going to rack and ruin. Now, how about some breakfast for you and the lady?"

Jacq shook his head. "We can't stop, Maggie. I don't trust de Vigny's word any more than I would a cracked anvil. I need to get away from the City now, before he sends the Guard after me."

Maggie laughed uproariously. "Don't you fret, Mr. Benet. I saw the young Captain leaving not long ago, with a face that would have spoiled fresh eggs. It just so happens he was met at the door by a deputation from the Citadel, with Colonel Deschamps in the lead. The Colonel was none too pleased with him, I can tell you, since de Vigny was supposed to be away early this morning on a campaign to the West. They had the Captain's horse with them, and he had to ride out without so much as a good-bye to your Auntie May. I think you have plenty of time to leave town. The Fourth Company boys were drinking heavy at the bar last night, and talking about how they might be gone for a month or more."

This unexpected news cheered both Jacq and Katkin. Jacq went down with Maggie to the main floor of the tavern, telling Katkin to join them after she finished dressing. Her heart still hammered painfully as she threw on her frock and packed her things in the leather satchel. She tidied up the room as best she could and stacked the broken bits of door by the fireplace. Looking at the pieces, she marveled at Jacq's tremendous strength, which had reduced the paneled oak door to nothing more than a heap of kindling.

Coming downstairs, she saw his tall figure leaning at the bar, deep in conversation with Maggie. Bread rolls and a mug of coffee were set out for each of them. Katkin ate heartily, still feeling the effects of yesterday's hunger. She laughed as she talked with Maggie about her interrupted performance of the night before.

After he finished his breakfast, Jacq stood apart, silently watching Katkin. Her appetite and cheerful countenance amazed him, given everything that had happened to her over the last few days. He reflected to himself that whether the Captain kept his word or not wouldn't matter, for he would never find them. Once he made her his wife, he planned to take Katkin as far away from St. Valery as possible. With this thought, Jacq clapped a hand to his face and groaned, "Gods, I completely forgot. I have done everything wrong."

Katkin laughed at his consternation. "What are you talking about? You saved my life this morning!"

"I meant to ask... that is, in the heat of the moment, something very important slipped my mind." He said nothing more, just crossed quickly to where she stood. Then he knelt down on one knee and took her hand in his own. Maggie looked on from behind the bar, beaming at them both. He said softly, "Katrione, will you marry me? Say yes, and I will be the happiest man in the world."

Looking down on him, her voice fled and she could not answer right away.

"Go on, girl," said Maggie, encouragingly. "Don't keep the man waiting."

"Yes," said Katkin simply, and burst into tears.

Jacq stood and swept her into an embrace, ending in a long kiss that almost took her breath away. Maggie turned around and wiped her eyes on her apron. She said, "Don't worry about the door, loves. Consider it a wedding present from old Maggie."

After saying goodbye to the barkeep, they went outside into the clear winter sunshine. Nestor stood on the street, yoked to a high-sided wooden cart. The back of the cart held a heavy wooden chest, with the words "Jacques Benet, Blacksmith" burned on it in black letters. Far more importantly, and to Katkin's immense happiness, Brinna stood nearby, munching from a feedbag. She hugged Jacq ecstatically, saying, "You got Brinna! But what about Pierre? You didn't give him any gold, did you?"

Jacq scratched his head. "No, he didn't say anything about gold. I just walked in and said I was taking Brinna. He didn't argue." Jacq flexed one huge fist and quietly said, "People hardly ever argue with me, and I always keep my promises."

Katkin stared at him for a moment, thoughtfully, and then asked, "But where did you get the cart? Did you hire it?"

"Nay, it belongs to my brother Barlow. He has loaned it to me for a time."

"Barlow? Doesn't he live in Belladore? How did you manage to get it from him?"

"Did I not tell you I would get no sleep last night?" he replied laughingly, and would say no more.

Climbing up on the cart, Katkin sat close to Jacq's side as he clicked his tongue and shook Nestor's long reins. Though she worried about the weight, the big horse handled the load easily.

Jacq smiled at her. "Don't worry, Nestor does not have to pull us for long."

"Jacq, I don't even know where we are going! Why won't you tell me?"

"What? And have all my hard work to keep it a surprise be for naught?"

They wanted to avoid the Citadel and the Yoke so Jacq found a ferryman willing to take them across the Mere and deposit them near the King's Road. From there they drove to Belladore, taking their time, laughing and talking in the weak winter sunshine. After passing through the village, Jacq drove the cart to Willow's little cottage that stood next to the mill on the far side of town. Willow and Yannick stood outside with baby Roseberry, and it seemed they were expected.

"At last! You are late, Jacq Benet," her sister chided playfully.

"We were unavoidably detained," he answered her, smiling.

As Katkin stepped down from the cart, Willow, plump and motherly despite her name, rushed forward to hug her. Immediately, with a look of concern, she asked, "Katkin, what in the world has happened to your nose?" There was a fresh cut and a bruise on the bridge from her fight with Tomas. Katkin had almost forgotten about it.

"Don't worry, Willow. It wasn't Jacq, if that is what you are thinking."

Willow shook her head firmly. "I know Jacq better than that, Katkin. That he might be responsible never entered my mind. He is the gentlest man I know and the kindest, besides Yannick of course." With this, she looked fondly over at her husband, who held Roseberry carefully in his arms. "Well, I can see there are some tales to tell and no mistake. You had better come inside so I can get you ready."

"Ready for what? Will someone please tell me what is going

on?" Katkin looked back and forth from Willow to Jacq to Yannick, waiting for an explanation.

Jacq laughed at her confusion. "Our wedding, of course. The Abbé expects us at the church at 12 o'clock, so you must be ready." He looked at her for a moment, his expression unsure. "Please say you are not angry at me. I know it is a bit sudden, but I have waited such a long time already." Then he asked her shyly, "You still want to marry me, don't you?"

She smiled in return and embraced him, touched by his nervousness. "Of course I am not angry, how could I be? I cannot think of anything I would rather do than marry you this day."

"I am very pleased to hear that, my love. Now I must go. Yannick and I have some important tasks to take care of before noon. Willow will help you in the meantime. When I see you again it will be in the church. I will be waiting for you there." Still he lingered, with his arms around Katkin, reluctant to leave her even for a little while.

"Come on, Jacq. Let her go for now. There will be plenty of time for such things later on. Your bride and I have much to do." Pulling Katkin away from Jacq, Willow gave Yannick a knowing smile and took her sister inside the house. Jacq untied Brinna from the back of the cart and turned her out to graze in the lush winter rye grass, and then he and Yannick rode away together.

They sat at the scrubbed pine kitchen table, and Willow said, "Now Katkin, I haven't had time to make you a dress, of course. We only found out about the wedding very late last night. You will have to wear mine, and I will need to take it in a little to fit you, I think."

Katkin looked confused. "Last night? How did you find out about it? Jacq didn't even ask me to marry him until this morning!"

Willow laughed. "Isn't that just like a man? Putting the cart before the horse, as usual. We thought he must have asked you already. Jacq came tearing up on Nestor last night. I heard the noise outside and woke Yannick. Honestly, it sounded like another invasion of the Mardonne or something. I grabbed Roseberry and Yannick stood by the door with the scythe in his hand. We felt a right bunch of fools when Jacq burst through the door, all out of breath. He said, 'I have to get married today. I need your help.' Of course we said we would."

Katkin seemed perplexed. "I didn't know Jacq had been here before. He never told me that."

"Jacq and Yannick have been best friends for a long time, though I only met him for the first time when Yannick and I married at the church. He has come here often in the last few weeks. I thought he seemed troubled and he confided much to Yannick, though not to me. They talked about you mostly, I guess. Finding you again brought him nothing but unhappiness for a long while."

Katkin nodded humbly. "Yes, I know. Last night much was said and much forgiven. Now everything is all right between us."

"Yes, it must be. I never saw anyone look as happy as Jacq did this morning when he came in. He and Yannick went off to wake the old Abbé and goodness knows what they told him, since it must have been five o'clock in the morning before they arrived there! They were gone for about an hour, and Yannick came back alone. Jacq had taken Nestor and gone back to his mother's house on the old Tintaren land."

Thoughtfully, Katkin asked her, "Are you happy, Willow? I mean, since we lost the land and all?"

Her sister paused before answering, looking slowly around her little one-roomed cottage, and at Roseberry lying quietly in her basket on the table. Willow kept the cottage spotlessly clean, and a pretty quilt she had made herself covered the double bed in the corner. Finally, she said, "Yes, I am, Kat. Yannick is so kind and he loves me very much. And I love him and we both adore Roseberry. We don't have very much, it is true, yet I wouldn't trade this house for a mansion somewhere else without Yannick. Of course, I miss mother and father, and I wish they were still alive, but do you honestly think they would have allowed me to marry a miller's son? Do you think you would be marrying Jacq Benet, today?" Katkin sat back in her chair abruptly, remembering Jacq's warning to her the day of the picnic.

Willow went to a wooden chest by the bed and pulled out a bundle carefully wrapped in linen. "I made it myself. I hope you like it."

Willow's wedding dress was lovingly hand made of white cotton fabric with tiny flowers embroidered all over it. It cinched at the waist with a woven belt of many-colored ribbons that crossed and tied at the back. Katkin thought it very beautiful and told her sister so.

"Now you must try it on," said Willow proudly. After Katkin had tried on the dress and found it to be a bit too big, Willow busied herself with taking it in. Katkin played happily with baby Roseberry. Willow spoke, her mouth full of pins. "This is your wedding day and mother should be here to talk to you. Since she is not, I will have to do. Katkin, do you know what will happen this afternoon, when you and Jacq are alone together? Do you fear it?"

Katkin shook her head firmly, saying confidently, "I am not afraid. Not with Jacq."

Willow smiled at her tenderly. "That is good. Sometimes it hurts a little the first time, even though he would never mean it to. You must be prepared for that. Soon though, my sister, what joy you will find with one another, as Yannick and I have. And then, in a little while, perhaps you will have a baby. A wonderful baby, like Roseberry. How happy that would make me, Katkin. I have missed you since you have been in the City. I am so glad you are coming back here to live."

"Am I? That is another thing Jacq never got round to telling me. I just ran off with him this morning without even finding out what we were going to do." She laughed at herself, "What was I thinking, doing that?"

Willow had finished the dress and arranged Katkin's hair. She said regretfully, "It is winter and we have no flowers, so I asked Yannick to pick some holly sprigs in the Acre and I made them into a bouquet with some mistletoe. Will it do, do you think?" She produced the bouquet, with red and white berries peeking out from the dark green foliage. Willow had carefully snipped every thorn off the holly.

Katkin hugged her sister gratefully and said, "Thank you for everything, Willow. This is the most wonderful day of my whole life."

"It does my heart good to hear you say that. I shall pray that all your days with Jacq are filled with such joy as the Gods see fit to provide."

Just before noon, Katkin and Willow, leading Brinna, walked

down the dusty main street of Belladore, towards the tiny church with its square stone tower. Children followed them, laughing and running about. It looked as though everyone in the tiny village had come out to see Jacq Benet's bride make her way to the church. "Good fortune, my dear!" the people called as she passed, and she smiled and waved shyly to them in return.

The arched wooden door of the church stood wide open but the interior was dark compared to the bright sunshine outside. She paused on the threshold, waiting for her eyes to adjust. Katkin could see Jacq, standing by the altar, looking back at her, his expression grave and just a little nervous. Next to him stood another young man with brown curly hair, not as tall, but strongly built.

"That is Jacq's brother Thaddeus standing up for him, and the gray-haired lady over there is his mother. You remember her, do you not? Jacq and Yannick fetched her this morning," Willow whispered to her.

Greenery filled the church, pine boughs and holly decorating every pew. Jacq and Yannick had obviously been very busy once they had left her at the mill cottage with Willow. Jacq's other brothers—Barlow, Nathan and Arkady stood next to their mother on the front row.

Yannick walked back to the doorway and offered her his arm. He spoke in his quiet, measured way, saying, "I am sorry your father is not here to give you in marriage and I would be honored if you would allow me to take his place." She smiled and thanked him, immensely grateful her sister's family could be with her, even if her parents could not. Placing her arm though his, she walked down the aisle of the church to join Jacq, his eyes shining, bright with unshed tears.

The old Abbé, smiling benevolently, took one hand of each in his own gnarled grip and spoke to them both. "Children, you have come here today to be joined together as man and wife." He led them through the vows, and each promised to love and honor the other for life. The simple ceremony lasted only a few moments. Jacq placed his mother's own gold wedding band on Katkin's finger. Afterwards they walked down the aisle together, holding hands happily as the bells pealed out a joyful song.

Jacq laughed when he saw Brinna's head poking through the

church door and asked his wife, "What is she doing here? Did she follow you?"

Katkin answered with dignity. "That pony is one of my best friends in the whole world. She deserved to be a guest so I invited her to our wedding. You don't mind, do you, my husband?"

"Nay, my wife, I am glad she is here with us. I would have you do anything that makes you happy on this day. And every day after this."

Jacq's mother waited on the steps for her eldest son and his new bride. She smiled when she saw Katkin, looking so radiantly pretty in Willow's wedding dress. Elisabeth said, "Well my children, it has been a long, difficult road for both of you. I still recall the first day Jacq brought you to me, my daughter. I gave you some seed cake, do you remember?" Katkin nodded happily. "When Jacq woke me early this morning to tell me you and he were to be married, I rejoiced in my heart, for my boy has loved you from the first day you met and has suffered much for it. Now there is happiness, for you are together at last. Welcome to our family, my daughter. Anything that is ours shall also be yours."

They walked back through the town together, to cheers and congratulations. At the hall, everyone in the village brought hastily made dishes to share for lunch, and the generosity of the people of Belladore, many of whom she hardly knew, made Katkin feel very welcome. She sat next to Jacq at a trestle table, talking and laughing with villagers she had not seen since she was twelve years old, and who remembered her still.

Finally, the new couple passed the loving cup and the impromptu wedding reception came to an end. Katkin had been wondering for some time what they would do next, for she had no idea where Jacq planned for them to stay. He surprised her by taking her hand and leading her back to the mill. Catching her up in his arms, he carried her across the threshold and up the three flights of stairs to the top floor as though she weighed nothing at all. Against one wall, he had created a pallet of straw covered in bearskins and another of Willow's hand made quilts.

Jacq put Katkin down and regarded her silently for a long moment, his gray eyes filled with longing. Speaking in a bashful whisper, he said, "I could not stay last night and share your bed, even though I wanted to, very much. Now this day I offer my bed to you, though it is a much poorer one than you deserve, my beloved. Will you share it with me?"

Katkin nodded slowly, not trusting her voice. As his fingers fumbled clumsily with the ribbons on her dress, she asked, "Shall I help you, my love?"

He replied softly, "Oh yes, my beautiful girl." So she guided his trembling hands around her waist, so he could undo all the bows in the ribbon belt, and found his mouth at the same time. Willow's wedding dress fell to the floor at her feet as she kissed him, until she could tell she had quieted his fears. Only then did she let him carry her to the bed and make love to her.

The heat inside Katkin's body swept over Jacq, and set his blood on fire—a feeling beyond anything he had ever imagined. Jacq thought he knew all about fire. Each day at his forge he used it, made it work for him. He was its master. But he could not tame the fire she brought to him, not like that. He lost himself completely in her, and wanted to stay lost forever, as she sighed his name and dug her nails deeply into his back. Her ecstasy broke over him like a wave and Jacq found he could hold himself back no longer. The moments that followed—in their sweet and powerful stillness—were so very much like flying, he wondered briefly if he had somehow grown his wings back.

Later as they rested together, under the quilt, she asked him, "That was your first time too, was it not, my husband?"

He blushed and nodded his head wryly. "How did you know? Was I that nervous?"

She laughed and said, "I could just tell, I don't know how. Why did you wait all that time? There must have been other girls..."

"I promised I would wait for you, that day by the lakeshore, remember? Anyway, I didn't want other girls. I have never wanted anyone but you, Kat. Do you remember the first day we met, out in the fields behind your house?"

"Of course I do," she said.

"After I walked you home, I told my mother then I had just met the girl I wanted to marry someday. My mother is kind, so she did not say I was a fool for choosing a thing so completely out of reach. Instead, she told me that such a dream might take a very long time to come true and I must be patient to the end. So I waited, though for a long time after Tintaren burned down, I didn't even know where you were." Just then, he tried to smother a yawn and Katkin smiled gently.

"Rest awhile now, my love. I know you must be tired." Jacq nodded sleepily and turned towards her, putting his arms around her waist. He buried his head under the quilt, on her belly, and soon was snoring softly.

Katkin lay awake in the darkened mill and stroked his hair, wondering, a little fearfully, about the devotion Jacq felt for her.

11

Thariens, the mountain tarn

(The Tollyn, Eleven)

Geya calls to Moonlight. Where is your vessel? We will have need of her very soon.

Raven answers for her. It is her wedding day, Geya. Can we not allow the girl and her husband even a little happiness? There is enough time for that, surely?

Geya snaps angrily. I can see only as far as the next twist in the Gyre, Raven. The Angellus may already be on their way. How do *you* know how much time we have left?

~~~~~~~~~~

Katkin woke from her nap and stretched. For a few seconds, she did not remember where she was, and then she heard Jacq by her side, still snoring gently. Rolling over, she watched her husband's massive chest rise and fall, the hair veiling it almost as thick and dark as the bearskins beneath them. She smiled, recalling his frantic travels of the night before and thinking how tired he must be after everything he had done. His face looked so young in the repose of sleep, almost as if he was fourteen again, as he had been the last time she saw him at Tintaren. She experienced a little shiver of sensual pleasure as she saw him stir, sighing, and roll over onto his stomach, pillowing his head on his arms.

Still he slept on, and Katkin would not have disturbed him for the world. The top floor of the mill was very dark inside because they had closed the windows to ward off the cold December winds, yet a narrow finger of late afternoon light penetrated through an ill-fitting pair of shutters and fell across Jacq's broad, muscular back, not quite covered by the quilt, and illuminated it. Katkin sat up carefully, so as not to wake him, intending to pull the cover up over his shoulders. Instead, she saw something that made her catch her breath sharply. Ever so slowly, she lowered the quilt so she could see all of his back, and softly began to trace her fingers down the many long scars she saw there. Her fingers touched almost every square inch of his back in their travels along those angry red roads of wounded flesh. She could not even begin to imagine what sort of torment might cause such scarring.

Jacq woke suddenly, his skin feeling chilled where she had pulled away the covers. He felt her hand on his back, felt her tense breathing as she sat by his side, and knew what she saw as her fingers traced the patterns there. Silently, he begged her not to ask him, but of course, she did—she had to.

"Jacq, my love, do you sleep?"

"No, I am awake," he said and rolled on to his side with his head propped on his hand. He looked at her worriedly. Even though he had known this hour would come, from the moment he took her upstairs to the mill, that knowledge did not make it any easier for him to answer the question he knew she would ask of him.

"Your back... I saw the scars, as you slept. I never knew they were there until just now. What happened to you? It must have been horrible." Her eyes, so full of concern, met his.

He said softly, "You know I would have no secrets from you, my love, unless it was something that would hurt you or endanger you if you knew it. So I don't want to tell you about my back. Do you understand?"

"No," she said stubbornly. "I want to know everything about you, Jacq, even the things that might cause me pain. You are a part of me now, and all you have experienced. So you must tell me. Please?"

He sighed and sat up, then crossed his arms over his drawn up knees, rocking back and forth slightly. "You remember the day I brought you home, the day you fell off Brinna and hit your head?" Katkin nodded, and a sick feeling began to grow in the pit of her stomach.

"Your mother took you into the house at once and left me outside with your father. He cursed at me furiously and would not let me explain what happened. Two of his hired men dragged me inside the barn and he punched me in the face and broke my nose, while the others held me. I fell down, so he kicked my stomach until I vomited all over the hay. I thought he might leave me alone after that, but the three of them dragged me upright, ripped my shirt off and tied my hands then hung me from one of the crossbeams overhead. I felt such fear then that I wet my breeches. He laughed at me, and called me a baby who couldn't take his medicine."

He paused, taking a deep, shaky breath. At his side, Katkin had begun to cry and he looked at her with concern. "Shall I stop now?" he asked quietly.

"No! No, Jacq, I must know the truth. Whatever you lived through must have been far worse than anything I feel now."

"Very well, my wife, you shall know. Your father took the horse-whip from the tack room and gave me three hard strokes with it. It hurt more than anything I have ever felt or thought I could feel."

Katkin felt bile rising up the back of her throat. She thought she might be sick, and she swallowed it down, saying thickly, "Go on. Don't stop."

"Then he said, 'Listen to me, young cur. If you don't wish to feel another lash, you will beg for my mercy and swear on your honor as a man that you will never speak to my daughter again.'"

She begged him, "Did you swear it? Please say you did... I don't care if you broke your oath."

He was looking at her, yet his eyes were far away, remembering. "I did not."

She choked back a sob, her horror almost overwhelming, and asked him in a hoarse whisper, "How long? How much longer did it go on for?"

"I don't know. After a long while I passed out from the pain. Your father and his men left me hanging there in the barn. I did not regain consciousness until my mother and brother came and cut me down. Afterwards, I could not move for many weeks, and by the time I recovered you had already been sent away to school in St. Valery."

She sobbed openly at his side. "I never knew. Goddess, if only I had. I could have..."

He sighed. "Could have what, Katkin? You were only a little girl."

She shook her head violently. "And you were only fourteen!

What kind of a monster would do that to a fourteen-year-old boy?" She answered her own question silently. *My father. My own father did this to him.* The revelation shattered her. "Jacq, I loved my father very much. I always thought of him as a kind man. Of course, he spent a lot of time in the fields, but in the evening he would come home and be very jolly and teach me to play his vielle. Yet all the time, inside he was this horrible animal, who could torture you, and I never knew it. I didn't know him at all."

"You and I grew up in very different worlds, my love. To you he was 'Father', and in your world he might have been kind and lovable. In my world, he was 'Lord and Master', and that is a very different thing. He needed us—me and my family and the other cottars—to work barefoot in the fields for no return other than a hovel and a little piece of land, so he could make a profit on the wine he sold. The old order ruled in his mind, and he thought it to be the only one that worked. I think he realized that you and I had become something more than friends and he feared that the old order was crumbling. So he tried to stop it, but in the end he failed anyway."

"Yet you worked to preserve the old order at the Citadel. I still don't understand why."

He sighed patiently. "I told you already. My family was desperately poor. At first, I just did it because I needed money for them. Later... well, in the end, though I cannot tell you why, I came to believe in what I worked for, very much."

She turned to him, her face still wet with tears, and he brushed them away gently. "It is long past, my love. Can you not let it go? Your father has gone to his grave, and I do not hate him for what he did."

Katkin could not forget so easily. She asked him sadly, "How can... How can you love me? After my own father did this to you?"

He smiled softly and laid back on the bear skins, then pulled her to him so her body rested on top of his. "How can I love you, my wife? Like this..." He put his mouth on hers and kissed her, until her tears finally stopped and she grew warm and moved restlessly in his arms. Afterwards, when Jacq made love to her again, Katkin felt her heartache about the past slipping away, leaving only the infinite promise of the present moment and the love they shared together.

When Katkin woke again she lay alone on the pallet. Her eyes strained in the darkness to catch sight of Jacq. Presently the door opened and he appeared, carrying a lantern in one hand and a large basket in the other. Squatting down beside her, he kissed her and asked, "Have you slept enough for now, my love? Willow has very thoughtfully provided us with this basket full of dinner, as she did not think we would like company just yet." He smiled sheepishly. "It is a good thing she did. My mind has been far from thoughts of food this afternoon, yet now I am hungry as a bear and you must be too."

Katkin sat up and pulled her shift on over her head. Her long chestnut hair, a mass of untidy curls, trailed messily down over her shoulders and she tried to comb it as best she could with her fingers. "Ugh. I must look a sight!" she said.

"You look more beautiful than ever, my wife," he said to her in return as he opened the basket and passed her a piece of chicken, roasted on a spit in Willow's hearth.

After eating a good deal of the chicken, some stewed vegetables and lots of freshly baked brown bread, Katkin wiped her mouth on a napkin and gave a contented sigh. Then she looked over at Jacq in concern, saying, "Willow and Yannick are too poor to keep on feeding us like this for long. What are we going to do now?"

He laughed fondly. "What an appetite you have, for food and for questions! Now you have eaten, perhaps I can answer the questions for you, too. As for what we are going to do, I haven't yet decided, but I do have an idea. I would like to go west, out past LeClaire, and find some land there. I will build us a house and send for you when it is finished. You can stay here with my mother or Willow in the meantime." He looked at her, silently hoping she would agree.

Katkin frowned slightly. "The land to the west is controlled by Reynard, is it not?" He nodded unhappily, realizing he should have known all along what her reaction to this proposal would be. "Why would we want to go there? I don't want anything to do with that man. I will not have him rule over me. Anyway, how long would it take you to build a house? Months, probably. I don't want us to be apart for so long."

"What would you have us do instead, my love? The most

important thing to me is that you be happy." He waited patiently, while she carefully thought out her response to his question.

"Could we just stay here? Close to Belladore, I mean. Everyone in the village is so kind and our families are both nearby. Willow told me today how happy she would be if I came to live close to her. She also told me a secret—she is going to have another baby next autumn! I would like to be here to help her when it comes." Here she paused and blushed slightly. "And when I am having your baby, which I hope will be soon, my husband, she will be able to help me, as well."

Jacq smiled broadly, charmed by her desire to be a mother so soon. "Very well, it is settled. We will stay here in Belladore. Yannick and I will clear some land so I can build a house for us. We can both live here at the mill until it is ready, and I will go hunting and kill some game for our kind hosts so that we may contribute to their larder. Does that please you?"

"Yes!" Wanting to give him a hug, Katkin launched herself towards him so hard he over balanced and fell back laughing on the pallet, taking her with him. She rested her head on his chest, listening to his heartbeat, slow and strong. "You don't mind? Not going west, I mean?"

Jacq looked up towards the dusty beams on the ceiling so she could not see his troubled expression. He said, "No, I want to stay here if that is what you want. Tomorrow, if you like, we will take Nestor and Brinna and go for a ride across the old Tintaren lands and visit my mother, as we used to when we were children. Perhaps she will even have a piece of seed cake for you."

She sighed blissfully. "That would be perfect! We can bring a picnic. Oh, Jacq, I am so happy. Everything I ever wished for has come true on this day. Except for one thing."

"What is that, my wife?"

She laughed and kissed him lovingly on the mouth.

12

Doubt

(Estate of Naer, Reversed Twelve)

Who is this Prime God? How dare he steal my believers? Already I feel weakened.

Geya smiles. Do not worry, Moonlight. I have a scheme to win them back and test the Innocent as well.

~~~~~~~~~~

A week after their wedding, Jacq took Katkin on a journey into the country outside Belladore. She rode before him on Nestor. As they reached some open, hilly ground, he covered her eyes with his hands.

"What are you doing, Jacq?" she said, laughing.

"I have a surprise for you," he said.

Nestor continued up the hill until they reached the top, with Katkin still unable to see. On the far side of the hill, sheltered by several mature oak trees, stood the crumbling stone foundations and chimney of an abandoned homestead. Jacq uncovered her eyes and said, "What do you think, Katkin? I know it doesn't look like much right now, but I can rebuild it." He peered at her anxiously, hoping she would be pleased.

She turned back to smile at him. "I think it is going to be perfect. But who does this land belong to, that they do not want it any more?"

Jacq did not say anything right away so Katkin knew the answer to her question. "It is du Chesne land, is it not?"

He answered her gravely. "It used to be, yes, but now it has grown wild and belongs to no one. This ruin used to be one of the cottar houses. I did not know the family who stayed here when your parents were alive, but it seems obvious they no longer need it. I can make it our home, if it will make you happy."

She said thoughtfully. "I will be happy no matter where we live, as long as we are together, but this place is especially beautiful. I don't care if it used to belong to Tintaren. That is all in the past now. Come and show me how you plan to rebuild the house."

They spent a few contented hours wandering around the ruined cottage and the surrounding lands. Katkin found the remnants of a kitchen garden, much overgrown, and an orchard of ancient, twisted apple trees. Jacq began to sort through the stones lying in great heaps on the ground, explaining to Katkin how he would lay them in courses with lime mortar to rebuild the walls. Then he would thatch the roof with bundles of river rushes, laid close and neat to keep out the rain and snow.

The view from the hill looked down into the lush valley of the Ariane River, carpeted with well-ordered fields and shelterbelts of tall poplars.

"Will you make a porch, so we can sit outside on fine days and see the valley? Please?"

Jacq smiled at her and said, "Of course I will." Pointing towards a huge, downed tree, he said, "I can use that fallen oak for the porch and the floor boards. It blew over two winters ago and will be sound and dry by now."

The next day and for many days after, he worked on the house, laying stone after stone in straight courses, making sure they fit together snugly to increase the strength of the walls. Each day Katkin and Willow put baby Roseberry into her basket and rode over carrying a hamper of food and drink for lunch. Katkin felt humbled by her husband's strength and skill as he manhandled each of the quoins into place, and the walls rose higher and higher.

Now he no longer worked at the Citadel, Jacq decided to let his hair and beard grow out, and soon he looked as wild and shaggy as a mountain pony. As Katkin passed him his lunch, she brushed his hair away from his eyes, which sparkled with joy.

"What shall we call our new house, my wife?" he asked her.

She bent down and retrieved a small nut from the ground close to the foot of the oak tree that sheltered their picnic spot.

"I think we should call it... Acorn," she replied and kissed him as he swung her up into his arms.

* * * *

Soon Jacq and Katkin traveled to the valley to collect rushes, which grew in profusion along the banks of the Ariane. Back at the building site, Katkin tied them into sturdy bundles and passed them up to Jacq as he perched precariously on top of the stone wall and laced them to a frame of round saplings.

After Jacq finished the roof, he and his younger brother Barlow cut the fallen oak into slabs with a pit saw. Twenty-one-year-old Barlow had his father's blue eyes and sandy colored hair. Jacq towered over his younger brother, so a lot of good-natured teasing and rough housing took place between the two of them about the difference in height. Barlow complained constantly about having to be down in the pit on one end of the saw while Jacq stood on top of the big trunk with the other end. Jacq, laughing at this, said, "It would take a month to dig a pit deep enough for me, my brother." Barlow had wiry strength and great endurance and he and Jacq made short work of the task. Jacq smoothed the thick planks with an adz and a plane on one side to create the floorboards for the cottage and the porch. Real glass for the windows would have been far too expensive, but the house had sturdy shutters to keep out the wind, as well as a heavy oak door with a bar across the inside.

"Looks almost like a fortress," Katkin joked to him as he fitted the door into place.

"Someday we may need it," he replied and did not smile in return.

One sunny day, as they sat together under the oaks near their almost-completed house, Jacq told Katkin that he and Yannick planned to go away for a few days. "I don't think I will be gone for very long, but we need to do some hunting."

After they left the next morning, Katkin sat at Willow's table and said, "Why do Jacq and Yannick have to go so far away to hunt, Willow? There is plenty of game around here."

Willow looked troubled. "I don't know, Sister. My husband and Jacq have been making these trips for as long as I have known him, and probably before as well. Jacq would show up from the City and Yannick would say they had to go hunting—although half the time they never even bring back any game. But they are very close, like two brothers, and share things between the two of them I am supposed to know nothing about."

"What sort of things? Secrets?" Katkin asked her sister.

Shaking her head, Willow said, "Maybe you will think this strange, but Yannick uses a different name for Jacq when he thinks I am not listening, and never in front of me. He calls him Dinrhydan. What do you think it means?"

Katkin stared at her, mystified, and said, "Well, as for what it means, that is easy enough. *Din* is the old tongue word for true and *rhy-dan* translates as of the heart. So together, the name would mean "true heart." But I have never heard anyone else, even in his own family, call Jacq such a strange nickname. I will have to ask him about it when he returns."

Willow regarded her seriously. "I wouldn't do that if I were you. Yannick doesn't like to talk about his relationship with Jacq at all. I gave up questioning him long ago, when he simply refused to answer me. I expect Jacq feels the same way."

Katkin felt a little shiver in her heart, as the first crack appeared in her relationship with her normally forthcoming husband. *I would keep no secrets from you, my wife, except things that would hurt you or endanger you if you knew them.* She wondered what kind of secret this mysterious name could be—the hurtful or the dangerous kind?

"Why do you think Yannick and Jacq make these trips, if not to hunt?"

Willow looked up at Katkin and said softly, "Yannick occasionally fights for the Rising. Sometimes I wonder if Jacq does, too."

Katkin said flatly, "Jacq would never do such a thing, Willow. He knows how I feel about Nicholas Reynard. Anyway, he is a blacksmith, not a soldier, and the gentlest man I have ever known."

Willow just shook her head and changed the subject. "How do you know so much old tongue, anyway? You didn't learn it at the St. Valery School for Girls, that is certain!"

Katkin laughed at the thought she might have learned such an archaic, guttural language at the exclusive girl's academy that she and Willow had both attended. "No, of course I didn't. Nurse taught it to me. She told me it was very important to keep the old ways alive."

"Really? I am surprised Mother let her. She used to be

quite against anything to do with the common folk, I seem to remember."

Katkin nodded. "She was, but I got the impression that Nurse intimidated her. But Mother and I did not get along very well, so we never discussed it."

"Yes, Nurse was a bit peculiar. The way she just showed up at the door one day, and said she would be taking care of us, remember? Then Mother just sent the old nurse away without a word." Willow looked at Katkin and smiled. "You are very like her, you know."

"Who? Mother?"

Willow nodded. "The same slim figure," and she sighed ruefully, looking down at her own ample hips, "And the same almond-shaped eyes. You have her coloring as well. Did you ever notice how Mother was always as brown as a field hand, even though she never went out in the sun without a parasol?"

Katkin was about to reply when suddenly little Roseberry cried out in fear and pain, and Willow whirled around to see what troubled her. While they had been talking, the child had toddled over to the fireplace and tried to pick up one of the pretty red glowing coals. She screamed and screamed and her frantic mother cried, "Katkin, what should I do? Look, her hand is so red and the skin is peeling away already. It hurts her so much, I cannot bear it." Willow started to cry along with her daughter.

Katkin wondered what she could do to help her niece, and then she remembered the phial of Lalluna's water she had taken from the Infirmarie all those weeks ago. An insistent voice in her head seemed to be telling her to fetch it at once. She told Willow to hold Roseberry's burned hand under some cold water, and then Katkin ran to the mill, where she still kept her things in the leather satchel against the day the house would be finished and they could be unpacked. Grabbing the glass phial, she hurried back, still unsure what she would do when she arrived. But still the voice continued to instruct her. Katkin put a little of the precious water in the palm of her hand and said to Willow, "Let me hold Roseberry."

The little girl, denied the comfort of her mother, cried all the harder and Willow frowned in concern, asking, "What are you going to do to her, Kat?" Katkin did not answer. She had already closed her eyes and withdrawn into herself as she held the little girl's injured hand loosely in her own.

The shock of the burning pain made her wince. Feeling something brush against the hand that held Roseberry's, she opened her eyes and beheld the ethereal form of the Goddess Lalluna, who had placed her delicate alabaster hand on top of Katkin's own sturdy brown one. Katkin's eyes widened and Lalluna gave her a serene smile. She said, "*Do not fear me, my vessel. You have been given eyes to see my true form, as none has before you.*" It was the voice she had heard in her dream in the Chapel. Slowly, Katkin felt the little hand cool in her own until Roseberry stopped crying and began to coo happily. The Goddess Lalluna withdrew her hand and slowly faded into a spark of nothingness. Katkin turned to Willow and saw her staring in bewilderment and not a little fear.

"Katkin, what have you done?" She took the girl back and looked at the palm of her hand. It was pink, and undamaged. "How on Yrth did you do that? Did they teach you such miracles at the Infirmarie? It is the most amazing thing I have ever seen."

Katkin shook her head, almost as surprised as her sister. "I did not learn anything like that as a Juvenie. I don't know how I knew what to do. It just came to me suddenly and I did it." Of her vision of the Goddess she said nothing, merely asked, "Did you see anything strange just now? As I held Roseberry, I mean?"

Willow looked perplexed. "No, I don't think so. I looked at you, and you sort of flinched and the tears in my eyes must have made my vision go blurry and white. When I rubbed my eyes I could see you again and Roseberry had stopped crying." Willow stood and hugged Katkin gratefully. "I don't know how to thank you."

She replied, "Don't give it another thought. I was happy to help."

When Jacq and Yannick returned home from their hunting trip three days later, Willow, full of pride and excitement, related the story of Roseberry's miraculous cure. Jacq stared at Katkin, his expression unreadable, as the normally soft-spoken Yannick said, "What is this blasphemous talk, my wife?"

Willow looked uncomfortable and said in return, "What do

you mean, Yannick? Katkin just wanted to help and she did heal Roseberry's hand."

"She practiced filthy witchcraft! I will not have such activities in my house."

Jacq spoke up, "Take care, Yannick, what you say of my wife." He moved to stand by Katkin, who was looking unhappily at Yannick, and put his arm protectively around her waist.

Yannick did not back down. "I am sorry to have to say this, Jacq, but what your wife has done to my daughter is absolutely inexcusable."

Willow defended her sister loyally. "Would you rather Roseberry's hand be blistered and scarred, my husband?"

Yannick, giving her an angry glance, answered inflexibly. "Yes, if Prime God willed she should suffer it in payment for some transgression. To go against that is to do the Devil's bidding. I will hear no more of this, wife, I have spoken."

Willow opened her mouth to say something more, and then retired into a hurt silence.

Jacq, shaking his head sadly, said to Yannick, "We have relied on your kind hospitality for too long, my friend. We will leave. Now. Katkin, go fetch your things and I will saddle Nestor."

"But Jacq, Acorn is not even finished yet," Katkin protested.

"I said *now*, Kat." He spoke more forcefully than perhaps he intended, for she gave him a little hurt look and left quickly, running back to the mill for her bag. Yannick stalked angrily out the back door and stood in the yard, his hands in his pockets.

Willow murmured, "I don't know what to say, Jacq. It is so sad the two of you have to go like this. Yannick has never acted this way before. He loves you both, and I don't think he meant what he said. Will you forgive him?"

Jacq ran his hands through his shaggy hair distractedly. "I know Yannick did not mean to hurt us, Willow. His rigid beliefs make him speak so. Anyway, we cannot stay here any longer. But you, my sister, are welcome to visit our house whenever you wish."

"And Yannick?" she questioned him.

"Yannick and I will always be brothers, Willow, even if we fight now and again about something. We have been through too much together to let something like this drive us apart. I am not angry with him. He would be welcome too, though I don't think he will be willing to come, at least for a while." Jacq looked at Willow gravely, his gray eyes full of concern. "My sister, please promise me you will not tell anyone in the village what Katkin did for Roseberry. You and I know she has a powerful gift for good, yet others may not see it so."

Willow colored slightly and said, "I wish I could. But I already told the Postmistress the story, yesterday. I didn't think it would do any harm. I am sorry."

Jacq sighed, saying, "Well, what is done is done and cannot be taken back. Now I must speak to Yannick before we go." Willow watched as Jacq went out the back door and stood by Yannick, holding a low but intense conversation.

Katkin finished packing her things and went to look for her husband. Passing around the corner of the house, she saw him talking to Yannick and stopped before they could see her. Feeling slightly iniquitous, she nevertheless tried hard to eavesdrop on their conversation, remembering what Willow had said about the secrets they sometimes shared.

Yannick spoke resolutely. "I know she means no harm, Dinrhydan, but she cannot come here again. I am a man obedient to the Prime God, not the old faiths. Such beliefs are pagan and wrong. You would do well to keep a close eye on your wife, because if word gets out into the village that she follows the old ways, there may be trouble for you. You know how important it is for you to stay hidden. They are looking for you, my brother, and they must not find you."

Jacq softly replied, "I take no unnecessary risks, Yannick, you know that. Yet I love my wife and her happiness is all I care about. I would have gone west before now, but for her wish to stay in Belladore."

Yannick said firmly, "You should have made her go. A wife must be obedient to her husband, as a slave is to a master, so it is written in the Book of Prime. But you must prevent her from practicing her witchcraft, if nothing else."

Jacq's voice was quietly commanding. "Do not make me choose between the two of you! You and I still have our work to do, and I would not have this disagreement get in the way. So we will not speak of it again, my brother. Do you understand?"

Yannick nodded his head. "Of course, Dinrhydan. Go with Prime God's blessing."

Katkin felt bewildered and a little frightened by this exchange. Yannick had used the mysterious name, Dinrhydan, and seemed to be saying Jacq faced some kind of danger here in Belladore. She stood quietly for a few moments, wondering who could be looking for him and why he must not be found.

She heard Jacq calling for her and she walked back around the house again. He had already saddled Nestor and Brinna, and packed their things on the sledge. Willow came to the door to bid them a sad good-bye. Yannick did not appear at all. Katkin could not help thinking as she rode away that the happy relationship with her sister had been damaged beyond repair.

For a long time, she and Jacq rode in silence, until they crested the hill and looked down on the oak grove. The empty cottage stood below them, its porch still only half-finished. Katkin, grateful for all Jacq's hard work, said, "Acorn is a beautiful house. I am very glad to be living here," but all the while she was remembering his words—*I would have gone west before now, but for her wish to stay in Belladore.*

He smiled gently and said, "I am pleased it meets with your approval, my wife. But it would be a better house if we had something to sit on."

She laughed and pointed to the sledge Nestor hauled. "We have the bed, and it is all we need, is it not, my husband?"

In the end, Jacq took some sawn rings of the felled oak and rolled them to the unfinished porch, placing them side by side. They sat together silently and looked down over the valley below, and Katkin wondered if she should ask any of the many questions that lay heavy on her heart. She decided to start with a simple one.

"Where is your kill from the hunting trip, Jacq?"

He looked up sharply, a bit startled by her question. "We shot no animals," he said in reply, but he did not look at her as he spoke.

She pressed him further. "You hunted for four days and you found no game in all that time?"

He growled back at her, "That is right, my wife. Now leave me in peace. I have much to think about."

166

I gave up questioning him long ago, when he simply refused to answer me...

Katkin shifted uncomfortably, sighing. Jacq was keeping things from her, and she could do nothing about it. Perhaps he felt angry about her healing of Roseberry—she could at least try to make that right. "I am so sorry about what happened with Yannick. I had no idea he would react that way. Why is Lalluna such a threat to him?"

He turned to regard her steadily, and his gray eyes were troubled. "It would be better if you did not mention her name again, Katkin."

Katkin stared back at him in surprise. Jacq had never shown any concern about her devotion to the Goddess before. What had happened to make him change so? She asked him in confusion, "Why do you say such a thing? Just because I have left the Unity does not mean she has stopped being important to me, and my Gift continues. I would use it for good, my husband."

He reacted angrily. "You heard what Yannick said, Kat. He thinks it is witchcraft. Others in the village may feel the same. People will start talking about us and word may spread. We have to be careful."

"Why? Captain de Vigny gave his word he would not press charges, and you are not wanted for anything else, are you?"

He stood and faced her and his agitation was plain. "I cannot tell you, my wife! You must just trust me. There are men in the Guard who would very much like to find me, and if they do I will be taken back to the Citadel and executed. Do you want that to happen?"

Her eyes filled with tears. "Of course not, Jacq! I just thought..."

"You thought what? That we could come here and settle down and live happily ever after without any more problems? Grow up, Katkin. There is a war going on and danger is all around us. So I say again, my wife, we have to be careful. Must I explain further or do you now begin to understand what your little adventure with Roseberry may cost us?" His angry words cut her to the quick. She said nothing in reply—just walked away from him to unload the sledge, not bothering to hide her tears.

Katkin heard his heavy step behind her as he left the porch

and ran to join her side. Putting his arms around her, he said, "Forgive me, my love. I should not have spoken to you like that. I know you meant no harm with Roseberry. I wish I could explain things more clearly, and someday when this war is at an end, I will, I swear it. To do so now would only endanger you, and that I could never do. Do you understand?"

She nodded her head tentatively, her heart still troubled. "No more answers now? There is much I would ask you."

He sighed unhappily. "No, my love, please ask me no more questions."

She looked at him with disappointment. "Very well, my husband."

As the weather grew steadily warmer, the oaks began to lose their winter bareness, and put on a lovely veil of green. Jacq worked hard, finishing the house, while Katkin cleared and replanted the kitchen garden. Life at Acorn was very quiet and somewhat lonely for her, after her years in the crowded Infirmarie. They had few visitors other than Jacq's family. His brother Nathan, who was a carpenter by trade, came to help with the furniture. After Jacq helped him set up his lathe in the dusty yard, they worked together for days—turning stools and table legs, and a sturdy four-poster bed to replace the pallet. Nestor, blinkered on one side, spent many patient hours walking in a circle to power the lathe.

One sunny day, Katkin asked Jacq if she could go to Belladore to buy some rough fabric. She wanted to make curtains for the windows to keep out the draughts and a ticking for the mattress that would replace the straw pallet when their new bed was finished. Willow had offered to come back to the house with her and help her sew it up. He looked up from his work, the wood spinning under his capable hands, as the shavings and sawdust flew out around him and fell like snow to the ground at his feet. "Of course you may. But you are not going to the mill, are you?" Katkin shook her head.

"No, just to the shop in the village. Willow will meet me there."

"Very well, my love. Please be careful and talk to no one. Do you understand?" Jacq braked the lathe and brushed his hands clean on his shirt before hugging her and saying, "Don't be gone too long."

He and Nathan watched her mount Brinna and ride away over the hill, heading towards Belladore.

Nathan looked up at his older brother. They shared the same gap-toothed grin and curly hair. He scratched his head and said, "Does she know yet?"

Jacq shook his head violently. "I am not going to tell her. It would bring her nothing but danger."

Nathan scoffed at this. "Come on, Jacq. You cannot keep it a secret forever. Sooner or later you are going to have to tell her something."

Jacq stared down at the gold band on his finger for a moment before saying quietly, "I just don't know if she will understand, Nate."

Nathan tried hard to reassure him. "Katkin is a strong woman and she obviously loves you very much. You know the longer you wait, the harder it will be to make her understand. Would you have her know the truth because the Guard has taken you to the Citadel? You should tell her yourself, right now or as soon as possible."

Jacq looked at him and shook his head once more. "I won't *get* caught. I just won't." He sighed, and after barking a command to Nestor, turned back to the lathe and began to work again.

As Katkin rode down into the village of Belladore, she reflected how different her life had become after those first few happy weeks as Jacq's wife. It wasn't as though her feelings for him had changed. If anything, she loved him more, as she watched him working so hard to make furniture for the house he had built for them, and put food on the table. They had been married almost four months now, and the walls he had raised around himself to protect her seemed to be growing higher each day. She simply never bothered to ask him where he was going when he rode off on Nestor to meet Yannick, who always waited for him at the top of the hill instead of coming down to the house. Sometimes, he would be gone for two or three days and she would be very lonely by herself, unless Willow came by to see her. She tried to stay busy with patching and mending their threadbare clothes, and weeding the new vegetable garden they had planted together.

If the solitude weighed on her too heavily, she would find

Brinna and ride across the old Tintaren lands to visit Jacq's mother. She always looked pleased to see her daughter-in-law. "How are you feeling, my dear?" she would ask, but her blue eyes could never hide her worry.

Katkin thought about her last visit to Mrs. Benet, when Jacq had already been away for several days, and she did not know when he would return. His mother had greeted her happily and arm in arm they went into the tiny house Elisabeth shared with Thad and Arkady. The kitchen was quiet and warm. A loaf of black bread cooled on the table. "Have some of the bread, my daughter, and I will make some raspberry-leaf tea for us. Now, you must tell me what is troubling you." She looked at Katkin with concern.

Katkin sighed. "I am all right, my mother. It is just that I miss Jacq so much when he is gone. I wish he would take me with him sometimes, but only Yannick goes." She paused. "Mother, who is Dinrhydan?"

Elisabeth Benet swore softly as she jumped and burned her hand on the kettle. "Where have you heard that name? You must not repeat it!" She moved to sit down at the table across from Katkin, and looked at her anxiously.

"I heard Yannick call Jacq that once, and Willow says he never does it unless they think she cannot hear. What does it mean, Mother? Will you tell me or are you, too, a brick in the wall my husband has built to keep me away?"

Elisabeth shook her head decisively. "Not to keep you away, never that. Rather to keep you safe. He loves you very much, you know that. Now I had better make the tea. Isn't the cherry tree outside the window lovely, my daughter?"

Katkin did know Jacq loved her, yet it wasn't enough, somehow.

She rode down the main street of the tiny village and left Brinna to graze on the common with the other horses. Walking back to the shop with a sinking heart, she noticed the stares of the villagers who passed her and heard their whispered remarks.

"She is the one who healed the little girl."

"Yes, the very same one who brought the cat back to life."

"It is obvious the Goddess favors her highly."

"Ssh... she comes, don't say more."

Katkin entered the little shop selling everything from food-stuffs to cloth to hardware and seeds. Willow greeted her happily. Her pregnancy had already begun to exaggerate her round figure. She carried Roseberry in a little sling at her side. "Hello, Katkin. How is the furniture making coming?" she asked.

Katkin hugged her sister. "It is slow and steady, Willow. I am looking forward to sleeping on a real bed again."

"What else has Jacq made for you?"

"Four chairs, a table, a couple of stools for out on the porch, and some wooden platters. Jacq makes everything very beauti-fully. I am glad to be married to a craftsman and not a soldier."

Willow gave her a quick glance but said nothing in reply. Instead, she asked, "What about a cradle?" She made no secret of the fact she could not wait for Katkin to join her in motherhood.

Katkin sighed tolerantly. "No cradle. We don't need one just yet."

Willow smiled. "You will soon. At least I hope so."

Katkin hoped so too, though she did not say it aloud. She thought if she became pregnant, Jacq's mysterious trips with Yan-nick might cease. Yet each month, as the full moon lit the sky, her body always disappointed her. Jacq was unconcerned, say-ing, "Never mind, my wife. It is early days yet. We can always try again." Usually this discussion would put him in the mood to try again right away, and he would catch her up enthusiastically and retire with her to the bearskins. Katkin was never happier than when he made love to her. She felt the stubborn wall between them melt away to nothingness then, at least for a little while.

With Willow's help, she selected some pretty cotton cambric for the curtains and a heavier, blue-striped canvas for the tick-ing. Katkin took some of their precious silver coins to pay for her purchases. Now Jacq had no regular employment, she thought they must watch every penny. Still, the little store of coins did not seem to dwindle and she often wondered how Jacq managed to replenish them. Like so many other things, she did not bother to question him about it.

Riding back towards her house with Willow, Katkin asked her sister whether Yannick had forgiven the healing of Roseberry. Willow sighed, saying, "He hasn't mentioned it for awhile. I don't think you should try coming to the house just yet though. That Prime God he worships is awfully fussy."

"Are there many others in the Village who worship this God?" Katkin asked.

Willow considered this for a moment. "A fair few, I think, though most not as seriously as Yannick. Certainly the church is full on Sundays."

"What about the old ways? Is there no one left who follows the Goddess?"

"Yes, among the old folk of Belladore I believe there are plenty. They don't like to talk about it much. I think people sort of frown on it out here in the country. Not like in St. Valery, where they have the Temple and the Infirmarie." Willow turned to look at her sister. "Do you miss being there, Kat?"

Katkin replied, "Yes, I do miss it, sometimes. I am frustrated because I know I should be helping people and Jacq will not allow it. Like the other day when Thad came over to help Jacq work the lathe. He cut himself quite badly with a chisel. I asked Jacq if I could try to heal Thad and he almost bit my head off. He thinks it is too dangerous to call attention to myself that way, even though it was his own brother who needed my help! So Jacq had to stitch up the cut with a sewing needle and some linen thread, while I stood by, doing nothing."

Willow sighed, saying, "People in a small village do talk, Kat. I never should have told the Postmistress about Roseberry. I just felt so pleased about what you did, I didn't stop to think about the consequences. I still hope it doesn't cause trouble for you, my sister."

Katkin decided not to tell Willow about the whispered comments that had followed her through town. There was no point in making her feel worse. Suddenly, Willow pointed excitedly down the hill. "Look, over there, your bed lies in the yard. Goodness, it is huge!" They had reached the crest of the hill, and now made their way down towards the house. The big four-poster bed had been temporarily assembled outside while Jacq used a hammer and nails to attach rope webbing on the frame to hold the mattress. Katkin smiled at him happily when she saw the carefully engraved acorn design on the headboard.

"It is a beautiful bed, my husband. I will get to work right away on the ticking. What will we stuff it with? Straw, I suppose."

Katkin thought their limited finances would not permit anything more luxurious.

Jacq stopped hammering for a moment and surprised her by saying, "No, my love, we have slept on straw for far too long already. Have a look in the bags over there." She went to examine the big hemp bags standing on the porch and found they held white goose feathers—fine and light.

"Where did you get these feathers from, Jacq? They must have cost a lot of money," she asked him, a bit suspiciously.

"They cost nothing. I traded some game for them a few days ago when Yannick and I went hunting. Do they not please you, Katkin?"

She smiled at him and said they did, and she would be happy to sleep on something softer than straw. Inside though, her mind quietly turned over the fact that Willow had told her Jacq shot no game on the last trip, at least according to Yannick.

So many lies on top of lies. Where will it all end, Jacq?

After he finished making the furniture, Jacq spent even more time away from home. He began clearing a stony field some distance from the house so he could plant a crop of barley to keep them fed throughout the winter. Using the smithy in Belladore, he had already forged a fine plow and some other tools to work the soil with. Now Katkin would say goodbye to him in the morning and not see him again until he trudged wearily home at dinnertime, leading Nestor by his halter. She felt very lonely most of the time, cut off from her sister and the people of Belladore.

One day, about a week after her trip to town, after she had made Jacq's breakfast and said goodbye to him as usual, she heard a very timid tap on the door. Opening it, she beheld a tiny little girl, no more than five or six years old. The girl had a halo of blond curls and a winsome expression. Katkin, immediately charmed, said, "Hello, my pretty little one. Why have you come to visit me?"

The girl spoke so quietly Katkin had to bend down to hear what she said. "Please, Miss, my Gram's sick. She's been coughing something terrible."

Katkin stared at her wide-eyed and asked, "How... How did you know where to find me?"

The little girl replied, "Our Jimmy saw you in the Village and followed you back here." She blinked hard as her blue eyes filled with tears. "My name's Tabitha. Can you please help my Gram, Miss? They says you can heal, just like the Goddess. My Gram looks after me and Jimmy. If she don't get better soon we will have to go to the work house and then we won't be together no more."

Katkin looked at the sad little girl in front of her and considered everything Jacq had told her about being careful. She made her decision and said, "If you will wait here for just a minute, I must fetch something before we go to her, then I will try to help as best I can."

Later, when Jacq complained about his dinner being late and grumpily wondered what she had been doing with herself all day, she merely offered, "Brinna wandered far, and it took me a long time to catch up with her. But look, I have these hips I gathered from the wild roses down by the quarry, and tomorrow I will make us some jam."

The bag of rose hips had actually come from the old woman, pressed into Katkin's hands as she left the hovel earlier that day after successfully healing the cough. "Goddess bless you, my angel," she said gratefully, and Tabitha and Jimmy had added their own small thanks.

"Please tell no one in the village what I have done for you," Katkin had replied.

Jacq did not question her further, just sat down at the table and began to eat. The stillness stretched between them like a gulf.

So, my husband, I shall have my secrets as well, it seems.

13

Dylloriah, the green valley

(The Tollyn, Two)

The Autochthones find the Innocent, Geya. They, themselves, insure their own survival. She carries the sign of the Dawnmaid within her.

~~~~~~~~~~~~~~~~

One late spring day, as Katkin bent over to dislodge a stubborn weed from the ranks of the radish and carrot shoots in the vegetable plot, she heard a snatch of song and the sound of harness bells drifting through the branches of the oak trees. She glanced up briefly but did not bother to investigate further. Though a kindred of Firaithi traders must be passing close by, Katkin knew they would neither stop nor talk to her. The Firaithi kept very much to themselves on their journeys through Yr.

As the sound of their caravans faded into the distance she went back to the weeding. The sun beat down on her bare head, and she looked up to the sky for a moment to try and judge the time. Probably almost midday, but Jacq would not be home for the noon meal. He had left with Yannick in the morning, saying he might not be back until tomorrow. She sighed and wiped the sweat from her eyes with the back of her sleeve, wondering, as she always did, where he was and what he might be doing. Katkin suddenly felt very lonely, and decided she would visit Jacq's mother once she finished her morning chores.

A cough close at hand caused her to look up sharply. A raggedly dressed woman, leaning on a twisted staff, stood at the edge of the garden plot. Her long gray hair hung in braids, adorned with many colored ribbons and shining glass beads. When she saw Katkin, her darkly wrinkled face broke into a toothless smile. Katkin stood, and brushed the dirt from her hands. Although the woman's strange appearance made her feel a little nervous, still she asked politely, "Did you come here for healing, Old Mother? How may I help you?"

The old woman croaked, "How you have grown up, my little Kitty Kat! But where are your manners? Do you not remember your old Nurse?"

Katkin stared uncertainly and then stepped forward with a cry to gather the old woman into an embrace. "Nurse! I am sorry I did not recognize you. You must come in, and let me make you some tea." She took the old woman's arm and led her eagerly into the cottage. Her nurse wandered around the single room, examining everything, while Katkin put the kettle on the hob to boil. After a moment she settled in a kitchen chair. Katkin sat down at the table, and pushed a plate of apple cake towards her. She had so many questions she hardly knew where to start.

"Why have you come to see me now, after all these years? How did you get here anyway?"

The old woman laughed. "Second question first. I came with the Firaithi. We passed over the borders of Beaumarais three days ago."

Katkin looked confused. "The Firaithi kindred that passed by just now? Why are you traveling with them?"

"They are my people. Our people, Kitty. Your mother was the daughter of their Tane*, Ifan Mare, and my daughter, for he was my husband. My real name is Neirin Mare."

Katkin stared at her while she worked through the implications of this. "But that isn't possible! That would make you my... Grandmother!"

The old woman blinked slowly a few times and her hazel eyes looked sad. "Yes, Kitty, I am indeed your Kymatre."

Tears sprang to Katkin's eyes. "Why did you never tell me? Where have you been all this time? If you only knew how lonely I have been..."

Her grandmother patted her hand sympathetically. "I am sorry, little one. We cannot always do what we would wish in this life. But now I must answer your first question. I came here to tell you a story, and to give you something." Neirin sighed and sipped

---

* The leader of a Firaithi kindred. Normally an inherited position.

her tea. "The tale is not a happy one. My daughter, Anwen Mare, was born under a full moon, in the early spring, when the buds were still tightly furled. That made her very beautiful, but willful and scheming. She always wanted the things the Gruagán* have, and with her light skin, she knew she could have them. When she was fourteen, the kindred came to Beaumarais for the horse-trading fair. Once Anwen saw your father, she knew he was the one to give her all she desired. Ifan and I could do nothing with her. When she danced the maiden's dance for him, her beauty stole his heart, as she knew it would. So he took her away from the Kindred of Anandi, and made her his wife."

Katkin stared at her grandmother, still stunned at her sudden appearance after so many years. Finally, she asked, "What happened after they married?"

"For a time Anwen was happy. She had the fine house and servants she desired. Of course we heard nothing from her—she wanted no one to know her humble origins. I found out things only through tossing the stones. A child came into the world, and then another. I went to the Elders and they said I must go to Anwen in her Gruagá house, to make sure the second child was brought up to know the true way of our Kindreds."

"You came for me? But what about Willow?"

Neirin shook her head. "Your sister Willow is a good girl, Kitty, but hers is the life of an ordinary woman. You are to be much more. The time ahead is dark, but you carry within you the spark of the Dawnmaid – the symbol of hope for our kind."

Katkin did not know what to say to this, so she asked, "But why did you not tell us who you were when you came, Grandmother?"

"Your mother would not allow it, Kitty. She wanted no one to know the truth. Her life, by then, was pretty miserable. The loss of her youthful beauty and slender figure had made her angry and bitter, and she blamed you children for it. She wanted no more, so she shut your father out of her bedroom, and they quarreled incessantly. You were the only light in his life. That is why he would never allow your mother to send you away. Of course, I always took his side as well."

---

* Firai word meaning "white devils."

Katkin shook her head in dismay. "I always knew Mother was unhappy. I guess I was just too little to understand why. But when I had to go away to school, what happened then? Did she tell you to leave?"

Neirin sat up straighter and said proudly, "I went of my own accord. I did not wish to spend any more time in Anwen's unhappy Gruagá house, believe me. I knew the time was coming soon when Lalluna would call you, and then you would learn what you needed from her. I had finished my work with you. So I packed my things and went back to the Anandi. Anwen wasn't sorry to see me go," she added dryly. "Since then I have traveled the greater Ambit* with our people, and waited for the moment when I could see you again."

"Why? You said you had something to give me?"

The old woman nodded slowly and removed a faded red pouch from around her neck. An intricate design of interlaced leaves and flowers was stamped on the leather. She untied the drawstring and emptied the contents out onto the table. Three octahedral stones, of bright ruby-red, immediately caught Katkin's eye. She picked them up carefully and studied the mysterious symbols incised on each face, feeling the silky smoothness of the gems, worn down over time with much use. But her grandmother reached for another object, carefully wound on a thong of leather.

Neirin said, "This periapt should have been given to Anwen as her birthright, but she lost her legacy when she married a Gruagá." Katkin studied the talisman dangling from her grandmother's wrinkled fingers. It appeared to be a preserved bird's foot, withered and yellow, clutching a pea-sized green crystal in its talons. She continued, "So I kept it, waiting for the moment when I could pass it on to the one who was meant to have it—you, Kitty."

"But, Grandmother, I am also married to a..." Katkin hesitated, not liking the old tongue word for the more settled residents of Yr. "...a Gruagá."

The old woman's eyes peered into Katkin's and she was aware

---

* The Firaithi recognize no political borders, and consider all Yr to be their rightful territory. They make a looping journey from north to south and back each year, through lands they privately call the greater Ambit.

of their sharpness and sudden, fathomless depth. "Are you? Is that man of yours like every other? I think not. Did he not once travel the paths of the dead with you?"

Katkin sat back, astonished. "How do you know of that?"

Neirin only shook her head. "I must go now, Kitty. Remember what I have told you. You must swear on the Un-Named One to keep the periapt safe, and secret." As Katkin nodded solemnly, she heard a tap on the door. Neirin, seemingly expecting the arrival of more guests, called to them to come in. A pair of Firaithi entered – an older man of about forty, and a girl of perhaps Katkin's age. She was the most striking young woman Katkin had ever seen, with flowing black hair reaching almost to her waist. Her peasant blouse left one shapely shoulder bare and she wore breeches and high boots. Katkin felt very provincial and dowdy in her presence.

The girl looked around the cottage with open disdain as Neirin introduced the pair. "This is my eldest son, Ander and his firstborn daughter, Cara. She is your cousin, Kitty." Cara's dark brown eyes flashed with anger at this introduction.

Katkin smiled and greeted her in a friendly manner anyway, pleased to think she had new family that she might get to know, but the girl rudely ignored her and sauntered back outside.

Ander spoke gruffly, with a thick accent, "I am sorry, Katkin. My daughter did not want to come this way, for she is betrothed and wishes to meet her future husband at the summer meeting ground as soon as possible." He switched to Firai, the old tongue of Yr, and Katkin found to her delight that she could still follow his speech with Neirin. "The girl's husband is on his way back here, Rha Tane, and we should be away before he arrives. We will have to make haste to reach the southern border by tomorrow."

The old woman nodded and turned to her granddaughter. Katkin's eyes filled with tears.

Neirin patted her shoulder. "Do not cry, little one. You and I may yet meet again. The stones tell me that you may one day take your rightful place and travel with the Kindreds once more. Until then, may the moon shine on your face, Kitty. Farewell."

Katkin caught her sleeve as she turned to go. "Can you not stay a little longer? I am sure Jacq would welcome you. The Firaithi could camp overnight here on our land."

Neirin and Ander exchanged worried glances, and then she shook her head sadly. "The Firaithi are not welcome in Beaumarais. The War has made all your people mistrustful. Both sides accuse us of spying for the other."

Ander snorted, "As if *we* would wish to get involved in a foolish Gruagán war!"

Katkin's grandmother continued. "No, it is best we go now, and if you will take my advice, you will not tell your husband a word about our visit today." She grasped her staff and slowly made her way out the door, with Ander at her side. Katkin sadly watched them leave.

She was still studying the periapt and wondering about its significance when she heard Nestor's heavy hoof beats echoing down the hillside. Remembering her promise to Neirin to keep the talisman a secret, Katkin hastily tucked it in the leather pocket she wore pinned to the inside of her shift. Despite her grandmother's warning, she rushed outside, eyes alight, ready to tell Jacq all about her unexpected company this morning.

He jumped down from Nestor and hastily embraced her, then went straight indoors. Katkin followed him, wondering what his hurry was.

"You are back sooner than I expected. Did your business with Yannick go well?" Then she plunged on, "You will never guess..."

Thoughtlessly, he interrupted her, saying, "I came back here early because I heard there were some Firaithi coming this way. I wanted to make sure you were safe. You did not talk to them did you?"

Katkin looked up at him uncertainly. "What? Why should I not talk to them?"

He ran his hands through his hair. "Just... because. I don't trust them. There are rumors that they carry messages for the enemy. Promise me you will not have anything to do with those darkies, should they pass this way again. Just go in the house and bar the door. Do you understand?"

She nodded dejectedly. When Jacq asked her a moment later what she had been doing all day, she said dully, "Weeding the garden, mostly," and turned away to the hob to cook his dinner. Jacq scratched his head, wondering what she could be upset about, and went to wash up. Once again, they ate in silence.

Later in the evening, Katkin forgot her unhappiness when Jacq suggested she take her vielle from its case under the four-poster bed and join him outside on the porch. When they sang together, the combination of her own sweet soprano and his bass harmonizing to the silly children's tunes she knew best always delighted her. Sitting with him, with the warm spring night all around and a million bright stars above, she could almost forget the gulf that lay between them, as they laughed and talked of everything and nothing at all. As a shooting star crossed the sky in a brief, glorious blaze of light, he asked her softly, "What do you wish for, my love?"

Katkin thought hard. More than anything, she wanted Jacq to dismantle the barricade he had built around himself, yet she wouldn't ask for that, not in front of him. Such a wish would bring their happy evening to a premature end. So she merely said, "I have everything I wish for already, why do you not use the wish?"

He looked at her gravely, and sighed. "I wish I could give you the happiness you deserve, my wife, yet I see in your eyes every day how I fail you." Katkin quickly protested, and he cut her off. "No, don't. I know it is true. I love you more than I can say. It is a bitter draught for me that all the promises I made on our wedding day have not been fulfilled for you."

With this, he stood abruptly and went inside. When Katkin followed him a minute later, after packing away the vielle, he had already gone to bed, and faced the wall, with his broad back to her.

As was often the case when he felt troubled, Jacq did not sleep well. His restlessness soon woke Katkin and as she lay beside him in the darkness she wondered what he could be dreaming of. She listened in amazement as he began to mutter in a strange tongue. "*Passeme nalaneralans sang rure truirn. Deres. Deres. Palos candi-cat sanien, iraos karimad tellubys ad anhanir. Geanfe iraos Dai.*"

Katkin was dead sure Jacq had never studied another language—he had never even been to school. She was just as sure the language he had just spoken was not one from Yr. How had he learned it? Where did it come from? Meanwhile, his agitation seemed to be increasing, so she shook him gently by the shoulder. "Jacq? Wake up, my love. You are dreaming."

He inhaled sharply and turned over, his hands searching in the darkness for something to connect with. For a moment she had the impression he neither knew where he was or who had woken him. Then he said softly, "Katkin... I am sorry. Did I disturb you?"

"No," she lied. "I was already awake. But you were talking in your sleep and you seemed uneasy. What were you dreaming of, my husband?" Katkin slid sideways, putting her head on his shoulder, and wrapped her arm across his chest. She could feel his rapid heartbeat and breathing, though he was doing his best to sound untroubled.

He did not answer her right away, and Katkin sadly wondered if he was concocting some tale, though she could not imagine why he would want to keep his dream a secret from her. But his reply, when it came, sounded genuine enough. "I dreamed I was flying, with you in my arms, across a sky full of the brightest stars I have ever seen. We soared ever higher, until the air grew thin, and you complained that your chest hurt and it was hard to breathe. So I stopped climbing, and watched as, one by one, the stars began to fall down in bright streaks across the heavens, and land in the sea below. They floated like lilies in the water. It was so beautiful and sad. I knew it was the end of the world, so I said a prayer to the dying stars. Then you woke me up."

Katkin said quietly, "You spoke out loud. You said, '*Passeme nalaneralans sang*,' and a whole lot of other words I didn't understand. What language is that?"

Again there was a pause, and then he said, "You must have been half asleep yourself. Or maybe my speech was just garbled." He chuckled in the darkness. "That dimwit Jacq Benet is just a blacksmith from Beaumarais. How could he know some strange tongue?" His voice was teasing, but his unaccustomed use of the third person distressed Katkin, and she sighed in the darkness.

"How indeed, my husband? Is this another secret I am not supposed to question you about?"

Now his voice lost its lightness. "I don't know what you mean."

"Yes, you do. Why don't you trust me? Tell me where you went with Yannick today." Katkin rolled away from him, onto her back, and stared up at the ceiling, fighting back tears. She said unhappily, "Tell me who you are." Then after a longish pause, when he sighed but did not speak, she said, "Tell me *what* you are, for sometimes I wonder if you are even of this Yrth, my husband."

He moaned and clutched at her, pulling her body back close to his. "You must not ask me. Not about Yannick." Jacq began to cry and Katkin felt a sudden stab of guilt and pity. He continued in a fierce whisper, his face buried between her breasts. "And... not about the demon in my head. Can you not just love me for what I am, right now?"

Katkin could only utter helplessly, "Of course I love you, more than anything. I won't ask you any more questions if you don't want me to. But would you not feel better if you told someone else? Maybe I can help you."

He spoke with rock-solid certainty. "Your love is all I need, Katkin. It is all I have ever needed. As long as I have that, then I will be all right. You must believe me."

As Katkin spoke again to reassure him, he covered her mouth with his own, and threw his arms about her tightly. Then he made love to her for hours with such feverish abandon it left them both exhausted and trembling.

As they lay entwined, and Jacq was almost asleep, Katkin murmured, "Do you remember when we were children, at Tintaren, my love?" He made some little sound of agreement so she continued softly, "You took me once to a silent place, where the sky was flat and white."

Jacq sighed. "I never should have taken you there. It was very wrong of me."

She said thoughtfully, "Even then I knew there was something very different about you, Jacq. I never understood how you did it. I still don't."

"I don't know either. I only went a few times myself and then I lost the knack of crossing over."

Katkin cast about with her hand and pulled the quilt up over the two of them as a cool breeze wafted in through the open window. Jacq's sweat in the midst of their passion had drenched them both. She shivered in the dampness of the covers, as she thought of the day, long ago, when they had gone to Old Man Bell's cottage together and peered through the curtained alcove at the white creature. Even now, after ten years, she could still picture it in her mind. It was roughly human in size, with a long worm-like body and a pair of muscular arms, all covered in pearlescent scales. But Katkin was most taken by the wings—beautiful wings that sprang out from its back, in a cascade of translucent feathery tendrils. At first, she had been fascinated, but when it looked up, and she saw it bore no face, terror filled her.

"When I saw that flat whiteness, just like the sky, it frightened me so much. I dreamed about it for weeks afterwards." She felt him stiffen as she asked, "This demon in your head, is he a part of that place?"

Jacq whispered. "I know not where he comes from. But he has memories that are not mine, of worlds filled with colors that have no name and light from the very heart of the stars. There are trees there, growing thousands of feet high, towering over me and somehow singing in a strange tongue. They fill my dreams, every night. And..." Katkin kept silent, waiting for her husband to finish. For a long time it seemed he might tell her nothing else, but at last he continued, in a voice filled with wonder. "Always in my dreams I fly. I soar and dive with feathered wings that feel as natural and real as my own arms—as though I have flown my whole life long. Flying like that gives me more joy than anything in my waking hours, except making love to you." Abruptly the wonder was replaced by a dull certainty as he insisted, "You see— it is madness—it must be. That is why I did not want to tell you."

He got out of bed, naked, and stalked across the room to get a drink from the pottery jug on the kitchen bench. The moon shone through the unshuttered windows, and for a disconcerting few seconds Katkin thought she could see the powerful sweep of shadowy gray wings down his back, almost touching the floor. Just then, a reminiscence stole over her, so faint at first she could only imagine it was a dream. But the more she looked at Jacq's indistinct form in the darkened main room of the cottage, the more she was convinced she had seen such a creature before. The feeling seemed intimately connected with the sensation of falling.

She gave a groan of frustration as Jacq stumbled back into bed and it slipped away from her again, akin to a butterfly taking flight.

Jacq fell asleep almost immediately but Katkin lay awake until the dawn, studying her husband's profile and wondering about his dreams of flying. Just as the sun rose and filled the cottage with rosy light, she thought instead of a token she had kept safe for the last year, ever since the day she ran away from the Infirmarie. She stole out of bed quietly, as Jacq turned over and sighed in his sleep, and crossed the room to where her clothes hung on a wooden peg. After digging in her leather pouch she retrieved the gray feather that had been lying on the ground next to her after she awoke from her three-story fall.

As soon as her fingers brushed against its softness the missing memory buoyantly burst from her subconscious, like a bubble breaking the surface after being trapped deep underwater. *He* had come to her, when she fell backwards from the third story of the Juvenet's hostel and carried her up into the sky on majestic gray wings... How *could* she have forgotten, until now?

14

The Knave, Dindal

(Arkirish Dynasty, Standing Six)

Go to your vessel, Moonlight. She has need of you.

~~~~~~~~~~

One brilliantly sunny morning, on the day when spring turned into summer, Katkin and Jacq sat at the table he had so carefully crafted, and breakfasted together. Jacq was telling her at length about his plans to build a sturdy barn close to the house. He described the structure in detail, growing animated as he explained to Katkin how it would help them become ever more self-sufficient. It would be a big project, taking many weeks, and she could not help thinking happily that it would keep him close to her, at least for a little while. Jacq's mysterious hunting trips with Yannick were occurring more frequently than ever. Katkin couldn't help wondering why, especially when what little news she heard from the outside world seemed so disturbing.

As the war between the Soldiers of the Rising and the King's Guard grew more intense, the Infirmarie overflowed with casualties and many villages had sustained damage from the fighting. Other distressing news came from the City, provided by the always-knowledgeable Willow, who had the Postmistress as an unimpeachable source. Tomas de Vigny had married Simone Beauchamps in a lavish ceremony at Havenwood. A few days later, his father had died from a pistol wound to the head. Though officially reported as an accident, gossip had it that the General's disapproval at the union had caused him to take his own life. Katkin felt a touch of sympathy for Tomas, despite the fact he had treated her dreadfully. She knew the old man, with all his blind and unreasoning ambition, had always been far too hard on his only son.

Katkin's reverie was broken as Jacq looked up sharply from his breakfast. He jumped up from the table, knocking his chair to the floor in his hurry to reach the door, left open to catch the summer breezes.

"Jacq, what is it?"

"Hoof beats. Someone riding hard, down the hill towards the house. Get away from the window, Kat. Close the shutter and bar it. Hurry, girl!"

Katkin could hear the rushing hooves now, and the sound filled her with fear. Jacq had already shut and barred the door, and now leaned against it, breathing heavily, his eyes darting rapidly back and forth as he waited for the rider to make his final approach. They heard the sound of running footsteps and then the door shuddered as someone pounded on it, insistently. Using his hand, Jacq signaled her to make no noise.

Yannick's voice rang out, "Jacq! Are you there? Open the door, I must speak with you."

Jacq breathed a sigh of relief as he turned and unbarred the door. Seconds later, when Yannick stepped inside, it became apparent Jacq's ease had been very premature. For Yannick pushed past him and seized Katkin by the shoulders, shaking her violently. "You witch! You wouldn't do as you were told, would you? Now they have come and taken Roseberry." He burst into a stream of vicious invective that left Katkin gasping.

Jacq grabbed Yannick and pulled him away from Katkin. "What is this about, Yannick? Who has taken Roseberry? You must tell me calmly so I can help you."

Giving Katkin a look of venomous hatred, he spat, "Ask your wife who has taken my daughter. She used to be one of them."

Katkin looked at him, eyes wide. "The Unity? The Daminem took her?"

"That is correct, witch. Three pagan harpies came to the house this morning with a detachment of Guardsmen riding post, and went right up to Willow, and said, 'The Apostate has used the power of the Goddess without our consent. We take her sister's child for the Solstice Observance, as atonement for this evil.' Then they did. Just picked her up and rode away. I heard Willow's screams and came running from the mill. They had too much of a head start for me to catch them and anyway I could not take on fifteen Guardsmen by myself. So I grabbed Turk and came straight over here."

Jacq looked at Yannick in horror. "Of course I will do everything I can to help you, my brother, but they must have made a mistake in taking Roseberry. Katkin no longer has anything to do with the Goddess or the Unity."

Yannick snarled back, "Really? Ask her who healed the Widow Batignon, and little Pierre Marcel, and lots of others in the village I could mention."

Jacq turned to her, his anger palpable. "Can this be true, my wife? Have you been doing the work of the Goddess here, after I expressly forbade it?"

Katkin, knowing she could give no explanation that would mitigate her terrible betrayal, just nodded her head silently and kept her eyes to the ground. Jacq gave an explosive groan and picked up a chair, then threw it at the wall. It shattered loudly and the pieces clattered to the floor.

For a moment, no one spoke, and then Katkin said quietly, "I know where they will have taken her, Yannick. We must go to the Temple. Now. There is not much time."

Yannick looked at her in disbelief. "Let you help? This is all your fault, witch. Why should I trust you now?" He said angrily to Jacq, "Are you coming to help me catch them, or shall I go alone?"

Katkin shook her head distractedly, and turning to Jacq, exclaimed, "You must reason with him, Jacq. Roseberry's life may depend on it. I am the only one here who knows where she is, and the only one who can enter there."

"What do you mean, my wife? Tell me quickly."

"The Temple of Lalluna. Each year on the Solstice there is an observance there, performed by the Maitress. I don't know exactly what she does because it is kept strictly secret. But I am afraid, my husband; I am very afraid for Roseberry."

Yannick, standing beside Jacq, began to cry quietly, his love and fear for his little girl conquering his rage. Jacq spoke decisively. "We must do everything we can to stop this from happening. Kat, get Brinna saddled and ride as quickly as you can for the City. I will be behind you on Nestor. We cannot take the Yoke, because the Guard might ask too many questions, so we will have to use the Redgate ferry. When does this observance take place?"

"At noon. We still have plenty of time if the ferry is on the right side." Katkin turned to go outside.

"Dinrhydan, wait. Let your wife go with me. You must not enter the City. It is far too dangerous. I only wanted your help to track them, because at that your skill far exceeds mine. I never meant for you to do this. It is suicide, my friend." Katkin looked over at Yannick in surprise, wondering at this devotion to her husband that overmastered even his dreadful fears for his daughter's safety.

"I *am* going and there will be no more argument. Katkin will not ride into any kind of danger without me beside her. I will fetch d'angwir and then we must go."

Jacq's voice sounded firm and Yannick knew it would be pointless to argue with him further. He said, "Dinrhydan, must you take d'angwir? If the Guard capture you, they will have no doubt of your identity. Will you not use my weapon instead?"

Jacq shook his head, refusing Yannick's outstretched sword, and studiously avoided Katkin's questioning glance. She wondered what they could be talking about. Jacq had no weapon other than the ancient matchlock gun he used for hunting, and he had never called it such an outlandish name before. She watched in amazement as Jacq, after pulling up an unfastened floor board close to the wall, bent and reached down inside. He retrieved a long, cloth-shrouded bundle. Katkin's eyebrows shot up, for until now, she had been completely unaware of this secret space or its contents. She put her hand over her mouth to smother a cry as Jacq revealed a beautifully worked two-handed sword, razor sharp. He fastened the belt around his waist with a quick grace undoubtedly borne of long experience. But she felt too worried about Roseberry to stand there wondering about this new mystery for long. The sword, named in the old tongue "justice for all," became just another entry in the long list of secrets Jacq had kept from her. Katkin, suddenly very afraid for her husband, quickly retrieved her little phial of Lalluna's water and shoved it deeply down into the leather pouch fastened to the inside of her shift.

They rode hard for the ferry, praying silently it would be waiting on the right side of the Mere. Following the King's Road, it took an hour from Belladore, skirting the Acre, to reach Redgate Ferry. Katkin pushed Brinna as much as she dared but the little pony could not keep up with Nestor or Yannick's chestnut mare, Turk, for long. The sunny day promised to be hot—already the horses were lathered in sweat. As they rounded the final bend in the road, they could see the ferry ahead of them, getting ready to leave the wharf. The ferryman was just unwinding the last rope from the big bollards. Jacq spurred Nestor forward and the horse responded with a burst of speed that left Katkin's and Yannick's steeds far behind.

When they caught up to him, Jacq had already negotiated for their passage to the City, so they led the horses onto the flat bed of the ferry. Katkin spoke in low tones so the ferryman would not hear as he poled them across the Mere. "Once we get to the Infirmarie, go straight through the gates and take the path branching off to the right. It winds steeply uphill through the cemetery, and ends at a locked gate. The key for the gate is given only to the Maitress, so one of you will have to break it down so we can continue up to the Temple."

Jacq stopped her. "You will remain below and point the path out to Yannick and me. I will not have you endangered if there is trouble."

She shook her head violently. "No! No, Jacq, you must stop trying to protect me from everything. You told me once to grow up. How can I when you will not let me?" He had nothing to say in reply to this and so she continued, "Once we reach the Temple, you two stay behind and keep the Daminem on guard from raising the alarm while I go and get Roseberry out of there."

Yannick spat angrily, "You have come merely to show the way. I don't want your help in this. I would save my own daughter, witch."

Katkin said flatly, "You cannot, Yannick. The Temple is dark and deep—the path to it winds on for a mile into the heart of Hythea, herself. You would wander in there a hundred years and never find the Source. I must go, for I, alone, know the way."

"You cannot stop me from following you," he stubbornly responded.

"Do you not understand? There will be no light beyond the entrance to the cleft. I must ask the Goddess herself to guide me. The Rule forbids all men from entering the Temple. She will not help me if you are there, I am sure of it."

Jacq looked at her, confused. "I thought you told me that the Maitress alone could enter the Temple, and only once a year. You were just a Juvenie in the Unity. How is it you know so much about the way?"

"I know because Lalluna sent me a dream, long ago. I did not know what it meant at the time. Now it seems certain she sent it to me to stop the Maitress from..." Here she stopped, not wanting to voice her dreadful fears and upset Yannick further.

Jacq asked quietly, "From what, Kat? We have to know what we are up against."

Katkin sighed. "From whatever it is she is going to do. I do not know what that is yet, my husband. But I will give my own life before I let her hurt Roseberry." Jacq said nothing, only put his arms around his wife and held her tightly, shaken to his very core. With all his strength, he could do nothing to protect her if she left him behind in the sunlight, to make her way alone in the darkness of the mountain to face an unknown peril. He buried his face in her hair.

She said to him confidently, "Do not fear for my safety. Lalluna will be my protector now. I have seen her face many times, and the bond between us is strong, for all it crosses the heavenly plane. I place my faith and trust in her and you must too."

Jacq lifted his head and studied his wife's face apprehensively, seeing for the first time the new maturity that had been growing inside her over the last few months. She had changed profoundly and he had been too wrapped up in himself and the War to notice. He could not help feeling somehow a part of her had been lost to him forever.

Yannick quietly gave voice to an expletive and turned away, shaking his head in disgust.

The ferry reached the jetty, and after disembarking, Jacq, Yannick and Katkin rode as fast as they dared for the Infirmarie. The great gates stood open, and once inside they followed Katkin's lead up the mountain path to the cleft in the side of Mount Hythea. After passing through the cemetery like a rush of wind, the three riders halted temporarily in front of the high locked gate leading to the Temple preserve. Jacq dismounted from Nestor. While standing on one leg, he brought the other up in a powerful side kick at the latch. The gate cracked but held fast. Another and another kick followed until suddenly the latch gave way and the gate flew open, scattering bits of wood on the ground.

The sun stood directly overhead now, and Katkin shouted, "We must hurry, time is running out." Jacq set Nestor off, and mounted him as he ran beside, jumping high and swinging his leg up over the horse's broad back.

A tumbled rocky cleft in the mountainside provided the doorway to the Temple, accessed by a narrow path of small white river stones set in the ground. They hurried up this path now, not checking their mounts at all. As they reached the entrance, Jacq and Yannick reined hard and swiftly dismounted, drawing their swords with a ringing whine of metal. Three Daminem stood guard and it shocked Katkin profoundly to see they also carried swords. Seeing the armed men approach, they immediately drew their own weapons and made ready to defend the Temple from the intruders.

"Go on, Kat, hurry! Find Roseberry. Yannick and I will deal with them," Jacq cried to her as he warily circled the armed Daminem. His code of honor would have prevented him from ever attacking a woman, yet he did not doubt these three meant to fight, whether he wanted to or not.

Yannick stood on the path back to the Infirmarie, intent on preventing any escape back to warn the others. He said, "Come, you harpies. Do not resist us, or you will lose your lives."

The Daminem, looking like angels in their white habits, attacked aggressively, their swords flying. Jacq, for all his superior strength, soon found it difficult to defend against them. Yannick was similarly pressed. After a few minutes of heavy sword play, one of the Daminem broke away and began to run back down the path.

"Dinrhydan, look! One is getting away," Yannick cried in frustration.

Jacq, with a mighty two handed slash, savagely beheaded the woman in front of him, and then took off down the path after the fleeing Damenie. The Damenie he pursued knew the terrain far better than he did, and to his immense disgust, she soon vanished into the thick holly groves dotting the cemetery.

Panting heavily, he returned to the cleft, and found Yannick holding his sword at the third Damenie's throat, forcing her back against the rock face. Jacq quickly disarmed her, and after ripping the bottom part of her habit roughly, tied her up and gagged her with the makeshift rope.

Yannick asked, "What of the other, Dinrhydan?"

Jacq shook his head. "I lost her in the cemetery, Yannick. Even now, she will be raising the alarm. I fear we will have more upon us shortly."

He walked over to look at the body of the slain Damenie. Her head lay to one side of her fallen body, still grotesquely attired in the flowing white habit of the Unity, now stained red with her blood. Reaching down, he respectfully closed the sightless eyes and covered her face with the wimple.

Jacq sighed and said sadly, "I never dreamed a woman could fight so well, Yannick. She fought as fiercely and skillfully as any man I have ever faced. I did not want to kill her but she left me no recourse. I pray there are no more of these Damenie-warriors inside the cave, as my Katkin carries no weapon at all."

With this, he set about methodically cleaning his sword, and marshaled his strength for the next battle, like the seasoned warrior he truly was.

Katkin ran into the open mouth of the cleft and down the path of white stones until the light from the outside failed her utterly. She stopped and said beseechingly, "My Lady Lalluna, give me now your aid, for I have come to stop the slaughter, as you charged me to do." The path in front of her, as it had in her dream, began to phosphoresce faintly and lit her way down into the roots of the mountain.

Katkin set off running as quickly as she could. She stumbled and fell many times in her haste to catch the Maitress, whom she was sure had Roseberry with her. The low cavern ceiling forced Katkin to slow her pace, and she shuffled with bent back through the narrow passages that branched and twisted, acutely aware she had little time left. Always the glowing stones stretched before her, and the way seemed endless.

Abruptly, she turned a corner, and through some trick of sound, Roseberry's wails reached her ears, though they sounded faint.

"Oh, Goddess, no. Don't let me be too late." She redoubled her speed, heedless now of the dangers of the low tunnel. Suddenly the walls fell away and the ceiling soared to reveal a huge cavern whose roof glowed with the same eerie light. Before her on a plinth, Katkin beheld a white marble statue of winged Lalluna, just like the one in the dream, but no tears of blood coursed down her face. Looking past the figure of the Goddess, Katkin could see the Maitress hobbling along, carrying Roseberry. The old woman, crippled as she was by arthritis, moved quite slowly. Setting off at a quick trot, Katkin thought with relief that she should easily be able to catch her.

A shower of stars suddenly intruded on her vision and her head exploded in pain. In her haste to catch the Maitress, Katkin ran hard into one of the many stalactites hanging from the cavern roof, and fell down, her head streaming with blood. Lying there, stunned and dizzy, she almost gave up hope, because it seemed she could not get up and go on again. *Roseberry will die some horrible death and I will have failed Yannick completely. He and Willow will never forgive me.*

A gently encouraging voice spoke to her. "My vessel, gather your courage and rise up. Do not allow the innocent to die. Please, stop this slaughter."

Somehow, Katkin found her feet, and grimly wiped away the blood that dripped from the gash on her forehead and stung her eyes. Her balance felt unsteady, but she staggered off as best she could in the direction the Maitress had taken. Whether the sound of the water covered her approach or the Goddess gave her some secret protection, Katkin did not know, but she managed to creep right up to the Maitress without the old women hearing her approach.

They had reached the end of the white stone path. Below them lay a vast pool of boiling superheated mud—it steamed and bubbled like some hideous cauldron with soft, sucking eruptions. The Maitress carried a lit torch in one hand, and the wailing Roseberry pressed close to her side with her other arm. Chanting softly, she placed the torch in a bracket in the wall and held Roseberry in both hands. The terrified child struggled fruitlessly.

"Stop, Maitress! Step back from there," Katkin shrieked frantically. The Maitress whirled around and almost lost her balance in her haste to see what infidel had followed her into this most sacred of spaces.

Katkin reached out to the old woman, grabbing hold of her habit and bodily dragged her away from that perilous edge. The Maitress looked at her with eyes full of hatred and fear. "You! What are you doing here, Katrione? The Rule forbids this place to all except the Maitress. The Goddess will be very angry."

Without answering, Katkin reached forward and quickly snatched Roseberry from her trembling hands before she could turn away again. Katkin began to back away from the mud pool until she had placed what she thought was a safe distance between her and the Maitress. The old woman shouted angrily, telling Katkin again and again that she must not interfere with the Observance.

Shaking her head firmly, Katkin said, "No, Maitress, the Goddess doesn't want these horrible sacrifices. She never has."

"How would you possibly know that? You aren't even one of us anymore. I am the Mother Superior of the Unity and I am following the instructions given to me by my predecessor. Throughout the long history of the Temple, every summer solstice we have sacrificed a female child to the mountain. The Goddess chose Roseberry and she will live gloriously in the afterlife because of her consecration."

Katkin scowled at her. "You chose Roseberry to punish me, Maitress. Do not blame the Goddess for that evil deed."

"Perhaps that is true, but I still have to sacrifice a child. It is my one important function as Maitress. You cannot take it away from me," she insisted. The Maitress stepped forward and Katkin quickly backed further away.

"Sacrificing a child is an abomination. No wonder you have lost your Gift, old woman. The Goddess grieves for the blood of these lost little ones. The sacrifices stop now. There will be no more." Turning away from the Maitress, Katkin clutched Roseberry to her chest and began to walk quickly back up the tunnel, the incredible heat of the mud pool at her back. With a strength borne of a frenzied rage, the Maitress ran after her and tried to wrest Roseberry from her. Katkin, already weakened by her head wound, felt her grip on Roseberry slipping. The child, caught in this gruesome tug of war, screamed and screamed.

Memory supplied Katkin with a defense, just when she thought the fight for Roseberry's life would be lost. She cast her mind back to the big barn at Tintaren, and twelve-year-old Jacq stood beside her. He had been teaching her fighting moves all morning. As they rested, out of breath, filthy and sweating in the dusty heat of the upper hayloft, Jacq said, "If someone has something you want, Kat, just twist their wrist like so, and their hand must open." Laughing, he demonstrated the effectiveness of this move to her and she howled in pain as he ground the bones of her wrist together in his big hand. "Now, you try, Kat," he said, patting her sympathetically, after she had wiped the tears from her eyes. She did try and found she could successfully perform this trick on him as well.

With one hand Katkin grabbed the Maitress' arm and viciously twisted the wrist, snapping the old woman's brittle arm bones in a last ditch effort to make her let go of Roseberry. Their struggle had taken them almost back to the edge of the precipice again and the sulphurous stench from the bubbling mud made Katkin want to vomit. Crazed with pain now, the Maitress lunged at her as Katkin kicked out with her foot, catching the old women square in the gut and causing her to stagger backwards. Katkin, fearing she would fall, made a desperate grab for her habit. She managed to catch hold of the heavy gold and silver moonstone necklace the Maitress wore as a symbol of her office and hung on for dear life, providing a counterbalance to the old woman's weight. The Maitress' eyes were pleading as Katkin tried with all her strength to haul her back. But the links on the soft gold chain broke, and with a scream of terror she plummeted backwards into the mud. Katkin stood at the edge, holding only the necklace in her shaking hand. The mud began to gurgle and hiss violently, effervescing up the side of the trench.

She turned away and fled as the mud rose higher and higher, overspilling the pool, and wished she could close her ears to the horror of the old woman's agonized screams as the boiling mud burned the flesh from her bones. The sound followed her back up the tunnel, going on for far longer than she would have thought possible.

Katkin shuddered, thinking of the Maitress' fifty year reign as head of the Unity of Lalluna—that she had thrown fifty baby girls into that pit of hell, and walked away listening to those same nightmarish screams.

Roseberry still sobbed, her little arms clasped tight around Katkin's neck, and Katkin cradled her closely, cooing and whispering little comforts to the child.

As she made her way back up the path she suddenly realized the winged form of Lalluna now traveled silently beside her. The Goddess said gratefully, "My vessel, you have not failed me. You and I are forever joined, due to your courage and obedience."

Katkin, unsure if she could converse with the Goddess directly, decided to try in that most holy of Temples, saying, "I could not have done it without your aid, Lalluna. But please forgive my ignorance and presumption, my Lady. Tell me, why did you never try to stop these monstrous sacrifices before now? They must have been going on for hundreds of years."

The Goddess' voice sounded sad. "I have not the form to intervene in human affairs directly. I must depend on my servants to do my bidding. I have sent such a dream as yours to the sleeping thoughts of one Juvenie of each generation since the inception of the Unity. No one interpreted it correctly or bravely acted on my wishes until now. I am forever in your debt, my vessel."

"You have helped me many times, as I healed the people of Belladore through you. I am very glad I could repay you in this way. Being your vessel has given me great joy. Now I must hurry, Lalluna. Jacq may be fighting for his life outside and I must help him however I can." She hugged Roseberry closer and broke into a run.

Outside the Temple, Jacq looked up from his sword cleaning and saw a company of Guardsmen, led by a single horseman, proceeding through the Infirmarie gates, far below them. His lofty perch on the mountainside gave him a clear view of their progress. They still had some distance to cover, but they moved rapidly up the path.

Jacq stood abruptly and said to Yannick, "Mount Turk, and be ready to leave as soon Katkin comes with Roseberry. Take your daughter and ride hard up the mountain. Katkin can follow you on Nestor. Try to find a way across country to the shore and steal a boat if you have to. Just get across the Mere somehow. Take Willow, Roseberry, and my wife and go west as soon as you can. If Kat objects, bind her and take her anyway." Shading his eyes with his hand, he looked down on the columns of marching men approaching and said grimly, "I will stay here and hold them as long as I am able."

"If she comes with the child, I will do as you say. Otherwise, you and I will fight to the death together, Dinrhydan. I will not leave your side unless it is to save my daughter," said Yannick earnestly.

At that moment, Katkin, carrying Roseberry safely in her arms, emerged at a dead run from the opening in the rock face. Yannick gave a plaintive cry of relief. Seeing him already up on Turk, she passed Roseberry up to her father, saying breathlessly, "Take her and ride straight up the mountainside. There is a path and a secret gate near the summit. Hurry, I see the Guardsmen coming!"

Jacq barked an order to Katkin. "Get up on Nestor, girl, and ride with Yannick away from here. Now!"

She said insistently, "No, Jacq. I will not run away! It was my foolishness that put you in this perilous place and I will not leave you here to die alone." Then, to Roseberry's father she said, "Ride, Yannick, you must save your daughter."

Yannick knew he did not have time to argue with the witch and still get Roseberry to safety. He had to choose. Yannick gave Jacq an anguished look and then spurred the chestnut mare up the mountain path, keeping under the cover of the trees—riding hard and not looking back.

The soldiers would be on them in another minute. Katkin went to stand by Jacq, and put her arms about him and said, "I am so sorry. This is all my fault."

Jacq shook his head. "Nay, Kat. Do not blame yourself for this. I knew the risks long ago when I first stepped on the path that led me here." His mouth found hers and he kissed her roughly, clutching her to him, one hand entwined in her hair, the other still gripping the hilt of his sword.

"Well, well! This is most touching, I must say." The strident voice of Tomas de Vigny rang through the afternoon air. He laughed delightedly, from his lofty perch on the black horse, Pollux. "Benet and his lovely wife, Katrione. I did not expect such a magnificent catch when the Daminem sent a message to say they had trouble at the Temple. Goodness me, to think I actually complained about my lunch being interrupted." Then, all business, he began shouting orders to his men. "Place this man under arrest. I want him shackled—both arms and legs. Don't even think of fighting back, Benet, unless you'd like to witness your pretty wife's death before your own."

Jacq released Katkin and placed his sword carefully down on the ground in front of him. He knelt down, laced his fingers, then raised his arms and placed his hands on the back of his neck, waiting silently with his head down.

"Oh, Jacq, my love," said Katkin, and could think of nothing else to comfort him. She sobbed quietly as the soldiers surrounded him and pulled him roughly to his feet, clapping his arms and legs in heavy irons and chains.

He stood defiantly, staring up at Captain de Vigny. "With what am I charged? I have done nothing."

Tomas made a little gesture with his hand and the soldiers under his command struck and kicked Jacq again and again, until he staggered and fell to his knees. A final blow across the back of the head with a musket butt sent him face down on to the ground.

Katkin, prevented from coming to his defense by a soldier who cruelly pinned her arms behind her back, screamed, "Leave him alone! He cannot fight back, you filthy cowards."

When his prisoner lay helpless and moaning in pain, the Captain moved forward, his horse's feet picking delicately over the rough ground. He rode to the fallen Damenie's body and dismounted. "The charge, Benet?" he said crisply. "The charge is murder, for now anyway. Later, after we have had a chance to chat, I am sure we can come up with a few other items as well."

Picking up Jacq's sword, d'angwir, he said casually, "Look at this, fellows, such a very fine weapon for a lowly blacksmith, wouldn't you say?" He held it up and admired the delicately damascened blade, gleaming brightly in the sunlight. Tomas handed it carefully to one of his men. "Clean it up, and make sure to leave it in my office, with the belt and scabbard."

Seeing the other Damenie lying near the rock wall, still bound and gagged with her own habit, Tomas cut her bonds with his own sword. The Damenie stood, rubbing her wrists to get the circulation back in her hands, and spat to Katkin, "Apostate, where is the Maitress? What have you done with her?"

"She is dead, Damenie," Katkin said tonelessly. "I tried to save her, but she fell into the pit." Walking slowly over to the Damenie, she placed the Maitress' broken necklace in the other's outstretched hand.

The Damenie, clutching the token of office to her breast, screamed in her face, "Murderer! You shall pay dearly for this trespass of the sacred Solstice observance. The Goddess herself will flay the flesh from your bones." From his position on the ground, Jacq groaned Katkin's name and weakly struggled to rise. The soldier standing guard over him placed a booted foot roughly on his bloody face and forced him back down.

"What about the girl, Sir? Shall we detain her as well? This Damenie has accused her of murder." A soldier moved towards Katkin.

Tomas spoke sharply. "Leave her, Corporal. I am hardly concerned with the accidental death of an old woman. Let the Unity deal with it as they may. Katrione has committed no crime I can see, other than being a lying whore. Seeing Benet's public execution next week should be a just punishment for that transgression. Escort her off the mountain with the horses and leave her to go where she will."

Turning to Katkin, he gave her a supremely polite smirk and bowed low. "Goodbye, my dear Katrione. It has been a great pleasure to see you again. Be assured we will take excellent care of your loving husband at the Citadel. I look forward to having some long and undoubtedly entertaining conversations with him, especially about that very special sword." Tomas sauntered away, and gave the order for his detachment to move out.

Katkin gave no reply other than an anguished cry. What could she say to change the awful reality before her? The Captain would take her husband back to the Citadel to be cruelly tortured and then executed. She watched in abject misery as his captors hauled Jacq roughly to his feet and dragged him away by his chains.

15

Irlimyrit, the frozen wasteland

(The Tollyn, Ten)

Must we? *Raven's black eyes are pleading.*
He is strong. Remember we use them for their good as well as ours.
But what if he does not survive?
Geya shrugs. There are many more of them.
Raven replies very quietly. I do not think so, Geya. Not like him.

~~~~~~~~~~~

Maggie Fenty watched over Jacq's wife, Katrione, as she slept in the double bed in the upstairs room at the Compass Rose. The doctor had been and gone—he had stitched the nasty cut in the girl's forehead and administered a sleeping draught to calm her hysterical crying. Now she slept fitfully, still hiccupping sobs, as if her sorrow remained wide-awake somewhere deep inside her.

It was morning when Katkin arrived at the inn. She simply hadn't been able to think of anywhere else to go in the City. Remembering the kindness of the barkeep the day Jacq had proposed, Katkin decided to see if Maggie would let her stay at the tavern so she could be close to the Citadel and her incarcerated husband. When she arrived, riding the nearly exhausted Brinna, Katkin gave the pony over to the groom to take to the big stable behind the tavern, ignoring his look of alarm as he took in her swollen, gashed forehead and wild hair, stiff with dried blood.

When she staggered into the empty tavern, Maggie had taken one wide-eyed look at her and said, "Upstairs with you and quickly. Whatever trouble you are in, it will be better if it is hidden away where others cannot see."

Katkin trod the stairs to the upper floor slowly—reluctant to revisit the first place she and Jacq had declared their love for each other. It seemed a million years and another lifetime ago.

Maggie came up the stairs right behind her, bearing a mug of strong coffee. Pressing the steaming drink into the girl's trembling hand, she sat with her on the bed and said, "Tell me."

So Katkin told her the whole sad tale, leaving out nothing, from the moment when her relationship with Jacq had begun to go horrifyingly wrong—the day she healed Roseberry. Maggie said very little, only asking a question now and again.

"Did the little bairn get safely away from the Temple?" she wanted to know.

Katkin sighed heavily. "I think she did. Still, I do not know for sure. Tomas had his men escort me away from the Temple. I thought he would want to keep Nestor, but he only seemed interested in Jacq. He told me to take both the horses and go. After the soldiers left me in front of the Infirmarie, I did not know what to do. I knew Jacq was in mortal danger but I could do nothing to help him. I thought perhaps he would want me to go to Willow and Yannick and help them instead. He always thought of others before himself." Her voice broke miserably and Maggie had to pat her back encouragingly to get her to continue.

"I took the Yoke, no reason not to, now I had lost Jacq, and went back to Belladore. I rode on Nestor, and led Brinna by her halter. When I reached my sister's cottage I could tell at once something was wrong. Willow always kept it so neat and tidy. Now the shutters were swinging open in the breeze. I looked inside and saw most of the furniture was missing. The house was practically empty."

Maggie murmured sympathetically, "Poor girl. That must have been a terrible shock for you."

Katkin nodded. "I could not imagine where they had gone to, so suddenly. I decided to find Willow's friend, the Postmistress, who knows all the gossip in the town. If anyone knew where they went, it would be she. 'Oh, Mrs. Benet,' she said, 'Yannick came flying through town on that big chestnut mare of his, as if the Devil himself snapped at his heels. Even stranger, he had Roseberry up on the horse with him and the poor thing just screamed and screamed. I ran out to see what troubled the child and heard him shouting for your sister to pack her things. Well, Willow was so happy to see that baby again, she just about cried. But Yannick looked in a fearful hurry and wouldn't let her stop to hold Roseberry for long. They piled everything into that big high sided wagon belonging to the mill and Yannick hitched up Turk to the traces and they were gone.'

"I asked her where they went and she shrugged. 'I don't rightly know, Mrs. Benet. They left on the road to LeClaire, though.' I could find out nothing else. My sister has gone, Maggie, and I know not where. I am all alone." She began to cry again, and the bitter loneliness of it broke Maggie's heart.

"Not alone, Katkin, not while old Maggie's here. I will do what I can to help you, and of course you may stay here as long as you have need." Maggie thought Katkin's tale must be almost done, yet far more sorrow remained to be told.

"By this time I felt nearly dead tired and my head throbbed like fire. I could think of nothing else to do except go home and try to sleep a little before coming back to the City in the morning. So I rode Nestor all the way, because Brinna looked nearly done in too, after that furious run to the ferry and trying to keep up with the big horses. When I crested the hill, I could not believe what I saw. Our beautiful house, that Jacq had worked so hard to build for us, had been burned down. Only the foundations and chimney remain standing. The Guardsmen must have paid us a visit after they arrested Jacq. They tore apart the inside of the house, looking for evidence against him, I guess. I could tell every single beautiful thing Jacq had made with his own hands had been wantonly destroyed—even things that could not possibly have hidden anything they wanted. They even smashed my vielle, Maggie, and they burned what was left. "So now I have nothing except memories to remind me of him."

Her voice took on a lifeless tone and the barkeep could tell that this unexpected blow—the loss of the house and the things Jacq had made—had been just too much to cope with.

"Why not rest awhile, my lamb? You don't have to tell me any more now if you don't want to." Maggie looked at the girl with motherly concern. She looked close to utter collapse.

Katkin shook her head. "I can't sleep. I just lie there and wonder what horrible things they are doing to him at the Citadel. It is unbearable. I would rather just talk to you a little while longer." Katkin's once sparkling green eyes, now clouded with unhappiness and fear, met Maggie's imploringly, and the barkeep nodded her head.

"Go on talking then, if it helps you, love."

"I jumped back on Nestor and just started to ride back up the hill. Brinna followed us. I could not think straight any more. I was almost mad with grief. I heard a horseman coming towards me and I panicked. It just seemed to me then that I had not a friend left in the world. So I turned Nestor's head, gave him a kick, and took off in the other direction as fast as I could. But the rider was Jacq's brother Nathan and he caught me before I could get very far.

"He said, 'Why do you flee from me, my sister? I am overjoyed to see you at least are safe. Mother has been worried sick. Will you not come back with me to her house now? It seems to me you need some attention for that cut on your head, and a place to stay until we can get you away from here.'

"Nothing he said to me made any sense. Why did he need to take me away? But I allowed him to turn Nestor and Brinna once again and lead me to Elisabeth Benet's house. On the way, he told me they already knew of Jacq's arrest and imprisonment, though I don't know how. Nathan was kind enough but I could tell, like me, he was out of his mind with worry for Jacq.

"Jacq's mother met us at the door and immediately took me inside and held me while I sobbed out the whole story. Of course, she felt horribly afraid for Jacq, although she did her best to hide it. She said, 'Katkin, it is not safe for you to stay here any longer. You must let Nathan take you away from here. It is what Jacq wanted—he made us swear to it on your wedding day. He loves you, and wants you safely out of this. Do you understand?'

"I shook my head. 'No, my mother, I do not. The Captain who arrested Jacq told me I could go where I pleased. I am not in danger. He is the one they wanted.' I asked her, 'Why do they hate him so much? What has Jacq done, that the Guard should arrest him and burn down his house?' Elisabeth looked at Nathan, and shook her head as he seemed about to tell me something. I felt so upset I screamed at the two of them, 'Why will no one tell me anything? Do I not deserve to know the truth of what my husband is before he dies some horrible death?'

"Elisabeth said, 'It would not be right for us to tell you things Jacq himself would not. Not while he lives anyway. Please understand, my daughter, we do not mean to hurt you.'

"But I did feel hurt, and I said so. All this has happened because of Jacq's misguided notion he must protect me from the truth of whatever he really is. He put me on a pedestal and told me not to ask questions. He even had a mysterious nickname I was supposed to know nothing about."

Maggie asked curiously, "Mysterious nickname? What do you mean?"

"My sister's husband Yannick called him Dinrhydan, Maggie. I don't know why and no one will tell me." She sighed deeply and said, "Sometimes, I feel as though I never really knew the man I married at all."

Maggie managed to hide her look of surprise before Katkin could see it. She had heard many tales of the heroic and daring exploits of the Dinrhydan—the men from the Garrison complained about him constantly as they drank and smoked in the tavern. Though it pained her to think that she, too, withheld information from the distraught girl, she decided to say nothing to Katkin about it. If Jacq truly was that man, and the Guard had captured him, Maggie did not think much of his chances. The King's Guard had been looking for the Dinrhydan for many years and he had a high price on his head.

"Tell me what happened next at Mrs. Benet's house, love," said Maggie, in an effort to distract Katkin from the nickname.

Katkin said, "I guess Jacq's mother knew how upset I felt because she told me to go and lie down in the bedroom. After I had left the room, I listened behind the door. She said to Nathan, 'I will make the girl a posset to send her into a deep sleep. We will wrap her up well and you can head west with her in the cart as soon as it gets fully dark. By the time she wakes, she will be with Willow. I hope someday she will forgive us, Nathan, but we have no choice except to follow Jacq's wishes in this matter.' I felt so betrayed. My husband's own mother wanted to kidnap me! I know what 'going west' means. Not stopping until we were in territory controlled by Reynard. I hate that man! He murdered my parents. So, I decided I wouldn't let Jacq's family treat me like a child any longer."

"What did you do? It sounds like they had their minds made up pretty well."

Maggie stood up and went to poke at the fire, which produced a shower of sparks. Katkin suddenly shivered, and said nothing for a few moments. When Maggie looked up, the girl's eyes looked very far away and she sat on the bed with her hands laced tightly together. Katkin was trying very hard to hold her grief in check now, Maggie could see that, but the effort seemed to exhaust her and she wondered how long she would be able to maintain it.

Shaking her head, Katkin forced herself back to the present, and her tale. "I lay down on the bed, and when Elisabeth came in with the mug of warmed milk I took a sip and pretended I found it too hot. So she left it for me on the side table and went out again. I opened the window and poured it outside. When she returned a moment later, she wished me good night and took the empty mug away. I knew she expected me to fall into a deep sleep, so in a few minutes I closed my eyes and let my breathing slow. Then, I heard her say to Nathan, 'The girl sleeps, my son. Fetch the cart and take her soon.'

"Nathan said to her, 'Mother, are you sure about this? I begged Jacq to tell Katkin the truth many times. Is it right we now take the girl against her will?'

"Elisabeth said, 'We must do as your brother instructed us to. It may very well be his last request of us, do you not see?'

"Jacq's mother went out with him, to help with hitching up the horse. I waited until they were well away from the house and then I followed the drugged milk out the window. As quietly as I could, I whistled for Brinna. They had unsaddled her, but I jumped on her bare back and rode as hard as I could for the Acre."

"Pet, you don't mean to say you went into the Acre at night?" Maggie asked in surprise. "That was a dangerous route to choose."

"I felt as though nothing worse could happen to me than I had already faced that day. So, I found a thicket and curled up on a drift of dry leaves. I prayed to the Goddess for her protection through the night. I could not sleep, but at least they hadn't made me a prisoner in a cart, and taken me to the west against my will. When the dawn came, I rode back across the Yoke and came here. I have nowhere else to go, and soon Jacq will be dead." With this, Katkin's eyes filled with tears and her lips trembled violently. There would be no damming up of that terrible grief any longer. Maggie held the girl as she sobbed brokenly, her back as thin and delicate as a bird's.

Jacq Benet, tightly bound with leather straps to a wooden chair, sat waiting for Tomas de Vigny to finish his lunch and join them in the interrogation room. By his side, a burly sergeant named Cheval hummed vacantly as he stoked the blazing fire in a little portable brazier. He poked two long iron rods well down into the red coals. Using two, Jacq knew, there was always a glowing red-tipped one ready to apply when they wished to persuade him to answer their questions. It became part of the little game the three of them played—Jacq, de Vigny and Cheval. That is how Jacq tried hard to think about it, at moments like these when he sat in this chair, alone with his thoughts and his terrible fears, waiting for them to begin. Soon, that little cock-a-whoop de Vigny would swagger in, remarking cheerily, "Well, Benet, I am so looking forward to another of our chats! I hope you will see fit to give us a little more information than yesterday. It disappointed me terribly when you passed out after only two hours." The Captain would always begin with this question; "Who are your contacts at the Citadel, Traitor?" Jacq would just press his lips together, saying nothing, and then Cheval would slowly draw one of the smoking red irons from the fire.

After a long while, de Vigny would tire of his stubborn refusal to talk, and then would come the part of the game Jacq liked least of all. "Let me tell you what is going to happen, Mister so-called Dinrhydan. You are going to die, very soon, my friend."

Jacq, his voice hoarse from screaming, would croak out, "I am not your friend, you shit," and de Vigny would slap him hard across the face a few times, thoroughly enjoying the feel of the pulpy, broken flesh under his hand.

"As I was saying, before you so rudely interrupted me, you will be dead. Who will rush to the rescue as I visit your pretty widow then, eh? You know, I think she always did fancy me more than you, Benet. Here is what I will do to her..." Then the Captain would launch into a description so graphically foul Jacq would be forced to close his eyes and concentrate on the only good memories he had left; the picture of her face in his mind, the smell of her hair, the touch of her hands, the way she sighed his name when he made love to her, the curve of her breast under his fingers. When he could ignore the pain no longer, then he would retreat even deeper into himself, and remember what it was like to fly. How his strong gray wings had once carried him between worlds, through the heart of the sun and beyond, to places so still and peaceful, where everything was white and as pure as the heart of a crystalline lattice.

The game ended for a time when he passed out—sometimes sooner, sometimes later. Jacq viewed his chances realistically. He knew he could not survive many more sessions. They had been working on him for five days now, for almost as many hours as he was conscious. He knew his heart would fail from the stress, sooner or later. If Jacq had his wish, it would be sooner. He felt certain of one thing though, they would not make him talk. He would never give away his allies in the Citadel, for to do so would condemn them to the same treatment he now received. On that point, he set his will irrevocably and nothing they did to him would break it. He knew also that as he died, the last thought in his mind would be of Katkin's face on their wedding day as she walked up the aisle in the little stone church on Yannick's arm. Nothing Tomas de Vigny said to him would change that.

Tomas de Vigny returned to his office and poured himself a stiff whiskey. He felt angry and frustrated by his failure to get Benet to crack.

A soft rap brought his head up and he saw Sgt. Cheval standing at the door. He saluted and said, "Begging your pardon, Captain, I need to have a word with you about the spy, Benet."

Tomas snapped, "Well, get on with it, man." Cheval, with his meaty hands and white pasty skin, always made de Vigny feel slightly grubby in his company.

"You want him alive for his execution, ain't that right?"

"Of course, I intend to make an example of him by having him publicly flogged before he is dragged to the gallows." Tomas smiled gleefully at the thought of this final humiliation for Jacq Benet, and then savored the last swallow of whiskey from his glass.

Cheval sighed. "Well, that's the thing, Sir. In my opinion, he isn't going make it through another interrogation alive. I know his type. A real hero. Though it doesn't happen too often, now and again we get a man who can't be broken and if you go on working on them, they just up and die on you. He's close, Sir, very close."

Tomas sighed heavily. "Are you sure about this, Cheval? We need that information!"

Nodding his head, the Sergeant said, "I've got a lot of experience with this job, Captain, and I'm pretty good at what I do. I'm telling you straight, Sir, Benet will die before he will talk."

De Vigny slammed his hand down on his desk and swore in frustration. If they had more time, he knew they could break Benet. But his superiors had given him just one week to extract the information from his prisoner before they publicly executed Jacq on the Citadel Commons in front of the big iron portcullis. The threat of a rescue mission made it too risky to let him languish in prison. Under no circumstances must the Dinrhydan be allowed to escape his punishment. The King, himself, had signed the order for it.

Sighing loudly, the Captain said, "Very well, Cheval. Tell the men to prepare a scaffold for the hanging tomorrow morning. I will not have that bastard Benet wriggle out of his own execution."

When the Sergeant had saluted smartly and left to relay his instructions to the carpenters of the Fourth Company, Tomas leaned back on his chair, feeling distinctly put out. He had been looking forward to another session with Benet in the evening hours. At last, smiling broadly, he thought of another pleasurable diversion to while away his afternoon. Reaching back into the cabinet behind his desk, he found a mostly full flask of brandy and poured himself a generous portion in the dirty glass on his desk. He called through the open door for his aide, saying, "Is Benet's wife still hanging around outside? Bring her to me, at once."

Katkin's days, since she returned to the City, had taken on a wearying sameness. Every morning she woke alone in the double bed on the top floor of the inn. Maggie would bring her breakfast and coffee. She would force herself to eat, but often, after the watchful Maggie had left the room, Katkin would vomit up her meal in the chamber pot.

After dressing herself in the same threadbare shift, Katkin

would walk slowly down to the Citadel and take up her usual position on a bench just inside the great portcullis gate. Occasionally, some uniformed man might walk by who looked important enough to be worth talking to. Katkin would stand and address him animatedly, asking, "When can I see my husband? When is his trial? Will he be allowed legal representation?" Most of the time, these busy men just ignored her. Occasionally, one would stop briefly, moved to pity perhaps, by her desperate expression.

"Sorry, Missus. Benet is not allowed any visitors," they would tell her and hurry away.

She never saw Tomas de Vigny, though if she had, she would have unhesitatingly subjected him to the same barrage of questions. Katkin had firmly decided she must put her anger aside—arguing to herself that such emotions meant nothing now. Helping her husband had become her only concern. If she could not help him then she at least wanted to see him, just for a few minutes, to tell him she loved him once more before he died.

So she sat and waited, marking the endless hours by the chiming of the great bells in the tower. When the gatekeeper made ready to close the portcullis, she would stand and stretch her stiffness away and then walk back, in the long sun of evening, to the Compass. Maggie would again try to get her to eat something, but the greasy tavern food always turned her stomach, and she would manage only a little bread or some soup before staggering upstairs again to get some sleep, so she would be ready for the same fruitless routine tomorrow.

On the fifth day of her vigil, Katkin, occupying her usual position on the bench, received with some surprise the news that someone within the Citadel wanted to see her about Jacq. She hurried after the Private, through the endless corridors, until they stood at last before the door of Tomas de Vigny's office.

He looked up when she knocked and said, "Well, Katrione, how nice to see you. Come in and sit down. I understand you have been making quite a nuisance of yourself outside since last Friday. Perhaps I can assist you with something?" He assumed a jaded expression and waited for her to speak, after taking a surreptitious look at the clock in the hallway. It would be amusing to see how many minutes it took to make her start crying and beg for his help.

210

Katkin did not start crying, nor did she beg. The Captain looked at her pale, thin face with sudden interest. Something had changed in the girl in the last week—that much seemed clear. The green eyes that met his so fearlessly were without extraneous emotion. She spoke crisply, and without rancor. "Thank you for agreeing to see me, Captain. I wish to request a visit with my husband, Jacques Benet. As you know, he is a prisoner here in the Citadel."

Tomas raised an eyebrow at her. This tactic on her part took him completely by surprise and he had to think hard before coming up with a suitably upsetting reply. "Of course I would like to help you, my dear Mrs. Benet. Unfortunately, your husband is being held in solitary confinement pending his date with the gallows tomorrow morning and is allowed no visitors." He sat back smugly, sure his words would demoralize her. He was wrong.

Her calm expression remained unchanged, and she murmured in reply, "Yes, of course, I understand that, Captain. I thought, perhaps, as a personal favor to me, you could make an exception, just this once."

This was too much. Tomas shook his head in amazement. "A personal favor? Why in the God's name would I want to do you a favor, you whore?"

Even this insult did not break that unshakable calm. Her green eyes rose to meet his cold blue ones and she held his stare for many long seconds before she spoke again, her voice soft. "Let me tell you a story. Once, a long while ago, I met a young man in the Acre. He had a terrible injury that would not heal and it made him deeply unhappy." At this, Tomas snorted derisively and she quietly insisted, "Captain, please let me finish. I risked my own life to save the young man from drowning and with the help of Lalluna, I healed his wound, so he could live his life unreservedly and without pain."

Tomas looked at the woman in front of him, suddenly no longer so sure of himself. Her eyes, as they met his, held nothing but warmth and kindness. She continued, "The grateful young man declared his love for me and I am deeply saddened to say, although he wanted me to very much, I could not return his affection."

The Captain shook his head, trying to break the spell her

words cast. He assumed that she wanted to make him pity her, to make him feel he owed her something. Yet the green eyes appeared to be without guile. His heart turned over inside his chest, remembering the day in the Infirmarie when she had thrown the water in his face and run away. All that happened after—the furious need to revenge himself against Benet—began on that winter's day. If only he had mastered his anger, before that blow had sent her to the ground, the story she told now might have had a very different ending.

He spoke, his usually strident tone softened. "Katrione, what do you want from me?"

Now her eyes grew bright with unshed tears, but Tomas had completely forgotten about the clock ticking the minutes away outside. He only stared at her, his thoughts now tortured with lost possibilities.

She said, "I just want to see him again for a few minutes, that is all. I know nothing of what my husband did, to make him such a hated man. Perhaps he even deserves to die. You see, Tomas, he never told me anything. I understand that you are a soldier, and it has been given to you to carry out Jacq's execution. I am not angry, because it is your job to do this, and you must follow your orders. I only ask that you remember what I once meant to you and grant me this request."

Katkin fell silent, and stared at her hands, folded and perfectly still in her lap. Tomas picked up the brandy flask on his desk and poured himself another generous portion, then drank it down without pausing. He found himself saying quietly, "You know I am not an honorable man, Katrione. If I were, I would grant your touching appeal, without question. It is in my nature, though, to want something in return for a favor. Is there some boon you would give me, for such a visit? I could take it from you anyway, soon enough, this thing I have always wanted. But if you give it to me now, freely, I will allow you to see your husband for fifteen minutes."

She looked at him with such burning intensity he felt sure she meant to refuse him, as she had so many times before. But instead she replied, "I would have your word on something, honor or no, before I agree. You must swear to me on the heart of the Goddess you will not tell Jacq of this before he dies. If you break your oath, Lalluna herself will lead me to you and protect me while I take your life. Do you understand?" Such was the spell Katrione cast on Tomas de Vigny on that summer afternoon in the Citadel, he swore the oath she requested, and did not break it. Then she said indifferently, "Very well, Tomas, you may take what you want."

Tomas rose and walked across the office unsteadily. He locked the door and she did not prevent him. Katkin moved towards the leather divan and stood still before it, with her eyes tightly closed. *Jacq, I do this terrible thing for you, so I may see you once more before you die...*

Later, a conversation she had with Maggie came back to her as she sat in the now empty office waiting for Tomas to return and take her to Jacq. Maggie had said, forcefully, "Listen to me, girl, and mark my words well. You may never get to see your man again, and maybe that's for the best." Katkin had protested, asking how that could be true. Of course she must see him if she could.

Maggie continued, "I have been the barkeep at the Compass Rose for thirty years, pet, and during that time I have listened to a lot of stories. Some of them were good. Others were not so very pretty—tales about unfortunate men who were arrested and taken in chains to the Citadel, just like your Jacq. None has ever walked out again. Your man is in there now, and he is fighting every minute. Not to stay alive, my lamb, never that, but to stay strong and sane and not give away information before they kill him." Katkin had given a little cry of horror and Maggie reached out to take her hand, gripping it tightly. "If you do get to see him, he is going to be changed. They will have done terrible things to him, love, things no man should have to endure. If you go in there and break down, because you cannot take seeing what he has become, you give him more misery. And more misery he does not need, not now. Unless you can guarantee his last look at you will give him happiness, you must not go."

Katkin thought long and hard about these words each day while she waited on the bench outside, not knowing whether she would ever be put to the test. Now in Tomas' office she closed her eyes briefly and went inside herself, finding the supportive presence of Lalluna. "My Lady, you must help me to be strong now, for Jacq's sake. Let me make his last day easier somehow. In this I cannot fail him, Lalluna."

The return of Captain de Vigny interrupted her prayer, and

213

he curtly ordered her to accompany him to the visiting room. It took a long time to walk there. They went down several levels, until Katkin thought that surely they must be deep underground. At last they stopped in front of a heavily reinforced wooden door, with a guard standing at each side of the threshold. "Open it, Soldier," Tomas said.

After the door swung open, Katkin stepped resolutely through, though her heart was hammering in her throat. But the room was empty save for two chairs facing each other on opposite sides of a small table. She could see another heavy door on the other side of the room. Tomas told her to sit down, and with a burst of his old jauntiness added, "Don't be too alarmed, Katrione, when you see him again. I am afraid your husband has rather let himself go since he has been lodging here with us." With that he left her, snapping to the Guard on his way out the door, "Fifteen minutes, and if they touch each other, the visit is over."

The door across from her opened and another uniformed guard appeared with a chain in his hand. A man in prison garb slowly shuffled in behind him, and except for his immense height, Katkin wouldn't have recognized her husband at all. He moved slowly and stiffly, as if every step he took was agonizing. Jacq kept his hands carefully behind his back as he lowered himself, with infinite concentration, on to the wooden chair across from her. Still he could not suppress a sharp little cry of pain as his leg brushed ever so gently against the table.

Katkin did not speak, not at first. She forced herself to look at his face. It appeared he had endured many beatings. His lips were split wide open in several places and one eye had swollen completely shut. The other streamed with tears. His nose had been broken and the nostrils were blistered and burned. They had cut his long hair and shaved his beard, and under the edges of his prison issue cap she could see the evidence of many more wounds on the naked scalp. That there were far worse injuries hidden by his clothes she had not the shadow of a doubt.

"Oh, my husband, I am so sorry," she whispered.

He looked at her with his one good eye, and that look was still as grave and steady as it had always been. "It does not matter, my wife. I have not told them the things they wished to know," he said quietly.

They sat at the table a minute without speaking. Katkin found it to be the most difficult ordeal she had ever faced, not to scream and run away from the nightmare apparition in front of her that had once been her husband, Jacq Benet. Somehow, she passed the test. Swallowing hard, she said, "I am very glad the Captain allowed me to see you, Jacq. I wanted to talk to you once more before..."

Jacq supplied the word she was reluctant to say. "Before I die, my love."

"Yes," she said simply, "before you die. I know you crave it, and I do not blame you, not now I have seen. Yet I will not give up hope, until I have nothing left to hope for."

Looking at her across the table, he drank in her beauty, as a man who has been lost in a desert and is mortally thirsty. The pain that tormented him every waking minute eased just a little. He whispered, "I am very glad to see you as well, my dearest, even though we have but a little time together. There are many truths I would tell you now, if I could, things I should have told you long ago. But mostly I just want to say I am sorry. Sorry you have to see me like this, and sorry I deceived you for so long. Can you ever forgive me?"

Katkin found this apology almost too much to bear. Only by digging her fingernails deeply into the palms of her trembling hands, hidden beneath the table, could she quell the tears threatening to spill over. "Do not speak of it, Jacq. What need have we now for remorse? I wish to remember our wedding day instead, and the first afternoon we spent in the mill together. Do you recall, my husband, how Brinna almost came into the church with us?"

He could not smile at her—his lips would not work properly any more, but he nodded his head in encouragement as she softly spoke of the events of their first happy day together. Her gentle words were a salve for his desperately wounded heart—an antidote to the interminable horrors of the last five days. He felt immensely grateful and told her so, as the guard said gruffly, "Let's go, Benet, your time is up."

Grabbing him roughly, the guard forced Jacq to his feet. In his haste, he almost caused the weakened prisoner to fall, and Jacq's hands came up instinctively to balance himself. Katkin's

215

eyes grew wide with shock and dismay. Every finger on his right hand was broken and twisted, their ends black and swollen where Cheval had used iron pincers to rip the nails off. The nails were missing from the left hand too, though the fingers were as yet undamaged. The Captain had been saving that particular piece of cruel entertainment for the next interrogation.

In that split second, Katkin fought inside herself the most heroic of battles—as heroic as any her husband ever fought against his enemies with his bright sword. She emerged victorious, though it cost her dearly. With tear-free eyes, she looked up at him and said, "Farewell, Jacq. My love for you will never fail. And I will hope on, until death takes you, and then I will pray the Goddess gives you peace and freedom from your pain."

Jacq said, "Seeing you this day has made everything all right, my beautiful girl. Now I will go to my death tomorrow with joy in my heart. Farewell, Katkin, I love you always, to the end of the Yrth." He bowed his head as the guard dragged him away through the door, which slammed shut behind them.

Katkin looked at the closed door until tears blurred her vision. They had taken Jacq away and now she had nothing except her memories. She tried hard to picture his expression as it had been on their wedding day and found, to her boundless dismay, she could not. The image of his gravely injured face was the only one that remained etched in her mind.

16

Loyalty

(Estate of Naer, Nine Standing)

Are you ready? It is time. Fly now, Raven, and take your place on Yrth.
You will become our enemy, and the enemy of all Yr.

Raven sighs. Why? You would have me become feral, Geya? Eat the
rotting corpses of men?

Geya nods. It is necessary this turn of the Gyre, my sister. By bringing
North and South together we force the fulfillment of the Prophecy.

A large crow appears in the mirror, and then spreads her black wings.

~~~~~~~~~~~~~

In a heavily fortified camp thirty miles west of the City, Nicholas
Reynard stood on a wooden platform, surveying the five hundred
uniformed men sitting before him on the grassy parade field. He
addressed them, saying, "Soldiers of the Rising, as you are all no
doubt aware, one of our own has been captured and even now
is imprisoned in the Citadel. It is the Dinrhydan, my comrades.
They torture him hourly, yet he has told his tormentors nothing—so say our contacts inside. Listen closely, my brothers. We
plan a rescue mission. But I must warn all of you now that such
a dangerous and untried effort will most probably fail and end
in the deaths of all who participate. Yet I believe we must do our
best to save the one man who has risked his own life time and
again for all of us and the Rising."

Reynard took a sip from a glass of water on the table at his
side. He continued, "I received a dispatch a few moments ago
indicating that two companies will depart the Citadel tonight
for Hislop. We allowed the Guard to intercept false intelligence
saying we plan to attack there tomorrow. That will leave the Citadel a little more vulnerable to assault, though not by much. It
is still heavily manned and the Dinrhydan will undoubtedly be

well-guarded." He paused and stared directly at his men, making eye contact with as many as he could and wondering who might volunteer to participate in what would most likely turn out to be a suicide mission. He hoped for at least twenty-five men.

"If you are willing, stand at attention now," he ordered, and watched and waited for the result. Within a few seconds, every man on the field stood up and cheered—the sound soon building into a fearsome war cry. Reynard stood at attention, his face grave before his men, and then walked among them to handpick the volunteers. Afterwards, he called for his equerry to ready his mount and then rode out alone.

Elisabeth Benet looked up at the sound of hoof beats and saw him racing towards her, across the fields of wheat. The green heads nodded and parted like a verdant wave. He rode Rufus, a red-brown gelding that rivaled Nestor in size and girth. This hurried journey from the west pressed the horse to its limits. At the horse's side ran an immense brindle wolfhound, tongue lolling. Elisabeth stood, straightening her tired back, stiff from hilling potatoes, and threw down the shovel.

It had been years since Kolya had come to her in the daylight hours. He visited in the darkness—a shadow that came and went through her unlocked window like a night breeze. Surely, this unexpected visit must have something to do with Jacq. She suddenly felt very afraid for her eldest son.

He reined Rufus to a halt and jumped down, obviously in a great hurry—still he patted the horse's blond mane affectionately before turning to Elisabeth. The dog, seemingly inexhaustible, bounded about the yard, scattering the hens that scratched there.

"Come inside, Kolya," she said urgently. He wore no distinguishing insignia of rank on his plain gray uniform but Elizabeth well knew the dangers this daytime visit presented to the leader of the Rising. "There are many unblinking eyes watching my farm." He nodded curtly and followed her through the open door into the house.

"Thad has taken Kadya hunting. They will not be back for some time," she said to him, and turned to the kitchen bench. Filling a pottery bowl, she placed it on the floor for the dog, who which drank it all, slopping water onto the dirt floor with every gulp.

He said, "Down, Fiann," and the dog obligingly sank onto his haunches and put his head on his paws. Her hands shaking, Elisabeth filled the cast iron kettle and hung it on a hook over the open fire. Nicholas sat at the kitchen table, saying nothing, patiently waiting for her to finish fussing with the tea and sit down before him. When she did so at last, he reached across the table and placed his hand over hers. Her eyes looked sad, though she did not cry. Elisabeth had never shed a tear in front of him, in all the years he had known her. He marveled at her tireless strength and the beauty of her lined face, aged by sorrow and the constant assault of the sun and the wind as she worked in the fields.

"Is it Jacq?" she asked fearfully.

"No, Elisabeth, he still lives, though we know not how well he fares. They will have done their best to break him by now, yet the Dinrhydan has told them nothing. My sources say his execution has been scheduled for tomorrow morning."

Mrs. Benet shook her head sadly. "I know I should rejoice for his sake, for he will be at peace. But there will be such a space left in my heart when death takes him, and nothing will ever be able to fill it."

Nicholas said quietly, "We plan a rescue, tonight, after midnight. Thirty hand-picked volunteers only, though every man in the camp would have gone if given the chance."

Elisabeth stared at him in shock. "Attack the Citadel? Kolya, this is madness! No one has ever succeeded in such an adventure. Will the deaths of another thirty men make Jacq's passing any easier? Who will lead this folly?"

Sure of her reaction, he sighed. "I go myself."

She cried, "Kolya, no! Would you have me lose two people I love in one night? Let them go with another in command, I beg of you."

His hazel eyes gazed steadily at her. "I would not ask any man to attempt something I would not do myself, beloved. Yes, there will be little chance we will succeed, but we have to try. It burns my heart those animals have had five days already to keep him in torment. If nothing else, I will have my revenge on that butcher Cheval. He will not live to see the morning."

"What does this revenge gain us if you do not see the morning either? Or Jacq?"

He spoke quietly. "Jacq is to be publicly flogged with the cat-o'-nine-tails before he is hung from the gallows. One hundred lashes."

Her faded blue eyes, the color of forget-me-nots, widened in horror.

"So you see, my dearest, we must go to the Dinrhydan, and if there is no rescue possible I will make sure his death is a peaceful one. Do you understand why I have to do this?"

She nodded wearily. "You will tell him I love him? Swear to me you will, before the end comes."

"Of course, but he knows it already."

"What of his wife, Katkin? Have your men been able to find her in the City? I would have followed Jacq's wishes and taken her out of it, but the headstrong girl ran away from Nathan and me. He searched all night for her without success."

Nicholas ran his hand through his silver hair, cut close to the scalp. "She has been keeping a vigil at the Citadel all week. Incredibly enough, she somehow persuaded that excrement de Vigny to let her see Jacq this afternoon for fifteen minutes. It must have done Jacq much good to have such a visit, though I suspect it was very hard on her. She left the Citadel at a dead run, and vomited in the street outside. So say my observers."

Elisabeth said in wonder, "That girl never fails to surprise me. I sense a powerful inner strength in her, borne of her devotion to Lalluna, I think. She has grown much in the few months they have been married. Jacq is blind to this, and in his utter devotion to her, meant to keep her forever in the dark about his under-cover activities. He told me again and again he only wanted to keep her safe. Secretly, though, I think he feared she wouldn't be able to cope with the truth. She and Jacq stand on either side of a terrible divide, my Kolya, because of what happened at Tintaren all those years ago."

Nicholas sighed in exasperation. "I begged Jacq to tell her what actually happened that night, and he flatly refused. He told me, 'I have already nearly destroyed her happy memories of her father with my scarred back. I would not have her hurt any more.'" He shook his head, smiling wryly. "The Dinrhydan was only ever irrational about one thing—that girl, Katrione. For her he would face any danger, even were it to go into the very jaws of hell."

Elisabeth smiled as well, fondly recalling the day when her ten-year-old son had come to tell her earnestly he had just met the girl he intended to marry someday. "His love for her is irrevocable, Kolya, and has been since the day they first met. I have no doubt it is her name that will be on his lips when he dies." She looked at him in concern. "Do you think Katkin will be in danger if your mission is successful? Should I send her a message?"

"If it is a success—yes, she may very well be. The King would stop at nothing to have the Dinrhydan back, even if it meant harming his wife, I fear. But it seems she has some divine protection, because de Vigny has left her untroubled this week, though I know not why. I believe the Guard is watching her movements and we cannot afford to tip our hand by warning her in advance. Once the mission is underway I will send a man to fetch her." He sighed again and stood, preparing to take his leave of Elisabeth.

She said softly, "I thank you from the bottom of my heart for this visit, dearest. But you did not have to come all this way to tell me of your plans. A message would have sufficed, for you must have much to do to prepare for this night."

Nicholas went to stand close beside her. "I came myself because I wanted to hold you once more, my love. To do so has always given my life a sweetness it would otherwise be sorely lacking. I have been a soldier all my days and seen much that is ugly and profane. Without you, I would be a bitter man, for I have lost many comrades. But at this moment, I know not whether I will see you again in this world and that is a bleak thought. Farewell, Elisabeth." He stepped forward and pulled her briefly to him in the quiet kitchen, and touched his lips to her graying hair, always so neatly brushed up into a bun on the top of her head.

"Farewell, dearest Kolya, my heart travels at your side this night," she said in return, her voice strong and untroubled. Only after she heard Rufus' loud hoof beats and Fiann's joyous barks fade away into the afternoon heat, did she put her head into her folded arms to cry quietly for her loss. No one ever saw her do this.

Maggie looked up in surprise when she saw Katkin walk through the door of the Compass Rose in the early afternoon. Usually the girl did not leave her vigil at the Citadel until they closed the portcullis at six o'clock. She kept her head down, and did not speak as she stumbled across the ground floor of the tavern on her way to the stairs. Maggie knew then that someone at the Citadel must have granted Katkin's wish to see her incarcerated husband. Drying her rough hands hastily on a dishcloth, she hurried up the stairs to the girl's room and found her lying listlessly upon the double bed. When Maggie sat down beside her, Katkin said nothing, only continued to stare up at the ceiling, her eyes dry and expressionless. Alarmed, Maggie said, "What has happened, pet? You must talk to old Maggie."

Katkin answered her in a lifeless voice, without inflection. "I saw him and I did as you said I should. He never knew how much it hurt me to look upon his face."

Maggie sighed and took her hand, squeezing it hard. "That must have been a powerful trial for you, love. You can be proud of yourself."

But Katkin did not feel proud—not at all. She found comfort only in the thought that her husband would soon be dead, and thus spared the terrible knowledge she had given herself to his hated rival, Tomas de Vigny.

"I have always been blessed with a desire to help others. With Lalluna's Gift, I have been able to heal many people, and make the world a happier place for them. I thought of myself as a good person because of it, yet I have learned differently today. The world is nothing but a tale of horrors, and I am first among them. I hate myself for what I have done."

Maggie stared at her in confusion, wondering what on earth had happened to bring her to this unhappy realization. "Don't take on so, dearie, it can't be that bad."

Katkin sighed deeply. "I just don't know anymore. I never dreamed human beings could treat each other the way they have treated Jacq. Perhaps I have been a fool, or just naïve. I always believed virtue and love would overcome everything. How wrong I have been. My soul has been torn apart by what I have done and seen on this day. I cannot heal myself."

"Come on, pet. You are just in shock about what's happened, that's all. Tomorrow, you will feel differently." Maggie squeezed her hand again encouragingly.

"Tomorrow he dies," Katkin said dully. She wished death

would come for Jacq right now. Anything to spare him the pain of another round of questioning. Katkin would have joyfully lain down at his side and let death take her as well, given the chance. She sighed. "Please leave me, Maggie, I just want to be by myself for a little while."

Shaking her head sadly, Maggie shut the door and left Katkin alone with her terrible hopelessness.

Jacq Benet moved restlessly on the straw-strewn floor of his dank and filthy cell, trying to find a position that caused him the least amount of pain. He was both surprised and gratified that De Vigny and Cheval had paid him no further visits. It seemed they were going to allow him to spend his last night on Yrth in relative peace. The thought of his imminent death did not trouble him overmuch. Seeing Katkin today had given him a desperately needed infusion of strength and serenity. He only regretted he had to leave her, so young, and so alone. But he knew his mother and all his brothers would make sure she would be all right— he had sworn them to that on his wedding day, before she had walked down the aisle of the church on Yannick's arm and struck him dumb with her beauty. It never occurred to Jacq to think she might be able to take care of herself, even though he had just witnessed first-hand her courage in the face of his terrible injuries.

He rolled over to face the wall, and used the edge of his shackle to scratch some wobbly words into the stone. Jacq had been working on this message diligently over the last five days, when he was able. Now, as he scratched the final letters of his name, he thought with satisfaction that he would leave behind the last word in the contest between he and De Vigny.

He listened wearily to the chiming of the great bells outside, only a faint sound by the time it penetrated the thick walls of the Citadel. Midnight. Almost time for the changing of the guard.

Suddenly an explosion shook the cell to its foundations. Jacq scrambled to his feet as quickly as he could, despite the pain, as clouds of dust and a hail of small stones rained down from the ceiling. Shouts rang down the corridor outside, and then Jacq heard the metallic clash of swords. As many booted feet hurried past his door, Jacq cried out, "What is happening?" No one paused long enough to answer his question. Knowing that the

Rising would never be so foolish as to storm the Citadel, Jacq could only think that the Mardonne might be attacking.

An acrid haze of smoke began to seep through the cracks in the stone. Jacq pulled his shirt up to cover his nose and mouth, and threw himself back to the floor, where the cooler, cleaner air lay. Outside, a curious rushing and gurgling had replaced the sounds of fighting,

Water!

Jacq was forced to his feet again as a torrent of freezing water suddenly poured under the door. He doubled over in agony as the smoky air caused a coughing spasm, forcing his cracked ribs to contract.

Just then, he heard the sound of a key being thrust into the lock. Jacq, even in his weakened condition, prepared himself to go down fighting if it came to it. He waded in his shackles across the flooded floor, now over a foot deep in water, and waited breathlessly, his one good hand clenched into a fist.

He shouted, "Come you dogs of Mard, I am not afraid!"

The door flew open and he looked into the startled eyes of his Commander, Nicholas Reynard.

"Dinrhydan, thank the gods, you still live. Can you walk? We haven't much time."

Jacq, almost overcome with shock at this sudden hope, said, "I can try." He staggered forward. Nicholas grasped him by the elbow and helped him out the door. The rising smoke and the screams of the dying gave a nightmarish air to their transit of the flooded hallway. After a few minutes, five more men of the rescue party joined them, bearing torches. Jacq could see their swords were stained dull red.

"How many are left, André?" Nicholas called quietly.

"We lost ten in the first engagement. Maybe three more since then," André replied. "But we must make all haste, Commander. We will not be able to hold the passageway to the breach much longer."

Nicholas sighed and encouraged Jacq's shuffling progress as much as he could.

The water continued to rise until it was waist high and churning wildly. Jacq pushed his way through, leaning heavily on Reynard and another man, trying to get back to the breach that his rescuers had blasted low in the Citadel wall where it dipped directly into Mistmere. Once they managed to get back through the hole in the revetment, a boat waited to take the rescue party to safety—those that remained, anyway. Fourteen men had given their lives so that the Dinrhydan might be freed. But at least Sergeant Cheval would torment no one else—the Commander of the Rising had split him open with his sword and left his body floating face down on the moiling waters.

Finally, they reached the revetment, and Jacq crawled on hands and knees through the breach while the inflowing water tried to wash him back into the Citadel. After this struggle, he felt too exhausted to climb into the waiting vessel. Four men picked him up as gently as they could and hauled him aboard. He tried very hard not to scream as they touched his burns and jostled his broken bones. At last, he lay in the bottom of the boat, soaked and shivering, as his comrades manned the oars above him. They pulled strongly, and headed for the shore of the Mere, as musket fire rang around them. One of the rowers took a ball in the back, and fell, screaming, into the water. He thrashed briefly and then sank, like a stone. Another man, cursing silently, took his place.

Katkin was dreaming. She and Jacq talked together in the room at the top of the inn—the room she now occupied alone. Jacq was telling her something and it seemed terribly important to him that she understood. She did not, and he grew more and more angry with her, saying, "Why do you not listen, Katkin? I am telling you the truth." He grabbed a chair and smashed it over the table. She sat up in bed, trembling violently. The noise continued unabated, and she belatedly realized someone was pounding urgently on the door. Jumping up, she slipped on the garish silk robe Maggie had loaned her and opened it. She let out of little cry of pure dread when she saw the identity of her visitor.

It was Tomas de Vigny.

He pushed through the door before she even had time to think of shutting it again, and fastened his hand firmly over her mouth so she could not scream. In her terror, she thought that surely he meant to kill her and she struggled in his arms.

He hissed at her in a furious whisper, "Stop fighting me, little fool. I have come to help you. Benet's escaped. The Guard is swarming all over the City looking for you. If I move my hand do you promise not to scream?"

Katkin, almost unable to believe what she had just heard, nodded desperately. Tomas took his hand away. She looked at him wide-eyed, and panted, "What is happening? Why are they looking for me?"

He turned to shut the door. "Did you not hear me? I told you, your husband has been freed. The King has issued a warrant for your arrest, so that they might force him to surrender. You have to get out of the City, now. Do you trust me, Katrione? You must, because I am your only chance to escape." His blue eyes met hers with directness and she could see that he was telling the truth. Questions crowded her mind, one after the other, trying to be voiced, and she bit them back and simply nodded to him.

Tomas smiled grimly. "I expect you want to know what is in it for me? Well, nothing. Not this time. Now, put these on and hurry!" He threw a bundle of clothes in her direction—a Guardsman's uniform of navy blue woolen breeches and a black shirt. Tomas had even provided some tall, black boots. Turning away from him, she disrobed and threw the black shirt on over her head. Pulling on the breeches, which were far too long, she stuffed them into the tops of the boots. In less than a minute, she stood dressed before him.

"Katrione, have you scissors? I need to give you a haircut." Tomas gave her a look of frustration when she shook her head.

He pulled a wicked looking pearl-handled dagger from his boot.

"Sorry, I am afraid this might hurt a little," he said, and began grabbing huge hunks of her long hair. He sawed them off about an inch from her scalp with the knife. A few seconds later, her luxuriant tresses lay in a pile around her feet.

"Tomas," she said urgently. "Where are you taking me? I must know."

"Now the cap," he ordered. "Quickly, we must go now. You can ask questions on the way." Bending down, he gathered up almost all the pile of fallen hair, and stuffed it into the fireplace, where it ignited on top of the last red coals. After she turned away from him, he carefully tucked one wavy chestnut lock in the front of his shirt, next to his heart. Katkin only had time to retrieve her leather pouch and stuff it in her pocket before he grabbed her arm and dragged her out the door.

Katkin followed Tomas through the mostly empty streets of St. Valery. He said, "Remember, we are meant to be on patrol, so try to look alert. If anyone stops us, just stay quiet and let me do the talking."

Tomas looked at her appraisingly. With her extreme thinness, she would pass easily for a boy, and with the War dragging on there were plenty of lads in uniform younger than she. Still, it was a hazardous ruse. He did not want to think about what would happen if the Guard caught up with them.

She walked by his side silently, and tried to take in the information he had given her. Jacq had been freed. Now the Guard searched for her instead and though it did not seem possible, Tomas de Vigny had decided to help her escape. The world had suddenly turned inside out.

As they crossed over Avenue de la Citadelle, Katkin said, "I don't understand. Why are you doing this? I thought you despised me."

They stopped in the shadow of the wall, waiting for a large company of uniformed Guard to leave through the portcullis.

"I don't despise you. In fact, I still..." Katkin saw Tomas take a deep breath before continuing. "That is to say, I still owe you a great deal, Katrione. You saved me from drowning on the day we met in the Acre, after I tried to take my own life. When you healed my knee, you gave me a reason to live again. Then you saved my life a second time—upstairs in the room at the Compass Rose." Katkin looked over at him in confusion. He explained, "You stopped Benet from strangling me the morning I came after you. Your husband has killed many other men, Katrione. He would have shown me no mercy, had you not begged him to spare my life." Katkin, who still had trouble thinking of Jacq as a soldier, took in this disturbing piece of information silently. Tomas continued, "So how could I hate you? You have done me no wrong. I have done many contemptible things and yet you feel no hatred towards me, do you?"

Katkin looked at him in surprise, amazed that he could sense her feelings so accurately. "You are right, I do not. But how did you know?"

"I could tell by the way you spoke to me yesterday. You pity me, Katrione. Even though I have treated you abominably, you still care. Why is that?"

Katkin shook her head, not sure in her own mind what the answer was. At last, she said thoughtfully, "I don't understand it myself, but the day we first met, in the Acre, I felt as though I already knew you. Perhaps Lalluna joined us somehow, when she came to us in the Mere. Such an attachment can never really be sundered. Do you see?"

Tomas nodded. "Yes. I felt the same way. So, how could I stand by and watch the Guard take you to the Citadel? They would have tortured you. I could not let that happen." He shook his head and said dryly, "Though I am a damned fool to care."

Katkin stood by him in the darkness, surprised and moved by his words. She said softly, "No, Tomas, never that. This afternoon I was convinced that the whole human race wasn't worth a groat, and myself included. But you have given me hope again and not just because of Jacq." Reaching over, she took his hand in her own and held it for a moment. His skin felt hot and dry. "I know what you risk in helping me, and I give you my thanks, for what it is worth. Had we better move? It looks as though they are getting ready to close the Portcullis."

Tomas led Katkin into the Citadel proper, and they hurried along the darkened pathways, heading for the gate to the Yoke. This, Tomas knew, was the most dangerous part of the whole insane escapade. Obviously the gate would be well guarded, and the Captain knew that if anyone started asking questions, Katkin would soon be caught out.

Together they approached the Citadel gate to the Yoke. They stepped into the brightly lit courtyard and the Captain spoke to the Sergeant in charge of the detachment of soldiers who patrolled the causeway. Katkin kept her head well down and pretended to be studying something of interest on the ground in front of her.

"Sergeant, this boy is replacing the dead man at the gate. Let us through at once," the Captain commanded.

The Sergeant, a grizzled veteran of many years in the Guard, looked at Katkin with interest and asked, "New lad, eh? What's your name, son?"

Tomas' heart quailed, and he thought all was lost, but Katkin replied breezily, her voice pitched suitably low. "Willem Laurier, Sir, from Aix Acre. I've only been here a week."

"Fine, good lad. Pass through, Private. Keep your wits about you down at the Mouth gate. You are escorting him, Captain?" Tomas hid his relief with a curt nod. The genial Sergeant unbarred the big gate and let them through, after passing a large bunch of brass keys over to the Captain. As they stepped on to the Yoke, Katkin could feel her heart pounding, but no one pursued them.

After they had walked in silence for a few moments, Katkin said quietly to Tomas, "I was very sorry to hear about your father's sudden death. Having Simone with you now must be a great comfort."

Tomas' laugh was bitter and brief. "I suppose she might be a comfort, if we were still married. She left me, only two weeks after the wedding. Had the bloody thing annulled—said I was a damned drunkard."

"I am so sorry. It hasn't been easy for you either, has it?"

He shrugged. "Simone is right. I am a drunkard. I started drinking to kill the pain in my knee and now I can't seem to stop."

The sounds of shouting and musket fire drifted across the Mere to them. She asked, "Did he make it, do you think?"

Tomas shook his head in the darkness. "I don't know. The rescue mission used gunpowder to blast into the Citadel wall, and dug through the earthworks to flood the lower levels. Once the water poured in, they fought their way down to his cellblock in all the confusion. He was taken away by boat, and that is the last report I heard." The Captain could not resist one gibe. "I was busy trying to save you, remember?"

Katkin laughed softly, her voice as warm as the summer darkness. "Aye, you were, Tomas. I still don't understand why." As she said this, they drew up to the locked gate at the other end of the causeway. The Captain, using the keys that the Sergeant had given him, opened it and waved her through.

He said, with studied carelessness, "I hardly know myself, Katrione. But now I must leave you to your fate. Pass through the inner courtyard and just keep going. I will tell the men you

229

are joining a scouting party in the Acre. I think your husband is in there somewhere. They headed the boat in that direction." He sighed. "I have to lead the Fourth Company there as soon as it is light, to search for you and Benet. You must take care I do not find you. When I am with my men tomorrow I can show you no mercy. Do you understand?"

She stood before him the darkness and said with emotion, "I cannot thank you enough for all you have done. You risked everything to save my life this night. I will pray we meet again in happier times. Farewell, and may the Goddess give you her protection." She hugged him hard and brought her lips to his for a brief kiss, and Tomas felt glad of the darkness, so she could not see his tears.

He laid his hand on her arm as she turned to go. "Wait, Katrione. Take this with you." Tomas unbuckled the sword belt he wore and held it out to her.

She shook her head. "I can't take your sword. You might have need of it. Anyway, I don't want to have to fight anyone."

He laughed grimly. "He really did keep you in the dark about everything, didn't he? This is his sword, d'angwir; not mine."

Jacq lay still and listened to the sounds around him in the darkness. He could hear the men of the rescue mission moving about the temporary encampment. They were waiting, in this hidden valley, to meet up with a second party of Reynard's men, who had been told to bring horses. Their arrival was imminent. Others were out in the Acre, looking for Katkin. Although Nicholas had sent men to the Compass after the rescue, she was already gone, leaving her clothes behind. Jacq increasingly felt a combination of fear for her safety and frustration at his own disability. He begged Reynard to allow him to join the men who were out in the Acre, already looking for her.

Reynard, shaking his head, said, "Dinrhydan, you must rest here with us and regain your strength. I haven't even seen the extent of the injuries those beasts have inflicted on you, my friend, but I know you would be of no use to the searchers as you are."

Jacq, exhausted by the rescue and in a great deal of pain, stirred restlessly on his pallet. The men had spread coats and cloaks on the ground for him so he could be comfortable as they waited for the horses. He strained his ears to catch conversations drifting around him, hoping for news of her.

"We cannot go on searching much longer, André, the Acre will be swarming with Guardsmen once it is light. Call the men back. The main thing is to get the Dinrhydan away from here and back to the Foxhole. We will have to leave the girl behind and let her take her own chances."

Jacq groaned at this. How could they even be thinking of leaving Katkin? She wouldn't stand a chance if the Guard caught her and took her back to the Citadel. Yet he knew his rescuers were practical men, and as far as they were concerned, they had already gained the prize they risked their lives for.

Reynard's quiet voice cut through the darkness. "Get ready to move out. The horses are here. I will tell the Dinrhydan." The Commander did not look forward to this task, for he knew Jacq would be angry. He walked silently through the darkened wood to the rough pallet his men had made for the Dinrhydan. It was empty. Squatting down in surprise, he used his hands to search the ground around the cloaks.

Katkin could see a distinct lightness to the east that blanked out the stars and heralded the dawn. She felt exhausted from stumbling around in the Acre for what seemed like many hours. Moving quietly from tree to tree, she had fruitlessly searched for Jacq or his rescue party until she managed to get thoroughly and hopelessly lost. For all she knew, she might have been walking in circles. In the darkness, familiar landmarks disappeared and any paths she found seemed to peter out into thickets of brambles and gorse. She began to feel panicked, remembering Tomas' warning about leaving the Acre before the dawn. The Guardsman's uniform she wore would be of little help if they found her out here, alone. Extricating herself from yet another bramble, she stopped to suck a scratch on her hand.

The sound of a horse's soft footfalls coming up behind her made her heart race. She dived into a bush, despite the pain from the wicked thorns. The horse and rider sounded quite close, and she prayed they would pass her by without stopping. Lifting her head slightly, she peered out through the brambles. She could only see the horse's feet. They were big, as big as plates, and the fetlocks shone glossy white even in the pre-dawn darkness. Katkin thought to herself in surprise—*that looks like Nestor.*

In a second, she had scrambled out of the thicket, Jacq's name on her lips. Her husband looked down on her, still wearing the uniform and cap, and said gruffly, "Wait there, boy, I would have some information from you." He clumsily jumped down from Nestor and drew the sword he had taken unasked from one of his comrades.

Katkin shook her head in confusion. She shouted to Jacq, "My husband, it is Katkin. Listen to me!" but his expression spoke only of pain and agitation. It was obvious he did not recognize her. Katkin began to back away from him, and he caught sight of the sword belt she wore buckled around her waist.

He roared, "How came you by that sword? It is my own—d'angwir. Give it back to me at once."

Not knowing what else to do, Katkin drew the sword so she could hand it to Jacq, hoping if she did as he requested it might calm him. But this action seemed only to infuriate him further. "So, you would fight me, young lad? I am the Dinrhydan, the mightiest of all warriors and I will slay you here and now. Prepare to die!" He stepped forward, his borrowed sword at the ready.

She screamed as he brought the sword around in a vicious slash that missed her midsection by a matter of inches. "This is madness, Jacq, stop, please, you must..."

In his anger at seeing his own precious sword drawn against him, Jacq's faint connection to reality snapped, and the blood rage took him completely. The Guardsman turned and ran before him, and Jacq laughed in the darkness. "Coward, come back and take your medicine. You cannot hide from me." He strode forward after Katkin, the pain of his wounds forgotten. She tripped on a tree root and fell headlong and suddenly he stood almost right on top of her, his sword raised high. Only the fact he had to fight left-handed saved her. As the sword came whistling down she managed to roll sideways and the deadly slash missed her by inches. The sword temporarily tangled in the same root and she quickly gained her feet. Though she knew had no chance of besting him in any kind of sword battle, Katkin realized she must defend herself until her husband's insanity passed. As he thrust forward, she parried as well as she could with d'angwir. Her mind went back once again to the hayloft in the barn, and another of twelve-year-old Jacq's lessons in self-defense. He had made her a carefully constructed wooden sword and though they spent many hours practicing, he was always the victor. She had no doubt Jacq could defeat her just as easily now.

Katkin's arm muscles screamed with fatigue as she swung the unbelievably heavy weapon again and again, trying to keep her husband from getting too close. She had long since stopped trying to reason with him, needing all her breath now just to move. As Katkin stepped backwards once more, she felt herself come up hard against a tree trunk. A quick twisting thrust from Jacq's sword caught her hand, and she dropped d'angwir with a cry of pain. Jacq stared down at her grimly and raised his sword for the final blow.

17

Sai Tammos, the roaring cataract

(The Tollyn, Fifteen)

Now we can know for certain who he really is, Moonlight. Search his mind, and tell us truly – Is he the son of Shiqaba?

~~~~~~~~~~~~~~~~

Tomas instructed his men to fan out and comb the section of the Acre assigned to the Fourth Company. Now, as dawn colored the sky, he felt very tired—he had spent the rest of the previous night after he left Katrione helping to restore order to the flooded Citadel. He saw no sign of the girl or her husband and he hoped they had been able to get away from the Acre and into Reynard's territory. Of his own treasonous actions in helping Katrione, he thought little.

Leading Pollux, the Captain moved out of sight of the rest of his men, pretending to search a thicket of trees, shrubs and brambles that lay off to his left several hundred yards away. His ears picked up the faint sounds of a struggle and the clash of swords. Breaking into a trot, he forced his way through the dense undergrowth and stopped in confusion. He could see Benet, looking like death, fighting a one-sided battle against a young guardsman that, in the low light, Tomas did not recognize. He saw the quick thrust that disarmed the boy and heard a curiously high-pitched scream. Benet was going for the kill now. He swung mightily and the boy ducked and narrowly missed being decapitated. His cap flew off his head and Tomas swore in alarm.

Jacq raised the sword again as Katkin, now sobbing aloud, cowered before him. The stroke, which would have cut her in half, never landed. Tomas de Vigny pulled his pistol from the holster on his belt and fired.

Katkin screamed again as Jacq, hit in the shoulder by the

ball from the pistol, crashed down like a fallen tree, narrowly missing her as she knelt on the ground. She scrambled forward on her hands and knees, and cried out in horror at the gaping wound in his chest. Looking around wildly, she spied Tomas, still holding the smoking pistol in his hand. Getting to her feet, she ran towards him, crying. "You shot him. You bastard, you killed Jacq!"

Tomas held her as she tried to strike him and covered her mouth with his gloved hand so she would not attract any more attention with her cries. He said urgently, "Listen to me, Katrione, I had no choice. I had to shoot him before he murdered you. Now shut up and let me think for a minute." He uncovered her mouth and she slumped to the ground at his feet, in shock and exhaustion from her battle with Jacq. Tomas knew the gunfire would surely draw his own men to them very soon. He grabbed the sobbing girl's arm and lifted her roughly to her feet, then slapped her hard across the face.

"Now, here is what you must do, Katrione. Pull yourself together. No more tears, no more panic. You have to heal him, now, as you healed me in the waters of the Mere. Get him on his feet and away from here, do you understand? I will lead my men in the other direction, but I cannot give you much time." Katkin looked at him as though she did not comprehend and he shook her roughly. "Do as I say, girl!"

Katkin took a shaky breath and nodded. "Keep your men away as long as you can. I will need a few moments to prepare myself."

She turned away from him, digging in the pocket of the uniform breeches for the pouch containing the little phial of Lalluna's water. Tomas saw her kneel down by Benet. Hearing shouts in the distance, he mounted Pollux and left her to it.

At Jacq's side, Katkin again examined the grievous wound left by the pistol ball. The two-inch wide hole had a red ragged edge. Blood poured from it in a steady stream, soaking Jacq's prison issue shirt and making a puddle on the ground. She listened in alarm to his labored breathing. Katkin knew she must hurry or it would be too late to save him. But first she must remove the lead ball from the wound, as otherwise the healed skin and bone would close around it. Steeling herself, she dug her fingers into the gaping hole, and felt inside. Jacq groaned and tried to move away. She had to straddle him with her own body to hold him still. At last, the ball lay in her hand and with an angry toss she sent it into the bushes. Then after moistening her bloody hands with the precious water, she went deep inside herself, seeking her centre and the reassuring presence of Lalluna. Nestor walked up beside her as she knelt, and stood quietly above his master's fallen form.

Nothing happened. She felt no warmth flowing to her hands, no touch of Lalluna's alabaster palm. Katkin cried out in alarm and frustration, "Lalluna, where are you? I need your help, Lady, as I never have before."

"My vessel, I am here." The voice came from above and Katkin looked up to see Lalluna, her iridescent wings folded gracefully, sitting astride Nestor's broad back.

Katkin cried, "Lalluna, why can I not heal him? I need my Gift and it has gone from me." She looked up at the Goddess beseechingly.

Lalluna looked down on her and Katkin could see pity in the moonlit eyes. The Goddess shook her head slightly, and her white hair stirred delicately, though there was no breeze. "You bear a life inside you, my vessel, and you cannot use my Gift any more. Not as you once did."

Katkin's mind whirled in horrifying confusion. "I am with child?"

The Goddess inclined her graceful head. "Yes, my vessel."

The sick feeling that built up inside Katkin almost had her reeling. She begged the Goddess, "Please tell me that it is Jacq's child I bear." Lalluna shook her head sadly and Katkin felt her world coming apart. Placing her hands over her face, she sobbed aloud, "Oh my Goddess, what have I done?"

Jacq moaned at her side, and she quickly dried her tears with the back of her hand. He spoke, though his voice was no more than an agonized whisper. "Katkin, my wife, are you with me? Or do I dream I hear your voice?"

Katkin bit her lip hard, hard enough to draw her own blood, and the pain brought her calmness. She said quietly, "Yes, I am here, my husband."

Jacq brought his mangled right hand up to find her and she

grasped it as softly as she could. Still he cried out in pain. She said, "My love, you must lie quietly."

His voice grew even fainter. "Can you... can you use your Gift, my wife? I think I have need of it now." Katkin took a deep breath, determined not to cry as his breathing grew ever more ragged and he coughed up a mouthful of bloody sputum.

"Oh Jacq, more than anything I wish I could. I cannot... I have lost my Gift, for I am with child." She put her head down into her hand to smother a sob. But Jacq's voice, when he had gathered the strength to speak again, sounded joyful.

"A child? You bear our child, Katkin?"

She did not hesitate even a fraction before she answered. "Yes, love, our child." The sun, rising now above the river bluff, sent a gleam of light that caught his face and she saw how peaceful his expression had become, despite his pain.

"Now I shall die in happiness, my beautiful girl, knowing a part of me will live on in you." He could not smile—still his injured face seemed suffused with joy. Katkin felt her betrayal tearing into her soul like the hungriest of wolves.

She begged, "Lalluna, please, you must help me save him. Is there no other way he can be healed?"

Lalluna looked down from her perch on Nestor's back at her faithful vessel and the mortal man the girl loved more than anything. "No way for you alone, my vessel. You must allow me to enter your body. I could use my power through you in that way, yet there is a grave risk to you and the child you bear. Such a blending of human and divine can pose a danger. When the curtain to the heavenly plane is cast aside many things may enter, and not all of them are benevolent." Then Lalluna gave a cry of dismay.

Jacq spoke slowly, obviously trying to marshal his failing strength. "My love, I see Death coming now, on his black horse. He waits for me, there, next to Lalluna and Nestor. Do you see, my wife?"

Katkin shook her head miserably. "No, it is not given for me to see Death yet, though I wish with all my heart I could."

He chided her gently. "Do not say such a thing. You must be strong for our child's sake. I have no strength left now to protect you. Farewell, my Katkin. I love you, always." With these words he passed into unconsciousness again and Katkin sobbed by his side, listening to the agony of his final breaths.

"Lalluna, before it is too late, enter me now. I care not for the danger." Katkin cried and raised her tear-filled eyes to look at the Goddess. Lalluna shook her head regretfully.

Tomas, riding back through the Acre, did not feel at all pleased to see that Katkin and Jacq remained in the dell. He had managed to lead his men in the opposite direction, but he knew the ruse would not last long.

"Katrione," he hissed in exasperation as he dismounted. "Why are you still here? I told you to get him out."

She lifted her face, tear-stained and miserable, to look up at him. "I cannot heal him. My Gift is forever lost to me. I am pregnant, Tomas. The child is yours."

Tomas stepped back as though she had struck him. "Mine? How do you know? How could you know... so soon?" he whispered.

"Lalluna told me and she does not lie. Because of my bargain with you, Jacq is going to die. Death already waits for him, and Lalluna can do nothing to help, not now." Katkin sighed and turned back to Jacq, whose chest still rose and fell with intense effort.

"Why can Lalluna not help you? She is a Goddess, is she not? I thought she could do anything," Tomas asked impatiently.

"When Death comes, he will not leave without taking a soul. It is too late to save Jacq now." Katkin kept her vigil next to Jacq, and it seemed with every passing second he could hold on no longer. Yet still his chest rose and fell.

Tomas, ignored now by Katkin, sat down by the tall oak tree that sheltered them all. Though he did not know why, he accepted every word she told him as the truth, unbelievable as it sounded. Perhaps it was because her emaciated face looked so ethereal in the morning sunlight. Tomas thought her beautiful enough to be a Goddess herself, at that moment. In the peaceful glade, only the sound of Katkin's quiet sobbing and Jacq's rasping breath disturbed the silence, until in the distance a crow began to caw stridently. A second later, unnoticed, it landed in the oak tree with a rush of purple-black wings.

Tomas mechanically removed his flintlock pistol from the

holster on his belt and began to clean it. His hands, so experienced in this procedure after years of warfare, needed no instruction from his brain on the task of reloading the weapon. Using his thumb, he half-cocked the hammer. He wondered to himself if Katrione would agree to marry *him* once Benet was dead. Judging from his breathing, he was not going to last much longer. The thought of Katrione as his wife gave him a momentary shiver of pleasure. His hands found the powder horn in his breeches pocket, and dispensed the proper amount into the muzzle. Still, Katrione did not love him, not like that, and might never be happy as his wife. Why was it so important all of a sudden, that she be happy?

Tomas called quietly over to Katkin, still keeping her lonely duty by Jacq's side. "The child, Katrione—is it given to you to know if it will be a girl or a boy?"

She answered him after a moment's silence, her voice raw from the tears she shed for her dying husband, "It is a girl child, Tomas. Lalluna has told me so."

Tomas sighed deeply. He took a piece of wadding from a small, delicately engraved silver box, and wrapped one of the deadly lead balls in it. A little girl. No doubt she would be as beautiful as Katrione. Perhaps she would even have golden hair, as he did. Taking the wrapped ball, he placed it into the muzzle, ramming it down firmly with the rod he detached from its holder under the barrel. He would be her father and she would end up despising him, just as he had hated the old man. The thought was unendurable. He added a small amount of gunpowder to the pan and closed the frizzen with a decisive click. Tomas left the loaded and half-cocked pistol on his lap, his fingers loosely entwined around the brass-tipped butt.

He whispered to her again. "Katrione, will you love our daughter as much as you would if Benet was the father? I know it must be difficult for you, knowing you bear the child of a man who has caused you so much pain."

Katkin said reassuringly, "It will make no difference to me. I will love our child with all my heart—you need have no fear on that score."

He sat back against the oak, unaccountably pleased, and the pistol felt heavy and cold in his hand. Thoughtfully he asked,

"Benet wouldn't be able to love her at all, would he? Not if he knew."

Katkin said in exasperation, "It hardly matters at this point, Captain. But, if you must know, I believe you are right. You and he will always remain enemies in his heart. He would not be able to look on the child without seeing your face."

Tomas thought then about those long conversations he had had with Benet in the interrogation room—about all the noisome things he said he would do to Katrione. His cheeks burned with shame now and he felt thoroughly loathsome. He raised the loaded pistol up towards his face, and studied it with interest.

"You must promise me that you will never tell Benet the truth. He must believe the girl is his own child. Swear on the heart of the Goddess as you had me do yesterday," Tomas begged. Katkin looked over at him in agitation.

"Tomas, what difference—"

"Swear it, Katrione, now!" The desperate appeal in his voice commanded her.

"I swear," she said, shaking her head in confusion at this irrational request.

"Very good, I thank you for that. I cannot give you much, but Pollux shall be yours. Use him to ride away from here when I am gone. My purse lies in the saddlebag and there is a little gold." His voice quietly faded away. Katkin, concentrating hard on the harsh sounds of her husband's breathing, barely heard what he said.

The pistol barrel, hard and cool, found its way into his open mouth then, and to his surprise, he could clearly see the figure of Death on his black horse, so like Pollux. Death moved slowly towards Benet now, and the horse's hooves left no marks on the soft ground. Tomas took the gun away and the vision disappeared. He said softly, "Farewell, my dear. Take good care of our child, always." After wiping his eyes with one gloved hand, he continued brokenly, "I lied when I said I did not know why I saved you. I miss you so much, do you understand? I still love you, even after everything that has happened. I wish to the Gods I knew how to stop—I cannot bear the pain of it any longer. But you belong to Benet now, and he will love you and our daughter in the way you deserve. Save him, Katrione."

Katkin, thoroughly alarmed by these last words, left Jacq's

side and rushed towards the Captain. Tomas pressed the back of his head hard into the oak tree, so the ball would penetrate the trunk after it left him. It would not do for it to ricochet and hit her. Then he put the barrel of the pistol into his mouth once again, closed his eyes tightly, and pulled the trigger.

Death reined the black horse and turned towards Tomas' body, as it slumped over next to the oak tree. Katkin stopped running when she heard the shot. She could hardly believe Tomas had just sacrificed his own life so she could save Jacq, but he had. Try as she might, Katkin could find no joy in his altruism. Blinking the tears from her eyes, she slowly turned away and said to Lalluna, "Lady, can you speak to Death? Can he tell Tomas something for me?"

The Goddess inclined her head.

Katkin said, very softly, "Tell him that I love him too."

The spirit of Tomas de Vigny, sitting astride the black horse, his face untroubled, gave her the gentlest of smiles, but she saw it not.

Lalluna said urgently, "Hurry, my vessel. If we are to save your husband, we must merge our spirits now. Though the soul of friend Tomas has called Death away for a moment, he will not tarry long before he returns."

Katkin nodded, unafraid. "I am ready, Lalluna. Enter me, if you will."

The Goddess stood on Nestor's back and, with the barest rustle of her luminescent wings, flew down to stand before Katkin. Never before had she seen the form of Lalluna with such clear purity and it took her breath away. The Goddess raised a perfect alabaster hand and touched the girl's forehead. Katkin saw her turn into a column of white fire and then the fire surged forward and engulfed her.

She felt burning pain and ecstasy intermingled, but such was the ecstasy, the pain seemed insignificant. Suddenly her senses sharpened, almost unbearably. She heard, in the distance, the sound of many men running and shouting—also the sound of the mice quietly cringing in the bracken around them. Her vision extended infinitely in all directions. Looking towards the City, she could peer through the Acre and across the Mere, to the Infirmarie, where she saw Becka Kent, wearing the moonstone necklace, sitting and writing at the Maitress' desk. She saw the Citadel, and the soldiers running like so many busy ants. She smelled and tasted the greasy food from the soldier's mess. The slightest breath of wind caressed her skin and she felt the touch of everything it had passed before it reached her. Every object before her, from the leaves on the trees to the body of Tomas, swirled in a rainbow of bright flame. The beauty of the world through the eyes of Lalluna overwhelmed her, and Katkin knew she would be forever transformed by it. The tiny clump of rapidly dividing cells in her womb began to glow like an ember and changed as well. The Crow in the oak cawed forcefully and disappeared, leaving behind a single back feather that drifted lazily down to land on the ruined face of Captain Tomas de Vigny.

Katkin moved to where Jacq lay on the bloodstained grass. Lalluna's voice whispered in her mind. "Would you have us heal just the wound that takes his life now, or every grievous injury he has suffered at the hands of his tormentors? Such a complete healing will cause you great pain and weakness, my vessel, though I will shield you as much as I can. You must not lose consciousness, or I must leave you before we are finished. Have you the strength for this?"

Katkin did not hesitate. To see her husband before her, whole and strong as he had once been, was the only thing she wanted now.

"I am strong enough, Lalluna. Use me to heal all his wounds."

Lalluna sighed, and felt afraid for the girl and her child. "Very well, my vessel. Kneel and place your hand over his heart." Katkin, with a steady hand, did as the Goddess instructed. She felt the burning of the white fire as it flowed from her fingers into Jacq's body. With a strangled cry, he stiffened, and his body rose up in an arc, so that only his head and heels touched the ground. Katkin looked on in wonderment as his body began to soften and blur until only the shadowy outline of a winged being remained. Then the pain of his wounds began and she could think of nothing else. Katkin screamed again and again in agony as each of his injuries touched her in quick succession. She felt each stroke of the horsewhip in her father's barn long ago, and each torment from the interrogation room. Redness began to seep into her vision, until it filled her eyes. Now it was the color of blood and growing ever darker. Something lay just beyond it—a pristine whiteness that spoke of peace and release from her torture.

Lalluna's voice broke through. "My vessel, do not fail now or all will be lost."

Katkin refocused herself with difficulty, accepting the pain and letting it flow through her. Love for Jacq and Lalluna filled her heart and brought respite, just as she thought she could endure no more. Tears streamed from beneath the lids of her tightly closed eyes.

"Attend to your husband, my vessel. See how he is changed," said Lalluna.

Katkin opened her eyes and looked at Jacq. He had returned once again to a human form. The hole in his chest was gone—the smashed bones of his fingers knitted once again and healthy new skin covered all his blisters and burns. Suddenly his body relaxed and fell back to the ground.

"It is finished, my vessel, we have healed him completely." Lalluna's voice sounded glad in her mind.

Katkin felt her consciousness slipping from her. She could not prevent it now, but Jacq lay beside her, alive and without pain. Nothing else mattered. As she slumped forward, Lalluna's misty form issued forth from her mouth and dissipated on the wind.

Jacq was dreaming. He shuffled through the Acre again, looking for his wife. When he caught sight of her in the distance, he tried to run. The pain of his wounds hindered him, until it felt as though his legs had become lead. Then Katkin saw him and came quickly to his side. It frightened him to see she flew on gossamer wings that had sprouted somehow from between her shoulder blades. The sun shone through them brilliantly, and they shimmered with a rainbow of shades. Her beauty deeply moved him, more so than it ever had before. But her face looked cold and perilous, and her eyes were the color of moonlight. He feared her greatly, this apparition that looked so like his wife, but was not.

She spoke to him, saying, "What are you doing here, Dai? Did you not curse us for allying ourselves with humanity?"

Jacq shook his head. He seemed incapable of speech.

Lalluna stared at him for a moment. Could she be wrong about his true identity? Finally she said gently, "Come back now from your journey to the Vastness, husband of my vessel. For through her you have been healed, and your pain is no more." Lalluna touched his face with her hand and he felt himself falling.

Jacq woke from this dream with a start and found he was lying on his back in a dell, sheltered by an enormous oak. His memories of the last few hours were sketchy. Hadn't he been with Reynard in the Acre, waiting for them to bring Nestor? He sat up and stretched, feeling the ripple of the powerful muscles in his back as they contracted. But Jacq did not think about his lack of pain—not yet. He lumbered to his feet, scratching the stubble on his chin in confusion. A few feet away lay the body of a young guardsman, face down. Yes, he could vaguely remember fighting the boy, who had so impudently drawn Jacq's own sword, d'angwir, against him. The sword lay on the ground, close to where Jacq had been sleeping on a patch of grass that was curiously black and matted.

The fallen boy still wore the belt and scabbard belonging with the sword. He would have those back. With a booted foot, Jacq kicked the guardsman roughly to turn him over. His horror and shock at the moment when he saw the boy's face drove him to his knees. Jacq gathered Katkin up in his arms, crying, "What manner of dream is this? I cannot have killed her in my madness. By the gods, make this nightmare end." He buried his head on her breast and sobbed aloud.

After a moment, she took a deep breath, and stirred in his arms. Hearing his cries, she said sleepily, "My husband, why do you grieve? Lalluna has healed your wounds, and you should be happy." He lifted his tear-stained face to peer at her, and the wild tufts of her impromptu haircut.

He whispered, "I thought I had killed you by mistake, my love, when I fought a guardsman who had stolen my sword. I know not what is truth and what is a dream. Am I now awake?" Confusion showed plainly on his face. "How did you get here, dressed like that?"

Katkin looked around her in alarm. She had no idea how long she might have been sleeping. "We must save the story for another time. Tomas' men will be coming soon, I fear. There is still danger all around us, and I would not have Lalluna's handiwork undone so soon." But, pleased to see him healthy and whole before her, she smiled and kissed him softly on the mouth. "I am very glad to see you well, my love."

The realization struck him at last as he looked down at his maimed right hand and found it healed—the skin on his massive arms was also smooth and unbroken. "You healed me? But you said... you said you could not, because you were with child. Was that just a dream as well?" He looked very distressed at this thought.

Katkin shook her head. "Nay, that was no dream. I am indeed with child. Lalluna healed you by using my body." She did not elaborate on the threat to the child or how painful the experience had been for her. With a cry of delight, Jacq caught her up in his arms again, despite the danger. His unbridled joy at the news she was truly pregnant felt almost physically distressing to Katkin. After a minute, firmly pushing his arms away, she said, "We must get away from here, love."

Jacq did not really want to let her go, not after she had been returned to him through some miracle he did not yet understand, still he saw the truth in what she said. They had many miles to cover before they would be safe. "Is Nestor here? We can both ride him." Jacq whistled sharply. Nestor appeared at a trot.

Pollux, sweating and frightened, still stood near the body of his old master, under the spreading limbs of the oak. Though she knew they must hurry, Katkin could not leave without saying one last good bye to Tomas, whose unhappy sacrifice had given Jacq new life. She walked over to him, and studied his face for a moment, then knelt and gently closed his eyes. Bending close to him, so Jacq would not hear, she whispered, "Fare well on your journey to the silent land, my love. I thank you with all my heart for both your gifts of life. May your spirit now be at peace."

Joining her side, Jacq said harshly, "Leave that rotting carrion for the crows, Katkin. They can have a feast with his carcass. I know not how he comes to be dead, but I do not rue it."

Katkin looked up at him and spoke sharply. "Speak no ill of the Captain. Neither you nor I would be here now if not for his steadfast courage." Jacq stared at her in fresh agitation. He could keep nothing straight in his head any longer.

She turned away abruptly but not before Jacq saw the tears

filling her eyes. He felt an angry stab of jealousy that she could speak of the hated de Vigny so kindly and weep at his death.

Katkin, mindful of the Captain's last gift, said, "I will ride Pollux, and we will be able to get away that much faster."

Jacq quickly disagreed. "You cannot ride him, Kat. Pollux is an untamed beast, every man in the Fourth Company feared him. He would bear no one but the Captain on his back. Leave him and come with me on Nestor." She shook her head and Jacq watched with wide, fearful eyes as she approached the restive Pollux, who snorted and reared. Placing her hands on either side of his head, she whispered soft words to the horse, which calmed immediately.

Katkin leapt lightly onto his back and said, "Do we ride, my husband?"

Jacq, shaking his head at this new wonder, caught Nestor and climbed up on his saddle. There seemed to be something very different about his wife now, though he could not say what it was exactly. Nevertheless, he felt a little shiver of fear in his heart. It seemed the brave woman who had healed him of his terrible wounds and tamed the fiery Pollux so effortlessly might no longer need his protection at all.

18

Cexcipet, the searing desert

(The Tollyn, Four)

Tell me of the prophecy, Geya.

Our grandmother says that when the four quarters of the compass are united, then the Dawnmaid will be born, and free the Autochthones.

Will she be able to defeat the Angellus?

That I do not know, Moonlight. Only Moera can say, and she does not speak.

Neither does Death, my sister.

~~~~~~~~~

The sound of a pistol ball whistling over their heads convinced Jacq and Katkin of the need to get moving. Nestor, responding to a hearty kick from his master, raced forward through the trees. Pollux followed closely behind. Wild shouts and the sound of many hoof beats pursued them, and Katkin would have been very afraid if she had not needed to spend every ounce of concentration keeping her seat on the breakneck ride that followed. Branches flew rapidly by, inches above her head, as the horses weaved through the densely packed trees. She leaned over and put her face next to Pollux's black neck to avoid being swept off the saddle.

Gradually they left their pursuers behind as they rode up a steep rocky slope, still in the cover of the Acre. Jacq headed back towards the place where he had last seen Reynard and his comrades—before he had taken that insane trip through the Acre and almost murdered his own wife. Though it seemed nothing more than an evil dream at the time, the reality of what he had done was inescapable. She had somehow pardoned him for that particular piece of madness; still he knew the moment would come, very soon, when he must tell her the truth about everything. He wondered fearfully if she would so readily forgive him this time.

Suddenly a cry echoed from the trees to their left and a figure wearing a yellow armband ran forward, sword drawn. Jacq reined Nestor sharply and dismounted, crying, "Yannick, by the gods, it is good to see your face, my friend!"

Katkin checked Pollux and watched the joyful reunion of her husband and Yannick Abelard without much interest. She still had not forgiven him for the things he said about Lalluna. Yannick, also pointedly ignoring her, said, "Dinrhydan, you have led us all on a merry chase. I am very glad to see you are alive." But of Jacq's restored health Yannick would say nothing, not in front of the witch.

"We are closely pursued, Yannick. I must get my wife away from the Acre as soon as I can. But if we ride west now in daylight, I fear the open country we would have to cross. We would be target practice for any Guard that happened to see us."

"Do not worry. The Commander sent for the hay wain this morning, in case we should find your..." Yannick did not finish the sentence, but Jacq knew what he meant and laughed.

"I am very much alive, thanks to my wife's ministrations. But we will find the wain very useful anyway, I suspect."

Baffled, Katkin broke in, saying, "How will we be any safer on a slow hay cart? I would rather stay on Pollux and take my chances as a faster moving target."

Jacq smiled at her confusion. "You shall see what a special hay cart this is and how we shall be perfectly safe once we are in it."

Yannick climbed aboard Nestor, sitting behind Jacq, and directed them forward through the trees to where the rest of the rescue party waited anxiously for news of the Dinrhydan. They rode hard for about fifteen minutes, to the edge of the Acre, where the big trees thinned and smaller pines and birches took their place.

Beyond the edge of the forest, Katkin could see an open country of rolling hills, dotted with farms and well-ordered fields. On the road before them, a group of about ten men gathered about a hay wain, which looked to have a broken wheel.

As Jacq and Yannick appeared from the trees on Nestor, the men let out a cheer and crowded round the big horse's flanks.

They offered their hands up to the Dinrhydan with congratulations and questions on his unexpected vigor. Jacq smiled at them but did not answer. Instead he cast a nervous glance towards his wife.

Katkin stayed well back, uncomfortably aware the truth about her husband's secret life was about to be revealed. A tall, silver-haired man, wearing a plain gray uniform, stepped out of the crowd around Nestor and approached her. He smiled and said, "Welcome, my dear. I am very glad to see you are safe."

She stared back at him and asked suspiciously, "Who are you?"

A terrible knowledge began to dawn in her eyes, as she recalled her sister's comment on the day Roseberry had been healed. *Yannick occasionally fights for the Rising. Sometimes I wonder if Jacq does too.* Katkin shook her head, remembering her firm denial to Willow—how convinced she had been her husband would never do such a thing. The signs had been there, all along, but she had ignored them, not wanting to know the truth. Suddenly she felt sick with fear and rage.

Jacq, hearing the exchange between Reynard and his wife, quickly left Nestor's saddle and went to stand by the Commander, who gave him a look of pity mingled with exasperation. Jacq shrugged miserably and said, "There was no time to tell her on the way."

Reynard paused for a moment and then spoke to Katkin, meeting her eyes with his own. "I am Nicholas Aleksei Reynard, Commander of the Soldiers of the Rising, and your valiant husband is one of my most trusted comrades."

Katkin said nothing in reply to this introduction—she merely jumped down from Pollux and turned her back on both of them, putting her hands up to cover her face. Jacq could see her shoulders trembling and knew that she wept. He stepped forward and put his arms about her from behind, and she thrust them away angrily, saying, in a choked voice, "Don't touch me, Jacq."

Nicholas Reynard spoke softly to him. "I will tell the men to ready the wain. We had it jacked up so we could linger here without suspicion. Five minutes only, Dinrhydan, then she must come, willing or no." He turned away, shaking his head sadly.

Jacq walked back to his wife and stood in front of her,

desperately wanting to say something to comfort her and knowing nothing would—not now she knew the truth.

"Katkin, look at me," he said sadly, and reached to uncover her face. She snatched her hand away as though his touch burned her. He could see his betrayal etched cleanly on her tear-stained cheeks.

"I know I should have told you, long ago. I am sorry... more sorry than I can say. But we have to go with him now—it is not safe for us here any longer."

She stared up at him and said stonily, "I am not going anywhere. Not with that murderer."

Jacq stared back and his frustration showed plainly on his face. He spoke sharply to her. "You wouldn't last five minutes out here before the Guard would have you. Shall I leave you and my unborn child to be slaughtered? You are going and there will be no more argument. On our wedding day, you promised to obey me, and now that promise must be kept. I am sorry."

She reached up and slapped him hard before he had a chance to catch her hand. "Don't you talk to me about promises, Jacq Benet! You promised me something that day in the church as well—to love and honor. Remember? How have you kept those promises, my husband?" She shook her head angrily. "I don't even know who you are any more. Willow tried to tell me months ago you fought for the Rising and I wouldn't believe her. I defended you! I told her the man I married was a craftsman, who made beautiful and useful things. Not a soldier, whose hands are stained with blood. How many men have fallen under your bright sword? How many have you butchered with d'angwir—as you would have butchered me if Tomas had not put a ball through you? Answer me, damn you!"

Jacq gave her a stricken look and whispered back, "I know not. Too many to count in all this long conflict. I take no joy in it, my wife; you must know that. I would be the craftsman you married if I could, were this war to end. Yet now my sword is needed more than my craft, and I cannot betray the men who have risked their lives for mine."

Reynard called to Jacq. "We must go now. Bring her, Dinrhydan." As Katkin turned to run, Jacq grabbed her roughly, hoisting her off the ground, and covered her mouth with his hand. She struggled, but his strength was ten times hers. It was like straining against bands of iron. Tearfully, he carried his wife towards Reynard and the wain.

In the centre of the bales of hay lay a wooden frame with a hiding space inside it, big enough for two people or a cache of weapons. Jacq ungracefully shoved Katkin into this space and followed close behind her. Reynard fitted the door into place, leaving them in almost complete darkness. The cramped interior felt very warm and stuffy.

Katkin could not get away from Jacq's body completely, so she curled up into the smallest ball she could and sobbed brokenly, "You bloody bastard. You said you always keep your promises. How could you take me against my will?" and then said nothing else for a long time.

After they hitched Nestor to the traces of the wagon alongside another horse, two of Reynard's men climbed up into the driver's seat and began the two-hour trip back to the main encampment, fifteen miles to the west. Pollux, forgotten by everyone, followed on his own, knowing somehow his new mistress was concealed in the wagon.

Jacq, feeling almost as unhappy as he had in his filthy cell at the Citadel, sat in silence, listening to the heart-wrenching cries of his wife. It would do no good to try to talk to her, not now. So he quietly sucked the blood off his fingers, where she had bitten him in her struggle to be free of him and his terrible secret. But, after a time, she surprised him by saying dispassionately, "You were a spy at the Citadel, weren't you? That is why you told me that your family did not mind your working there. They knew all along. Everyone knew the truth—except for me."

"Yes, I was a spy. From the time I was sixteen, until I left, right before we got married."

She voiced her disgust. "How could you live and work with those men for so many years and then betray them all? What kind of a man would do that?"

He sighed in the darkness. "I never made friends with any of them. I kept to myself. That was the only way it was possible for me to do what I did."

"Even Trudeau? Wasn't he your friend?" she asked bitterly. Then with sudden understanding she asked, "Where did you see him in LeClaire, Jacq? On the opposite side of a battlefield? Did you kill him after he told you about the letter? Is that why he couldn't give you the rest of my message?"

Jacq said quietly, "No, Katkin. He was already gravely injured when I rode past. He recognized Nestor and called my name, and told me about the letter. Then he died, in my arms. It was not easy to see him die like that, believe me. His commanding officer sent him back into battle with his leg in plaster. When our men overran the lines he couldn't get away."

Katkin spoke more softly still, and yet her voice sounded as brittle as glass. "Yes, no doubt you feel a great deal of remorse over his death, and all the other deaths you have caused. But you tell yourself that you have saved lives in the Rising by your actions. Is that right? I just want to understand how you can live with yourself and how you can sleep at night."

"I believe in what Commander Reynard and the Rising stand for. A country where no other children will die in misery, the way my sister died. You don't understand what it is like to be hungry, Katkin. How could you? Your parents—"

She cut in, her voice rising again, "Are dead. And my home destroyed. All because of that murderer you believe in. How did you come to fight for Reynard? The boy I knew and loved at Tintaren would not have done such a thing. I cannot believe you have changed so much."

Jacq sighed. At least she was still talking, even if it was to insult him and the Commander. He tried to stretch his legs in the cramped space and ended up almost kicking her. "He is not a murderer, Katkin. I need to tell you the story of what actually happened on the night he attacked Tintaren. I should have told you long ago, but I did not want to hurt you."

She said cruelly, "What is this fairy story, Jacq? Another carefully constructed rampart of lies? In that way only, you remain the craftsman I married."

"No!" he hissed at her. "No, this is the truth. I swear it, on my honor as your husband."

Her laugh was not pleasant to hear. "Your honor?"

"Listen to me, Katkin. I love you more than heaven and Yrth. The only thing that kept me sane in prison when they tortured me was that love. You saw what I looked like when they had finished with me. I am not proud of taking you against your will—but I would do it again if I had to. How could I leave you behind for the Guard to find? They would show you or our child no mercy, my wife."

Katkin sat quietly in the darkness, her anger at his betrayal still running hot in her veins. She said, with feigned indifference, "So... this fairy story. Tell it to me, my husband. It will help to pass the time until I can get away from you and this airless box."

Jacq took a deep breath, determined not to be provoked. "I had just turned fifteen when Tintaren Manor was burned down. My mother knew of the attack in advance so she took all of us and hid in the cellar of the pitiful ruin of a house your parents had given us to live in after your fall off Brinna."

"How did your mother know of the attack?"

Jacq hesitated for a moment and said, "That is her own story and you should ask her if you want to know the answer. She waits for us at the Foxhole, with Thad and Kadya. Willow is there too, safe, with Roseberry. She will be very glad to see you, my wife." He paused to pull the filthy, blood-matted prison shirt off over his head, shoving it as far away from them as he could. In the stuffy interior of the wain, it smelled truly disgusting. Then he continued with his tale. "Commander Reynard surrounded your parent's house with his soldiers and sent a man bearing a white flag for a parley. Your father shot him dead from an upstairs window."

She said nothing to this, so he went on. "Still they did not attack because the Commander knew women and servants remained trapped in the house. I swear he wanted no bloodshed. He sent five men to break into the house from the rear, to get your father and his pistol out. Your father shot two more men before they overpowered him. He broke away, and ran upstairs again. There were many other guns in a locked cabinet on the landing."

"Yes," said Katkin. "I remember it."

"He took all the guns he had, and the servants helped him load them. Reynard's men stayed below, afraid to go up the stairs and be picked off one by one. They sent a message out asking for reinforcements and the Commander sent every man he could."

Katkin said angrily, "Go on with your tale. What happened

then? Tell me how those men murdered my mother and father. Even if Reynard did not pull the trigger, he ordered it to be done."

Jacq shook his head in the darkness, but she did not see. "It did not happen like that, my love. Your father... He must have gone insane. He turned the guns on the servants, and when he finished with them, he..." Jacq could not say any more, knowing how much pain this next part of the story would bring her.

"I would hear the rest of it, my husband." Her voice sounded icy and he wondered if she believed anything he had said.

Jacq said quietly, "He shot your mother in the head as she crouched in a wardrobe." Katkin, hearing this, gave a strangled cry of protest. Jacq wanted so much to hold her, yet he knew she would not allow it. He must finish the grim tale first. "Your father took every lamp he could find and smashed them all. The fire soon engulfed the upstairs rooms and he perished as the house burned to the ground. You see why I could not bring myself to tell you the truth, though I should have long ago. I am sorry, Katkin." Jacq sighed deeply and said no more.

Katkin did not want to believe this new and much more chilling version of events. She had long hated Reynard and had constructed her own account of that terrible night in which he starred as the chief villain. Now Jacq had demolished that story with his appalling tale of her suicidal father killing both her mother and all the servants. It did not seem possible, but she thought of the dreadful scarring on her husband's back. A man who would horsewhip a fourteen-year-old boy might be capable of any atrocity.

She shook her head, trying to make sense of it all. Jacq's lack of trust hurt her deeply. Why had he not told her from the very beginning he fought for the Rising? Suddenly, all her caustic remarks about Nicholas Reynard came back to her one by one, and then she understood. As a child, she had worshiped Jacq. He had always been her hero. After the wedding, she still held him to that ideal, when in truth he was only human. She knew her hatred of Reynard had put him in an untenable position. He wanted to go on being the hero in her eyes, because he knew she expected it of him. At the same time, he had to fight for the cause he believed in. So he had tried to do both, as well as he could, until the terrible day the Unity had come for Roseberry.

She realized now why Yannick had begged Jacq to remain behind. Yet he had given himself into the hands of his enemies to protect her. She recalled how brutally they had beaten him in front of the Temple, as she looked on, unable to do anything to help. He had endured far worse in the Citadel, but had not betrayed the men who depended on him. Katkin began to weep again, very quietly. Now she knew the truth, she would have taken back all the hurtful words she said to Jacq in her anger, but she could not.

Jacq, sitting across from her in the darkness, battled with an overwhelming desire to comfort his wife. Impulsively, he reached out, pulled her close to him and held her tightly. She did not struggle against him, not this time.

After a little while she said, "I am so sorry. I shouldn't have said all those awful things to you. Can you forgive me?"

He sighed in the darkness. "I deserved every one of them and more for leaving you to find out everything the way you did. Nathan tried to convince me long ago I should be honest with you but I kept telling myself you never needed to know. You hated Reynard so much—I thought you would stop loving me if you knew the truth. It is I who should be begging your forgiveness."

"I forgive you, though you needn't have asked. I will never stop loving you, my husband. I had just forgotten, for a little while, the things that are most important to me—we are together again and you are well and whole." She sighed happily as she lay against his chest and brought her lips to his for a long kiss.

"How long will it take to get to Reynard's camp, my love?" she murmured presently.

"At least another hour, I am afraid. This is not the most comfortable form of transport, I realize, but at least we are safe from prying eyes."

"Yes, very private," she said thoughtfully, and kissed him again with an urgency he recognized right away.

"Katkin, you cannot be serious! In here? We hardly have room to move, and anyway I stink to high heaven." He laughed softly in the darkness.

"I know you stink, my husband. I have a nose on my face after all," she said equably. "And I do not care. Can we manage, do you think?"

255

Nicholas Reynard, leaving the transport of the Dinrhydan and his uncooperative wife to his men, rode hard for headquarters with his usual escort. The Guard did not know his face well, but he preferred not to spend too much time in open country, especially that not under his direct control. He breathed a sigh of relief when he crossed the Ariane River and entered his own territory.

They rode towards the range of high hills purpling the horizon ahead. The villagers of St. Germain terraced the hills for agriculture and the sunny slopes grew many vital foodstuffs. A solidly built stone château overlooked the valley. Reynard had won this grand house early in his campaign against the King's Guard. After evicting the wealthy Lord of St. Germain and his family, Reynard divided the lands among the cottars and the village, and took the house for his headquarters. It had an excellent outlook high on the hill and had been made easily defensible by the addition of high stone walls and trenches around the perimeter. The property backed on to the territories of the Mardonne, and no King's Guard detachment would willingly cross over the border to attack from the rear. This château headquarters, now renamed the Foxhole in honor of the Commander, served as a home base for about three hundred soldiers of the Rising.

Reynard and his men passed through the village swiftly and headed up the steep road to the Foxhole. They passed the outlying sentries and rode for the main gates along a palisaded section of the perimeter wall. Four soldiers stood on guard. When they saw the Commander approaching they broke into a cheer and one called, "What news of the Dinrhydan, Sir?"

"He is well, my brother, and travels slowly behind us hidden in one of the wains. It will be another hour before you see them make their way up the road. Send a runner when you do, so we may have a welcome waiting in the courtyard." Reynard gave the password to the gatekeeper, and he admitted them into the compound.

The Foxhole retained a shadow of former glory when approached from the winding tree-lined driveway. But as the riders came closer, the canvas tents set up on the broad green lawn, ammunitions dump, stables and scattered pieces of artillery gave it a distinctly martial air. It had been Nicholas Reynard's home for the last five years, when he was not on a campaign with his men.

The horses drew up noisily in the cobbled courtyard and men hurried forward to see to the mounts. Fiann bounded about, ecstatically pleased to see his master again. A tall young man came forward and took Rufus' reins. Reynard's equerry said, "Welcome back, Commander. I hope your mission was successful." When Reynard nodded tiredly to him, he continued, "Your lady has been asking for word, Sir, and we could tell her nothing other than the news that came by pigeon last night, saying you had gotten the Dinrhydan out of the Citadel. Will you go to her now, or shall I carry a message?"

Sighing, Reynard said, "I cannot go myself. I have an unhappy duty to carry out first, and I must not delay it. Tell her the Dinrhydan and his wife are safely on their way, but the girl had to be brought against her will. Ask her to make ready a secure room, in case we have to lock Katrione up to stop her escaping back to the City."

Reynard shook his head—troubled by the thought that Jacq's wife would have to be kept a prisoner at the Foxhole.

Calling Fiann to his side, he walked into headquarters, heading towards his office and the cheerless yet compulsory task of writing personal messages of condolence to each of the wives of the men who had been killed on the mission to save the Dinrhydan. He carefully told each widow how to apply to the Paymaster for a pension. Though the Commander's time and attention were constantly in demand in the oversight of the war, he would let none of his assistants do this assignment for him. Over the years he had had to write many such letters, but he never got used to it.

Some minutes later, a shout in the courtyard caused him to look up from his task. The runner from the gate had arrived to announce the sighting of the wain. Reynard left his half-finished letters and hurried back outside, calling for several aides to accompany him.

The Commander had three men arranged in a semi-circle around the back of the wain as the hay bales that hid the door were unloaded. If the girl made a break they had been instructed to stop her if Jacq could not. Jacq stepped through the door first,

257

shirtless, drenched in sweat and covered with wisps of hay. Smiling broadly, he turned to reach back into the secret space and pulled his wife out and into his arms. He kissed her intently, holding her a foot off the ground, as her arms twined about his neck—ignoring completely his Commander and the other men who stood ready to welcome him. Nicholas smiled sheepishly at the three men near the wain and sent them back to their duties. It seemed the Dinrhydan's wife would not need to be caught after all.

Pollux skittered into the courtyard, his eyes white and terrified. He would let no man near him, rearing up at each approach. "How did that animal get in here?" asked Reynard, perturbed.

"I don't know, Sir," said the runner. "He did not come in with the cart when they brought it through the gate."

Reynard asked, "Who does this wild beast belong to? Can no one control it?"

Katkin walked confidently towards Pollux, her hand outstretched.

"Dinrhydan, your wife..." said Reynard, concerned for her safety. Jacq just shrugged. She touched the horse's face gently to calm him and he suffered himself to be led away to the stables by his mistress. Once there, she unburdened the horse, lugging Tomas' heavy saddle and throwing it over the stall divider. Inquisitively, she poked about in the saddle bag and found the pearl-handled dagger and his leather purse, which contained several gold ducats.

Reaching down to the bottom of the purse her fingers brushed against a soft bundle. She withdrew something very curious—a chestnut lock of her hair that Tomas had carefully braided with a length of his own long blond hair and tied with a ribbon. Katkin looked at it sorrowfully for a long moment, again feeling keenly the loss of Captain Tomas de Vigny. Katkin could not bring herself to burn the braid, though she knew for Jacq's sake she should. Instead, she shoved it down in her pocket. Thoughtfully, she placed all the other items back in the bag, and buried it deeply out of sight under a large pile of hay in Pollux's stall.

Jacq soaked happily in a deep marble tub in one of the upstairs bathrooms of the château, as his comrades brought up bucket after bucket of hot water from the copper outside. Though his commander wanted to meet with him and learn the details of his five day imprisonment, he had ordered him to have a bath and be deloused first. The debriefing could wait until he smelled sweet enough to be indoors with.

Katkin sat on the edge of the bath and recounted the whole story of how she came to be in the Acre in a Guardsman's uniform as he scrubbed away a week's worth of accumulated dried blood and filth from the Citadel. Jacq shook his head incredulously at the Captain's role in her escape. It did not seem possible to him that de Vigny could have developed a conscience, not after all the things he had said and done. But when Katkin told her husband of Tomas' final sacrifice on his behalf, Jacq was frankly disbelieving.

"He must have been suicidal already, either because his wife left him or his father's death. That devil would never have traded his life for mine," he said, adamantly. Katkin made no reply to this. She could not argue with his conclusion, firmly based on his experiences with Tomas de Vigny. After all, he did not know the whole story and he never would.

"Wash my back for me?" he asked her, and leaned forward in the water. Katkin took a sharp breath and dropped the soapy rag in the bath. "What is the matter? Does the sight of my scars still upset you so?" he asked her in concern.

She shook her head in surprise. "The scars are almost gone. They must have been healed at the same time Lalluna and I dealt with your other wounds. It was so dark in the wain I never knew it until now." He happened to be looking directly at her face, lit by a sunbeam from the bare window, and so glimpsed the shadow of pain that passed across it before she could chase it away with a smile.

Jacq sat back in the bath abruptly, sending a wave of soapy water onto the marble floor. Leaning his head back, he closed his eyes against the magnitude of what he had just witnessed, and asked a question he would have rather not known the answer to. "It hurt you, didn't it? As much as it did me. Don't pretend. I saw the truth in your eyes just now."

She sighed deeply and looked away from him. "Yes, my husband. I felt it all, just as you did, but Lalluna was there and she helped me bear it."

259

Reaching up, he pulled her down into the bathwater with him and held her close. "I can never repay you for all that you have suffered on my sorry account," he said sadly. "I have caused you nothing but pain since you married me."

Katkin disagreed with him. "You are wrong, my husband. I have had much more joy than pain."

Jacq, with his arms around her in the bath, felt how thin she had become—he could easily count her ribs with his fingers through her wet clothes. He wondered how she could be so strong when there looked to be so little left of her, for he felt then that her strength must almost equal his own. Strangely enough, Jacq took no comfort at all in this thought, for he still wanted only to protect his beloved wife from everything.

A soft knock at the door disturbed them and Katkin heard Willow say, "Jacq, are you in there? Do you know where Katkin is?" Laughing, Katkin stepped out of the bath, wringing the water out of the guardsman's uniform she still wore and went out to see her sister.

Later, while Jacq met with his Commander, Katkin sought out Jacq's mother. After wandering though many forlornly empty rooms and passages she finally found Elisabeth in a small sitting room on the first floor. The room held only a couple of chairs and a small table with an oil lamp. Most of the items in the great house had been sold to raise money for the Rising or chopped up for firewood. Even the tall windows were bare—the curtains had been torn down and ripped up for bandages and wadding. Elisabeth stood and put down her book when she saw Katkin approach. She hugged her briefly, and held her at arm's length to study her face and her unusual haircut, then sighed, saying, "I don't know how you survived everything that happened, my dear, but I am very glad to see you here. You saved my son's life, and for that I must give you my thanks." Her light blue eyes regarded Katkin seriously and at that moment they reminded her very much of her husband's. "I am sorry for what Nathan and I thought to do with you on the night you came to us. Can you forgive me?"

"I understand why you had to try, my mother, and you must understand why I ran away from you and Nathan. I believed that Reynard murdered my parents, and I did not want to be taken anywhere near him. Now I have learned differently, though there is still much I don't understand." Katkin rubbed the stubble on her head distractedly. Willow had given her a dress to wear and she felt a little strange in it. She certainly preferred the trousers of the uniform for comfort. But she had hidden them away carefully, with the black shirt and the cap, in the saddlebag that now resided in the pile of hay in Pollux's stall, against the day when they might be needed once more.

Jacq's mother sighed. "That you have questions, I do not doubt. Much has been wrongly kept from you, my dear, and not just by your husband. I, too, have secrets that I hesitated to share with you, knowing your feelings about Commander Reynard. Ask your questions now, daughter. I will hold nothing back."

So Katkin asked her how she had come to know about the attack on Tintaren.

Elisabeth's eyes went blank and far away for a moment. "I knew because I received advance warning from Nicholas Reynard. He is my lover, Katkin, and Kadya's father. And Jessie's, may she rest in peace."

Katkin stared at her, dumbfounded. Of all the explanations she expected to be given, that one had never crossed her mind.

Elisabeth smiled at her shocked expression. "Yes, I thought that might be your reaction. Let me start the tale from the beginning, while you find your tongue again. When he was ten years old, some Guardsmen caught Jacq throwing stones at their horses as they passed. The leader of the detachment brought him back to me and told me the sorry tale. I felt so bad about what my son had done that I invited the officer inside for a cup of tea. To my surprise he accepted, and stayed an hour. He told me of his home in the far north and how much he missed his family there. Mr. Benet had been dead two years and I had no friends among the other cottars, so I was happy to spend an hour with this soft-spoken soldier who seemed to be as lonely as I."

She paused to smile again at Katkin. "I suppose you have guessed by now that the soldier was Nicholas Reynard, though he introduced himself to me as Kolya. I have called him that ever since. To my surprise, he came back to see us the next time he passed through Belladore, and the next. He became a regular visitor. I learned much about his life in the City and he learned of mine at Tintaren. One night, very late, after Jacq and his brothers had gone to bed, Kolya knocked on my door. Rebels had killed fourteen of his men that day in an ambush, and he looked care-worn and sad. It never occurred to me to ask him why he had chosen to come to me instead of going home to his own wife. I just took him into my bed, and he stayed the night, leaving before the dawn to get back to the City on time. After that, I never knew when he might appear, but it always pleased me when he did. Before long, I found I was pregnant."

"He already had a wife when you bore him a child?" asked Katkin. "Why did he not divorce her and marry you?"

Elisabeth sighed. "Though she had a lover of her own, his spiteful wife would not give her permission. When I gave birth to Kadya, it gave Kolya great happiness, though I did not share it."

"Why, my mother?"

"I was struggling to feed the four children I already had, Katkin, and another hungry mouth was not going to make my life any easier. Kolya helped me as much as he could with Kadya but his wife spent extravagantly and he had little left at the end of each month. Later, I got pregnant again with Jessie. My dire situation made me very angry and I did not see how I could possibly go on. So, I sent Kolya a letter telling him never to return." She sighed deeply and Katkin felt acutely sorry for her parent's former worker, whose life had been so very difficult. In all her years at Tintaren it had simply never occurred to her that the cottars who worked the fields might suffer from hunger and want, while she herself had every luxury.

Elisabeth continued. "I had Jessie the year the potato crop failed, and we had nothing much to eat. The older children went out to glean the dried wheat stalks left from the harvest in the fields, or pick dandelion weeds—anything we could subsist on. But my milk dried up anyway and Jessie starved to death when she was two months old." She paused to wipe the tears from her eyes, saying sadly, "It never gets any easier to tell that story. I still miss her—my only little girl child."

Katkin thought about her own baby girl, growing inside her. How would she feel if she had to watch the child die of hunger, and could do nothing to prevent it? The thought could not be borne. She said, "I am so sorry, my mother. It must have been terribly painful."

Elisabeth nodded. "I tried to contact Kolya, just before the end, but he had been sent far from the City on a campaign. Hunger preyed on all the poor that winter. Some of the cottars tried to take food stores from their masters by force and the King called out the Guard to put down the uprising. One day, about a month after Jessie's death, Kolya came to see me again. He cursed at me furiously when I told him what had happened and rode away on Rufus like a storm from the east. I thought I would never see him again. A little later I heard he had been killed in an ambush north of the City and the news devastated me, for I still loved him very much."

"What? How could that be true?" Katkin asked, thoroughly confused.

"He led a detachment of soldiers north to subdue a group of renegades. Without his knowledge the men brutally abused the captives before killing them all. Kolya cannot abide cruelty in any form and he decided then he could no longer fight for the Guard. Later the same day, other cottars, seeking revenge, captured some of Kolya's men, locked them in a barn and set it alight. The fire left nothing but an unidentifiable heap of ash and bone. Kolya deserted his regiment and allowed them to think he had perished in the blaze with his men. So, he left his career in the King's Guard along with his last name, and became Nicholas Reynard, Commander of the Rising. That is why no one in the City knows who he is."

"And you, my mother? You thought he was dead. How did you find out otherwise?"

"He came to me one night, not long after, as he used to. When I opened the door, I thought I saw a ghost." She smiled and said wryly, "He soon convinced me otherwise. And that is how I came to know of the attack on Tintaren beforehand. Have I answered your question, Katkin? Do you have another?"

Katkin thought of Jacq's disturbing memories and her own visions of her husband bearing magnificent gray wings. She asked suddenly, "Who is Jacq's real father?"

Elisabeth looked stricken, but answered in a monotone. "I thought you knew that already. Jacq's father is Francois Benet. A blacksmith I met at your parent's estate. He was a very ordinary man, Katkin. Jacq is nothing like him." The subject seemed to be a painful one for her mother-in-law and although Katkin was positive she was hiding something, she decided not to press her further.

Elisabeth sighed and looked out the window at the rising moon. She said softly, "I am not gifted, as you are, with Sight, but still somehow in my heart I know my son's fate belongs to the whole Yrth."

Katkin regarded her curiously. "What do you mean?"

She paused, unsure whether her daughter-in-law would understand what she was trying to say. "You were chosen by Lalluna, were you not? She has given you Gifts beyond the ken of any mortal." When Katkin nodded uncertainly, Elisabeth continued, "Jacq has been chosen too. Ask me not how I know it, but I do."

A breeze stirred through the open window and the candles guttered on the wall. The shadows deepened and Katkin realized it must be quite late. She stood and stretched, then said thoughtfully, "Good night, mother. Goddess grant you peace."

With that, she went to seek out her husband and her bed.

19

Dread

(Estate of Naer, Two Reversed)

Geya watches over the sleeping mountain, Hythea. It was time for her to wake.

Moonlight, now is the moment for you to return to your people. Soon the Prime God will have no power left in St. Valery.

~~~~~~~~~~~~~~

Katkin slept peacefully next to Jacq on a mattress that lay on the floor of an elaborately plastered room, upstairs in the main wing of the Foxhole. Other than the mattress, the room held nothing except a spindly table sitting on the uncovered floorboards. The bare windows stood wide open to allow the summer breezes to enter. Neither Jacq nor Katkin woke as the room began to tremble gently, though Jacq stirred, and turned over, sighing deeply. In the office of Nicolas Reynard, where the Commander slept alone on a narrow camp cot, Fiann woke and whined quietly, suddenly afraid. The sentries on duty at the perimeter fortifications noted the time and went back to their patrols. The shaking lasted perhaps thirty seconds and ended without a trace.

Lalluna, wings folded gracefully, watched from her perch on top of the table. She looked sadly at her vessel and the man the girl loved more than anything. Then, closing her moonlit eyes, Lalluna sent Katkin a dream.

The dream began in a darkness so overpowering that Katkin could see nothing. The sound of her own breathing and pulse filled her ears with whispered staccato drumbeats. High above her, a red glow began to shimmer, until it appeared the very fires of Hell had been somehow transported up into the heavenly firmament. The moon rose in a smoke-wracked sky, gravid and blood red. The sight of it made Katkin very afraid, and she tried to run away, but her legs would not bear her far. White flakes rained down from the sky and landed softly, like snow, in her hair. Black ashes and pieces of cinder covered the ground as far as she could see.

Looking around her anxiously, she knew she stood in the Infirmarie compound, yet it looked very different in this hellishly-lit darkness. Some unknown force had damaged the main buildings severely. The muck falling from the sky slowly buried others. Fires burned out of control all around her. Going inside the main wing, she opened the door to the first ward. Black shrouded patients occupied a line of beds against the wall. Pulling back the covers from the first body and then the next, Katkin cried out in terror at the sight of their faces, so hideously burned the bones poked through the shriveled, blackened flesh. The bodies began gliding upwards with fleshless hands outstretched, and then backed her into a corner, where she sank to the floor, covering her head with her arms.

Jacq sat up in bed, his heart hammering painfully, eyes searching the darkness to find the source of the noise that had woken him. He groped for his sword automatically, and touched it reassuringly where it lay on the floor next to the bed. Then he realized that Katkin tossed and shivered uncontrollably next to him, seemingly in the grip of some nighttime horror. Releasing his grip on the sword, he shook her shoulder gently, trying to wake her. Her eyes snapped open at once, but they appeared blank and far away. In a strange, low-pitched voice she said, "I hear the cries of my sister the Yrth..." With another strangled cry she truly woke, her eyes shining bright and frightened in the darkness.

"Katkin, wake up. It is all right, my love, you just had a bad dream. Look, I have you now." Jacq put his arms around her stiffened form and slowly she relaxed into his body.

"Oh, Jacq, what a horrible nightmare," she whispered. "Everything was destroyed, black and burned. And the people..." She could not describe the terror of those faces.

He said comfortingly, "Do not be afraid, my wife. It is over now and I am here with you." His arms tightened around her and she rested her head on his broad chest, listening to his strong and steady heartbeat. Soon, by the sound of his low and sonorous snoring, she knew he had fallen asleep again. Katkin lay awake for many more hours, replaying the images from her dream. She wondered if it was some message from Lalluna, but if so, she had no idea what it might mean. But the words she remembered chilled her to the bone:

I hear the cries of my sister the Yrth. No more shall blood from the bright swords of men stain the ground. All shall perish. All shall be cleansed with the fire. Hythea has spoken.

The day dawned clear and sunny. The dream faded back into the recesses of her mind, as Katkin rose with Jacq to have breakfast in the great ballroom of the château, which now served as a mess hall. Reynard did not appear, being busy with the overnight reports of the sentries, and an early messenger from the City.

Jacq kissed her goodbye after the meal and said he would be away most of the day, training new recruits. He studied her face for a moment and said, "You look so tired, my love. Try to get some rest today while I am gone." Patting her stomach affectionately, he said, "You must take better care of yourself now we have a baby on the way."

But Katkin found lying in the empty bedroom enervating rather than restful, so she got up and sought out her sister. Yannick opened the door to their room and said abruptly, "What do you want?" Katkin, still very uncomfortable in his presence, turned away without speaking, but he called her back. "I never thanked you for saving Roseberry. You risked your life for my child and for that I should be grateful," he said quietly.

"I am very glad I could help," she said.

He hesitated for a moment before saying, "And as for the Dinrhydan, you saved his life as well, didn't you? All of us owe you our thanks for that." She nodded, and did not say anything about Tomas' death or Lalluna's assistance, thinking Yannick would not understand.

This thawing of relations with him emboldened her to ask a question that had been on her mind ever since she arrived at the Foxhole. "Yannick, how did Jacq become the Dinrhydan?"

Yannick shook his head and said, "The Commander is the only one who knows the full answer to that question. You should ask him yourself, if you can find him unoccupied for a few minutes during the day."

267

After finding out that Willow had gone for a walk to calm the teething Roseberry, Katkin went outside in the cobbled courtyard to look for them. The sun already blazed in the cloudless sky and it promised to be a hot day. Beyond the courtyard, Katkin could see a grassy parade field and a group of ragtag soldiers, all wearing yellow armbands, practicing close order drilling. Jacq's tall figure strode among them, encouraging and instructing. She shivered as she watched him—it seemed she would never get used to the idea of his being a soldier rather than the humble blacksmith she thought she knew.

Nicholas Reynard came and stood beside her. "It must be difficult for you to see him like that."

Katkin looked at him in surprise. His comment so neatly matched her thoughts she wondered if he had sensed them somehow.

"Yes," she said. "He is very different now than the man I thought I married."

He regarded her steadily, and asked, "Are you so sure? For the qualities which drew you to him—his honesty, courage and compassion—are all the same things that make him a natural leader of men in battle."

Katkin nodded. "That is true, yet I would have him use those qualities for peaceful ends if I could." At that moment, the ground began to tremble again, and she said in alarm, "What is happening? Commander, do you feel it?"

Reynard nodded and said, as the shaking subsided, "It is because of these tremors I sought you out. Another happened last night, though you must have slept through it. I would speak with you in my office, if you have a moment." He turned and she followed him inside, wondering apprehensively what on Yrth the leader of the Rising could want to talk to her about.

Fiann rose, stretched, and ran to greet his master as Reynard entered the office. Sumptuous oak and mahogany paneling once covered the walls, but now most of it had gone for firewood and the bare lath and plaster gave the room a most disheveled look. After patting the dog and distractedly scratching behind his ears, Reynard sent him back to his bed in the corner. But the dog disobeyed him and instead loped over to Katkin, who had just entered through the double glass doors. Rearing up, he put both feet on her shoulders so that his head rose well above hers. The Commander, embarrassed at this display of bad manners from his normally well-behaved dog, began a sharply spoken rebuke, and then cut it off in surprise. For Katkin, obviously unperturbed, had placed her hand on the dog's face and was talking to him softly. Fiann stood completely still and Reynard could almost believe the dog understood what she said. Finally, after giving her a comprehensive lick on the face, Fiann dropped down to all fours again and padded off to his bed, looking very thoughtful indeed.

Shaking his head in wonder, Nicholas invited the Dinrhydan's wife to sit down. He found this uncanny ability to communicate with animals fascinating, but he had no time to question her more closely about it. The earth tremors and the strange report he had gotten from the City this morning needed his full attention.

"Yannick has told me the story of Roseberry's rescue, and it is of that I would speak with you, if I may," Reynard said.

Katkin nodded tentatively, unsure of what details he could possibly want from her.

"A message has arrived from one of our contacts in the City. A cloud of smoke and steam crowns Mount Hythea. Some people have reported seeing a red glow from the summit at night."

Katkin's eyes went wide. The Commander was telling her about the tremors in the City and the surrounding countryside, but she hardly heard him. Now he looked at her expectantly, awaiting an answer to a question he must have just put to her.

"I am sorry. What... What did you ask me, again?" she whispered.

"I asked whether you saw any evidence of volcanic activity when you followed the path down to the centre of the mountain. When you went in after Roseberry, I mean." He stared at her, perplexed by her agitation.

Katkin sighed, and said, "I would rather not talk about my experience in the Temple in any great detail, Commander. Such a place is sacred to me. But I will tell you there is a pool of boiling mud at the end of the cave." She closed her eyes, hearing the final agonies of the Maitress once more and remembering how the mud had frothed over the side of the pit, almost as if it had been a living thing.

269

"Will you confide to me nothing else? I swear it will not leave this room," he said in frustration.

"No," she said firmly. "There is nothing else to tell."

"Very well," he said, resigned to her reticence. Jacq's wife seemed a fey creature sometimes, yet he did not underestimate her power. What mastery over hurt and disease did she possess? He knew it would be fruitless to ask such a question of her. She would not answer.

She smiled shyly at him and it struck him how young she was, in truth, for all her mysterious power. "I would ask a question of you now, Commander, if you have time."

"Of course, and please call me Nicholas," he said, smiling in return and hoping in this way he might win her trust.

"I wanted Yannick to tell me the story of how Jacq became the Dinrhydan, but he said you were the one who knew it best."

Reynard asked gravely, "Has Jacq not told you the tale himself?"

Katkin shook her head, and said, "Jacq would never tell me stories of his own heroism. He is far too modest for that. I would like to know all the same, though."

"Then I will tell you, my dear, as much as I can. It is a long story, and I have only a little time to spare this morning, before I must ride out to inspect another of the camps. Some time, perhaps, when this War is over, you shall hear the tale in full, because there will be songs sung to celebrate the exploits of the Dinrhydan and his bright sword d'angwir, do not doubt it." He sighed, settled back in his chair and looked into the middle distance, remembering.

"I first made Jacq's acquaintance when he was ten years old, and a proper young rapscallion he was, too. Elisabeth met me at the door the first day I brought him to her and boxed his ears while I watched. Then she invited me in for tea. We became friends at first and later, lovers, so I saw a lot of young Jacq. Life had been difficult for him and he already possessed courage and maturity far beyond his years."

Katkin nodded in agreement, remembering his refusal to bend before her father.

"After his sister Jessie died, he finished growing up more or less overnight and decided to go off to the City to train as a blacksmith.

270

After I made up my mind to leave the Guard and throw my lot in with the Rising, he came to me and offered to become an agent for us. Because he was only fifteen, Katkin, I turned him down, thinking him too young to be of much help. Jacq kept his eyes and ears open anyway and soon he began sending me valuable information from the Citadel through Elisabeth. His duties as a blacksmith and farrier meant he always knew when the Guard needed horses for patrols and action outside the City. He gave us advance warning on several attacks planned by the Guard. I warned Elisabeth how dangerous this unofficial spying could be for him, but he would not listen to his mother or me. Because of Jessie, he believed very strongly in the cause we had taken up."

"That makes sense," said Katkin. "I asked him again and again how he could be working for the Guard when it seemed obvious his sympathies were with the Rising."

"By age twenty, Jacq had become my most trusted and senior contact in the Citadel. Still he wanted to do more, so I assigned him to a group of men carrying out sabotage and escort duties. He began taking leave from his job at the Citadel whenever he could. His first such mission, escorting some wounded soldiers back to the Foxhole, became a baptism of fire. A force of Guardsmen ambushed them at the bridge over the Ariane River. Jacq held the bridge alone against thirty men, after running back to help one of the wounded that had not been able to get across. After he had driven back the invaders he carried the injured man to safety."

Katkin looked at him in amazement. "Jacq held off thirty men, all alone? Did the man he helped make it back alive, too?"

Nicholas nodded. "It was Yannick Abelard. Ever since that day, he has been your husband's most devoted friend. I knew after hearing about the ambush that Jacq could acquit himself extraordinarily well in the arena of battle, and I gave him more responsibilities within the Rising. Now he commands his own unit. He leads by example and his men are completely devoted to him. They gave him the name Dinrhydan. For even in heavy fighting, Jacq will always go back for a fallen comrade and carry him to safety, as he did on the Ariane River Bridge with Yannick. He has risked his own life many times over the years on such rescues."

Then Katkin asked him about the sword, d'angwir, describing

her astonishment when Jacq pulled the bundle from under the floorboards.

Nicholas smiled and shook his head. "I can well imagine your shock, my dear. Once Jacq made up his mind to fight for us, as well as acting as a spy, he knew he needed a weapon. But an ordinary sword would not do, because of his immense strength and height. He forged d'angwir himself, working late at night at the smithy in the Citadel. So it is a very special sword, distinctively long and heavy. But by using a full face helmet during combat and the code name Dinrhydan, Jacq was able to keep his true identity secret until the day you had to rescue Roseberry."

Katkin nodded, for the first time understanding Tomas' interest in the sword, when he picked it up outside the Temple.

"Jacq would have gone on spying at the Citadel indefinitely, but de Vigny made his life pretty difficult once he knew Jacq was his rival for your affections. He asked for leave and I granted it willingly. A few days later, he woke me very early in the morning to ask if he could marry you! I was very surprised at that. Of course I said he had no need to ask my permission."

Katkin smiled, remembering the urgent business Jacq had said he must take care of before he proposed to her.

"After he left the Citadel and the two of you were married, he continued to lead missions for me as often as he could, and he almost always accomplished whatever I asked of him with few casualties."

"So all those hunting trips with Yannick were merely a cover?" she asked him.

"Most of them were, yes. Jacq wanted to keep you safe, my dear. At the same time, he wanted to go on helping the Rising in any way he could. He felt torn in two, and it caused him much pain," said Nicholas.

Katkin sighed. "I know now it would have been far better for him if we had come west right after we were married. Jacq suggested the idea to me, but I wanted to stay in Belladore to be close to Willow and he agreed. I wish he had told me the truth from the beginning, Nicholas. So much anguish might have been averted."

"You must not blame yourself, Katkin. How could you have known what dangers lay ahead? He gave you no information, thinking he could continue to do his work for me without your knowledge." He smiled. "I told him he was a fool, but Jacq was ever stubborn, especially about you, and he wouldn't listen to me."

Katkin smiled at this, yet Reynard thought he saw a trace of sadness in her green eyes.

Nicholas looked at her intently and asked, "Now you are here, are you happy? I know the events of the night we surrounded Tintaren have been a terrible burden for you and I feel responsible for that. You lost your home and your parents. How could I blame you if you still harbored resentment against the Rising and me?"

It took her a long time to answer his question. "I don't hate you or the Rising any longer, Nicholas. On my wedding day, Willow helped me to understand what the loss of Tintaren really meant, and I do not rue it, not now. Still, I will not be happy until Jacq can put away his sword and we can live together in peace." She leaned forward, her expression intense. "When I was a child I thought of you as my enemy. I felt a simple comfort in blaming my unhappiness and loss on one man. Now I know my true adversary is far stronger and much more deadly. It is the War itself. I have no doubt in my mind this enemy will eventually steal from me everything I care about. All of you—the Rising and the King's Guard—align yourselves against me with your bright swords and your unquenchable desire for the blood of your enemy. We stand on opposite sides of this greater conflict— the one between peace and war—and I shall willingly fight to the death to save the things I love."

He looked at her in confusion. Her words, which he did not understand, were spoken with a conviction and maturity far beyond her nineteen years.

The tremors continued and so did Katkin's hellish nightmares. Visions of the City, burned black and buried in ash and cinder, haunted her each night. Jacq tried, without success, to convince her to drink one of his mother's possets to help her sleep. She stared at him wide-eyed, saying, "I cannot ignore the dreams or suppress them, my husband, do you not see? They are a message from Lalluna. I must find out what they mean before it is too late. Something terrible is going to happen."

Jacq seriously wondered if the pressures of the last few weeks had made her unstable and worried constantly when he had to be away from her. He enlisted his mother and Willow to keep watch over her. But Katkin often eluded them and would walk the perimeter walls for hours, like a caged animal, her only companions Pollux and Nicholas' big wolfhound, Fiann. Inside her, the conviction grew that she would have to leave very soon. A storm gathered on the horizon, and it would be far more deadly than this little conflict between the Rising and the Guard. Lalluna called her, but still her love for Jacq made her hesitate.

Reynard looked at his lieutenants, arrayed around his desk at the Foxhole. Jacq and Yannick attended the meeting, as well as representatives from every other camp.

He spoke gravely. "My comrades, the events in the City over the last few weeks have caused great fear and confusion there. Hythea has been spewing hot ash and cinders, and since the summer has been dry, many fires have broken out in the City. The Guard have been kept very busy. Their numbers are thinly spread across the whole of the mountain and they have not engaged us in the field for some time." He spoke decisively, "This is the moment we have been waiting for, comrades, the moment when we can attack the Citadel with everything we have and be victorious. The City of Isle St. Valery will fall to us in two days time and many old wrongs shall be righted. Now, I would hear from each one of you. Tell me your thoughts."

In the heat and silence of that midsummer afternoon, one by one, the men around the desk spoke softly and nodded their heads in agreement. Only Jacq Benet hesitated briefly, thinking of his wife's ill health and wondering what such a campaign would do to her already fragile state of mind. After a moment, he nodded in turn and made the decision to protect her by once again keeping the truth to himself.

Another presence in the room watched with apprehension. Lalluna shook her head sadly. The fools wanted to march right into the middle of the holocaust and she could do nothing to prevent them.

Everything rested now on the shoulders of her vessel.

Katkin was dreaming again. This time, instead of the burned out City, she found herself in Nicholas Reynard's office. Jacq stood there, along with a lot of other men she did not recognize. The Commander, standing up behind his desk, spoke to them. Katkin heard every word, and saw each man nod in agreement—even Jacq. Though she did not wake up screaming, this dream was by far the most horrifying of all the nightmares, for it meant time had run out. She could delay her departure for the City no longer.

Rising quietly, Katkin stood and looked for a long moment at Jacq, sleeping peacefully, his curly brown head pillowed on his outstretched arm. "Good bye, my love. I hope you can understand why I have to go. Lalluna has need of me."

Not daring to touch him, lest he wake, she sent a kiss through the air and turned away. In Nicholas Reynard's office, the dog, Fiann, stirred and whined quietly.

Outside, the full moon rode high in the cloudless night sky. Her figure cast a flat black shadow as she crossed the cobbled courtyard. Once inside the stable she crept over to Pollux. He stood quietly in the darkness, wide awake, as though he had been waiting for her. He made no sound as she hefted the saddle across his back and tightened the girth. She found Tomas' saddlebag in the hay, and threw on the Guard uniform and boots, which hung even more loosely on her emaciated frame.

She mounted Pollux and would have ridden towards the open stable door, but she saw then that her husband stood before her, wearing only his breeches, and he held d'angwir in his hand. The blade shone like liquid silver in the moonlight.

"Where are you going, Kat?" he asked her quietly.

"I must go to the City, Jacq. Something terrible is going to happen and I have to stop it." She sighed and looked down upon him. His stormy expression clearly showed he did not believe her.

"Listen to me, my wife. You are unwell. All this..." here he made a sweeping motion with his arm as if to include the War itself. "All this has been too much for you. Come back inside with me now and let me hold you in our bed until dawn. I promise I will stay awake with you and keep your dreams at bay. When morning comes, I will go to the Commander and tell him I am leaving the Rising. Together, we will travel far away from here and I will start afresh with you, as if it was our wedding day once more. I will be the craftsman you loved, and put my sword away forever, I swear it." He raised his hand up to her. "Nothing is more important to me now, only that I heal you of this terrible sickness. Just get down off Pollux. Please, my love."

His tearful entreaty cut her to the quick. He would give up everything he fought for, because of his love for her.

Sadly, she shook her head, though she would have given anything to be able to do as he asked. "You think I am mad. I am not. I must go, for Lalluna has need of me."

Jacq felt his exasperation mounting, though he struggled to hide it from her. "I think you are frail and infirm, my wife, and I blame myself, completely. The nightmares are just a product of your disturbed mind." She shook her head again and he said angrily, "Why do you not believe me, Katkin? I am telling the truth." He stepped forward a pace and Pollux snorted in alarm and backed up.

Katkin spoke softly. "I had a different dream this night, my husband. The Commander of the Rising told his Lieutenants he planned to attack the City in two days time, with every man and weapon at his disposal. Was that a product of my unhappy mind?"

He looked at her in wide-eyed disbelief. "How could you possibly know that? We were all sworn to secrecy." Then he whispered, "You frighten me so much. I know not who you are any more."

His unconscious repetition of her own words to him by the wain was a cruel irony that hurt her very much.

Still she answered firmly, "I know because Lalluna told me. When Reynard attacks the City, everyone is going to perish. Now I *must* go, so please get out of my way. Though I love you more than anything, I cannot do as you ask."

Jacq shook his head. "No! I will not let you throw your life and the life of our child away for this madness. I have to stop you, and someday you will thank me."

Reaching down into Tomas' saddlebag, Katkin retrieved the pearl-handled dagger and held it up before him. "You will have to kill me then, for I will not go with you willingly, my husband."

"Kat, no, don't make me fight you. Gods, please girl, I beg you, don't do this." He was crying openly now and it broke her heart to see him so unhappy. Only her dedication to Lalluna prevented her from jumping down from Pollux and throwing herself into his arms.

Then she saw Jacq's expression harden as he raised his sword a fraction. He had decided his only chance to save her was to kill Pollux with a vicious slash to the throat. Though it might injure her when the pain-crazed horse reared, at least she would still be with him and alive. As he stepped forward, something incredibly heavy hit him hard in the middle of his back and he went sprawling face down onto the hay-strewn stable floor. His sword flew from his hand and out of reach.

Fiann snarled menacingly as Jacq stiffly turned over, seeking the thing that knocked him down. The dog stepped on to his chest and stayed there, slavering, with his teeth bared and hackles raised.

Katkin said, "Don't hurt him, Fiann. Just hold him until I am safely away." Jacq saw her urge Pollux forward. Saying, "Farewell, Jacq, I love you always," she left him crying brokenly on the stable floor.

After a minute, Fiann lost his grim look and licked Jacq's face apologetically. Jacq slowly rose to his feet, rubbing his elbow where it had been slammed into the stable floor. Fiann weighed over two hundred pounds and had hit him like a cannon ball square in the back. He had no doubt his wife had somehow called the dog to her aid. Jacq walked across the stable and retrieved his sword, which had impaled the wooden wall of the tack room. Turning away, he made the unhappy trek back to the Foxhole to wake his Commander and tell him of Katkin's mad desertion.

Reynard, presiding over a hastily called meeting of all his lieutenants, had just been given a report by one of the sentries on the perimeter wall. Though Jacq immediately sent word to the main gate for them to stop his wife at all costs, she had never appeared there. Instead she and Pollux had apparently ridden hard for the east perimeter fence. The sentries on duty reported hearing a female voice say, "Pollux, you must carry me back the way you came into the Foxhole. Give me all your strength now, great heart, for Lalluna has need of it." As they ran to confront the speaker, the sentries saw Pollux, running as swiftly as a wind from the west, jump high and sail over the six foot tall stone wall with Katkin clinging to his back. He landed cleanly on the other side and melted into the shadows. The pursuers had found no trace of him or the Dinrhydan's wife.

Yannick, now bitterly regretting his earlier overture of peace to Katkin, said angrily, "That witch will betray us all to the Guard! She was ever a turncoat, Dinrhydan. Only your love for her prevented you from seeing it."

Jacq turned on him furiously, his huge fists raised. He growled, "My wife is ill, Abelard, not a traitor. It would be very wise for you to retract what you just said."

Nicholas Reynard stepped hastily between the two men and spoke quietly, trying to calm them both. "Dinrhydan, for the god's sake, sit down. A fight between you and Yannick is the last thing we need right now. For what it is worth, I don't believe your wife has gone to the City to betray the Rising. She follows some inner prompting, perhaps, that seems irrational to the rest of us. She can do no harm though, for she knows nothing of the planned invasion."

Jacq sank into a chair, putting his head in his hands, and said nothing of Katkin's last dream.

Reynard continued, "Of course I fear for her safety, for if she is arrested and taken to the Citadel they will try every method they can to extract information from her."

Jacq groaned, his face still hidden. The others looked on him with sympathy, except Yannick, who muttered to himself about the just penalty for witchcraft.

"We must go ahead with the invasion as soon as we may, and perhaps we will be in time to save her. You must not give up hope, my friend." Nicholas placed his hand on Jacq's trembling shoulder to comfort him. But he, too, felt terribly worried about the girl and her sudden urge to go to the City. He thought about her last words to him on the day he asked her about Hythea:

All of you—the Rising and the King's Guard, align yourselves against me with your bright swords and your unquenchable desire for the blood of your enemy. We stand on opposite sides of this greater conflict—the one between peace and war—and I shall willingly fight to the death to save the things I love.

He remembered the intensity of her wide-eyed stare as she spoke. Now he wondered more and more what she meant.

20

Prince Carolet

(Arkirish Dynasty, Three)

Why must we use my vessel in this way, Geya? She has already proved her worth in stopping the sacrifices.

Geya's voice is cold. You need her to win the hearts of your people, Moonlight. Her suffering is of little consequence to us.

Moonlight shakes her lovely head, deeply troubled by her elder sister's callousness.

~~~~~~~~~~

Katkin reached the lakeshore in a little over four hours, riding over thirty miles in that time. Pollux was stumbling tiredly when they finally stopped by a rundown shed and quay close to the water. One of the many independent ferries that crossed the Mere daily docked there. No doubt the ferryman slept inside on his bed and Katkin hoped, with the help of Tomas' gold, to persuade him to get up and pole her across Mistmere. She planned to leave Pollux behind, for she knew he would be of no use to her once she reached the City.

Pounding on the door, she roused the man, and heard him complain, "All right, all right, don't break down the door. I'm coming." When at last he arrived, she saw he was unkempt and probably drunk, for he smelled strongly of ale and sweat.

Katkin, remembering at the last moment she was meant to be a lad, had to lower her pitch in mid-sentence and hope it sounded as though her voice was changing. She said, "I need to get to the City, Sir. I deserted my regiment three days ago, now I have changed my mind and want to get back in time for muster. Would you take me?"

The ferryman shook his head, cursed, and made to slam the door in her face.

Then she said, "I have gold."

"Pollux," she said sadly. "I cannot take you with me. Make your way back to the Foxhole in your own time by the safest and most secret ways. Let Jacq take care of you, great heart, and I will come back for you if I may. May the Goddess Epona protect you, Pollux. Farewell." She fondly held the black horse's head close to her breast for a moment, as the ferryman swore colorfully in his impatience to be gone.

Crossing the Mere, she sat very still and quiet as the ferryman tried to engage her in drunken conversation. He took his time, poling lazily, telling her, "Haven't had no business in two days, Lad. Benedict's shut off the City and no one's getting out or in. Mighty surprised you want to go back. I've heard there's been rioting in the streets. You'd be much better off in the countryside where you can get away if Hythea blows her stack."

Katkin lowered her voice and said firmly, "Then we must hurry, Sir, for the King will be in need of my help." The ferryman only grinned drunkenly and continued to push the quant slowly through the dark waters of the Mistmere.

"The King? He don't need no one's help," he muttered after a moment. "He's safe enough in the Citadel on his fancy throne, if you ask me. But he knows right enough that if word gets out about the mountain, the Mardonne or the Rising will be knocking on the Yoke Gate 'ere long. That's all he cares about, not the commoners like you and me, Lad. We can all fry long as he stays safe, I reckon."

Katkin took in this information silently, knowing that if she could not stop Hythea then everyone in the City would perish from the poorest of the poor to the King, even though he had locked himself away in the Citadel. The thought made her feel numbed and useless.

The water slipped slowly by, and they appeared to be making little progress. As the ferryman continued his drunken ramblings, she used the time to plan her next move, once she reached St. Valery. Katkin had no idea what she needed to do in order to stop the eruption that threatened to destroy the City and the surrounding countryside. She quickly decided it would be useless to approach the King with a warning; he would probably not believe her and might very well call the Guard to make an arrest, since she was still a fugitive. Then she thought of Becka, her former best friend at the Infirmarie. After all, Becka, in her role as the Maitress, might have useful information about Hythea. Katkin could not help thinking the key to the puzzle would be found somewhere in the Temple of Lalluna, on the grounds of the Infirmarie.

She had been so deep in thought it took a few moments for her to realize the ferry had silently glided to a halt. The moon had set some time ago and the Mere looked as still and black as obsidian. The ferryman slowly removed the dripping quant from the water and placed it carefully across the stern.

"What is wrong?" she asked. "Why do you stop, Sir? I have to make haste to get to my muster on time." Though she tried hard to sound unworried, her voice echoed shrill and strained in her own ears.

The ferryman staggered forward and dropped down beside her on the low bench.

"What's yer hurry, laddie? Fine lookin' boy like you gets a lonely man thinkin'. You're almost pretty enough to be a girlie and I think I'm too pissed to notice the difference. So how about you and me gettin' friendly?" As he spoke, he groped drunkenly at her legs in the darkness, trying to remove the Guardsman's breeches she wore.

Reaching inside her black shirt, Katkin removed the pearl-handled dagger and pressed it against the ferryman's throat. He stopped moving immediately. Not bothering to disguise her voice further she hissed, "Get your filthy hands off me, you swine. Now, if you would not have your throat cut from ear to ear, you had better get back to your quant."

The ferryman's quick twist caught her by surprise. In a second he had disarmed her, and throwing the knife down on to the bench, held her in a grip of iron, his breath hot and fetid in her face. "Well, well, well. I thought you was awful pretty for a laddie. Turns out I was right, eh missy? Now I'll have some real fun..."

Katkin screamed and struggled with him on the deck of the ferry, as the boat tipped this way and that. As his hand went to cover her mouth, she bit into his thumb as hard as she could. He howled in pain and loosened his hold on her. Retrieving her knife, she turned and executed a dive off the side of the boat into the cold waters of the Mistmere, spitting out the one inch piece of his flesh still lodged between her teeth. She let the dive carry her deep underwater, and turned so she surfaced at the stern. Reaching up, she seized the quant and hurled it as far into the darkness as she could. It landed with a dull splash a fair distance from the boat. The ferryman screamed abuse to her as she carefully tucked the knife back into her shirt and swam away.

Katkin had once been a strong swimmer and she set off confidently for the dark outline of the City in front of her. But the privations of the last few weeks soon caught up with her and she found her strength flagging. The chill of the Mere, even in the summer night, made her teeth chatter. Soon, she found herself floundering about in the dark water rather than progressing towards the peninsula. Desperately, she called out to Ancamma, the Goddess of the Mere, and to Lalluna for help, fearing her quest to save the City might end before she even set foot on the shore.

After a moment, the whisper of wings surrounded her. Five large white swans dropped down into the water, two on each side of her and one in front. Tentatively she threw her tired arms over their backs as they glided quietly along, half expecting them to squawk indignantly and fly away. But the swans patiently bore her forward until her hands brushed a floating mass. Ancamma had provided a large willow bough, recently dropped from one of the trees by the shore and still quite buoyant. Gratefully, she grasped it with both hands and rested, able at last to catch her breath. She knew the cold would drown her if she stayed still for too long, so she began to kick her legs, and made her way slowly towards the shores of the City. The swans stayed by her side and she appreciated their gentle company in the cold and silent water.

Looking up, she saw a red tint to the heavens and thought thankfully that the sunrise must not be too far away. A second later, her eyes widened in fear, for she realized the fiery shades did not herald the dawn. They gathered over the summit of Mount Hythea like a bloody crown.

A little later, as true dawn colored the sky, Katkin reached the shore of Isle St. Valery. The swans lifted themselves gracefully off the water and flew away. She found she had washed up close to the wharves across from the Compass Rose. Many ships were berthed there and she swam between them, keeping in the early morning shadow as much as she could.

Soon she found her feet scrabbling on shingle and she hauled herself out of the water. She headed for the inn, where she hoped Maggie might find some dry clothes for her and perhaps an early breakfast. Feeling wet and disconsolate, she walked across Wharf Lane and prepared to pound on the door of the Compass, which lay dark and silent before her. A printed notice tacked to the window frame caught her attention and she stopped to read it. It said, "Closed, by order of King Benedict."

Racing around the corner, she sought the stables and found them as dark and empty as the main building. Katkin wandered around gloomily. She had been counting on seeing Brinna and Maggie again.

Her soaking wet clothes were making her shiver, so she decided to bury herself in a large pile of dry hay in the back of one of the stalls, hoping to keep warm. Later, when she had rested, she would set off for the Infirmarie. She could steal something else to wear on the way and ditch the Guardsman's uniform before going to visit Becka.

Jacq paced distractedly back and forth in the coolness of early morning, as he supervised the muster of all the Rising. His thoughts rested with his wife, and he wondered whether or not she had yet finished her insane journey to the City. So far, there had been no word from Reynard's contacts inside the Citadel, though they had promised to send a message by swift carrier pigeon if they learned of her whereabouts. Jacq gave a worried sigh as he sent a detachment of men over to the armory to receive muskets and ammunition.

Just then the sound of approaching hoof beats brought his head up sharply. A black horse appeared in the courtyard and Jacq's heart sank utterly as he recognized Pollux, returning to the Foxhole—riderless. The horse skidded to a halt directly in front of him and stood perfectly still as Jacq put his hand up to touch him. He bent his proud head, allowing the man whom his Mistress loved more than anything to lead him to the stable and remove his saddle and bridle. Once inside the darkened stall, Jacq buried his face in the horse's jet black mane and cried bitterly, knowing the men who depended on the strength of the Dinrhydan would not be able to hear. Pollux could do nothing to comfort him.

As the clock in the Citadel Tower chimed nine times, Katkin brushed hay off her very damp and disheveled uniform. Cutting through the back of the stable and in to an alley, she soon found an unattended yard behind a high wooden fence. She could see a lot of clean washing fluttering on a line and a dress she thought might fit her. Hoisting herself over the fence silently, she dropped down into the yard and hastily removed the dress she had her eye on. Suddenly, a ferocious barking made her jump. She had alerted the family dog. Catching it by the collar as it growled and snapped at her, she spoke to it softly and it became docile at once. Unfortunately, the barking had already disturbed the master of the house, who shouted down to her from an upstairs window, "Oi! What do you think you are doing, boy?" Katkin fled over the fence, taking the dress with her, and ran back to the stables, eluding his pursuit.

The dress, a shapeless and worn affair in white, probably belonged to one of the servants of the house. She slipped it over her head, grateful to be clean and dry again. The boots from her uniform had been abandoned in the Mere during her early morning swim and she had no other footwear. Katkin sighed as she realized she would have to walk the several miles to the Infirmarie barefoot.

After one last check made sure the alley was deserted, Katkin stealthily left the stables, heading for Tinker's Lane, which crossed the City roughly parallel to the much more heavily traveled Lampwright's Street. The persistent smoky pall in the air and the occasional flutter of ash made her very apprehensive. She traveled slowly, making her way through alleyways and vacant lots, as the ever present Guardsmen swept the empty streets looking for curfew breakers.

It took Katkin almost all morning to reach the Infirmarie by the circuitous route she was forced to employ. She decided her first stop would be the Springhouse. The presence of the Goddess had always been strong for her there, and she hoped if she spent a moment in the peaceful confines of the bathing room she might be given some inspiration as to her next move. She knew the empty paths criss-crossing the green sward in front of the main building presented as much risk as the ones in the City, so Katkin chose a longer route, hugging the outer wall and approaching the Springhouse from the rear.

Once inside the door, she stopped in confusion, for the interior seemed unexpectedly cool and quiet. Katkin gasped aloud as she passed into the main hall and saw all the copper bathing pools were empty and dry. The fountain of Lalluna, with its beautiful verdigrised statue of the Goddess also stood silent. Katkin sat down on the edge of the fountain and asked, "My Lady, what has happened? Where have your healing waters gone?"

Lalluna's voice, strong and quiet, entered her mind. "*My daughter, Hythea, has taken them all, my vessel. Very soon we must go to her and heal her of the terrible anger she holds in her heart.*"

"How, Lalluna? I don't know what you would have me do now. Please tell me, my Goddess, or send me a sign."

If Lalluna answered her question, Katkin did not hear it. A sharp blow to her temple rendered her instantly unconscious.

Back at the Foxhole, Elisabeth Benet and Willow Abelard sat together at the wide kitchen table, sipping tea. Willow said regretfully to Jacq's mother, "He asked me to watch over her, and I failed them both. Roseberry kept me very busy, and Kat often walked for hours, with only that wild horse and the dog for company. Though I knew something troubled her deeply, I could do nothing to help." She began to cry softly.

Elisabeth patted her arm comfortingly. "You must not blame yourself. All of us watched her as well as we could. But she could not ignore the dreams tormenting her. Katkin truly believed all of us would perish if she did not act."

"She was mad, Jacq said so," Willow insisted.

Jacq's mother shook her head. "I am not so sure about that. Your sister has power far beyond our understanding. Jacq has always underestimated her strength. Because of his overwhelming love, he felt he must protect Katkin from everything. Even now I don't think he sees her as she truly is."

Willow stood and looked out the open window, remembering the winter's day when her sister had healed Roseberry's burned hand. She still did not understand how Katkin had done it, but she did see what Elisabeth meant about a mysterious power.

"I just hate to think of her out there, all alone. Maybe she has been captured already. I might never see her again." She sighed and wiped the tears from her eyes.

"Let us not give up hope for her. She is stronger than you know, for all her frail appearance. Wherever she is right now, I will wager it is not in the Citadel."

Willow nodded bravely and gave her a smile.

Elisabeth rose and said, "Now I must go find Jacq and try to make him eat something. He has had nothing at all since last night's dinner and he must keep up his strength somehow. Too many other men depend on him." She picked up a wrapped plate of food and went out to the parade field.

Katkin woke, feeling sick and disoriented. Squinting from a painful headache, she tried to move her hands to rub her eyes. She discovered to her dismay a gauze bandage circled her wrists tightly. A quick wiggle of her feet indicated her ankles were similarly tied. Her heart began to hammer as she realized her former best friend must now be holding her prisoner.

Just then a tall Damenie peered at her face and said, "The Apostate stirs, Maitress."

Becka said softly, "Sit her up and leave us, Damenie Carmine. Katkin and I have much to discuss."

Damenie Carmine pulled Katkin up to a sitting position, none too gently, and tucked several pillows behind her back. Katkin could see now that Becka had placed her in one of the wards in the main building. Other beds, all unoccupied, surrounded her. Becka, now wearing the habit of the Maitress, fingered the heavy gold and silver moonstone pendant as she walked towards Katkin's bed.

"Becka, why on earth am I tied up?" Katkin asked. "I have come here only to seek your help. I swear it on the Goddess."

Becka did not display the most welcoming of expressions. She raised her hand and slapped Katkin hard across the face, once and a second time. "I gave you the first in return for the time you slapped me in our room, Kat, and the second to remind you I am now the Maitress and you are to address me as such." She smiled maliciously at the tears that sprang to Katkin's eyes.

"So, Apostate, what brings you back to the scene of your crime? Did you think you would be able to just waltz in here and take over without a struggle?"

Katkin looked at her in confusion. "Take over? What on earth do you mean, Becka?" Another quick slap made her ears ring and Katkin began to understand how deeply her former room mate seemed to resent her presence at the Infirmarie. "I am so sorry," she said, with undisguised sarcasm, "I meant to say Maitress."

"Do not pretend ignorance, Apostate. I have known for years you desired the power of the Maitress' position," Becka said firmly.

Shaking her head, Katkin said, "If I had wanted to be Maitress I had only to stay. The former Maitress offered the job to me a few days before I ran away from the Infirmarie."

Becka's eyes narrowed and her words were obviously tinged with jealousy. "Yes, Katrione, always the old woman's pet, weren't you? With your perfect test scores and your magic healings. The old Maitress used to talk of nothing else. I always came in second to you. You could have had everything—the handsome Captain de Vigny, a new mansion and all his money. But you threw it all away for a coarse and low born blacksmith! Of course, after a few months of living in abject poverty, you discovered you'd made a terrible mistake, so you came back here to ask the Maitress' forgiveness. When she refused to grant it, you murdered her and took the sacrifice from Lalluna to revenge yourself on the Unity. Not being satisfied with that devilry, you have now come back to kill me. Why else would you be carrying this?" Becka produced the pearl-handled dagger from within her habit.

This twisted interpretation of the events leading to the former Maitress' death appalled Katkin. She tried to explain to Becka about her dream, and the horrible sacrifice of the child. Becka cut her off, saying coldly, "I am quite familiar with the details of the Solstice observance, Apostate. I am the Maitress, after all. You can rest assured the tradition will be upheld as long as I hold the office." She looked smugly down at her former rival as the other blanched.

"Maitress, I came here only to ask your help. Lalluna has sent me many dreams about the imminent destruction of the City..."

Becka interrupted her yet again. "Proper little oracle, aren't we? You always thought you had some cozy relationship with the Goddess, with all those dreams and magic voices."

287

Katkin, sure she had never mentioned anything to Becka about her special ability to communicate with the Goddess, asked, "How do you know about any of that?"

The new Maitress' laugh sounded brittle. "I read your private journal, Katkin, every day for years and years when we shared a room together. I know everything about you and your relationship with your imaginary friend, Lalluna."

If Katkin could have moved her arms, she would have made the sign of the Goddess at this blasphemy. "How can you say Lalluna is imaginary? You are the head of Her Unity."

Becka retorted petulantly, "Why should I not? She has never appeared to me, or even sent me a dream."

"But, Bec... I mean Maitress, what about your Gift?" Katkin asked. "Where did that come from, if not from the Goddess?"

"My Gift is weak and what little I have will be taken away as soon as I perform the Solstice Observance. If the Goddess is real, why would she do that? It is all just a fairytale for fools to believe." Becka gave her a look of sheer hatred and said acidly, "Of course, I know you would have made a much better Maitress than me, but you are not going to get the chance."

Katkin cried out to her, "I don't want the chance, Becka! I came here because Lalluna told me the City will be destroyed in less than one day's time. I need your help to stop it from happening. Why do you not believe me? Have you not seen the fires at night over Hythea and felt the ground tremble?" Her eyes met Becka's in a silent plea for understanding.

Becka appeared troubled for a moment and forgot to slap Katkin for this additional use of her first name. "Of course I have seen the signs from the mountain. King Benedict has told the people not to be concerned. He says Hythea just murmurs in her sleep and soon will slumber again. You frighten me with your words, Katkin. Do you really believe the City will be destroyed?"

Katkin nodded desperately. "I don't just believe, I know it is true. You must untie me and let me go to the Temple. In my heart, I know the answer to the riddle Lalluna has set for me lies there. There is little time. I beg of you, Becka... my old friend, let me go now, before it is too late. If not, by tomorrow we shall all be dead."

Becka looked confused and thoroughly unhappy. "I cannot. When the Sisters first brought you up to the ward I called for..."

She did not need to finish her sentence. Katkin's eyes widened in horror as she saw four armed Guardsmen step through the door and into the ward.

Forty miles away, at the Foxhole, Nicholas Reynard watched over the almost-completed muster from his office window. Outside on the parade field, in the dusty afternoon heat, Jacq still strode doggedly back and forth, shouting orders to the assembled soldiers. Nicholas turned to the man who stood at his side and asked, "How much longer do you think the Dinrhydan can keep going, Yannick? He has not stopped moving since his wife left last night. We have a long march ahead of us. He should be resting."

But Yannick felt no such concern.

"He is better off without that witch, Sir, if you will pardon my forthrightness. She brought him nothing but trouble. Has she been captured yet?" he added hopefully.

Reynard shook his head angrily, saying abruptly, "We have had no word. Go and check on the supply carts, Abelard."

Yannick saluted and left the room, passing a soldier who entered through the open office door. He handed the Commander a small silver cylindrical message holder, saying, "A pigeon brought this from the City a few minutes ago, Sir." The soldier saluted and left him alone, yet Nicholas Reynard could not bring himself to read the dispatch right away.

Finally, sighing deeply, he unscrewed the top and pulled out the tightly rolled slip of paper. It said simply, "Katrione Benet has been captured and taken to the Citadel." Nicholas, swearing hotly, balled the paper up and threw it down on his desk.

The leader of an army must make many decisions in a day, and they can never be taken lightly as, more often than not, the result of those choices might be to condemn one man or another to death. Reynard, the seasoned veteran of several wars and many such decisions, sat down at his desk and rested his head in his hands for a moment. Though he knew Jacq should be told the information contained in that cylinder right away, he also knew it would probably render him unfit for the coming conflict. Reynard desperately needed the Dinrhydan's legendary strength and courage for the attack on the City and so did every other man in the Rising. The outcome of the whole war could depend on it.

After a few moments of vacillation he reluctantly determined he had no choice but to keep this latest intelligence report from the City a secret, at least for the time being. He hoped some day his most trusted Lieutenant would find it in his heart to forgive him for this most difficult of decisions

Katkin, chained to the wall in a grimy cell in the Citadel, idly wondered if it could be the same one Jacq had been detained in. Certainly it might have been recently flooded, for a couple of inches of scummy water remained in puddles on the floor. The room held nothing except an overflowing bucket of night-soil. The powerful stench in the closed space sickened her and she had to concentrate hard on her breathing to stop herself from vomiting. She passed the time counting the scratch marks on the mildewed walls, and sending occasional prayers to Lalluna for strength. Katkin harbored no uncertainty that she would now be questioned and that every method, however cruel, would be used to make her talk. She knew she must not divulge Jacq's location or the plans of the Rising, but what if her resolve failed before the end?

A guardsman unlocked the door and entered the tiny cell, then hauled her to her feet roughly. She asked him anxiously, "Where are you taking me, Soldier? Am I to be tortured so soon?"

He looked at her with disdain. "Right now, you are to be taken before the King. The interrogation can wait until afterwards."

The walk from the lowest level holding cells up to the King's Chamber in the shining Citadel Tower took a long time. Katkin shuffled along as best she could, but before long the iron loops on her bare ankles and wrists wore bleeding holes in her flesh. As they traversed a long hallway, another tremor rocked the Citadel and her guards swore in consternation.

Opulent purple and gold tapestries decorated the walls of King Benedict's throne room. A huge crystal chandelier provided light from high above their heads. Katkin looked around her, temporarily in awe of so much grandeur. Then she remembered that this King, Benedict, had closed off the City and prevented his own subjects from evacuating to safety from the wrath of Hythea. His stubborn need to cling to power would be the death of them all.

The King, his voice high pitched and reedy, said to her imperiously, "State your full name for the record, young woman."

Katkin said promptly, "Katrione Estelle du Chesne Benet, your Majesty." She thought that this question would probably be the last one she would want to answer.

King Benedict had reigned for the last three decades, and had become fatter with each passing year. With his hairless pink pate he reminded Katkin of a pig, dressed up in purple and ermine and sitting on a fancy throne. He waved a hand at her and every beefy finger bore a jeweled ring. "Approach our throne, Katrione."

She hobbled forward painfully, the irons still grinding into her bloody ankle bones. Katkin remembered Jacq had endured five days of this agony and much, much worse. The thought gave her courage. "Your Majesty, on what charge am I being detained?" she asked quietly.

"Silence! We will ask the questions," he thundered in return, as two Guardsmen threw her down onto her knees. Katkin kept her head down, waiting to see what the King would do next. His next statement did not come as a surprise to her.

He said, "We know you are married to an agent of the Rising known as the Dinrhydan, and we will have information from you as to his whereabouts. Know you will be tortured if you do not comply with our request, and being a woman will not excuse you. We have no scruples during war time, my dear. Now, tell us, where is your husband?"

Katkin said nothing, although one of the Guards kicked her roughly in an effort to make her answer. Her thoughts lay with Jacq at that moment, as he strode the fields of the Foxhole, shouting orders to his men. Though he was now a soldier rather than the craftsman she married, Katkin knew in her heart she still loved him more than anything. She would never betray him to the King.

His voice softened. "You should fear us. We can have you executed tomorrow if we wish it."

"On what charge?" she asked, and her guard kicked her again for her insolence.

The King's laugh softly mocked her. "What does it matter? We could make one up if we had to, but you have given us plenty already. The murder of the former Maitress, interfering with the

Solstice Observance, performing healings outside the auspices of the Unity—each one of these things is punishable by death. But you have information we need and we are willing to grant you a stay of execution in return for it."

Katkin laughed in turn, but hers sounded harsh. "I will tell you nothing. What difference will it make to me or you or anyone else on this cursed rock? Everyone in this City is doomed to die tomorrow morning, including you, old fool. There will be no stay when Hythea is the executioner. She is determined to cleanse the earth of the blood from the fallen and no man can stop her. I tell you truly, the Goddess Lalluna has spoken to me in my dreams."

The king stared at her in alarm, as Katkin raised her bloodied hands towards him. He wanted very much to believe she was insane, and her words were just the ramblings of a diseased mind. Yet her eyes appeared crystal clear and pierced him to his very marrow. Benedict said shakily, "What is this doom you prophesy? Our City will never fall, for we have done nothing to deserve this punishment."

"You think you have done nothing, old man? Who has presided over the bloodiest civil war in the history of Beaumarais? The Guard and the Rising have fought long, brother against brother, and the blood of the fallen cries out to Hythea. It is this blood that has sentenced us all to death, for we all bear the guilt, King Benedict. Both sides wanted victory rather than peace, and for that Hythea will show us no mercy, not now. Do you think it was worth it, my King?"

Benedict shook his head angrily. He said, "We do not believe our honorable prosecution of the war against the peasant rabble of Reynard has caused this difficulty. Of course we must strive for victory—otherwise we would lose the conflict."

Katkin's answer to this did not reassure. "The cottars have legitimate grievances, and they too will fight until the death for victory. Would that the two of you had met at the table instead of the battlefield. How many innocent deaths might have been averted? Now it no longer matters, for we all are going to perish. My dreams do not lie, O King."

Her eyes seemed to burn into the King's soul with a blazing green fire, and for the first time since Hythea had woken, he felt fear stirring in his heart. Angrily, he said, "You must not threaten us, or we will silence you forever. Now tell us of these dreams. Quickly, woman."

Katkin wondered what had caused this sudden change of heart, but she did not understand the effect her words had on those around her. Her guards, all young men from the City, became increasingly agitated and disheartened as she told Benedict graphically of the terrible destruction of the City and the message of Hythea. The King, looking ever more fearful, called over a pageboy and whispered an order to him. The page went from the throne room and returned a moment later, announcing, "Maitress Rebecca Kent, as your Majesty requested."

Katkin saw Becka nervously approach the throne.

The King asked, "You are acquainted with the defendant, Katrione Benet?"

Becka swallowed nervously and said, "Yes, Your Majesty. I have known her for many years. We served as Juvenet together before she became an apostate."

"You heard her describe her dreams of the destruction of the City to us just now?" Becka nodded and the King continued, "Do you think she speaks the truth? You, who are head of the Unity of Lalluna, should know if anyone does."

Katkin muttered to herself, "I wouldn't count on that, old man."

Becka drew in a deep breath and said firmly, "I believe she is correct about the annihilation of the City, your Majesty." Katkin looked up at her in surprise. She had not expected the new Maitress to come to her defense. A moment later she said something even more unexpected. "I do not believe, though, the Apostate speaks the truth about its cause. The King's glorious battle against the hoi polloi of Reynard could never bring about such a disaster."

Becka paused to lick her lips anxiously as King Benedict smiled, obviously pleased with her flattery. "Continue, most highly esteemed Maitress," he said.

"She, herself, has brought this judgment down on the City, by her wicked interference in the sacred Solstice Observance. As long as this ceremony has taken place, the mountain has slept peacefully. After the Apostate murdered the former Maitress and took the sacrifice away, the thermal springs dried up and the tremors started."

Katkin shook her head, bitterly regretting her decision to go to Becka for help that morning. She could see that the girl, with her festering jealousy, was playing to the King's arrogance. But Becka had not finished yet. She continued, her voice growing stronger and more persuasive. "Therefore, your Majesty, it is my considered opinion that the only way we can stop this imminent destruction is for Katrione, herself, to be given to Lalluna as a sacrifice by casting her into the pit of boiling mud in the Temple as soon as possible." Katkin, despite the dire nature of Becka's words, looked up at her old roommate in joyous disbelief. Did she really know what she suggested? Becka stared straight ahead, but Katkin saw her quickly cross her fingers.

The King, however, could not be convinced so easily. "Katrione Benet has information we need, Maitress, about the whereabouts of her husband, the Dinrhydan. We will have to extract that information from her before sending her to her death. Can we not delay a day or two?"

Becka only had time to shake her head before a tremendous roar filled the Citadel, from the lowest dungeon to the highest rampart. The King cried out in alarm as the most prolonged of all the tremors shook the room violently. The purple and gold wall hangings fell to the ground along with the chandelier. It landed inches away from the throne and showered the King in broken crystal. He clutched the arms of his throne, terrified by this newest display of Hythea's power. A huge piece of stone falling from the ceiling crushed one of the men standing guard over Katkin. His mangled arm lay inches from her face.

The King's page cried out in alarm. "Your Majesty! A sheet of fire pours from the top of the mountain." Unsteadily, King Benedict made his way to the balcony, and in the late evening's twilight saw a scene of devastation so total he closed his eyes in disbelief. Half the buildings in the City seemed to be damaged and fires blazed out of control. Shouts and screams floated up from below as people tried to extricate themselves from the fallen structures or help their loved ones do the same. When he saw the wall of flame creeping down the mountain he moaned in terror.

Katkin, still on the floor in her chains, cried out, "Take me to the Temple, I beg of you! Now, before there is nothing left to save!"

King Benedict, after staring at her in confusion for some moments, finally nodded his head in agreement. "Though we do not understand why you appeal to us for your own execution, Katrione, we grant your request forthwith." He spoke to the Guardsmen still surrounding her. "Quickly! Take her now to the Temple and cast her into the pit. Gods protect us all if it is not enough."

The guards blanched and muttered to each other, then finally complied with the King's order.

Becka stood beside Katkin as her remaining guards pulled her upright. In all the confusion they were able to have a quick conversation.

She whispered, "What do I need to do now?"

Katkin smiled at her gratefully and said, "You have done enough, my sister."

The new Maitress looked very afraid. "Katkin, I convinced the King to have you thrown into the sacrificial pit. What can you do to stop the eruption if you are dead?"

Katkin shook her head as the guards began to drag her away. "Do not worry. Once I am inside the Temple, Lalluna will show me the way, I am sure of it, Becka. Go down into the City and try to save as many as you can. The people will have more need of the Infirmarie than ever. You must lead now, and I have every faith in you. Go with the Goddess."

Becka looked on in disbelief as Katkin went to her immolation with an expression of joyous acceptance.

21

Mellasarat, a high mountain pass

(The Tollyn, Twelve)

Geya sits alone and turns the tokens one by one. She considers the outcome of her careful plans, and wonders if Dai could be right. Such thoughts do not trouble her for long.

~~~~~~~~~~

The bells on the Citadel Tower chimed eleven times as Katkin's guards made ready to take her to the Temple and cast her into the pit. They placed her in a tall, narrow cage, just large enough for her to stand upright. Her guards hung her shackled hands from a loop in the top so that she had to stand on her toes. It was all she could do to keep her feet under her as the men lifted the cage unsteadily on to a cart, pulled by a team of black horses. The excruciating pain from the iron cutting into her wrists forced her to find her centre and call on Lalluna.

As the cart moved slowly through the streets, with a detachment of mounted Guardsmen as an escort, Katkin took in the nightmarish scene about her. Fallen rock and debris made the way almost impassable and they were forced to detour many times. Shouts and screams rent the smoky air. The Guardsmen brutally shoved aside or rode down those panicked citizens appealing to them for help or guidance. Since King Benedict refused to leave the Citadel, or release any of his personal guard to aid the City, her people now had a new monarch – Fear.

To anyone else it might look as though Hythea had already spent her anger, yet Katkin knew differently. She thought back to the penultimate dream Lalluna had sent her, showing her the final destruction of the City. It began with a huge, black many-branched cloud rising up from the crown of Hythea, as dark and menacing as the depths of the underworld. The earth trembled in fear. Then came a sound so deafening it had seemed the mountain itself roared in her fury. The memory of that all-consuming howl terrorized Katkin, even now. Behind the roaring came the burning breath of Hythea, and before it flew the seeds of destruction of everything and everyone in the City. The wind tore down the mountain at many times the speed the fastest horse can run. Larger boulders bounced along like stone hammers, and smashed everything in their path. Air from the forges of Hell flowed down on top, and like a liquid cataclysm, bathed the City in Hythea's cleansing flame. Men, women and children burned alive as they huddled in their houses or tried to flee in uncomprehending terror.

Not satisfied with the death of all thirty thousand residents of the City, the glowing wind roared across the Yoke, for Hythea also desired the annihilation of Nicholas Reynard's Rising.

This vision of death occupied Katkin's thoughts all the way to the Infirmarie.

The front gates stood wide open. As the cart passed inside, it did not surprise her to see the interior of the compound looked much as it did in the first dream Lalluna had sent her at the Foxhole. The roof of the Springhouse had caved in. The earthquake had seriously damaged the main wing as well. As the cart made its slow progress up the mountain path to the Temple gates, Katkin's guards began to leave her, one after the other. The terror of the fire-lit night and the continuing aftershocks, on top of her dire predictions, proved too much for their courage. Soon only the driver of the cart remained and she prayed to Lalluna that he too would not desert and leave her locked in the metal cage. He feared the wrath of Hythea as much as his comrades, yet he did not stop the cart until they had passed the Temple gate and stood before the cleft in the rock. Katkin saw a strongly made wooden door now blocked the space, apparently to make it easier to keep out intruders.

The remaining Guardsman, a lad of eighteen, climbed quickly down from the cart. With quivering hands, he unlocked the cage and removed her shackles from their support overhead. Katkin cried out in pain as the blood rushed back down into her numbed hands. Shaking his head, the guard looked on her with fear and pity. Then he unlocked her shackles and leg irons, leaving her standing free before him.

He urged, "Run away, my Lady, as fast as you are able. You are too beautiful and courageous to die such a horrible death, and I will have no hand in your execution, though it means treason. I will tell my superiors I have cast you into the pit. Now go."

The young man's desire to save her from the boiling mud touched Katkin deeply. She asked him, "What is your name, Guardsman?"

"Philip Tremayne, Lady."

"And are you frightened, Philip?" she asked him.

He answered her unsteadily. "Yes, Lady, I am very afraid. I know in my heart the terrible destruction you prophesy is true and I will not live beyond sunrise this day. I would have you go and seek your end in any way that seems best to you, and I shall do the same."

Katkin's heart was moved with pity for this brave young man who wanted to give her an easy death. "Although you would spare me, I must indeed go into the Temple and face whatever fate awaits me there. Do not lose heart, my brother, for I hope I will be in time to heal the wrath of Hythea, with the help of the Goddess Lalluna. So, come now, unlock the final door for me and you may go where you will."

He looked at her with awe. "You are still determined to go? Truly you are a Goddess yourself, Katrione Estelle du Chesne Benet. Such courage is beyond my understanding."

Laughing merrily then, for it seemed to Katkin his words must be for someone else, she said, "I am certainly no Goddess, just an ordinary woman with a task to complete, and I must go now. Have courage, for you may yet live to see the dawn if I succeed."

She turned away from him and strode resolutely through the open door into the Temple passage.

Nicholas Reynard, on Rufus, rode through the moonlit country-side towards the City. The Dinrhydan, on Nestor, rode beside him, silently despondent now he could no longer maintain his frantic pace. Five thousand men marched or rode behind them. The long procession had several more hours of steady travel before it reached the Yoke. The fact they met no resistance encouraged them to make haste. The column left the Foxhole much earlier in the day, marching fifteen miles without stopping. Then Nicholas had ordered a halt and commanded his men to set up camp, to make it look as though they intended to go no further that day. As soon as darkness fell, however, they had abandoned the false camp and now the men of the Rising intended to march to the City overnight. With luck, they would arrive shortly after dawn, and proceed with the attack as soon as they could launch the boats.

Reynard glanced over at Jacq, whose face looked grim by the moonlight.

"We may yet be able to save her, Dinrhydan. You must not give up hope."

Jacq said nothing in return, merely shaking his head in despair. Reynard prayed silently that Katkin would still be alive when they reached the Citadel, and that they would be able to free her in the attack on the City.

A cry from the rear of the column interrupted his thoughts. A single horseman, riding at a gallop, shouted, "Make way! I have an urgent message for the Commander." The marching soldiers parted and let the man through, as Reynard reined Rufus to a halt. Jacq, on Nestor, stopped beside him, and Reynard looked over at him in deep concern. If this message concerned Katkin, he would have to tell Jacq of its contents.

The messenger, dusty and sweat-stained, drew level with them and handed Reynard another of the silver message cylinders, saying, "This came three hours ago, Sir. I brought it as quickly as I could." The Commander thanked him and anxiously removed the rolled paper, aware of the Dinrhydan's impatience at his side. He read the message silently and then slowly dropped his hands, saying nothing.

Jacq, in an agony of fear, questioned him sharply, "What does it say? Read it to me."

Nicholas could not even look at him or speak a word of comfort—not now. He stared down at the curled paper in his hand and spoke the message aloud tonelessly. "Katrione Benet was sentenced to death by King Benedict. The execution is to be carried out at midnight." After Jacq gave a choked cry, he stopped reading, though the message contained more information about the last major earthquake and its devastation in the City. Reynard looked on at Jacq with grave sympathy. He had dropped Nestor's reins and now sat miserably hunched over on the horse's back, with his hands covering his face. Nicholas said softly, "Take Nestor and a few men and ride back to the Foxhole, where you may grieve in peace. Let your mother take care of you, my son. You do not need to be here with us, not now."

He waited patiently until Jacq, obviously still trying hard to master his emotions, could reply. Finally, his hands dropped away from his face. He spoke harshly. "Nay, Commander. I will not go back. What need have I for grief now?" Nicholas saw Jacq bite his lip so hard the blood welled up, and then he continued. "Now I need only one thing—death. My own and as many of her executioners as I can take with me. They have taken from me my wife and child, and they will pay."

Though Nicholas did not want to ask it, he knew he must, for the sake of the other men that Jacq would lead in the attack on the City. He said, "Dinrhydan, I cannot let you take men into battle if you would put them in harm's way by your own desire for death. Are you able to put your hurt aside and do what is necessary for the good of the Rising?"

Jacq shot him an angry glance. "Have I ever endangered any man without cause?"

Reynard shook his head, but could not help thinking that in the past Jacq had not been mad with grief, as he was now. Jacq continued to stare at his Commander until finally he nodded his agreement and gave the order for the march to resume. The Dinrhydan rode beside him as silent as stone, with the fell look in his eyes of one who goes to meet his death joyfully and without reservation.

Walking through the unlocked door into the Temple tunnel, Katkin struggled to breathe in the incredible heat and noxious gases issuing from the cavern. Stopping just inside, she tore a wide strip off the white dress and soaked it in a muddy puddle, then tied it tightly over her nose and mouth. The darkness lay thick inside and Katkin, as she had previously, asked Lalluna to light her way. But the glowing stones did not appear and she wondered fearfully if Lalluna had already abandoned the City to the destructive breath of Hythea.

Katkin began to pick her way down the tunnel, without being able to see as much as a hand in front of her. The air felt oppressive, and the soles of her feet soon grew uncomfortably hot. Turning a corner, she saw a faint light ahead—it glowed orange and wavered unevenly on the tunnel wall.

Fire.

Suddenly Lalluna appeared. "My vessel," she cried. "You have come at last. I cannot hold her much longer—even now she would burn through her bonds if I did not prevent her."

"I am ready, Lalluna, use me as you see fit," Katkin said calmly.

But Lalluna needed to warn Katkin of the true nature of her request. "When we heal Hythea, my vessel, you must touch her, as you touched the man whom you love more than anything."

"Of course, my Goddess," said Katkin. "I understand that. I am not afraid."

The Goddess shook her head. "You would feel fear if you knew. For my daughter, in her rage, is made of firelight, and to touch her is to cast your hand into the living, molten rock."

Katkin blanched at this, and her heart hammered painfully in her chest. Still, she said, "I must do it for the sake of the City, and for Jacq. Even though the fire consumes me, I will not run away. It must be done, so come, let us make ready."

Lalluna inclined her head gracefully and said, "Thus I knew it would ever be, when I chose you long ago. You carry the blazing heart of a star in your small human frame. Together, you and I must go to Hythea, and touch her. We will heal her of the madness that has caused so much destruction."

"And after that?" Katkin asked her.

Lalluna said sadly, "I do not know. Perhaps the heart of Hythea will consume us both, and we will be no more. It will take all of our combined strength to prevail. Nor can I say whether the child you bear will survive. She is only a tiny spark."

"Let us begin," Katkin said bravely. "I know my life and the life of my child will be sacrificed for something worthwhile, even if we do not survive."

Lalluna turned into a column of moonlight, as she had before in the Acre, and lit up the cavern around Katkin, outlining the rocks in sharp relief. Once again, she felt the pain and ecstasy of the Goddess' form as she entered. But she could not enjoy her heightened senses for long, because Lalluna was already urging her forward down the tunnel. Katkin found to her surprise that her feet no longer burned. In fact, her feet no longer touched the dusty floor of the cavern. She flew along the tunnel with wings that had appeared between her shoulder blades. This feeling of effortless flight felt quite calming to Katkin, almost as if she were in a waking dream. She could breathe with the power of the Goddess, and the heated and noxious air no longer troubled her at all. Very soon, they reached the Temple, awash in flames, and Katkin saw the statue of Lalluna lying on the ground surrounded by ferociously burning white flame. The marble figure cracked and split as the fire consumed it.

Lalluna cried out within Katkin, saying, "As soon as Hythea rises from the ground we must join with her, my vessel. My image no longer binds her. You must keep in contact with her until I am able to complete the healing. As her fire incinerates your flesh, you must give her more. Do you understand? It will be the most difficult undertaking I have ever required of you. Are you ready?"

Desperate fear filled Katkin and her serenity fled. What if she could not do this thing Lalluna asked of her?

The fire formed itself into the figure of a woman—she burned with an unquenchable flame. This was Hythea, daughter of Lalluna.

Lalluna said quietly, "You must touch her now, my vessel. We have no more time left."

Katkin stretched out her trembling hand to the pillar of fire standing before her. Her last conscious thought was of Jacq, and she reached out in her mind to find him so she could tell him she loved him once more.

As the men of the Rising stopped for a fifteen-minute rest break, Reynard kept a watchful eye on Jacq, who had not uttered a single word since the news of his wife's execution. Nicholas always spent the last few hours before a battle reviewing every potential exigency and creating strategies to deal with them. Seeing Jacq drowning in his repressed grief caused him to think instead of Elisabeth, whom he had left behind at the Foxhole with Willow and Roseberry and a handful of others, mostly old men and young boys, who were willing to stay and defend the camp.

When he sought her out for a few stolen moments before he had to depart, she had been sitting and holding a book, but he could see her thoughts were far away. "I have to go soon, Elisabeth, and I would hold you once more before I do. Though it seems a bitter parting now, soon after the dawn breaks tomorrow, we shall be free of this terrible war forever. That will be a joyous day for us, my love, for it means that we will be able spend the rest of our lives together without the need for secrecy. Please temper your sadness at this farewell with that hope."

"Until it is certain you ride to victory, my Kolya, I cannot hide my grief nor temper it with hope. For if you fail I will lose not only you, but Jacq and Thad as well. My daughter has already left me, and Katkin's fate is unknown, though I hold little hope for her now. I do not know how many more losses I can bear." Then, although she was strong, and had suffered much in the past, she broke down and cried in his arms.

Nicholas Reynard gave the order for the columns to reform so the Rising could complete the last part of the overnight march to the City. The men moved quietly and in an orderly fashion. Reynard, sitting on Rufus as he waited for the men to regroup, thought confidently of their success.

A shout from one of the men brought his head up sharply. "Commander, look! The Dinrhydan!"

Reynard hurried towards Jacq. He had fallen to his knees beneath an elm tree, his hands clenched close to his chest. His stiffened body and arched neck spoke of some incredible torment. He cried out in his agony, "They are burning her alive! Ach, the pain. I cannot bear it."

As Nicholas reached him, his eyes rolled back in their sockets and he fell onto his face, unmoving. Nicholas instructed some of the men surrounding Jacq to turn him over carefully. The Dinrhydan's eyes opened, yet seemed to be sightless, for he did not respond when his Commander leaned over to examine his face. His chest rose and fell raggedly, and his pulse felt quick and light. Nicholas stared down at Jacq's prone form for a long moment. Then, sighing, he gave instructions for four men to drape Jacq as carefully as they could on to the back of Nestor and take him back to the Foxhole. He hoped Elisabeth would have some idea what to do for her eldest son. Reynard would miss him sorely, but the invasion must proceed with or without the Dinrhydan.

Lalluna, filling the body of Her Vessel, battled with the spirit of her daughter, Hythea, as Katkin screamed in agony. Hythea's white-hot rage had already incinerated Katkin's fingers and palm, consuming the bones as well as the flesh. She forced herself to push the stump of her arm further into the glowing form of Hythea and almost passed out as the fresh flesh quickly ignited in the intense heat. Katkin felt her soul shrinking further and further into oblivion, until only a tiny spark of consciousness remained. The pain blinded her as she gave Hythea more flesh and bone.

As four men lifted the Dinrhydan, he moaned and struggled against them. Reynard, already walking back to Rufus, turned around, saying, "Put him down!" Jacq, now conscious, sat by the elm tree, with his back propped against it. Reynard squatted before him, and looked intently at his face. "Jacq, what happened to you? Can you tell me?"

Jacq was trembling, and answered his question unsteadily. "I walked to the tree, and I was thinking I could not believe she was dead, because I thought I would feel it somehow if she was, and I had not. Suddenly, I felt her presence all around me, in the air, like a... scent or something. I do not know, I cannot describe it." He paused to wipe his tear-filled eyes and Reynard patted his shoulder sympathetically. "After a few seconds the pain started, as if I had taken my arm and thrust it deeply into my old forge at the Citadel. I have never felt anything so keenly. Somehow I knew..." here Jacq had to stop, for he could not describe the terrible knowledge that had come to him, as she burned alive and he could do nothing to stop her agony. In a moment, as his Commander looked on him with deep sadness, he forced himself to continue. "The pain stopped just as suddenly, and I felt the connection sever. They must have thrown her into the volcano."

Then Jacq fell on to his side and lay there for a long while.

Lalluna cried out, "My vessel! I have finished, Hythea has been healed." Her daughter melted into a creature of smoke and ash and blew away in the fresh wind now filling the cavern.

Katkin felt the fire leave her, though the pain hardly lessened as a result. Steeling herself, she looked at the remains of her arm, now just a smoking, blackened stump that ended just below the elbow.

Lalluna said, "I am sorry you have suffered such great hurt. Yet we still live and so does your child. I can take away the pain of the flesh that remains but I cannot put back what Hythea has burned away."

Katkin said stoically, "The loss of my arm does not matter. Heal me as well as you can, and let us go into the City. Nicholas Reynard means to attack soon and we must prevent the bloodshed, lest Hythea wake again."

Katkin left the Temple and began to fly back down the passage towards the entrance to the cave.

Now the Goddess had become a part of her, Katkin could no longer tell where she ended and Lalluna began. She felt much older, and wiser, yet the girl who had once dedicated herself to the Unity still remained. A panoply of experiences, from many lifetimes, filled her with wonder and fear. She saw herself, as the vessel of Lalluna, touching and healing thousands of lives. In each tableau she looked upon from her past, two recognizable figures stood out—Jacq and Tomas.

Now she felt herself passing through the present and rapidly into the future. An utterly black, pulsating Void, in a blasted heathland, stood before her. Many small black creatures poured forth.

"The Angellus." Lalluna's voice spoke in her mind. "Geya believes that Dai let them into the outer pellicula."

But Katkin surprised her by saying hotly, "Dai is no traitor. I have seen and talked with him. He told me the dark ones are not the enemy."

Lalluna's voice was sharp. "Don't be absurd! You are not of the Amaranthine. How could you have done this?"

"He saved my life, about six months ago, the day I ran away from the Infirmarie."

The Goddess laughed, not altogether kindly. "You do not know of what you speak, my vessel. These remembrances of yours are childish dreams, nothing more. The Angellus have destroyed many turns of the Gyre. Now we fight them as best we can, Fyn and I and the others."

Katkin questioned her further, but Lalluna said only, "There is one whom I love, as you love your husband, but our stars are crossed and we can never be together."

As Lalluna spoke, Katkin wanted desperately to reach out to Jacq. The Goddess said, "Though I know you did not mean to, you have already grievously hurt the man whom you love more than anything, my vessel, when you sent your thoughts to him during the healing of Hythea. Use my eyes and you will see."

Katkin saw Jacq's prone form on the ground under the elm tree. Nicholas Reynard stood over him, and sighed. "You must go back to the Foxhole, Jacq. I cannot linger here any longer. Already we have delayed too long."

Jacq stubbornly shook his head. "Commander, why do you not see that I am ready for battle? I have nothing else to live for. Will you deny me this last chance to revenge myself on my wife's murderers?"

Nicholas shook his head, sighing.

22

Kal Jheriad, the lofty peak

(The Tollyn, One)

Did she say she went to one of the outer Pellicula? Rythis? How could she travel there, Moonlight?

Moonlight sounds very troubled. I do not know, Geya. She said she spoke to Dai there. But it is not possible. It *must* have been a dream.

~~~~~~~~~~~~~

Lalluna swiftly left the Temple and made her way down the mountainside, her wings just a glimmer in the moonlight. With the healing of Hythea, the tremors stopped, as did the sheet of lava creeping down the shoulder of the mountain. The cock's crow heralded the sunrise, and as people walked the streets in confusion, they saw the winged form of Lalluna over the City. Before her came a rising wind that blew away the smoke and wrack from the sky.

A page told King Benedict the news as he sat in the ruined throne room. Fear filled his heart, for he knew now in sending Katrione Estelle du Chesne Benet to her death he had woken something very different and much more powerful—an Avatar. If the Goddess came seeking revenge, he knew his life would be among those forfeit. Licking his lips nervously, he called for his servants and bade them make ready his personal ship.

From the throne room the King could step out onto a private balcony high above the Citadel Commons. Benedict stood at this balcony now and observed the scene below him. Almost all the surviving residents of the City had gathered in the Commons, as well as many Guardsmen, although there had been no call for them to assemble. They appeared to be quietly waiting for something, and the King had a feeling it was not an address from their monarch.

Lalluna flew onto the balcony, with a whisper of wings. The King stepped back through the open door in terror and ran down the stairs from the throne room. Lalluna allowed him to flee like a frightened hare. One insignificant monarch did not interest her. She wished to address the assembled people below so she could impress upon them the importance of bargaining for peace with the Rising.

As she stood above them, her wings gleaming whitely in the first light of dawn, the people of the City waited silently. They could see that the Goddess, though still exquisitely lovely, had been terribly maimed in her battle to save the City.

Lalluna said, "My people, I stand before you now, joined with the flesh of my vessel, Katrione Estelle du Chesne Benet. We are no longer two beings, but one new creature with the power of both the Yrth and the Amaranth—we have become the Arkafina. Together we healed my daughter Hythea." At these words, a clamor of approval echoed from the people of the City. The Arkafina continued, "There has been much suffering, and many deaths, as a result of the wrath of Hythea. We would not have this terrible thing happen again, my people." There were cries from below as some asked her how they might prevent such a tragedy.

She answered them in this way. "For many years this land has been torn by a civil war. This War has set brother against brother, father against son, and wife against husband. The blood of the victims poisoned the ground, and it was this poison that infected the spirit of Hythea with rage. There were legitimate grievances brought forward by the Rising, but they foolishly chose to fight. Your own King, Benedict, wanted victory and would allow no quarter. He spent the lives of Guardsmen like pieces of silver. Both sides have suffered from want, and disease and death. We stand before you now to say this War must end—so that Hythea does not again vent her wrath on Beaumarais."

The cheers echoing up from below were deafening. The Arkafina smiled her beautiful serene smile and flew down to land among her people. The crowd parted reverently as she walked among them. There were many there who knew of Katrione Benet's healing work in the village, for she had been known as the angel of Belladore and her fame had spread to the City. Now everyone felt great joy, though not one would approach her—such was the awe the people felt before the Arkafina. All but one.

A young man stepped forward, wearing the uniform of a Guardsman. He walked boldly up to the Arkafina and knelt before her on the stone pavement of the Citadel Commons. In a clear voice that carried through the whole assembly, he cried, "Command me, Lady, for did I not say to you early this morning I believed you to be a Goddess?" Philip Tremayne offered his sword by the hilt to the Arkafina and she received it with grace. Then more and more Guardsmen came forward, as if they had only been waiting for one to show courage enough to lead them.

The King, Benedict, quietly seething, stood close to the edge of the assembly on the Citadel Commons. Unable to remain silent at this defection, he screamed at the Guardsmen, "This is treason. I will have every one of you hung, drawn and quartered for this. Get back to your positions at once. Would you have the City fall to Reynard's peasant horde? I say we will never agree to talks with that rabble-rouser..." His voice trailed off uncertainly as a group of Guardsmen approached him. They pushed him off his feet unceremoniously, and Philip Tremayne snatched the gold circlet from his head.

Holding it up high, Philip exclaimed, "Shall I give this back to the old man who almost brought about the destruction of the City? The man who would let no one leave, though danger threatened us all?" An overwhelming cry from the people gave him their answer. So he spoke again. "Who would you have lead us now? Speak, citizens of St. Valery!"

When the cheers had gone on long enough, Philip carried the circlet back to the Arkafina. As the Goddess inclined her neck gracefully, he placed the crown upon her head with trembling hands. The Arkafina, her voice joyful, said to him, "Philip, by your steadfast courage in the face of darkness and firelight, you too, have brought about the salvation of this City, and we give you our gratitude."

Maggie Fenty stood among the crowd and watched in amazement as the girl she had known as Katkin Benet spoke to the assembled people of the City, her iridescent wings pearled in the light of the dawn. Though Maggie feared to approach the Arkafina, the pony at her side did not. Brinna heard the gentle call of her Mistress in her heart and walked forward. The Arkafina greeted her old companion with joy. Then the Arkafina, with her hand resting lightly on Brinna's back, spoke again to the crowd.

"My people, would you have me lead you through the dark days ahead? For a great endeavor lies before us all—to heal the wounds brought about by the War and the wrath of Hythea. We cannot rest until the City is the shining jewel of the Mere once more. Yet there may be more suffering to come. Even as we speak, Nicholas Reynard marches through the Acre towards the City with five thousand armed men, grave and fell." A cry of consternation met this news. Lalluna said, "Do not fear, for if you will it, People of St. Valery, I will stand alone and hold the Yoke against the invaders."

"Not alone," said Philip Tremayne, quietly.

The roar rose up into the dawn sky, and the Arkafina bowed her exquisite head in assent.

The Rising reached the shores of Mistmere just after sunrise, after a quick march through the Acre that had seen them cover the last five miles in a little more than an hour. The men wearily looked on the smoke-palled City from the mouth of the Yoke, and they were very surprised to see the gate stood open before them. Nicholas Reynard held up his hand and the five thousand men behind him stopped as one.

In the early morning air, the Mere lay quiet, and as still as glass. Patches of mist clung to the hollows of the bank. The silence shattered as a flock of white birds, disturbed by the arrival of the Rising, flew up into the air, squawking loudly. Rippled rings spread out across the water until they lapped against the shore, where the five thousands of the Rising awaited the order to attack.

Yannick said to his Commander, "What sort of devilry is this, Sir? Has the City no wish to defend herself against us? I fear it is a trap. Let us strike now, with everything we have, before they spring it." The Dinrhydan, at his side, nodded grimly in agreement, his hand resting on the hilt of d'angwir.

Nicholas Reynard shook his head uncertainly, and using his spyglass, surveyed the Yoke. He saw someone standing in the middle bay—a petite woman, with raggedly cut hair, who wore a ripped and bloodstained frock that might, at one time, have been white. She appeared to be gravely injured, as there was nothing

310

but a blackened stump at the elbow where her left arm should be. The woman stood alone, save for a single Guardsman who stayed well behind her, just inside the Citadel gate.

The Commander gave a cry of amazement and handed the glass to the Dinrhydan, saying, "Look, my son, it is your wife! She lives still, though it seems she has been badly hurt."

Jacq, after looking hopefully through the glass for a long moment, shook his head sadly, for he recognized the perilously fair figure of his dream in the Acre—the creature with eyes the color of moonlight. He said, "Nay, Commander. She is not my wife, though I know she resembles her. My wife died in the heart of Hythea. Look again—do you not see the wings of the Goddess?" Reynard took back the glass and saw. His heart was troubled, for of all the exigencies he had planned for in this attack on the City, the appearance of Lalluna was never among them.

The Arkafina, with a shiver of her translucent wings, approached the Rising and landed in front of them without so much as a whisper. She wore a gold circlet on her head, and Nicholas Reynard wondered at this. The soldiers behind him murmured in consternation and once again he held up his hand. He walked forward until he stood before her on the Yoke.

Yannick, his eyes wide with fear, said anxiously to the Din-rhydan, "Do you think she will ever forgive me for calling her a witch? I must have been blind not to see she is an angel." Jacq merely shook his head, thinking to himself angrily that Lalluna was no benevolent creature.

Nicholas Reynard looked upon the Arkafina, and her moon-lit eyes met his. She said, "Hail, Commander of the Rising. Do you wish now to attack and right the many wrongs you feel your people have suffered? The City stands before you and she is defenseless." She held up her one good hand and swept it towards the Isle, as if to invite him to proceed.

Reynard smiled grimly at this, and answered, "Lady, as long as you stand on the Yoke, I hardly think the City is undefended. I know you have powers far greater than the Rising. But what is my alternative? My men have marched all night for this final campaign. They wish to end the War we have all grown so weary of. King Benedict will not parley with us. He seeks only our destruction."

311

The Arkafina informed him gravely, "The people deposed the King early this morning. I stand before you now as their representative. Now the fate of Beaumarais must be decided, between you and me. I would have you choose peace and the redress of the wrongs of the past, Nicholas Reynard. Will you come with me, to the table? We cannot bring back your daughter Jessie, yet together we *can* prevent the deaths of many other children." The Commander looked at her in surprise at the mention of his child's name, and saw the sympathy in her eyes.

Nicholas stood silent. His weather-beaten face remained carefully without expression as he made his decision. He had marched all night with five thousand men to vanquish the City completely, so that the death of little Jessie Reynard could at last be avenged. There would have been much bloodshed before that victory, he knew, yet it would not have given his daughter life again. He considered his lover, Elisabeth, waiting anxiously for news of him and her sons, and of all the other wives and mothers who did the same for all his men. Would they not press him to choose the bargaining table instead of the battlefield? But could he trust the Arkafina that stood before him, who insisted she wanted peace and justice for all her people?

A Commander must make many decisions in a day, yet never was one more important than this. As Lalluna stood by, her wings shimmering, waiting patiently for his reply, Nicholas Reynard decided, at last, to choose peace. He smiled, and extended his hand, and she took it willingly, saying, "Will you come with me now to the Citadel? We have much to discuss, Nicholas."

He nodded, feeling almost as if he dreamed. But knowing Jacq still waited anxiously behind him, Nicholas asked her, "Lady, is there any message you would have me give the Dinrhydan? His heart is heavy with grief for his wife—for he thinks she is no more." She looked at him, her eyes full of cool pity, and he was reminded once again that this unearthly creature was not Katrione Benet.

The Arkafina said, "Tell him only that he must wait. The fate of Beaumarais balances on a knife blade and we must attend to the needs of all our people first."

He turned and left the Arkafina and walked back to where Yannick, Jacq and the others waited. They looked at him expectantly, fingering their weapons, awaiting his order to begin the attack. He smiled and said joyfully, "There will be no battle today, my brothers. I go now to the Citadel with the new Voice of the City and she has promised us a fair redress. Wait here for me, men of the Rising, for when I return the war will be over at last."

The men lifted their voices in a resounding cheer. All but one. Jacq Benet stood by, watching the rejoicing of his comrades, and then he said quietly to Reynard, "Did she have no words for me, Commander?" Nicholas sighed deeply and repeated the message from the Arkafina. Jacq turned away without speaking and stalked off alone into the Acre. He took d'angwir from his scabbard and slashed wildly at a young green sapling until it lay in shreds at his feet. Reynard watched him with a heavy heart, but he could do nothing to help the Dinrhydan. His first duty had to be to all the Soldiers of the Rising.

For the next day and many days after, Nicholas and the Arkafina met in the quarters of the King in the Citadel Tower. The Mayor and the Council, the Maitress of the Infirmarie, Rebecca Kent, representatives from all the villages and other Lieutenants of the Rising, joined them. Only Jacq would not come to speak of peace with the Arkafina.

After the first meeting, when Reynard went back to his men, he told them, "The City has been devastated by the wrath of the mountain, Hythea. Her people need all of your strength and courage to help with the rebuilding. A steadfast young man named Philip Tremayne will lead the effort, and he is coming to meet with you now. Please follow his instructions as if they were my own." So the men of the Rising put aside their enmity and went to work to create shelter for all the displaced peoples of the City.

The agents for all the various factions met in the King's private library, around a long table. Around them stood shelf after shelf of rare illuminated manuscripts the King had hoarded away. The Arkafina, knowing her people must be free to choose their own fate, insisted, "Hold elections for a Chamber of Deputies as soon as is practical. One hundred delegates, gathered from all the towns and villages, must meet each year to decide the future course of Beaumarais."

This suggestion was welcomed by all, but there was a great deal of argument on how to balance the power of the City against the rest of Beaumarais. Once again the Arkafina spoke out. "I have chosen Nicholas Reynard to serve you as Prime Minister for the next two years. He will insure the concerns of the countryside are not overlooked as they have been in the past." Though the present Mayor and Council grumbled at this, they realized that their comfortable days of political patronage had ended when Philip Tremayne took the crown from King Benedict's head.

Reynard graciously accepted his new post, saying, "I have been a soldier for far too long, and my words are not as gentle as they might be, but I promise to speak for every person in Beaumarais as fairly as I can, and always listen to their concerns." Turning to the Arkafina, he continued, "What will you do, Lady? The people would have you lead them, as their Queen. I would have you stay as well, for I need your wisdom," he added humbly.

The Arkafina said, "The time will come, soon, when I must depart my vessel, for I am greatly wearied by this corporeal form and I have many other pressing needs to attend to. The people must decide then who they wish to lead them. For now, we will remain, though our main concern is to go into the City and heal as many of the injured and sick as we can. Now you have been given the task, it is up to you to organize the government as you see fit. We have faith in your discernment, Prime Minister Reynard."

Time passed, and the Arkafina still busied herself, night and day, with the needs of the people.

Jacq rode Nestor back to the Foxhole and lived there, virtually alone. On the day the remaining members of the Rising made ready to join the others in St. Valery, his mother came to his room.

"Will you not change your mind, Jacq?" she begged him. "Nicholas says he needs you in the City to help with the rebuilding. There is a lot of blacksmithing work to be done."

Jacq shook his head and would not meet her eyes. "I will linger here awhile, and keep an eye on the Foxhole," he said tonelessly. "You go on without me." With a last sad look, his mother and Willow departed. Only Nestor and Katkin's horse, Pollux, remained to keep him company, and he spent many lonely hours in the stable caring for the only things he had left that she had once touched.

"*Jacq...*" she said softly. He stirred from his sleep and felt her lying there, next to him. The moon burnished her naked body with a silver flame. At once he was filled with an inexorable need. "*Make love to me, Jacq,*" she whispered. "*I want you so much.*" With a moan, he pulled her close and she pressed her body eagerly to his.

"Katkin, my love," he cried. "Are you truly here with me?" Her hand stroked him in the darkness, inflaming his desire, and he surrendered to it, without knowing the answer to his question. She was ready for him—drew him in so deeply he felt he might be lost forever. There was no holding back. Jacq felt her nails rake his back, heard her cries of ecstasy, as his own shattering climax took him.

After he had awoken and found himself alone once more, he wept. Jacq decided then he must leave Beaumarais and ride until he found a place where memories of his wife did not haunt him. He could think of nothing else to do, other than take his own life, and his code of honor would never allow such a cowardly act.

Packing up what little he had left, he went to the stable and led Nestor and Pollux out into the courtyard. Taking off the black horse's bridle he said, "Go, Pollux, and run free. I can care for you no longer, and there is no one else." The black horse looked at him intelligently but did not run away. When Jacq mounted Nestor a few minutes later, and rode from the courtyard to the open Foxhole gates, Pollux followed, sure in the knowledge that the man his Mistress loved more than anything would lead him to her.

Jacq took the road north, towards the villages known as the Three Sisters, and did not look back. As he rode he considered that he might yet be able to find an honorable death. Perhaps, in time, he could hire on with some mercenary force that would have a use for his sword, d'angwir. The thought gave him a forlorn sense of hope.

On a rainy morning in the City, the Arkafina met with Nicholas Reynard and the Maitress of the Infirmarie, Becka Kent. Becka had just agreed that the Unity would never again practice the

Solstice Observance. The Goddess, her moonlit eyes bright, ordered firmly, "The door to the Temple must be closed forever. I trust you in this matter, Maitress. Do not fail me!" Becka nodded her head nervously. Even though the Arkafina looked something like her old roommate Katkin, she still felt very afraid of her.

Reynard offered the Maitress the assistance of Philip Tremayne and the men of the Rising to reconstruct the Infirmarie buildings that had been damaged by the earthquake.

Becka asked, "What of the healing springs? If the waters do not return the Infirmarie will be useless, anyway."

The Arkafina replied, "The waters flow again, Maitress, it is merely the pipes that need repair."

Then the Arkafina lifted her head sharply. "I must leave here. He is going and I must stop him for my vessel's sake, for she loves him more than anything. Farewell."

With a whisper of wings, she left hurriedly through the open door to the balcony.

Jacq rode Nestor through a flat land of fens and marshes, as a warm summer rain fell steadily. He kept his head down, letting the horse pick its way without much guidance. Rushes and willows grew in profusion on either side of the narrow dirt track.

Nestor stopped suddenly without a command, for he had seen Lalluna land on the path before them. Jacq looked up as the breath of wind stirred by her wings touched his face like a caress.

Staring up at him, Lalluna said sadly, "Why do you journey alone, husband of my vessel? Can you wait no longer for her to be returned to you?"

Jacq spoke harshly, for he had not forgiven her. "You will never return her to me, Lalluna. Katkin and my child are dead, by your hand. You have had your revenge. Now be gone from me, for I will speak no more with you, murdering harpy." He urged Nestor forward and the Goddess raised her one remaining hand. Though Jacq kicked him cruelly, Nestor would not move past her.

Inside her, Katkin said, "Lalluna, it is time for us to part. My husband has need of me, and I love him. If I have served you well, please release me now."

She said in return, "Of course you must go to him, my vessel, but what of our people? I will be pleased to leave the cares of this world and your cumbersome human body behind for a time, yet they will look to you still for guidance."

Jacq, from up on his horse, saw that Lalluna seemed to be carrying on some internal debate, for her moonlit eyes held no expression, and she stood silently before him. He again tried to spur Nestor past her, and then stopped in confusion as Lalluna opened her mouth. A column of white light issued forth from her parted lips and formed into the shape of a winged woman, as insubstantial as smoke.

She said, "You are wrong, Dai. Revenge was never *my* motive. I am deeply sorry I had to keep your beloved for so long, but all Beaumarais is in her debt. Until we meet again, farewell." The figure melted into nothingness on a rising breeze.

Jacq jumped down from Nestor, and threw himself forward, just in time to catch his wife as she fell to the ground. He cradled her closely, watching her chest rise and fall, still not daring to believe she had been returned after all his hopes had gone astray. All around him, birds burst into song as the sun peeped out from behind the clouds. On the damp ground beneath his knees, many small white flowers bloomed, like bright stars in a green sky.

He said to her, through his tears, "Katkin, my love, awake. I would hear your voice so I know I do not dream."

Her eyes fluttered open at his words. She whispered his name and twined her good arm about his neck, pulling his face down close to hers. "I am so sorry I had to leave you that night in the stable. I know how much it must have hurt you. Can you ever forgive me?"

He smiled and said in return, "You need not ask my forgiveness, nor should you sorrow on my account. All you did was for the salvation of the City and the Rising—I know that now." Jacq sighed. "Ever since the day we met I have tried to protect you, because I did not want to believe you had strength equal to my own. Now I understand things differently. You and I will be partners, and care for each other in the future. Come back with me to Acorn and there will be no more walls between us. The War has ended, and I can again be the craftsman that you loved."

Katkin kissed him and said, "I loved you as a soldier, too. I have never stopped loving you." She smiled at him, but he could see the lingering worry in her eyes.

"What is the matter, my love? Now we are together there can be no cause for unhappiness."

She said, "The City impatiently awaits my return. I am still Queen, at least for a little while. Will you share me with the people of Beaumarais? I fear it will be some time before we will be able to rebuild the stone house we once lived in together."

"As long as I do not have to be king, Katkin, I am happy to share you. I would be the Dinrhydan only, and I will help you as much as I can. Is that all right?"

Pollux stepped forward and put his head down in between the two of them and Katkin, nodding happily, patted the black horse's mane. "You brought Pollux? Did you think I would want to ride him?" she asked.

Jacq shook his head, saying, "Nay, Kat, he followed on his own, almost as if he knew you waited for me on this road, though I myself did not. I thought I had lost you and our child forever, my wife." His arms tightened around her as she brushed the tears from his eyes.

She smiled and said, "Pollux can follow us back then, for I wish to ride on Nestor with you, my husband."

All his years of working as a blacksmith had made Jacq very strong, and he found it easy to climb up onto the tall back of Nestor, still holding her in his arms. She turned to face him on the saddle, so that her legs wrapped around his body, and kissed his mouth with such ardent longing that he dropped the reins altogether, and put his arms around her instead. But it did not matter, for Nestor, that wise old horse, needed no guidance from anyone to find his way back home again.

Katkin and Jacq passed over the Yoke and into the Citadel. They sought out Prime Minister Reynard, and found him in his office, the former throne room of King Benedict. "Well, my dear," said Nicholas, smiling at Katkin, "though I will always appreciate the help of the Goddess in our time of need, it is very good to have you back again. You gave your all for the City and Beaumarais and we are forever indebted to your courage."

Katkin, embarrassed at this lush tribute, blushed and dropped her head, saying, "I could not have done it without Jacq. The Din-rhydan is just as deserving of your praise." Jacq, sitting beside her, reached across, took her one hand in his own, and kissed it. She smiled at this, but then said, "What should I do now, Nicholas? I am still Queen, and yet I know the people chose the Arkafina to lead them, not me. I am just an ordinary woman."

The Prime Minister shook his head firmly, and said, "Not so, Katkin, that you have never been. But why not let the people decide? In ten minutes, I go to the balcony to address them, as I do each day at this time. You must come with me and we will put the question to them directly. Will you do this?" She nodded uncertainly, a little nervous at the idea of addressing so many people without Lalluna.

When Katkin stepped onto the balcony, the people of St. Valery greeted her with such a sustained roar of approval she had to hold up her hand for silence. Jacq stood by, his arm protectively around her waist, as she spoke in a clear voice, "People of the City and Beaumarais, I stand before you, no longer as the Vessel of Lalluna, but as an ordinary citizen."

The cries from below interrupted her, as the people shouted, "You are the Angel. The Angel of Belladore!"

Katkin had to hold up her hand once more. She continued, "It was Lalluna you chose to lead you through the difficult days ahead, for she has the wisdom of ages in her eyes. Now she has departed and I have no such special gift. Therefore I would take the crown you gave her off my head, and give it to whomever you choose to lead you, from this day forward."

With a trembling hand, Katkin reached up to remove the gold circlet. The crowd below remained silent for a few seconds. Then with one voice, they began to call her name again and again.

23

The Sage, Rathyss

(Arkirish Dynasty, Seven Reversed)

Geya sits alone before her mirror, outside of time and space. She will rest for a time, while the child grows, and then the next phase of her design will begin. There is much yet to be done in the war against the Angellus, this turn of the Gyre. But she is content.

~~~~~~~~~

Queen Katrione Arkafina rides wearily through the darkened streets of Isle St. Valery. An escort of four Guardsmen, bearing the standard of the white swan, follows close behind her. When Katkin reaches the gates of the Infirmarie she slips through unnoticed and heads for the Spring House. It is deserted at this time of night, but the restorative waters continue to flow, filling the copper-lined pools and splashing down the stone steps of the reservoir. Katkin dismisses the guard, and they form a worried knot outside the double doors, wondering what impulse has possessed their Queen to make this late night visit to her old home. Once inside the bathing room, she closes and bars the doors, then slumps down on a bench by the fountain. The candle lantern at her side barely pierces the gloom and the arching beams high above her head are clothed in shadow.

A steamy mist clings to the statue of the winged Goddess, towering above the bathing pools. Katkin inhales sharply then slowly lets the breath out, almost like a sigh, and feels the pungent scent permeate her body. It is soothing—calming. Katkin whispers, "Lalluna," and again it sounds like a plaintive sigh. After a moment, a vision appears before her.

The Goddess speaks, but only Katkin can hear her voice. *"I know why you have come, my vessel. I wish the tidings I have to offer were not so grave."*

Now Katkin stares at the vision, as insubstantial as the mists that surround the fountain. She says softly, "Tell me the truth, my Goddess. What is wrong with Gwenn?"

Lalluna's voice sounds sad. *"Your daughter carries the spirit of a vengeful demon within her."*

Suddenly, everything becomes clear. Katkin asks, timorously, "This demon—is her name... Ketha?" She has heard Gwenn whispering to this invisible friend many times over the years.

"Yes, Keth Dirane. When we joined together that day in the Acre, to save your husband, she crossed the heavenly plane. Now she lives on in your daughter, in the form of a carrion crow."

Katkin says bitterly, "So it is as I have suspected all these years." She shakes her head, ruefully. "I tried for a long time to pretend to myself that Gwenn was only an unruly child. Her size and strength even as a young girl made it easy for her to pick on other children. Now she has been expelled from every school in St. Valery for fighting and disobedience. She is becoming more selfish and quick-tempered with each passing year. I even begged Jacq to discipline her, but he says her difficulties will pass. 'Youthful high spirits' he calls it. And what's worse, he has been teaching her everything he knows about swordsmanship. Every day she becomes more like the warrior he once was."

Lalluna chides her gently, *"You are still her mother, my vessel. Will she not heed you?"*

Katkin shakes her head sadly and the droplets of mist clinging to her chestnut curls drip down into the reservoir like falling tears. "She knows the truth and she blames me for everything. If she tells Jacq..." She leaves the sentence unfinished, unwilling even in the privacy of the Spring House to utter her darkest secret. Instead she asks, "Who is Keth Dirane? What does she want with us?"

"She is a sister Goddess, but not a benevolent one. Keth Dirane desires to feast on the flesh of men. I fear she will bring death and destruction to all of Yr. Her hunger will never be assuaged."

Katkin's eyes widen in horror. "Is there nothing I can do to stop her?"

As she begins to fade away, Lalluna says, *"Soon I will no longer have the power to come to you, my vessel. The Prime God has stolen my believers, and thus my very life-force is fading away."*

321

The Queen cries out in alarm, "No, Lalluna! You cannot leave me. I need you..."

A whisper clings to the mist. "*Gwenn's father does not sleep. He will bring you comfort when you have no one else to turn to. Go to him. He waits for you, under the oak tree.*"

The vision vanishes and now Katkin sits alone in the Spring House, with only the sound of the rushing waters for solace. Many more minutes pass whilst she repeats the Goddess' words in her mind, and tries to fathom their meaning.

After a time, Katkin leaves the bathing room and rejoins her men outside. The autumn air feels icy after the warmth of the thermally heated baths. Katkin shivers and one of the guards hurries forward with her woolen cloak, which he drapes about her shoulders. She remounts her brindle pony, Alis, missing, as she always does, her old friend Brinna, dead these five years.

Once they reach the confines of the Citadel, Katkin gives Alis over to her equerry and dismisses her escorts. Climbing the stair to her private apartment in the Citadel Tower, she wonders what she should tell Jacq of her conversation with Lalluna. Would he understand? That Jacq loves Gwenn as his own she never doubts, for Katkin has kept her oath to Tomas de Vigny. She only wishes her husband would feel as much love and pride for his own son, Tristan Dinrhydan, born two years after Gwenn.

As she enters the spacious bedroom she sees Jacq sitting up in bed, holding a book on his lap. A candle, already more than half-consumed, flickers by his side. He watches admiringly as she shrugs off her simple white robe, and slips into a woolen nightgown.

"I waited up for you. Is everything all right?"

She replies, "I am fine. I just had some business to take care of."

"Tristan was in here earlier. He wanted to show you the prize he won at school."

Katkin smiles proudly. "Another one! What was it for?"

Jacq shrugs and says vaguely, "Um... The Mathematics Cup, I think. I had just come in from practicing with Gwenn so I didn't pay too much attention."

Katkin begins a rebuke then bites it off when she sees the bandage on Jacq's right forearm. "What is that? Are you hurt?"

He looks distinctly uneasy. "Gwenn accidentally nicked me while I was giving her a lesson. But it is fine, honestly. The garrison surgeon put a few stitches in it, just to be on the safe side." Jacq knows all too well how his wife feels about sword fighting so he adroitly changes the subject. "You ought not to be working so hard, Kat, especially tonight. Tomorrow is going to be a big day for you."

She looks a little startled. Katkin has been so wrapped up in her worries about her daughter that she has almost forgotten about the morning. She crosses the room and sits on the edge of the double bed. "What time do the Quindecennial Celebrations start?"

He pats the space beside him. Katkin joins him under the covers, curls her body into the curve of his, and rests her head on his shoulder. "The main parade and review starts at ten o'clock. Our children will both be marching with the Queen's Guard. Did you know the quartermaster had to make up a special uniform for Gwenn?" he continues proudly. "Turns out she is taller than almost all of the men in the Garrison."

Katkin says flatly, "Well, I will be happy when the whole thing is over. I don't need my subjects to make a fuss of my reign as Queen."

Jacq laughs softly. "You won't get away with that. Your people love their Queen Arkafina too much. There are balls and celebrations planned for the next two weeks. But there is another commemoration planned for tomorrow night as well. I hope you haven't forgotten about that too?"

She looks slightly guilty and then says, "Of course I haven't. It is your mother's and Nicholas's fifteenth wedding anniversary. Are all your brothers coming to the celebration?"

He nods. "Everyone but Kadya. He must still be traveling in the east somewhere. Mother thought he might be back in time, because she had a letter from him a few weeks ago saying he was on his way home, but it doesn't look as though he will make it now. But Jessamine will be coming from boarding school. Gwenn was pleased to hear that. She hasn't seen her in awhile." Now Jacq's gaze shifts into the distance and he says, "The only way I could get Gwenn to agree to come to any of your tributes was to tell her that Jessamine was going to be there too." He chuckles, oblivious to the hurt his words will cause. "What on earth have you done to make her so angry at you, Kat?"

Katkin shrugs. How can she tell Jacq all her fears about Gwenn? It would break his heart. So she says, "I think she is irritated with me because I told her she couldn't have any more private tumbling lessons if she didn't stop threatening her tutors."

Jacq gives her a reassuring squeeze. "Don't worry, she will get over it. It is only..."

"Youthful high spirits, I know," Katkin finishes for him, and sighs. "I hope you are right about that." Then, to take Jacq's mind off Gwenn, she asks, "What is that book you have in your lap?"

He looks at the volume in his hands and says, "I found this book on the principles of flight in the library. I wondered if you would read some of it to me before we go to sleep, if you are not too tired." Katkin smiles and nods. Though she is very tired, she loves to read to her husband—for it is the one thing he cannot do for himself. Her worries about Gwenn slip away as she turns the pages and softly reads the text aloud. Jacq lays at her side, entirely content, and closes his eyes. In a little while he sleeps, snoring gently, and his face, weathered now with the passage of time, still poignantly reminds her of the ten-year-old boy she met once in the fields of Tintaren. Katkin lovingly kisses the gray stubble on his cheek, pulls the quilt up high to shelter them from the cold and blows out the candle.

Appendix I

The Tokens of the Luckcast

Estate of Naer—the twinned tokens (the symbol)

Love (*heart*) – A new love or friendship begins.

Hatred (*clenched fist*) – A strong feeling of dislike for someone or something.

Courage (*horse*) – Gain strength from each other.

Dread (*storm cloud with lightning*) – Trouble ahead.

Serenity (*dove*) – Peaceful times.

Anger (*hammer*) – Beware of someone's fury.

Passion (*torch*) – A very strong feeling for someone or something.

Indifference (*torch, extinguished*) – Apathy will destroy something important.

Happiness (*mermaid*) – A time of joy and contentment.

Sorrow (*willow*) – A time of unhappiness and discontent.

Hope (*seabird*) – Help is on the way.

Despair (*black chain*) – The situation may get worse before it gets better.

Truth (*white feather*) – The answer may be trusted.

Falsehood (*black feather*) – The answer may not be trusted.

Beauty (*rose*) – A person or thing possesses inner beauty, though the outside may be ugly.

Ugliness (*thorns*) – A person or thing is ugly inside though the outside may be beautiful.

Loyalty (*dog*) – A situation calls for faithfulness and trust.

Betrayal (*snake*) – Beware of treachery.

Beginning (*hourglass, full*) – A beginning.

End (*hourglass, empty*) – An ending.

Yes (*open arms*) – A positive answer may be expected.

No (*crossed arms*) – A negative answer may be expected.

Certainty (*rock*) – You may be sure of the person or situation.

Doubt (*sand*) – You have doubts regarding the person or situation.

Plenty (*grapevine*) – A good harvest.

Need (*an empty bowl*) – A time of want.

Strengthen (*arrow*) – Reinforcements are coming.

Devastate (*fire*) – Potential ruin.

Birth (*acorn*) – The gestation of a child or an idea.

Death (*the scythe*) – A matter comes to an abrupt conclusion.

The Tollyn – A mythical landscape

Kal Jheriad – The snow-capped peaks of the Kal Jheriad portend the climbing of new spiritual heights and the triumph over adversity. But one must remember that with the ending of one quest comes the beginning of another— frequently the view from the top of Jheriad is of another higher mountain in the distance.

Dylloriah – This lush green valley is home to a well-ordered and prosperous community in a temperate land. Dylloriah represents matters pertaining to hearth and kin.

Gessach Mebd – A meandering river always speaks of travel and adventure. Gessach Mebd foretells a journey or an attack of wanderlust or discontentment.

Cexcipet – The sands of Cexcipet guards many secrets. Just as an oasis may lie hidden beyond the next dune, so this card portends mystery and the unknown.

Thanis – The vast ocean. The moon moves the ocean tides and Thanis holds the lover's hearts in her sway. This card pertains to all aspects of romantic love.

Hithluel – This rocky outcrop, on the shores of Thanis, represents the inevitable workings of fate, in the same way the ocean is fated to meet the land.

Tarcisany – An abyss on the ocean floor has depths unplumbed. Tarcisany represents the covert world of dreams and memory.

Arrereons – This verdant plain speaks of partnerships, property and accumulated wealth.

Cittak – The remote island archipelago, lost somewhere in the vastness of Thanis, foretells a time of isolation and abandonment.

Irlimyrit – Everything remains frozen and unmoving in this icy wasteland. Irlimyrit presages stagnation, obstacles, or stalled progress.

Thariens – The water is crystal clear in this perfectly still tarn on the lofty shoulder of the mountain. The surface reflects like a mirror, just as drawing Thariens reveals new understanding of a person or situation.

Mellasarat – A high pass through the Kal Jheriad—speaks of hope and a way through seemingly insurmountable difficulties.

Pencathe – Close to Hithluel lie the rocky arms of Pencathe, a natural harbor. Thanis unexpectedly returns something or someone from the past.

Varing – A warning to those who wander in the Varing, the trackless fen. This card predicts loss, confusion, and chaos.

Sai Tammos – A journey on Gessach Mebd can prove dangerous if one chances upon Sai Tammos, the thunderous cataract. A sudden change of heart or fate is predicted by the appearance of this card, or perhaps even a miracle.

King Elfair – A strong outside force will become involved.

Queen Elleranne – Predicts the arrival of an individual with the ability to heal.

Prince Carolet – A person who through ignorance or ill will consistently makes bad choices.

Princess Arellen – Foretells the acquisition of wealth and possessions or their loss.

The Hero, Aages – A brave and steadfast person will offer their help.

The Knave, Dindal – An untrustworthy person.

The Sage, Rathyss – Represents judgment and consequences for actions both good and bad.

The Innocent, Citchet – The child-like spirit.

The God – The male spirit of the heavens.

The Goddess – The female spirit of the heavens.

The Priest, Taleyear – Spiritual matters need more attention than material ones.

The Priestess, Cahunine – Pertains to matters of learning and education

Sister/Brother – refers to peers.

Mother/Father – refers to elders.

Daughter/Son – refers to children.

Appendix II

Glossary

Abiding vows – The vows taken by a Damenie of the Unity at age twenty-one. The vows include strict adherence to the Rule of Lalluna, the acceptance of poverty and the promise to perform all healings under the auspices of the Infirmarie.

Amaranthine – Seemingly immortal beings from the future. Have the ability to traverse the continua at will.

Ambit, Greater – The journey undertaken through Yr by the Firaithi every other year.

Anafireon – The spiritual energy that inhabits the body.

Ancamma – The Goddess of the inland sea known as the Mistmere.

Angellus – The mysterious dark beings that are the enemy of the Amaranthine.

Arkafin – Male angelic spirit.

Arkafina – Female angelic spirit.

Astrelet – Spirit body, receptacle of the anafireon.

Autochthones – Amaranthine name for the Firaithi.

Azimuth – Part of the Amaranthine system of addressing points on the Continua.

Beaumarais – A small country in the continent of Yr. Bounded to the east by the Mistmere and Mardon to the west. The northern border is shared with Secuny and the southern with Spanja. The capital is Isle St. Valery, an important trading hub on the inland sea. For more information on the history and geography of Beaumarais see Appendix III.

Belladore – Village about thirty miles west of the City of Isle St. Valery. Katkin's father was the Lord of Belladore and their ancestral home, Tintaren, was close to the village.

Citadel Commons – The broad paved plaza just outside the main gate of the Citadel. Home to the weekly market as well as many parades and executions.

Citadel, The – The five-sided fortress that overlooks the City of Isle St. Valery. The abode of the ruling monarch and the Guard.

Isle St. Valery – The capital city of Beaumarais. Population approximately 35,000. (For more information on the history and geography of Isle St. Valery, see Appendix III.)

Continuum – The Amaranthine term for the "worlds between worlds" or other dimensions. *Pl. continua.*

Cottars – Tenant farmers and laborers who work in return for a house and a small piece of land. Entire families normally enter into service with a particular Lord, and they are bound for life. Some Lords treat their cottars well, providing decent housing and medical care, as well as educational opportunities for the children. But others regard the cottar scheme as a guarantee of cheap labor, and offer little in the way of wages and benefits.

D'angwir – Jacq Benet's sword. Called "justice for all" in the old tongue.

Dai, the Irrakai – Winged Amaranthine. Known as "the seeker of paths between the stars."

Dinrhydan, The – Jacq Benet's code name. Translates as "true heart" in the old tongue.

Damenie – A Sister of the Unity. *Pl. Daminem.*

Epona – The Goddess of Horses.

Firai – The language of the Firaithi.

Firaithi – A wandering people, comprised of twenty tribes, who traverse Yr trading in horses and handcrafts. Their earliest history is unknown to outsiders, but it is surmised that they may have come east a thousand or more years ago from the mountainous region now known as T'shang. They speak an obscure language unrelated to the other tongues of Yr. The Firaithi peoples are dark skinned with brown or hazel eyes. They tend to be small in stature with a wiry build. Their hair is thick and lavish, and both men and women prefer long tresses, done up in braids. Their Goddess, whom they refer to as "The Un-Named One" is Hana, the Eastern Star.

Geya – A Triple Goddess of the Amaranthine. Her sisters are Raven and Moonlight.

Gruagá – Firaithi name for the settled peoples of Yr. Means "white devil." *Pl. Gruagán*

Havenwood – Home of the de Vigny family.

Infirmarie – The compound of the Unity of Lalluna, on the shoulders of Mt. Hythea. Ill and injured folk from throughout Beaumarais and beyond seek healing in the waters there. Founded in the earliest days of the City after Antoine St. Valery discovered the thermal springs. Home to the Daminem and Juvenet of the Unity. The Temple of Lalluna, a secret cavern deep in the heart of the mountain, can only be entered from the Infirmarie grounds. It is the source of the healing waters.

Juvenead – An apprenticeship in the Unity of Lalluna.

Juvenie – A junior Sister of the Unity, who has taken Prime Vows. *Pl. Juvenet.*

Keth Dirane – The name that the Amaranthine Raven was given by the Firaithi when she came to Yrth. *Lit. "Death's Shade."*

King's/Queen's Guard – The military force of Beaumarais.

Kymatre – Firai word for grandmother. *Lit. "elder mother."*

Lalluna – The name that the Amaranthine Moonlight took for her own when she appeared on Yrth. The patron Goddess of Beaumarais.

Lauds – Prayers before breakfast.

Linnun – The divination method of the Dalvolk also called "the water runes."

Luckcast – The divination method of the peoples of Yr.

Maitress – The Mother Superior of the Unity. Appointed for life from the ranks of the Juvenet.

Mardon – A neighboring but unfriendly country to the west of Beaumarais. Several wars have been fought between Mardon and Beaumarais over disputed territories. Citizens from Mardon are called the Mardonne.

Mistmere – The large inland sea that brings trade and exchange to Beaumarais. Isle St. Valery is on a peninsula that extends into the Mere.

Moonlight – Amaranthine. Sister of Geya.

Pellicle – Part of the Amaranthine system of addressing points on the Continua.

Prime vows – Vows made by a Juvenie when she is accepted into the Unity.

Raven – Amaranthine. Sister of Geya.

Refectory – Dining hall for Daminem and Juvenet at the Infirmarie.

Rule of Lalluna – An important element of the vows that the sisters of the Unity agree to abide by. The Rule requires Juvenet and Daminem to remain both chaste and childless.

Reynard, Nicholas – Leader of the Soldiers of the Rising.

Secuny – The neighboring country to the northwest of Beaumarais.

Solstice Observance – A secret ceremony performed by the Maitress of the Unity on June 21st each year to ensure the continued flow of the thermal springs from Mt. Hythea.

St. Valery's Acre – The vast forest that clothes the western shores of the Mistmere.

The Rising – The militia formed by the Cottars after the cruel winter of '52 killed many children.

Tintaren – The ancestral home of the du Chesne family. The land is suitable for the cultivation of grapes for wine.

Triske stones – The divination method used by the Firaithi. Consists of three octahedral bone carvings—each face is incised with a different symbol.

Unity of Lalluna – A group of anchorites dedicated to protecting the thermal springs issuing from the side of Mt. Hythea.

Vielle à roue – An ancient musical instrument consisting of several gut strings bowed by a revolving wheel. Tangents attached to keys change the pitch of the strings. May also have several drone strings and a buzzing string, called a chien or dog.

Yoke – The land bridge between the shores of the Mistmere and the City of Isle St. Valery. Narrow and paved with cobbles, the Yoke is gated on both ends and heavily guarded.

Yr – The continent on which Beaumarais is located.

Yrth – A watery world, with only one main landmass, the vast continent of Yr. The residents have fire and steam power, but not electricity. Several large islands exist to the west of Yr, mostly unexplored.

Appendix III

A Brief History of Isle St. Valery and Beaumarais

Traders from the crowded eastern margins of Yr founded the City on Isle St. Valery in the twelfth century. They recognized the potential of the uninhabited peninsula which pointed, like a finger, to the middle of an inland sea called the Mistmere. At one time the peninsula had been an actual island, formed by a once-fiery volcano, but the lowering of the water levels over time had created a narrow isthmus to the mainland. The traders set about felling trees and soon built a trading post and stockade in the wilderness. As word spread, St. Valery quickly grew in size to a lively village. Although many hostile forces called the surrounding lands home, the young community could be protected from invasion by defending the narrow Yoke, as the land bridge was known.

The village continued to grow, with the influx of shopkeepers, craftsmen, and settlers looking for work and more space to house their families. After a few hundred years, St. Valery had become a busy and vibrant city, with broad avenues that climbed up the steep sides of Mount Hythea. The mountain remained the living heart of the City, with the Infirmarie nestled on her side, near the source of the healing waters. The thermal springs drew many people seeking solace and cures, and the Daminem of the Unity of Lalluna cared for them and the Mountain herself.

Once the peninsula became crowded, the new arrivals spilled over into the countryside surrounding the Mistmere. The thickly forested shores were cleared and planted, except for a rocky and uninviting district known as St. Valery's Acre. This vast stretch of forest remained untouched, and became a hunting preserve for Kings and gentry. The outlying villages grew in size, but still looked to Isle St. Valery for protection. After the first invasion of the Mardonne, in 1560, the City and countryside united to form the Kingdom of Beaumarais. A monarch was appointed from the oldest of the ruling families. The small realm rapidly grew in stature and influence, fueled by the endless opportunities for trade provided by the Mistmere. The City, especially, grew in power through the profits of this trade, and the King rewarded generously those he thought deserving. He handed over great swathes of countryside to a few elite families to develop as they saw fit. Cottars tended these farms and preserves in return for a scrap of land of their own and their Lord's protection in times of trouble. Most were treated little better than slaves by their wealthy masters.

A disturbing divide between City and country, and rich and poor, began to trouble Beaumarais thereafter and the ruling King recognized the need for further defenses. The addition of a pentagonal Citadel on the western edge of the peninsula increased the military presence dramatically. It served as both the King's Guard garrison and the abode of the King himself. Later still, the entire City was surrounded by a high wall to provide further protection for her residents. All the citizens of Beaumarais were taxed equally to pay for these improvements and resentment in the country villages ran high.

In 1760 a period of prolonged drought resulted in a famine that gripped Beaumarais for several years. The privileged, snug in their mansions and villas, were able to import the foodstuffs they needed from neighboring countries, but the cottars starved miserably. As many children and old folk perished, the old antipathy between master and servant finally boiled over into the Cottar Revolt. Though the King brutally put down this uprising in 1762, the cottars quietly regrouped under the aegis of a charismatic new commander—Nicholas Reynard. Shortly thereafter, the rebellion grew into an out and out civil war. No one could say when it would end. Men from both sides convinced themselves of the virtue of their cause and would not compromise. Many died. Mount Hythea, with roots deep in the earth, soaked up the blood of the fallen, and mourned. Keth Dirane, the battle crow, feasted in delight.

This volume covers the period from immediately before the start of the civil war until its end. When a peaceful reconciliation is reached through the efforts of the Arkafina, Beaumarais, for a time, becomes a land of tranquility and prosperity once more.

About the author

Suzanne Francis believes the genesis for her inventive Song of the Arkafina series lies in her chronic travel sickness as a child and young adult. While growing up in England and on the Continent, she happily participated in many family and school trips, though riding in the back seat of a car often left her suffering from nausea for hours on end. To help pass the time, she began telling herself stories, serialized over many days and weeks, often featuring the landscapes through which she was traveling. These imaginary adventures, along with a life-long love of reading good books (but only when sitting still) sparked her interest in writing. Since then she has penned many fantasy short stories and sonnets, as well as two novels.

After earning her BA in Geography, Suzanne worked for several years as an urban planner in the USA, before retiring to have children. A series of part-time jobs followed, everything from migrant farm worker to dishwasher, retail manager to massage therapist. Her appetite for voyaging has taken her to such far-flung places as the Cook Islands, Mexico, across the deserts and Deep South of America and on many adventures through the capitals of Europe. She has drawn on these life experiences to amplify and embellish the unique characters and settings of her novels.

In addition to writing, her passions include neo-paganism and playing a perversely difficult musical instrument called the hurdy-gurdy.

She is a member of the Troth, and the Otago Writer's Guild.

Presently, Suzanne lives in rural Dunedin, New Zealand with her husband Michael and four children.

Author's Acknowledgements

There are many people who gave unselfishly of their time and energy to help me make this book, but first on the list would be Mike Goodwin, writing buddy extraordinaire. Without his unstinting criticism and generous encouragement, this book would not have been published. I would also like to thank Martyn Folkes at Mushroom eBooks for his patience with my many inquiries. My family, both in New Zealand and the United States were both supportive and patient with my eight to ten hour writing days.

Dale Benson, Maureen Collins, Benjamin Durrant, Fiona Glasgow and Fabienne Lecomte also read earlier versions of the manuscript and provided much-needed support, suggestions and advice.

The following is an excerpt from *Ketha's Daughter*, the next installment in the *Song of the Arkafina* series from Suzanne Francis and Bladud Books.

~~~~~~~~~~

Later, resting on the blanket, the night breeze cooled the sweat on her skin and she shivered in his arms. The fire had died down to glowing red ash and he could barely see the outline of her face in the darkness. Arkady whispered, "Who are you? Will you not tell me your real name, my beautiful crow girl?"

She turned to face him and her voice sounded bleak. "I cannot, dear Kadya. She would be angry with me."

"Who would be angry?"

"Ketha. I must do as she says." She sighed deeply. "Sometimes I wish I did not have to."

Arkady rolled onto his side and rested his head on his hand so he could see her face more closely. He said, "I don't know much about you, but I can see you are in some kind of trouble. You don't have to tell me anything else if you don't want to. Let me help you. We can both ride from here right now on Ajax, and by tomorrow we can be far away from this place. Trust me, I will make sure, whoever this Ketha is, she cannot find you."

She shook her head miserably. "Ketha will always find me. There is nothing you can do to stop her."

He begged her, "Please, I want you to stay with me. What hold does Ketha have on you? Will you not say?"

"Don't ask any more questions!" she cried in frustration. "We have so little time to be together before she returns. There is only one thing you can do for me this night." He could not see the tears clinging to her lashes but he tasted them as she turned her face to his and sought his mouth once again.

Afterwards, utterly spent, Arkady fought a losing battle to try and stay awake. But as her fingers lightly stroked the hair on his belly, he felt his eyes closing, and forced them open again. He knew instinctively she would be gone when he awoke, so he whispered, "Don't go, Krikka. Please don't leave me." She said nothing in return, just waited patiently for him to fall asleep. Then she rose very cautiously and dressed herself. She located the pearl-handled dagger in the sand and shoved it back down into her boot.

Ajax rested quietly in the lee of a dune and made no sound as Krikka saddled her. The girl carefully unpacked the rest of Arkady's food and the water skin and left it by the fire. She placed the rolled silk painting of Hana next to it. Krikka wore a periapt tied with a leather thong around her neck — a withered crow's foot clutching a green crystal. Thoughtfully, she slipped it over her head and dropped it on top of the painting. She walked slowly back to where Arkady slept on the blanket and said, very quietly, "Farewell, Uncle."

A large black crow flew down and landed on her back. For a few seconds it looked as though the girl had sprouted a pair of black wings, and then the crow disappeared. Krikka bit her lip so the pain would not make her cry out. Then she led Ajax away through the dunes and headed north towards the coast and the Fynära.

"What took you so long?" Ketha croaked angrily. "I told you we should have just killed him and taken the horse. We could have been miles away by now."

"I am sorry, Ketha. You promised me I could see him before

we left. I don't want him to die because I care about him. Do you understand?"

The battle crow laughed harshly. "He will die soon enough, when the Fynära pay a visit to Beaumarais, my pretty girl. Ketha will have plenty of carrion to feast on then."

When Arkady woke the next day, the sun was already high in the sky. As soon as he saw the pile of things she had left, he did not bother to look further for Krikka or Ajax. Spying the crow's foot, he picked it up and gazed at it for a long moment. Krikka's face came back to him, and her eyes. As blue as the skies of T'Shang. He shivered slightly, thinking of their feverish encounter of the night before. If she hadn't stolen his horse, he might have thought it all some wild, fey dream. As he placed the charm around his neck, Arkady wondered if he would ever see her again. He shouldered the satchel that held the food and his water skin and turned away from the ashes of last night's fire, sighing deeply. It would be a long, slow walk to Beaumarais.

www.ingramcontent.com/pod-product-compliance
Lightning Source LLC
Chambersburg PA
CBHW020530020726
47494CB00006B/1708